# STONEHEART

# STONEHEART

## Charlie Fletcher

Hyperion Paperbacks for Children
New York

an imprint of Disney Book Group

First Hyperion Paperbacks edition, 2008

3  5  7  9  10  8  6  4  2

Library of Congress Cataloging-in-Publication Data on file.
ISBN-13: 978-1-4231-0176-5
ISBN-10: 1-4231-0176-6

Visit www.hyperionbooksforchildren.com

*With love and thanks to my parents,
Margaret and Paul Fletcher, makers of a
happy childhood and much else besides . . .*

# TABLE OF CONTENTS

Things men have made with wakened hands,
and put soft life into are awake through years with
transferred touch, and go on glowing for long years.
And for this reason, some old things are lovely
warm still with the life of forgotten men who
made them.

*"Things Men Have Made"*
*—D. H. Lawrence*


Our happiness here is all vain glory,
This false world is but transitory,
The flesh is weak, the Fiend is slee
*Timor mortis conturbat me.*

*"Lament for the Makers"*
*—William Dunbar*

# STONEHEART

# CHAPTER ONE

## Belly of the Whale and the Monkey's Teeth

George never spent any time wondering why he wanted to belong. He just did. Things were like that. You were in or you were out, and in was a lot safer. It wasn't the sort of thing you questioned. It was just there.

On the class trip before this one, they'd been to the War Museum and learned all about trench warfare. George had thought that's what life felt like: just keeping your head below the parapet so you wouldn't get hit.

Of course that was last year, in the past, like all the other things about being a kid. He still thought about them sometimes. He still remembered what being a kid was like. But he was over that. He was twelve. Real Twelve, not "Only Twelve," as his father had called it the last time they'd spoken. He knew *his* twelve wasn't anything like his dad's because he'd seen pictures of his dad as a kid looking clueless and specky and fat, all of which—in George's twelve-year-old trench—would be the equivalent of sitting on top of the parapet with a big round target painted on your head, yelling, "Cooee! Over here."

George could remember talking and laughing about stuff like that with his dad, before his dad moved out and there was too much talking altogether.

He didn't say much at home anymore. His mother complained about it, usually to him, but sometimes to other people late at night on the phone when she thought he was asleep. Somewhere inside it hurt when he heard her talk about it—not as much as when she said he used to have such a lovely smile, but nearly.

And nowhere near as much as never being able to say anything to his dad ever again.

The thing was, he wasn't *not* saying anything on purpose. It was something that seemed to have just happened, like his baby teeth falling out, or getting taller. Mind you, he wasn't getting taller as fast as he would have liked, and right now that was part of the problem.

He was average height for his age, maybe even a bit more—but somehow he *felt* shorter, the same way he sometimes felt older than he was. Or maybe it wasn't exactly older, just a bit more worn and rumpled than his classmates—rather like his clothes. His clothes were all thrown in the same washing machine, colors and whites together, and though his mother said it made no difference, it did. It made everything pale and gray and washed out, and that's exactly what George felt like most of the time.

It was certainly what he felt like today, and not being able to see properly was making him feel more insignificant than usual; all he could make out was the whale's belly and the back of his classmates' heads as they clustered around a museum guide showing them something interesting. George tried to push forward, but all he got was an elbow in his ribs. He sidled around the pack and tried to get another view, careful not to push anyone.

He found a place where he could nearly hear and edged closer, peering through the thin gap between a circular stand full of pamphlets and a boy about four inches taller than he was. As he rattled the stand with his shoulder and reached to steady it, the boy turned and registered him.

George smiled at him on reflex. The boy didn't return fire on the smile. He just looked away without comment. George wasn't too worried about being blanked. In fact he was relieved. The boy was the name-maker, the one with the gift for finding the cruelest nicknames for his peers, then making them stick. He'd *almost* been a friend of George's when they'd all been new together, but finding his gift had given him a kind of easy invulnerability, a power that meant he didn't have to have friends anymore, only followers. That's what made him dangerous.

The boy turned back around. This time he spoke. "Something I can help you with?"

George froze. Then tried to hide the freeze with another smile and a shrug. "No. Uh. Just getting a better—"

5

"Don't stand behind me."

The boy turned away. But several others had seen, and in their eyes George saw something he recognized. Not interest, certainly not sympathy, not even much dislike. Just a pale gratitude that they weren't the target this time.

So George swallowed and stayed where he was. He knew enough not to be seen being pushed around. He knew once you did that you were sunk. He knew there was a level below which you couldn't afford to sink, because once you were down there, there was no ladder back up. Once you were in that pit, you were fair game for everyone, and everyone unloaded on you.

So he looked down at the square of marble he stood on and decided he'd stick to it. There were teachers present, anyway. What's the worst that could happen?

The boy calmly reached backward and toppled the stand, right into George. George stepped back, but there wasn't enough room, so he batted at the metal column with his hands to protect himself. It hit the floor with a loud metallic crash, spilling pamphlets all across the tiling around him.

The room suddenly went very quiet. Faces turned. The boy turned with them, innocent-looking amazement quickly morphing into shocked surprise.

"Chrissakes, Chapman!"

The cluster of boys around him dissolved into hooting anarchy, and the three adults—two teachers and a guide—were left looking for the culprit. And with everyone else doubled up and pointing, there he was, head above the parapet, feet bogged down in a landslide of bright-colored paper booklets.

Mr. Killingbeck fixed him with a sniper's eye, crooked a bony trigger finger at him, and fired a one-word bullet.

"Chapman."

George felt his face reddening. Killingbeck snapped his fingers at the other boys.

"The rest of you clear Chapman's mess up! You— follow me."

George followed him out of the whale room back into the central hall of the Natural History Museum. Mr. Killingbeck stopped in the middle of the room beneath the dinosaur skeleton and beckoned him closer.

George had enough experience of Mr. Killingbeck to know not to start what was coming. So he just waited. The man's mouth worked slowly, as if everything that he said tasted bad and had to be spat out before it caused him more pain and discomfort.

"Mmm, tell me, were you trying to be rude, Chapman, or does it just come naturally?"

"It wasn't me, sir."

"Who was it, then?"

There was no answer that George could give. He knew it. Killingbeck knew it. So he didn't say anything.

"Moral cowardice and dumb insolence. Neither very appealing, Chapman. Neither what you were sent here to learn, are they?"

George wondered what planet Killingbeck was on.
Planet 1970–something, probably. Not a planet where
George could breathe. He began to get choked up. His
face began a slow burn that he could feel without seeing.

"That was unforgivable, boy. You behaved like something wholly uncivilized. Like that ape over there."

The bony finger jabbed at a monkey in a glass cage,
baring its teeth in the grimace that would be the last
message it ever sent to the world. George knew what it
felt like.

"You're uncivilized, Chapman. What are you?"

George just looked at the monkey, thinking how strong
and frightening its teeth looked. More like fangs, really.

Killingbeck worked his mouth.

George found the blob of plasticene in his pocket and
began kneading it with his fingers. It still had the knob-
bly contours of a face he'd sculpted on the bus.

"I think it's worth something more than sullen
silence, Chapman. I think it's worth an apology, for a
start."

George's thumb coasted over the open mouth in the
plasticene face and wedged it a bit wider.

"Get your hands out of your pockets."

George smashed the nose on the plasticene and
pulled his hand out of his pocket.

"You're going to say sorry if you have to stand there
all day. Do you understand?"

George worked the plasticene in his fist.

"Or you can tell me who did it. Do you understand?"

George understood. There was a rock. There was a hard place. And then there was him, jammed up between the two. He couldn't grass on another boy, even a bully, because grassing would drop him into a place so low in the eyes of the other boys that, not only was there no ladder back up, but there was no floor either. Rat on someone, and the rest of your life would be spent in free fall down a pit that just got deeper and darker and never stopped.

That was the rock.

That was simple.

The hard place was less simple, maybe because it was so big, so immovable.

The hard place was everything else.

The hard place was his life.

The hard place was everything that led to this moment.

And the moment was clamping around him and giving him nowhere to run.

"Chapman?" Killingbeck's finger tapped impatiently on the side crease of his trousers.

George looked at the monkey's fangs. How easily they'd snap through that impatient stick of flesh and brittle bone. He'd like to have those teeth in his head. He'd like to bite that finger off and spit it back at Killingbeck. He'd like it so much that he could feel the crunch and crack and almost taste the blood. The feeling was so immediate, so real, that he was suddenly frightened by it as it hung black and treacly in his mind. He'd *never* had a thought like that. The shock made him reel inside and forget that he wasn't speaking.

"Sir?"

"Well?" Killingbeck's voice jerked him back into the now, back between the rock and the hard place. He didn't know what he was going to do. But he suddenly knew from the prickling in his eyes that there was one treacherous possibility.

George was not going to cry. And knowing what he *wasn't* going to do suddenly made it all clear—he knew what to do, what to say. And he knew to say it very slowly, very calmly, so as not to let the thing rising in his throat choke him.

"I understand that's what you think I should do, sir—"

Killingbeck looked at him with the surprise of a hungry man whose dinner just bit back. His mouth stopped chewing at the next thing George was going to say.

"—I just don't agree with it."

The pupils in Killingbeck's eyes irissed down to the size of periods.

George knew he'd made a mistake. He knew, with a sudden flash of intimacy which scared him more than the finger-biting image, that Killingbeck wanted to hurt him. He could feel the itch in the man's hand as the bony fingers blunted into a fist.

"Well. Well, well, well. That's fine." Killingbeck closed his eyes and ran his free hand through the thick gray hair that curled back around his skull, as if he were trying to massage the very thought of George out of his head. "You'll stay here until you decide to apologize. If you haven't done so by the time we leave, you will be in more trouble than you can imagine. You will stand straight, you will not sit down, you will not put your hands in your pockets, you will not chew at sweets, you will not move from this spot. The museum guards will not let you out unless you are with the rest of the party. We will pick you up in an hour and a half, and you will apologize then, in front of everyone. Do you understand *that*?"

His eyes snapped open. George didn't flinch. "Yes."

Killingbeck 180'd and strode off after the rest of the class.

George listened to the click of his heels across the stone floor.

Then he put his hands in his pockets. Then he sat down on a bench. Then he put a piece of chewing gum in his mouth.

And then he got up, walked to the door, and out into the drizzle that was soaking the steps in front of the museum.

The guards didn't give him a second look.

# CHAPTER TWO

## The Horror

George felt the cold wind slap him as he stepped out of the museum. He felt horrible. The black treacly feeling was still bubbling in his head, and the chill on his face only made it worse. He didn't know what to do next. He just knew he'd had to get out and be alone for a moment.

George knew that it was safer and easier to be alone. He'd decided this right after his dad had died, when life had suddenly filled with too many people saying all the wrong things, as if their words could begin to fill the new dull hole in the middle of him.

Being a loner seemed like a hard road, and sometimes his weakness betrayed him: for example, he hated himself for smiling at the boy who'd toppled the pamphlet stand on him; it had been sheer, unthinking weakness.

He'd betrayed himself.

Smiling had been like trying to be friends when they

weren't. Smiling had been a gutless, needy thing to do. And George had definitely decided he didn't need anyone, friends or otherwise.

Rain spat at him, and he looked up, thinking that alone was the way to be, because alone meant you were in charge of what could get to you and what you could keep out.

Above him, high on the decorated facade of the museum, there were carvings of imaginary animals, nearly real but not quite. Lizards that only existed in the mind of the sculptor alternated with alarming pterodactyl-like birds. The pterodactyls had nasty pointy teeth jagging out of nasty pointy beaks, and ugly hooks stuck out of their featherless wings. Their eyes had the wide-open glassy stare of someone you don't want to cross.

He felt the cold air on his gums and wondered if he was smiling or grimacing. The more he looked the more he saw that the whole front of the building seethed with stone carvings of animals. They made him uneasy. He didn't know why, but he didn't like them. He felt watched. Maybe it was the windows in the facade—the people who could be looking out, seeing him with a red face and eyes pricking with frustration and tears that he wasn't going to let come.

He knew enough about self-pity to hate it. He hated it more than Killingbeck, more than the rock or the hard place. So he turned from the facade and wiped his eyes to be sure no one saw him nearly cry.

He looked at his watch: 3:42. They'd be in there until four thirty at least. He didn't know what he was going to do. He turned away and leaned back against the building.

Something jagged into his back.

Behind him, at waist height, on the corner of the front portico of the museum, a little nubby carving of a dragon's head stared up at him.

It reminded him of the things his dad made—used to make—in his workshop. Not the big stuff, the serious stuff, but the little animal toys he'd sometimes squidge out of clay to make George smile when George was smaller, on days when George found him at work but not too busy.

The memory didn't make him happy. Maybe because he'd thought about his dad too much for one day anyway, or maybe because the dragon had fangs and the fangs reminded him of the monkey, of the taste in his mouth, of Killingbeck.

Whatever the reason, the result was strong and sharp.

He hated the carving.

He hated it a lot.

His fist was bunched and in motion before he thought about it. Once he thought about it, he knew this was going to hurt. He knew there'd be blood, split knuckles, maybe even broken bones. He knew he didn't mind. He knew in a place that was closer to wanting than knowing that all this was likely, and all this was okay.

His fist was the size of the dragon's head. His fist was not made of granular stone. In the microsecond before impact, he realized he didn't know what this would feel like. He realized he was going to break his first bone. He felt more air on his gums as his grin rictussed wider.

He didn't feel the impact. He heard it—a sharp, ugly crack—and the world jerked a bit.

Something hit his foot.

He closed his eyes and cradled his hand instinctively, waiting for the wave of pain. From the cracking noise alone he knew that bad damage had been done. Now that he'd done it he wished he hadn't. He didn't want to look at his hand in case something was sticking out of it. Like a bone. He checked it with his good hand, carefully. No bone, but definitely wetness.

Something hissed at him.

He opened his eyes. He must have imagined it. As he turned to check behind him, his foot stumbled over an obstruction. He looked down.

It was the stone dragon's head.

He'd knocked it off.

He looked at the portico. There was the stump of its neck, sheared off neat as a scalpel cut.

Now he looked at his hand. No bone. No blood, even. Just wet from the rain. It was fine. He picked up the dragon's head. He couldn't believe it. Something had changed. It wasn't looking at him anymore. It wasn't looking at anything. Unless he was going mad, it had been looking at him. Now its eyes were closed. He decided it must have been a trick of the light.

There was another hiss from behind him. Then a wet scrape and a dry squeal.

He knew without looking that the noise must be one of the museum guards, maybe even Killingbeck coming out to give him a real beasting about leaving the hall. He had no idea how Killingbeck was going to react to seeing that his least favorite boy had just broken a carving off the museum wall.

So as he turned, he jammed the dragon's head into his coat pocket, hoping to hide it but knowing he wasn't going to get away with it.

It wasn't Killingbeck. It was something worse, something so much worse that if he'd had time to think he would have given anything for it to be Killingbeck instead.

It wasn't anything human.

It wasn't anything possible.

It was, however, peeling itself off the stone facade of the museum and looking at George with flat, blank hatred. And not just hatred—hunger, too.

It was a pterodactyl.

Its eyes were wide and unblinking, as if permanently surprised to find there was room for them at all in a skull that wasn't so much a head, as a long, heavy beak that tapered back into a ribbed neck, bent under the strain of holding up all those teeth. Its body was small and surprisingly pigeon-chested, but was more than made up for by the large batlike wings and the sinewy legs that ended in bent knuckles and ripping talons.

Something like breath hissed from deep within its stony neck.

George's body had entirely forgotten to breathe.

The thing jerked off the frieze with a final effort. It tried to spread its wings, but only succeeded in getting one uncurled before it disappeared from view, plummeting below the level of the balustrade.

George heard a noise like a sackful of wet suitcases hit the grass below. Unable to stop himself, he peered over the balustrade. The monster continued unpacking itself and getting all its wings and talons in the right order. It had its back to him. It stretched itself like an old man working a kink out of his neck.

And then it turned.

It looked right at him with dead stone eyes. And as the rest of the body twisted to follow the head and point itself at him, George knew what those eyes were doing.

They were locking on. Acquiring a target.

And that target was him.

As if to confirm this, the pterodactyl raised its beak to the lead sky and chattered its teeth in a noise like a drumroll played on dead men's bones.

Then it lowered its head and began to lurch forward, dragging itself toward him on its wing-knuckles,

swinging its body and foot-talons along between them,
like a demon on crutches.

George ran.

# CHAPTER THREE

## Old Running

He hit the corner of Exhibition Road, skidded into the turn, and started sprinting, careening off the crowds filing into the Science Museum. By the time they started to protest, he was just a memory of blurring feet, fifty yards up the road.

A traffic warden tried to grab him with the reflex action all men in uniform have when someone young runs really fast in their direction. "Hey, there . . ."

George tore out of his grip and kept going. One fast look over his shoulder gave him a horror shot of the pterodactyl clipping along the pavement behind him, with a terrible jerky lope. It appeared to run with its legs and simultaneously pull itself forward on the hooked knuckles of its wings.

Nobody paid it any notice.

George screamed and doubled his speed, ducking into a side street, then almost immediately turning into another. He shouted "Help!" but London's a busy city, and by the time people heard it he was gone.

He got a stitch.

He kept running, pounding through the backstreets, heading for the park.

Usually you can run through a stitch and get over it. This one must have been a different kind. This one just got another one on top of it and hurt twice as bad.

He didn't slow down.

Running from nightmares is how nightmares begin. Our bodies have really old memories that our minds know nothing about. And these memories made him speed up as he skidded into the road that runs along the bottom of Kensington Gardens.

He couldn't see how to get into the park, so he turned right and kicked harder.

Behind him, the pterodactyl pulled itself around the corner and sniffed the air. George ran. Looking back, he saw it getting smaller. It seemed to have stopped to look at all the greenery in the park. He ran and ran until a lorry pulled across the pavement and he couldn't see it anymore.

As soon as he couldn't see it, George had time to feel the pain in his side. He stumbled and went sprawling as his feet hit a paving-stone edge.

He bounced up on his feet and looked back. Clear.

He didn't see the tramp until the tramp grabbed him and stopped him dead on the edge of a junction.

George whirled.

"Wha—?"

A lorry thumped through the junction, right over where George would have been.

The tramp let him go. George looked over his shoulder. He couldn't see anything. He gave in and bent double, gasping with pain and exhaustion, wondering if he was going to be sick.

"Don't mention it . . ." wheezed the tramp.

George pointed back down the empty road. The tramp looked back along his arm. The pterodactyl stepped out from behind a tree and looked at them. Then it scuttled behind another tree.

"Did you see it?" George gasped, trying to get the right amount of oxygen into his body as he grasped at the receding wisp of his normal world.

The tramp shrugged and shook his head.

"Just 'cos you're paranoid don't mean they ain't after you, mind," he said, and dissolved into a series of lumpy giggles that sounded like he was being choked.

George gulped air. Everything hurt. His feet, his muscles, and his lungs. His head hurt worst of all.

There was no movement from the distant tree.

There was movement closer to him. There was something above the tramp's head, on the side of the building.

On an elaborate drainpipe, a carving of three fantastical lizardly salamanders fanned out, their tails decoratively plaited together, their heads facing down, each about eight feet long. That wasn't what had caught George's eye.

What caught his eye was the fact that they *moved*.

George's jaw fell open.

Above the tramp's head, the three architectural details had started to writhe. He could hear the hiss and slither of scales against scales as the tails began to unplait themselves. He could see the salamanders' eyes turn to him, their noses sniffing.

Cold fear wrapped his neck. He pointed. The tramp followed his gesture. He looked puzzled. "What?"

One of the lizards got its tail free of the others and reared back, hissing at George. He looked at the tramp for a fast second.

"Can't you see?"

George heard a distant clack. He tore his eyes from the new horrors on the building wall to see the pterodactyl awkwardly loping toward him, only thirty yards away.

George was running again. He ran past joggers, past dog-walkers, past cyclists.

Nobody stopped. Nobody looked. Nobody helped.

But he didn't slow down. The one time he did snatch a look back, he could see the salamanders scuttle and slither along the gutter beside the creature, with an unlizardly sidewinding motion he'd seen in a program about rattlesnakes. It was a movement that was horrible in itself, full of threat and power and evil.

George pumped down the pavement, now running alongside Hyde Park past a modern red-brick building with a tower and a soldier and a horse outside.

The soldier didn't give him a moment's look.

He could feel each pace through the soles of his shoes, like the pavement was hitting him, rather than the other way round. He could hear his breath like it was someone running beside him. His chest hurt as if it were being burned inside.

He risked a look behind him.

"Hoi!"

He hit the street cleaner's barrow at full tilt, smacking all the wind out of his body and sprawling in a mess of brooms and rubbish bags across the pavement.

"HOI!"

George found a breath, and another one, and then a lot more ones that each hurt worse than the last. He wiped tears from his eyes.

"You mad?" the street cleaner wanted to know.

George shook his head, no words left in him.

"You clean that up, pal," said the sweeper, coming out of the gutter. "You clean that up right now!"

George started to cry.

The big sweeper stepped back. Spooked. "Oi. Steady."

Snot ribboned out of George's nose as he sobbed. The sweeper looked around, scratched himself, and looked as embarrassed as a man with a bulldog tattooed on his neck can do.

"Steady, mate. It's . . ."

He looked around again. People in the bus stared at them, like they were on TV. Disconnected. Bored. Passing the time. People in cars ignored them and concentrated on the car in front. A motorcycle despatch rider roared past.

The sweeper picked up two halves of a broom.

"You broke my broom, you . . ."

George froze. Behind the sweeper's shoulder, on the other side of the road, as a red bus jerked forward, he saw a flash of scale. A sliver of beak. And a dark, dark glint of eye.

The pterodactyl had been pacing on the other side of the road, on the park side, using the traffic as cover.

The bushes on his side rustled again, and this time he turned fast enough to see three salamander tails disappear into the foliage.

"Wha—?" asked the sweeper.

But he was talking to thin air. George had gone.

# CHAPTER FOUR

## The Gunner

George ran into Hyde Park Corner, the busiest junction in London, a sea of traffic grinding around a roundabout full of thick monuments and thin grass.

He pinballed across the slow flow of cars, bouncing from boot to bonnet and back again. Cars hit their horns, and a cyclist hit the brakes and shrilled a whistle at him, but George plowed on, pushed by the mind-killing panic that follows cold fear. A truck screeched its air brakes as he slammed in front of it and hit the concrete and railings on the other side. He looked back.

The pterodactyl followed him in an implacable straight line, deliberately, without hurry, like something that now knew it had gotten him.

And worse than this slow horrible thing that clattered its leathery wings and chattered its teeth as it came, was the fact that George now knew that no one else could see it.

It pulled itself toward him over car bonnets in front of the eyes of drivers who just looked through it.

It scraped over the roofs of taxis, and the drivers didn't stop talking for an instant. No one in the bus looked around, no one registered that this prehistoric nightmare of bones and teeth was stalking a child through the most crowded thoroughfare in London.

The thing hopped up onto the backseat of a motorcycle and looked right at him for a long moment. The motorcyclist didn't notice, even when it threw its head back and snapped its beak to the skies in a mocking victory clatter.

People say you're never as alone as when you're in a crowd, but being alone in a crowd when something's hunting you down and the crowd can't see it is a *lot* worse.

George dragged himself backward over the railings before he realized what he had done.

He backed up until he was stopped by seventy tons of white Portland stone. He had backed into the Royal Artillery War Memorial.

He looked around and for a moment thought the pterodactyl was impossibly hanging above his head, ready to drop on him and end the nightmare in a horrible and painful way.

Then the last bit of his mind that could think straight realized he was looking up at a dark statue, a soldier, a gunner in a World War One uniform, tin hat tipped down over his eyes, arms spread out against the stone, like he was resting. And over his shoulders was a waterproof cape that, for an instant, George had mistaken for wings.

There was a clatter in front of him. He looked around, and with a freezing twist in his guts, saw the pterodactyl slowly pulling itself up onto the railings only six feet away.

His body, thinking for itself, began to edge right along the base of the war memorial. Amazingly, the monster looked away. He edged consciously now, reaching for the corner.

The corner of his eye must have caught the movement, because he wasn't looking for it. He stopped before he knew why.

There, slithering into view, was one of the stone salamanders. George scuttled back along the memorial, toward the other corner.

Again he heard his feet scrape to a halt on the gravel before he knew why. The other two salamanders reared slowly around that corner, mouths open in a silent, gaping hiss.

George had run out of ideas.

The pterodactyl turned to look at him, slowly, easily, hatefully. And the hate in its eyes was an old hate, a hate that George didn't understand, but felt right in his core. And on top of the hate was cruelty and glee.

It *knew* it had him.

It seemed to grow bigger in front of him as it raised

its reptilian wings in triumph and blocked out the last of the sun. Its mouth began to open, and from inside came an ancient smell, fouler than anything George had ever smelled, a smell that was old and inhuman and purely frightening.

George had nowhere to run.

He felt nothing but fear and the wall at his back. His mouth made shapes. No sound came out. He saw his tears hit the ground in front of him.

But one word made itself and spilled quietly out of his mouth, falling to earth too silently for anyone but him to hear, as the thing got down off the railings and started toward him.

"Please."

The monster opened its beak and reared back for what George knew was the killing blow. If its long fanged beak wasn't already one big grin, you'd have said it grinned even more as it hissed and flexed its sharp talons.

"Please . . ."

It was over. The thing struck.

*Blam!*

The thing stopped.

*Blam!*

The thing looked surprised.

*Crash!*

Something else landed in front of George.

Something with steel tacks on its boots.

Something with a gun.

Someone.

The pterodactyl looked at the two holes in its chest. Shook its beak in disbelief. In rage. Coiled itself and leaped for them—

*Blam, blam, blam!*

The first shot stopped it. The second shot dropped it. And the third shot smithereened it, blew it into shards of stone, turned it to dust.

George looked up. He saw a man made from tarnished bronze from the bottom of his army boots to the top of his tin helmet. The Gunner from the war memorial looked back down at him as he broke the revolver in his hand, shook out the spent shells, and reloaded in a movement so fluid that he didn't seem to need to look at his hands while he did it.

He moved so fast that he snapped the reloaded revolver back together while the shells were still tinkling at George's feet.

George felt his nightmare wasn't over. He scooted away from the Gunner, but not fast enough. The Gunner grabbed him and yanked him back against the wall and then stepped in front of him. Protecting him.

Over the shoulder of the rain-cape, George saw the three salamanders boil across the ground and meet in the pile of dust that had been the pterodactyl.

They writhed blindly as if trying to find it, to smell it out, and then they turned and looked at George and the

Gunner. George saw it again. The ancient hatred multiplied in three pairs of eyes.

The salamanders hissed and lashed their tails together, sliding them in and out of one another until they were braided, as they had been when he'd first seen them sliding off the side of the building. Then they reared up like a three-headed cobra, moved—and the Gunner fired.

*Blam, blam, blam, blam, blam, blam!*

Six shots rapid-fire stopped them and spun them, jerking into them, and then the revolver clicked out and there were no more bullets. One lizard twitched and rolled its way out from under the bodies of the others.

The Gunner took off his tin hat and dropped it into George's arms. He wiped his forehead and stepped across the gap to the salamanders, fumbling with the ammo pouch at his belt.

As the salamander struggled free, he smashed his boot across its neck, pinning it to the ground, reloading the big heavy revolver as fast as before. Two shots sent it to dust. He stepped back and sent the other two bodies the same way.

When he stopped, all there was to see was a faint dust smudge to show where the nightmares had been real.

He reloaded and reholstered the gun before he turned to look at George. George just clutched the tin hat the same way he used to clutch his teddy bear.

The dark statue crouched in front of him. George could see that his eyes were gray, like a pencil drawing of eyes in the black-tarnished face. The gray eyes seemed to look through him. Then the Gunner took the hat and scratched his neck. He stretched his neck like he was working kinks out of it, in a gesture George later felt was strangely familiar.

Right now, George just watched.

It wasn't that his mind hadn't caught up yet. It hadn't even *started*.

The Gunner propped the hat against the war memorial and hunkered down next to him, picking something out of his uniform pocket.

Cigarettes.

He—it—the whoever—scratched a black match on the white stone and produced a yellow flame that he applied to the cigarette between his lips. Gray smoke plumed, disappeared inside the statue, and reappeared in a perfect smoke ring. They both watched it shimmer and fade in the London air.

George couldn't think what else to do. Except: "Thanks."

The Gunner turned and looked at him. Took another puff. Kept looking.

George came up with something else to say. But all it was was:

"Um."

He looked at his feet. At least they were familiar.

An unfamiliar voice came from the Gunner's throat. A gravelly voice. A cockney voice.

"Thank me when this is over, mate."

George looked up to see the gray eyes still looking at him. Because they didn't blink, he could see the white bits were now a very light gray and the pupils were getting even blacker.

The Gunner took another puff and blew it out on a half-laugh.

"Blimey. You got no idea what you just started, have you?"

# CHAPTER FIVE

## Caged Heat

Deep in the City something had been woken, something so old and so ordinary that people had been walking past it for centuries without giving it a second look.

It was so commonplace and undistinguished that anyone who came looking for it couldn't fail to be disappointed with what they found, not that anyone had come looking for a very long time. Nothing about it gave a hint as to its purpose or its power. It looked like a roughly hewn lump of old masonry: whitish rock, about the size and shape of an old milestone. The only clue that it was more than the nothing it seemed was its setting.

It was caged.

It sat in the side of a building that was younger than it by at least two thousand years, and it looked out on the street through a thick lattice of iron bars.

Given its antiquity, people who noticed this usually thought that the bars were to protect it from the public.

Only a very few—and a very strange few at that—knew that it was precisely the other way around.

The grille of iron had become a wind trap for the rubbish that swirled around the building on the eddies from the looming high-rise opposite. A gutted packet of crisps was stuck on top of the thing, glinting silver and brown. A fragment of label proclaimed "Barbecued Be—" to anyone who chose to peer in and see what flavor its long-gone contents had been.

If the person peering in had been a connoisseur of coincidences, they would no doubt have smiled at what happened next, given that the label turned out to be a prophecy as well.

There was a low-frequency hum, the kind that old refrigerators make in the dead hours of the night when they think no one is listening. And then the crisp packet slowly shriveled and shrunk and finally burst into a bright and short-lived flame, before disappearing completely.

And it may have been nothing, or it may have been the two narrow blood grooves on the rounded top of the stone; but cleared of the debris, it now suddenly looked vacant and ready as a mortician's slab.

# CHAPTER SIX

## The Choice

Now that everything had stopped, George's legs began to shake for real. Once more he felt like crying; once more—but only just—he decided he wouldn't. He felt very tired, the kind of tired that sucks you toward sleep like a dark undertow, the kind of tired you know you have to fight because the sleep it's pulling you down into may not be a good sleep at all.

He looked around to see if the Gunner was still hunkered down next to him. He was, his eyes panning back across the traffic in front of them.

From high above came a keening whistle.

George looked up at the triumphal arch on the other side of the grass. A vast statue of a woman and a chariot pulled by plunging horses loomed overhead. The whistling came again, this time sharper, this time so high and urgent that it drilled into his ears and hurt.

The Gunner nipped the end of his cigarette, pocketed

it, and stood up in one decisive movement.

"What is that?" asked George.

The Gunner's eyes followed his look up to the frozen horses in the sky.

"That's the Quadriga."

"No—" said George.

The whistling came again, and now there was no mistaking its message.

"—that," he finished.

"It's a warning," the Gunner said.

"What about?"

The Gunner scanned the rooftops over the road.

"This isn't the time for questions, son. This is the time for a choice."

George opened his mouth. The Gunner rode right over to him.

"Choice is stay—or go."

Tiredness sucked at George so hard that he felt like stopping swimming and sinking into it instead. Closing his eyes seemed like such a good thing to do that he let them flutter before he shook his head and tried to think.

"I don't know what's happening," he began.

"Yeah, you do. You're choosing. Now. Go or stay? Live or die?"

Suddenly and without knowing why, George got angry.

"That's ridiculous. . . ."

The Gunner spat.

"'Course it is. Death's always ridiculous. So what? Life's a joke an' all. That's why you might as well have a laugh and enjoy it while you're 'ere. But it's your shout. Which way you gonna jump?"

George's leg shake turned to a disjointed yammering against the stone. When he spoke, it came out more like a whine than he meant it to.

"I really don't know what's happening."

The whistling became staccato and even more intense. The Gunner grabbed George's arms and lifted him until they were nose to nose.

"I do."

George's mind fused. He couldn't say anything. He couldn't really think anything. The Gunner shrugged.

"Right. I'm getting back up on that plinth and I'll watch what the thing that's on the way here does to you, because if you're too stupid to save yourself, you're too stupid to bother about."

He dumped George back on his feet and turned. George grabbed his arm and clamped on.

"No. Help me."

The black face looked back at him for a long beat. Something changed in the face, maybe the set of the jaw, maybe the eyes crinkled.

"God helps them what help themselves."

"What does that mean?"

"Means hold my hand and run like a bastard."

George let his hand be enfolded by the big, black

hand. He had just enough time to wonder at the fact that the metal felt soft and pliable and not as cold as he'd expected, before his arm was almost yanked out of its socket as the Gunner headed for the underpass.

They skidded into the fluorescent-lit tunnel and clattered down the low ramp, heading north, beneath the traffic. Halfway down the underpass there was a busker strumming a guitar, singing an old Simon and Garfunkel song about being safe in a fortress deep and mighty, with more attack but less accuracy than the original.

His eyes watched George approach. He gave no sign of seeing the Gunner, or of hearing the hobnailed crash of his ammo boots on the concrete floor. He just watched George's approach with boredom then disgust. He cut the song long enough to spit an ironic "Thank you" as George passed the open guitar case without adding to the spattering of coins in its scarlet interior.

George was still looking back as the Gunner dragged him up the steps into the darkening, tree-shrouded end of Hyde Park.

"He didn't see you!"

The Gunner just kept running, weaving through the pedestrians heading home through the neon-enhanced gloom, heading away from the traffic, deeper into the park.

"None of them can see you!"

The Gunner tugged George's arm just in time to make him look ahead and sidestep the tree trunk that loomed out of the orange-tinged darkness.

Which was a pity. Because if he'd kept looking back he might have noticed that he was wrong.

One pair of eyes had seen them. One pair of eyes stretched in something more intense than disbelief. The eyes stared out from beneath a long sweep of dark and shiny brown hair. They were wide-spaced eyes with hooded lids set in a creamy white face.

On the top floor of a red double-decker bus speeding west on the open bus lane, a girl of George's age wrenched out of her seat and stumbled back through the standing passengers, eyes locked on something disappearing into the park, as the bus drew her farther and farther away.

She yanked the stop cord and serpentined down the stairs, oblivious to the complaints of the other passengers, ignoring the "Hoi!"s and the hands that plucked at her long sheepskin coat as she launched onto the rear platform of the bus, eyes raking back into the darkness, searching for something she could no longer see.

The conductor grabbed her.

"Oi, missy, simmer down."

She didn't even look back.

"I have to get off!"

The bus hammered down Rotten Row.

"Next stop in a minute," said the conductor, not letting go.

The bus slowed for a taxi. The girl twisted her head

like a snake and bit the conductor neatly between his thumb and forefinger.

As he yelped and let go in surprise, she leaped off the back of the slowing bus, stumbled, fell, got up, dodged another bus that braked hard, and ran off into the park. The girl—whose name was Edie—didn't seem to mind the new graze on her knee any more than the honking and shouting behind her.

But then the other thing about the pale face beneath the shiny hair was that it was tough beyond its years, a toughness that came from having decided she wasn't going to mind about little things ever again.

And it had the look of a face hard on the trail of something big.

# CHAPTER SEVEN

## Parking

The Gunner pulled George to a halt in the intricate tracery of shadows cast by a neon light above a spreading plane tree. He looked all around.

George concentrated on getting oxygen into his lungs. He waited until he'd gotten enough for a short question.

"Are we safe?"

The Gunner just set off again, but this time George noticed that it wasn't a headlong run. It was more like a game of hide-and-seek, where the Gunner flitted them from one pool of shadow to the next, always keeping an eye behind them for whatever it was that seemed to be stalking them.

Now that they were moving slower, George's brain had room for more than just terror and the hard job of breathing despite the stitch in his side. Thoughts tumbled into his head, hopping in on top of each other before he could really focus on them, like watching TV while someone else held the remote and speed-hopped the channels. He thought of Killingbeck. He thought of home, the empty house where his mother would not be there to miss him yet. He wondered if and when she'd notice. He flashed a horrible image of the pterodactyl crawling toward him over the stationary traffic. He thought of his mobile phone, stuck in his backpack, unclaimed in the dark recesses of the museum cloak-room. He saw the stone salamanders writhing into a strike in front of him, ready to kill.

And then he was sick.

As the Gunner tried to pull him on, he kept his hand on a thin plane tree and bent over and was sick. Twice. Then his stomach tried for a hat trick, but there was nothing left but a hot prickling sensation all over the back of his neck, and a tremor that calmed as the Gunner put a big hand on his shoulder.

"All right now?" he asked.

George shook his head.

"You done well there. Didn't get any on your shoes or anything. Hold on."

He suddenly hoisted George into his arms and stepped over a low wall on the edge of the park. George opened his mouth, but then the lurching sensation of falling into a deep space took the words out of him unsaid. There was a jolting instant of rushing vertigo before the Gunner's boots crashed to the concrete.

George looked around to see that they had jumped over the wall into a fifteen-foot drop, that ended on the ramp, into an underground parking garage. The Gunner set him on his feet and walked him very quietly down the ramp into the subterranean space.

The parking garage was empty of people and full of cars. Somewhere in the distance came the lonely sound of a tire shrieking in protest, but right now the Gunner and George were the only figures among the bonnets and windshields stretched out below the fluorescent lights. The Gunner walked between two cars, found a shadow behind a concrete pillar, and hunkered down again.

George looked at him. "What are we doing?"

"Waiting."

"What are we waiting for?"

"For it to go away."

"What is it?"

"Dunno. Want to go back up there and have a look-see?"

George didn't.

"Besides, you're run out. That's why you just chucked it all up. There's a point of exhaustion, and you just ran through it. S'like horses. You just need to lie up for a bit. . . . I was good with horses."

George noticed that the Gunner had a bridle chain tucked into his belt, under the cape. The Gunner noticed him looking.

"Horse Artillery. We pulled the guns through the mud

and tried not to kill the old nags doing it. Lose a horse, lose the guns. Lose the guns, lose the battle. Lose enough battles, and well—"

He seemed to catch himself. George thought it looked like he was pulling himself back into the here and now from somewhere a long way off.

"Anyhow. This ain't about that. Get your breath."

The Gunner retrieved his part-smoked butt and fired it up.

George looked at him, then at the fire sprinklers in the ceiling. The Gunner's eyes stayed on George's through the smoke curling roofward from the cigarette.

"What?"

"I don't think . . ." began George.

"Yeah?"

"I don't think you can smoke in here."

The Gunner's eyes held steady, but something rippled under his dark bronze skin, something near his mouth. Despite himself, George felt an answering twitch on his face. The last thing in the world he felt like doing was smiling, but as the Gunner's face cracked, he felt his face going with it. And like the small crack that signals the dam is going to burst, as the Gunner began to laugh, so did he.

"Can't smoke? *Can't smoke!*"

The Gunner was laughing like a deep rolling bell. George's laughter fired along underneath it, sharper, thinner, and echoing with hysteria. Somehow all the fear and incomprehension found a voice in his laughter. He had no idea why things were so funny, only that the laughter was right. He flashed a memory of his dad belching at the dinner table, and responding to his mum's disapproval with a cheery "Better out than in." That's what this felt like, this laughing on the shank end of terror. He had no idea what was finding voice in his laughter, but he knew it was better out than in. Keeping it in would have burst something inside. The Gunner wiped his eyes.

"Can't smoke? I can step off a monument in the heart of the city and shoot me four taints and drag you through the park double-time, and no beggar sees me, no one turns a hair—and you say I can't spark up? God's truth!"

He stopped laughing. George rolled on for a bit and then dried up as inexplicably as he'd begun, as he felt the Gunner waiting for him.

"You need to pay attention, son. Because, whatever you woke up thinking were the rules? Well, up's still up and down's still down—but everything in between? All bets are off. It's a whole new ball of chalk."

He kept George in the grip of his eyes as he blew a long plume of smoke right at the fire sprinkler.

"What do you mean?"

"I mean: you want to survive this, you need to think first and ask the right questions. And 'What do you mean?' ain't the right question."

George started to shiver. He opened his mouth. Thought some more. Shut it.

The Gunner grunted approvingly.

"That's good. Engage the brain before running your mouth. Don't worry about the shivering. It's shock. It'll pass, or you'll go doolally for a bit."

"I don't want to go doolally."

"Might not be the worst thing that could happen."

George looked at the damp concrete at his feet.

"I think I went doolally a while ago. I think all this is doolally. I think someone's put drugs in my food or something. I think this isn't happening."

The Gunner just looked at him. George wondered if he'd gone back to being a statue.

"Look," George said after a pause, "please tell me what's happening. Please tell me what you are. Tell me what those things are. Please."

The Gunner tapped his chest.

"I'm a statue. They're statues—carvings—whatever. That's all we got in common. I'm a spit, they're taints. Taints hate spits, spits don't care much for taints because of it. You could say there's been zip between us since the first man thought of carving something and putting a little of himself into it. We're both 'made,' see? Both created by craftsmen or even artists—don't matter which, we call them both 'makers'—but we're as different as chalk from cheese."

"Taints are evil?"

"Dunno about evil. They're just bad. See, there's nothing human in them. They was made to frighten, to be ugly, to leer at you off church roofs and put the shivers up you."

"Gargoyles."

"Yeah. Sort of. I mean, all gargoyles is taints, but not all taints are gargoyles, if you follow me. But things like gargoyles was made to remind you about hell, meant to outshout the devil. Nothing human in them. Empty. And like all empty things, they're hungry. Not for food, though. Hungry for what makes you you, and me me."

George thought of the pterodactyl's toothy beak, and the look in its eye, and knew just what the Gunner meant.

"Though, of course, I'm less me than you're you, me being a spit and all."

"What do you mean?" asked George; although, as he asked it, somewhere inside him he thought he knew, thought he'd been told this before, thought that if he stopped and tried he could remember the answer. Before it came to him, the Gunner spoke.

"A spit is a statue that the 'maker'—sculptor, stone carver, whatever—has made to represent someone human. And because of that, while a maker works, something of that must flow into us, and fills that hole the taints have eating away inside them. I mean, a statue of Lord Kitchener ain't Lord Kitchener, but he's—well, he's what the artist thought and knew about Lord Kitchener.

It's like he's got a spark of Kitchener's spirit in him. He's the spirit and image of Lord Kitchener. The spit and image if you like. That make sense?"

George needed to think before he answered. He knew about sculptors. He remembered talk about "putting something of yourself" into things, other talk of things "coming alive beneath your hands." He felt the plasticene in his pocket. He nodded slowly.

"So who are you?"

"I'm the Gunner. No one special. Just a soldier. From the Great War. The only other name I got's the name of the man what made me. Just like you got the name of the man what made you. Whatever your name is . . ."

"Chapman. I'm George Chapman."

"I'm Jagger. My maker was Charles Sargeant Jagger. So I'm a Jagger. You got a big family?"

"No."

"I got a few. There's Jaggers all over London. Jagger did well out of the war. People liked what he done, making us look like heroes, but nothing crowing about it. Made us look like men who knew about mud and dying first, then made us look like heroes after. For them that had lost sons and husbands, we looked like the men they wanted to remember them as, the men they hoped they'd become before the bloody generals sent them out to be butchered."

"So I call you Jagger?"

The Gunner had gone still and was looking up.

"Wh—"

The Gunner looked at him and held a finger to his lips.

"Quiet as mouse."

He eased his revolver from the holster.

"Cat's on the roof."

# CHAPTER EIGHT

## The Cat on the Roof

The parking garage had a roof made of concrete reinforced with a grid of metal rods. It was about two feet thick. Above that was eight feet of earth, thick and sticky, like modeling clay. The earth was reinforced by its own web of tree roots, criss-crossing over and under themselves as each tree sent feelers out into the clay in a microscopically slow explosion, searching for water and food. This network was itself laced with tunnels made by earthworms burrowing blindly beneath the park as they went about their business. And on top of all this was the grass—white roots in the clay, green shoots above it, reaching into the air, trying to breathe something clean through the exhaust fumes from the sea of traffic endlessly growling past on Park Lane. In the three inches of grass that topped the clay was a tiny world of insects going about their daily grind as thoughtlessly and relentlessly as the human inhabitants of the city around them.

There were ants, there were ladybirds—and for a moment there was a beetle.

Edie saw it quite clearly, its shiny black back reflecting the orange glow from the streetlights as it moved slowly from a discarded cigarette packet toward a pile of vomit. She knew the little pyramid in the grass was vomit because she could smell it. She could smell it better than she would have liked because her nose was on the ground like the rest of her, splayed beneath a bush, hardly breathing. She knew the beetle *was* a beetle—but wasn't anymore—because she saw the gargoyle land three feet in front of her, and she saw its stone claw plash into the clay beneath.

Edie edged farther back into the shadows under the bush, trying to move as imperceptibly and silently as the tree roots beneath her. In her left hand was a small glass disk, glowing blue between her fingers. It was also hot. She slipped it in her pocket without taking her eye off the stone claw four feet in front of her nose. She didn't need a warning glass anymore. The thing was here. It was much too here for comfort.

It was a limestone gargoyle with the face of a snarling cat and the horns of a small devil. It had wings, but no arms, and long powerful legs that ended in the beetle-crushing foot claws Edie was staring at. Its eyes were blank stone like the rest of it, the set of its eyebrows was fierce and angry. A century and a half of weather had stained the stone in streaks of black and gray, and somewhere in the past, a hard frost had expanded the water in a crack in its right wing, and a section had fallen off, giving it a lopsided, battle-worn quality.

Edie knew she was good—unnaturally good—at not being seen when she wanted to remain unnoticed. But she wished she was even better at it as she watched the cat-gargoyle bend low to the ground and sniff. As it breathed out, she heard a low whistle, like someone blowing across the mouth of a bottle. It moved its head from side to side across the ground, trying to pick up a scent. Edie decided to stop edging backward and tried to make herself invisible instead.

The cat-gargoyle moved away from her toward the parapet over which George and the Gunner had disappeared. As it turned away to make its sniff-and-whistle noise scenting along the top of the wall, Edie allowed herself a deep breath. She also had a good opportunity to see the sharp ridge of vertebrae running down its back, like a line of giant thorns trying to burst through the taut stone skin. She could see the dense feline muscles bunch and relax as it moved to and fro, as if it were dancing in a slow trance, led by its nose.

And then Edie saw the woman with the stroller and the spaniel, hurrying through the orange gloom, obviously late for something and unhappy about it. The spaniel was running ahead of the woman, ears flapping happily. And then it stopped and its ears went back and it growled.

Edie's first thought was that it had seen the cat-gargoyle six feet ahead of it. The cat-gargoyle turned and looked at the dog.

The woman snapped her fingers at the dog as she passed on the strip of pathway. "Bramble. Come here. Bramble!"

Bramble was frozen in a trembling rigor in front of the cat-gargoyle. Spaniels don't get many ideas, so when one takes hold, they tend to stick with it. And with a horrible feeling in her stomach, Edie realized that the thought Bramble was having was *not* about being able to see the gargoyle. It was about sensing her under the bush.

"BRAMBLE! Come!" the woman called. She left the stroller and walked toward the dog and the gargoyle. The gargoyle took a step backward and crouched, drawing its wings open, parallel to the ground, ready to scythe into action. Edie noticed that the ends of the wings had sharp hooks on them. She'd seen a bullfighter once on the TV, and he'd made the same gesture with his cape, stepping back, spreading the cape behind him, hiding the sword, seeming innocent but ready to kill when the bull got close enough.

The woman walked right past the gargoyle. Edie thought she must have brushed it with her coat, but she clearly could not see it any more than her dog could. She grabbed the spaniel and clipped a leash to its collar.

"Come on, bad dog, there's nothing there!" she

snapped as she pulled the spaniel away. The dog started to bark back over its shoulder, the bark getting louder the farther his mistress pulled it. The bark ended in a yelp as the dog was swatted over the nose and attached to the stroller, whose occupant had now started squealing and yelling. There was a flurry of wind in the trees above, and the woman grimaced. She pulled an umbrella from the bags hung on the back of the stroller and opened it one-handed.

"Come on. It's going to rain. We've got to get home. Good dog."

The smack on the nose had dislodged the thought of Edie from the spaniel's mind, and she trotted after the cooing mother who trundled off into the darkness, putting a rain hood over the baby as she went.

Edie was about to breathe again when she realized something chilling. The cat-gargoyle remained braced and ready to attack—but its head had slowly turned, and it looked back over its shoulder in the direction the dog had barked.

Toward Edie.

Suddenly—so fast your eyes had to twist to keep up—it switched the position of its body so it faced her bush. Keeping the claw-tipped wings spread in a nasty echo of the umbrella Edie had just watched the woman unfurl, it crouched lower to the ground and sniffed toward her.

Very slowly, one wing tip pushed the bush aside, and suddenly Edie had nowhere to run. The stone eyes looked at her. Edie had time to note that the whistling breath came from a corroded copper pipe sticking straight out of the thing's mouth, like a gun barrel.

Edie reached into her pocket and pulled out the disk of glass. Where it had glowed blue, it now blazed like a torch, like a blue-green torch. She held it out straight at the end of her arm, with only the merest fraction of a shake. The rest of the shake was in her voice.

"Go away."

She cleared her throat. Lost the shake from her voice and tried again.

"GO AWAY! You have to GO AWAY!"

One stone eyebrow rose in a question. And then the fierce snarl stretched even farther back, and the horns flattened like the dog's ears had. And it didn't go away at all. It stepped toward her, pulling the bush apart, opening her to the world and whatever it was about to do.

And then the rain came—a spitter, a spatter, then all at once like a block falling from the sky. Edie set her jaw and glared defiantly at the stone eyes through the falling water.

"You. Don't. Scare. Me," she lied. "Nothing scares me. Not anymore. You can't hurt me. You have to GO AWAY!"

The cat-gargoyle shook itself in a shiver, looked her in the eye.

"You don't scare me. . . ." she lied again.

And then the cat-gargoyle jumped.

Backward. Up into the sky. Into the rain. Away from her.

Edie stared very hard at the place where it had been, until her eyes had convinced her brain that there was nothing to see except rain and grass and the ugly orange light.

She looked at the glass disk in her hand. As she was staring at it, the light died in it, and it looked like what it was, an old piece of sea glass, the bottom of a bottle washed to and fro by the tide, worn smooth by the pebbles and sand. Something anyone might find on a day at the sea. She stuffed it back in the pocket of her sheepskin jacket. Took several deep breaths, and headed across the grass down onto the ramp of the parking garage.

# CHAPTER NINE

## Parked Up

George and the Gunner stared up at the concrete ceiling. The gunner smiled.

"It's gone."

George slumped back against the wall and stared at the radiator grille of the Mercedes in front of them. "What was it?"

"A taint."

"A taint?"

The Gunner shrugged and scratched himself with more human pleasure than you'd expect from a statue.

"Probably a gargoyle. It was flying. Most of the flying taints are gargoyles."

George filed this under "New Information" and found he was overloaded in that department.

"Wait a minute. The thing that chased me from the Natural History Museum. The three lizard things that came off the building. The things you shot. Were they taints?"

"There you go. Catch on quick, you do. Keep going like that you might even make it through the night."

George was opening his mouth to ask a question he didn't really want the answer to, when there was a scuff of feet approaching. The Gunner held him still with a hand on his knee. The footsteps stopped in front of them. There was the scrape of a key in a lock, the solid *click-clunk* of a Mercedes door opening and closing, and then the boom of an engine coming alive behind the radiator grille in front of their noses.

"Er . . ." said George.

The headlights came on. George and the Gunner were splashed against the raincoat gray of the walls by the high beams, like cartoon prisoners caught in a searchlight.

"Help?" George shouted hopefully to the face behind the steering wheel in front of him. The face looked through him, then away as it craned around to back out of the parking space.

"He can't see you," said the Gunner.

The lights swept off them as the Mercedes chunked out of reverse, found drive, and squealed away down the rows of parked cars, looking for the exit.

"Why can't he see me?" he asked, feeling like he shouldn't have shouted help, as if it had somehow, given his situation, been rude.

"Oh. Well, he can see you. His eyes work, but he can't

*see* you in his head. His brain won't let him."

"Because?" said George.

"Because he's a normal rational bloke—apart from driving a German car—and normal rational people don't believe you can walk around London with statues. Stands to reason—it's impossible. So his mind won't believe his eyes. It's a protection thing. If he could see us he'd know he was, y'know . . ."

"Doolally."

"That's the ticket."

"Why can *I* see you?"

The Gunner indulged in some more scratching, then stood up suddenly and stretched out the kinks in his neck.

"Because you done something. Dunno what, but it must have been bad to get the taints so angry. Suppose we'll have to find out what it was, but I'll tell you this, and I'll tell you for nothing an' all—it was bad enough to drop you out of your London, into my London. And that ain't good. Not for you."

"What do you mean, your London?"

"I mean the London where the taints hate the spits, and things that stay still in your London move and hunt and fight. Didn't think your London was the only one, did you? London Town's more than just any old city. It's like the rock and the clay and the dirt it sits on. It's got layers. You just fell through one into another. Now, come on, we got to go ask the sphinxes how we can best solve—"

He stopped. Ears pricked. George stepped closer to him without thinking about it.

"What did you hear?"

"Nothing. I mean, I heard something stop, but the something was so quiet I didn't notice it until it suddenly wasn't there."

Footsteps started again, this time easily audible, heading for them. The Gunner relaxed.

"It's all right. It's just a person. Stand easy. Nothing to worry about."

"Nothing to worry about?"

The Gunner shook his head in disappointment.

"If you ain't going to listen there's no point me flapping my lip, is there? I told you. Normal people can't see us, because to them we, I, am impossible, right?" He pointed. "So she can't see us. Look."

A twelve-year-old girl with dark hair and a sheepskin coat walked toward the empty car bay they stood at the end of. The Gunner waved at her. Looked at George.

"See. Nothing. Try it. Make a face. Blow a raspberry. She won't be able to see you, I promise."

He nudged George. George waved at her. Her face didn't change. He stuck his tongue out and made a face.

"See," said the Gunner, "she can't see us because her mind won't let her."

"I can see you fine," said Edie. "I'm just waiting for you to stop making stupid faces and say something sensible."

The Gunner stared at her.

George stared at the Gunner.

The Gunner looked down at George.

"Ah," he said. "Interesting. That's not meant to happen. Unless . . ."

His voice trailed off like the smoke from his cigarette. And they all stood there for quite a long time, not saying anything, just looking at each other. George looked at Edie, Edie looked at the Gunner, and the Gunner looked right back at her. George felt the tiniest bit left out of the staring contest. So he broke the silence.

"Who are you?"

Edie didn't answer.

"Okay. Why are you here?"

She broke eye contact with the Gunner long enough to shoot George a look that was fierce and contemptuous in roughly equal proportions.

"I followed you. Obviously."

"Why?"

"Because I've seen statues move. Lots of times. But I've never seen anyone else see it. So."

Now she gave up trying to outstare the Gunner and looked at George. He realized her eyes were the same deep dark brown as her hair, as deep brown can get before it becomes black. So dark that you couldn't really see where the eye stopped and the iris began. This was a little unsettling. For all he knew, the irises were pinpricks of hate.

"So what?" he asked.

"So I thought you might be like me."

"He ain't," said the Gunner, still looking hard at her. "He's nothing like you."

Edie lifted her chin. Maybe it was to look up into the Gunner's face. Maybe it was just defiance. George thought it was probably both, but what he thought on top of all that was that the only thing weirder than finding yourself talking to a statue that talked back and shot things was seeing someone else do it. Somehow, standing to one side and watching something impossible happening made you a lot more woozy than doing it yourself. He found his hand had excavated the lump of plasticene in his pocket and was kneading it nervously.

"Why not?" asked Edie.

"Because," said the Gunner, as if that ended it, and walked past her, heading for the exit ramp. George and Edie looked at each other.

"Er," he said. That didn't sound impressive. So he tried "Um"—which sounded just as pointless as the last time he had used it. The black eyes blinked at him once. Then turned away as Edie strode off after the Gunner.

"Hey," she spat, "'because' isn't an answer. Why isn't he like me?"

The Gunner stood on the ramp, looking up at the rain coming down.

"I'm talking to you."

The Gunner turned very fast and grabbed her wrist.

She went to bite him, striking in the same swift snake action with which she'd bitten the bus conductor, but stopped before her teeth hit the bronze hand. Instead she growled in anger and kicked him. All she hurt was her foot. He reached for the collar of her coat and lifted her until they were eyeball to eyeball.

"I heard you," he said.

"So why isn't he like me? He can see you. He's just like me. He's—"

The Gunner cut her off. "He ain't like you. Ain't like you at all. No one's like you. . . ."

She struggled against the grip on the scruff of her coat, but it was about as effective as kicking him.

"No one's like you. No one's been like you for years. I ain't seen nor heard of someone like you for more than years. For decades. No one has. Some of us even think you're . . ."

Rain dripped into a growing puddle at the base of the ramp as he stood there trying to think of the right word. When he found it he rolled it around his mouth like a favorite sweet before letting it out.

"Extinct."

"I don't know what you're taking about. I'm not gone. I'm here. I'm a—"

"You're a glint."

"A what?"

"A glint. You're a glint."

She looked at George. He shrugged.

"What's a glint?"

"A glint is what you are if you can see all this. You're a glint, a seer, a bright spark; someone so sharp and shiny they cut themselves, so sharp they slice between all the different layers of 'what is' and 'what might be' and end up chopping right on through into the 'what was.'"

There was a flicker of something close to panic in Edie's eyes for a moment, then she pushed it away and jutted her jaw at the Gunner.

"I don't know that. I don't know what that means. I'm just me—"

"Glints is dangerous. Glints is trouble. Glints is so much bleeding trouble that they attracts more trouble. A glint is the last thing we need if we want to get where we need to go. So you stay here—and we're going."

"Don't tell me what to do," Edie growled. "Put me down."

"Or what?" asked the Gunner with a dangerously good-natured smile.

Edie squirmed her hand in and out of her pocket, and brandished the sea-glass disk in his face.

"Or I'll use this," she spat.

He looked at the dull glass circle with interest. He reached his hand toward it. He tapped it. It pinged dully.

"You'll use your bit of glass, will you?"

Edie concentrated savagely and nodded.

"What does it do?"

"It glows when there are gargoyles around, and they

fly away when they see it. It's powerful."

He pinged it again. She began to feel silly holding it out. He put her down suddenly.

"Frightened a lot of gargoyles with it, have you?"

"Yes. No. One. Just now. The one that was sniffing after you. It came after me, and I held it out and it flew away."

The Gunner looked at the rain falling out of the black rectangle over their heads.

"And why did you hold it out? Did you know it was powerful?"

"It gets hot when they're about. It gets bright. It senses them. . . ."

"And it's a weapon, is it?"

"It must be. It flew away."

"That why you got it out?"

"No. I got it out because I couldn't think what else to do." The Gunner's smile was getting on Edie's nerves. "Anyway. *Why* doesn't matter. It *worked*."

"Was it raining?"

"What?"

"When you thought you defeated the mighty gargoyle, was it raining? Had this rain just started?"

Edie thought. And nodded.

"Wasn't your glass. Your glass is just a warning stone. Not a weapon."

"But it flew away!"

"It flew away because it's a gargoyle. S'what a

gargoyle is. Just a jumped-up waterspout. A really ugly bad-tempered waterspout. That's its purpose. When it ain't raining, it can go where it likes, but soon as the first drop hits the roof of its building, it's got to go. Vengeance and spits don't mean a thing to it. It's got to do what it was made for, same as everything else does. It can't deny its First Purpose. It's got to do what the maker intended."

George coughed.

"The Maker? You mean God?"

The Gunner laughed and shook his head, sending an arc of rainwater spinning away from himself.

"Don't know anything about gods. A maker's just the bloke what makes us. I told you mine certainly wasn't any shape of a god, not Jagger. He was just a soldier himself, fought in the Great War, come out alive with a headful of what he'd seen, and making-hands to help others see a bit of it too. The gargoyle's maker was probably some medieval stonecutter with a foul mouth and a belly full of sour beer, more'n like. 'Makers make the made, and the made must follow their makers meaning.' That's how it goes. It's how it's always gone." He turned to Edie. "Your glass didn't save you, so don't try it again. Rain stopped play, or it'd have had you. It's not a weapon. It's a warning, no more, no less. Now we'll be going. Goodbye."

He snapped his fingers at George.

"Come. We can move fast and safe while it's raining, and we got a lot of city to cross before we make the river."

"Why are we going to the river?"

"Asking the wrong question again. Just come."

George threw a glance at Edie. She was standing in the rain, looking down at the glass in her hand. Two steps would have taken her under the shelter of the over-hang at the lip of the ramp, but she didn't seem bothered. She looked bedraggled and sad and a little like a puppet with some of its strings cut.

"Why can't she come?"

"I told you. She's a glint."

Edie looked up. There was a flash of lightning above, and in that flash she flinched. And for an instant, and only a very short instant, George thought she looked much younger and less certain. She pocketed the glass and wrapped her arms around herself, as if she had sud-denly noticed the cold.

"But I still don't know what a glint *is*!" she said, frus-tration straining the edges of her voice.

"Glints is uncanny. And what we got to do is going to take all the canniness I can muster. Glints is bad luck. Sorry, but that's the truth on it. Now we got to go."

"Okay," she said. "Go. Fine. But I'll follow you."

"Don't," said the Gunner, and strode off up the ramp.

She waved George after the Gunner.

"Go on, then. Off you go. You have to go. Otherwise I can't start following, can I?"

George felt a tug in his guts. He wanted to stay close to the Gunner, but something made him feel bad about leaving this girl. Maybe he was feeling sorry for her, he thought. Maybe he was feeling sorry for himself. Or maybe he just wanted company in his nightmare.

"Look," he started, "I'm sorry—"

*Whap.* She slapped him. The stinging smack to his face shocked him almost as much as anything he'd experienced so far.

"What the . . . Why did you . . . ?"

Edie bunched his shirt collar in her fist as she spoke, fierce and low.

"Don't be sorry for me. Don't treat me like I'm soft. And don't like me."

He felt the red handprint on his face. "I don't like you. Don't hit me again."

"Good. Then we'll get along fine. You better hurry up."

George looked up the ramp. The Gunner was gone. He didn't stop to think. He just raced up the wet incline, shouting, "Wait!"

# Chapter Ten

## Higher Ground

There are steep roofs on the north side of London's Euston Road, roofs pierced with clock towers and turrets and spires and chimneys. They are so high, and the sweep of the building is so fiercely decorated that no one looking up at its gothic exuberance really notices the watchers looking back at them. But above the sixty million bricks that make up St. Pancras station and the hotel attached to it, there is one of the largest rookeries of gargoyles in London.

On the north side of the building, its stone eyes staring out over the sweep of wet rails heading out of London beneath it, a cat-gargoyle arched over the gulf of air between it and the glass train shed below, as water spouted from the copper pipe jutting from between its snarling teeth. It was the same as all the other gargoyles on the roof, except for one thing. It was steaming, like a racehorse after a long hard race.

It didn't know much, but what it did know was this: it had failed. The other gargoyles of St. Pancras knew this. Next time, perhaps more than one would have to take to the air, and hunt in a pack. And next time they would not fail.

# Chapter Eleven
## Running on Shingle

Perhaps because it was still raining, the Gunner no longer ran. Instead he walked fast and purposefully down Park Lane, keeping the well-lit massif of Mayfair's western edge on his left shoulder, and the tree-filled void of the park on his right. Even though he wasn't running, George had to trot to keep up. George didn't say anything as they pressed on through two more underpasses and into Green Park. He had a head full of questions, but perhaps because he felt bad about leaving the girl behind, he said nothing. He knew if he asked another question right now, it would lead back to her in some way. So he left well enough alone. What he did do was glance back when he thought the Gunner wasn't looking, and saw that she was trailing them, about forty feet behind.

Edie watched the boy as she trailed them. She noticed him looking back, then turning away in case he was caught looking. He was only a couple of inches taller than she was, but then she was tall for her age and he seemed sort of hunched apologetically in on himself. His hair was longer than most boys his age, and it wasn't spiked or gelled or anything. His jacket flapped as he hurried along, too big for him—bought to grow into, no doubt—and as if to compensate, his ankles poked out below trousers that had clearly failed to keep up with a growth spurt. She remembered the look on his face as he'd said sorry. It had been an honest face, and he'd looked her right in the eye as he said it. He seemed kind underneath the sadness and fear. Which is why she had hit him.

She followed them into an underpass—only to find the fork in the tunnel, and that she suddenly had no idea which way they'd gone. She headed left, running, deciding if they had gone right she'd sprint back and catch them up.

In the right-hand tunnel, the Gunner had broken into a run of his own. George didn't catch him until they'd burst back out into the air.

"Why are we running?"

The Gunner jerked his head back.

"We're losing the baggage. Come on."

He pulled George through a hedge and ran on.

Under their feet, Edie realized she had taken the wrong turn. She doubled back and took the other tunnel. By the time she made it back out into the evening air, there was no sign of them.

She kicked savagely at the gravel. She did it again. Then she started running, cutting a wide arc through the trees, heading toward St James's Park and the river beyond. The Gunner had said they were going to the river. Maybe she'd catch them there. As she felt gravel spit under her running feet, she thought of the beach. And why she was running.

Edie knew the Gunner was right about one thing: she was bad luck. The thought caught at her like a riptide, sucking her back and down into a dark place where she found it harder and harder to breathe. The more she tried to run her mind away from the thought, the stronger the feeling grew. She knew the feeling was panic, and she knew giving in to panic was dangerous, because she'd stop thinking clearly. And thinking clearly was how Edie survived. Trying to escape the panic wasn't easy. It was like running in pebbles, like trying to scramble up a steep shingle beach, when every step forward slides back in a scrabble of unstable stones, and the faster you try and move, the more tired you get.

Edie had got very tired once, running up a shingle beach. Someone had been chasing her. She had run from the water across the sand and up the steep shelving wall of pebbles, hearing him behind her. The pebbles close to the sea started small, and got bigger as the slope rose toward the railway line at the top. Her feet made a crunching noise as she ran up the gravel-size stones; as they got bigger the noise changed to a scrabble, then a clacking as bigger stones cracked against each other, dislodged by her bare feet scrambling toward the top of the mound.

She had heard no noise behind her, so she risked a look. For a moment she could see nothing but the shingle and the gray sand beyond, and in the distance the wind blowing whitecaps across the rollers coming in from the Channel. Then she saw a flash of red as he came over the wooden beach divider, and she turned and ran faster. In panic.

She didn't see the half-buried tire that caught her foot and sent her sprawling on the very lip of the slope. It sent her crashing to the ground, smacking her cheek on a sea-flattened piece of flint; but it saved her. She found herself looking down into a deep trench, maybe six meters deep. On her side of the trench the pebbles sloped sharply down until they met a wooden wall that rose even higher than where she was. It was new wood, massively cut beams—three times as thick as a railway sleeper bolted together—to make a new beach defense. In the distance she saw yellow bulldozers and a construction shed, but it was too far away and on the wrong side of the wind for anyone to hear her even if she screamed, and there was no one there that she could see anyway.

It was Saturday afternoon, after all, and nobody works on a Saturday if they can help it. She was alone, and behind her she could hear crunching footsteps changing to clacking. She got to her feet, took one step forward—and fell again. Her ankle had turned. In the distance she heard a train approaching. She looked behind her. He was puffing up the last part of the slope, face as red as his anorak, almost as red as the blood staining the handkerchief he held to his cheek. His eyes were hot and angry but he was smiling. He wasn't smiling like a villain in a film; his smile wasn't saying "Gotcha." It was much more frightening than that, given what he'd said and what he'd tried to do, and what she'd done to stop him. It was a smile that said "I'm your friend—we're pals."

She knew the smile well. Out of that smile came lies and promises and threats and the smell of The Red Lion and the rank stale reek of rolling tobacco. Out of that smile came the sounds and smells of pain and betrayal and fear.

He stopped, and puffed and sucked air. He looked at the blood on his handkerchief. He scowled briefly around at the empty beach and the railway line beyond the deep trench and the beach defense.

"I'm going to have a heart attack, you carry on like this."

He smiled at her.

"Come on. Stop this nonsense. It'll be all right."

Edie would have been a lot more likely to believe him if he hadn't still been carrying the open lock knife in his other hand.

"Come on. It's just you and me. Don't be silly."

Edie heard the train approaching. It was coming fast. It would pass quickly and be gone, and she would still be here alone with him and the knife and nothing but the wind and the sea and the big heavy stones under her hand.

He spat and put the handkerchief away in his pocket. "It's just us."

The train boomed around the curve and into sight, suddenly upon them. The wire mesh on the rusting fence posts rattled in protest. Edie lurched to her feet and waved at the train—her cries for help drowned by the noise. The train was empty. The only pair of eyes belonged to the driver at the front. He misunderstood, smiled and waved at what he took to be a happy girl and her father on the beach, and was gone. Edie watched the empty windows flash past like hollow sprockets, with no human shape breaking their rectangular uniformity.

With another boom and the thump of empty air closing in behind it, the train was gone—and suddenly she was looking at the sea marsh beyond the rails, and the farewell flash of yellow as the last carriage pulled away, headed for the small town where nobody was expecting her home for tea.

And then she felt three distinct things all at once. She felt his hand grip her hair. She felt panic. And she felt the heavy smoothness of the rounded flint in her hand.

She knew she was bad luck. And she knew all about

panic. That's why she would always do whatever she could to steel herself against it. She would always stare at her fears rather than ever turn and run without thinking again.

She stopped running. She *hadn't* been thinking. She'd been remembering. She'd been looking back. She needed to look forward. She stood in the dark and tried to calm her mind enough to think ahead. Her right hand reached unconsciously for the sea-glass in her pocket. It closed tightly around it as she steadied her mind, eyes closed, concentrating on getting her breathing steady and her mind clear. And then her eyes opened as it came to her: before they had seen her, she had seen them, while she was creeping up on them in the underground parking garage; she'd heard them talking.

She'd heard the Gunner say they needed to talk to sphinxes. She hadn't walked all of the streets of the city, but she knew a lot of them. And she could think of only one place where there were sphinxes.

And it was by the river.

# CHAPTER TWELVE

## The Riddle of the Sphinxes

The rain was easing off when they turned off the Strand and headed downhill toward the Embankment. As they slowed a little, George asked a question that had been troubling him.

"What happens to statues when you shoot them—like you did—and they sort of go to dust and blow away?"

The Gunner spared him half a glance and less of a smile and kept on walking.

"You don't kill all statues like that. Not spits, anyway. But you kill a taint, they do go to pieces, and the wind or something takes them and winnows them off. I mean, they're gone from the walking world. They do end up reconstituted back on their perch or their plinth after turn o'day, but they never walk again. They're just lumps of rock or metal."

"And spits are different?"

"Chalk and cheese, mate. We don't go to pieces like

taints do. It's like we got more to hold us together—the spirit part. At least that's how I see it. It's like a sense of who we are is just enough glue to stop us getting blown away like a taint. We can get hurt, mind, and if we're hurt too far from home, same thing happens to us. But if we get back on our plinth or whatever before turn o'day—that's midnight to you—we get better."

"You get better?"

"It's like we wake up next day mended. Recharged, like a . . . like a . . ."

"Like an electric toothbrush," said George, getting it.

"A what?" said the Gunner, almost offended.

"Like an electric toothbrush," said George.

"Electric toothbrush, my Aunt Fanny!" snorted the Gunner. "No such thing. What kind of banana would put electricity in their mouth? Stress is getting to you, mate."

"No—" began George.

"Adam Street." The Gunner jerked a thumb at the street sign as they passed. "That's a good omen, if you believe in 'em."

George didn't know what to say.

"Not really sure what to believe in after today."

The Gunner jumped over the railings into Victoria Embankment Gardens and lifted George after him.

"Well, believe in good luck, then. Got to be good luck coming to the Sphinxes down Adam Street. Adam being the first man, and all. I mean, this is man's business you're on now, young 'un, so a good sign don't do any harm. There they are."

He hunkered down behind the railing and pointed with his chin. George crouched next to him and looked across the traffic to the edge of the Thames. A tall stone obelisk soared up into the night sky, and on either side of it, looking in opposite directions up and down the river, lay two crouched figures with the massive bodies of lions and the smooth faces and ribbed headdresses of ancient Egyptian royalty.

"It's Cleopatra's Needle," whispered George.

"'Course it is," said the Gunner. "I said we needed to talk to the Sphinxes. Though don't call it Cleopatra's whatsit if it comes up in conversation. They're a bit touchy on the subject."

"Why are they touchy?"

"Because they're Sphinxes and they're stuck in London and it's a lot bloody colder than Egypt—how do I know? Anyway. They don't like the rain, one of them really doesn't like people, and they get really narked if you call it Cleopatra's Needle."

George remembered walking past this place with his dad and mum when things were great and he was smaller.

"Right. It's *not* Cleopatra's Needle. It's an obelisk to Thutmoses or Tutmosis or someone. . . ."

The Gunner dropped his head and watched the last of the dwindling rain pour off it and splash on his boots.

"Probably shouldn't have said that. I mean you're right, but . . . you probably shouldn't have said that."

"Why?" George asked.

The Gunner stood up and swept his cape back over his shoulder, staring across the road.

Edie's voice came from behind them.

"Because they heard. And now they're looking at you."

The Gunner's eyes flicked at Edie and then dismissed her. "Both of them. And we only wanted to talk to the nice one. Enough trouble getting a straight answer out of her as it is. Come on . . ."

He stepped over the railings and hoisted George over after him. Edie stood there with her hands on her hips.

"What about me?"

The Gunner shrugged.

"Not my problem. You got in there, you get out. But I'm telling you for real this time. Stay away. I won't harm you. I'm a spit. Them Sphinxes, half-human, half-animal? . . . well, they're something in between: half-taint, half-spit. Get on the wrong side of them, it could go either way."

He pulled George across the traffic, oblivious to the cars and buses swishing past, but avoiding them as if by magic or blind luck. He spoke quietly into George's ear.

"It's because they're half-spit, half-taint that we're talking to them. If you've stirred up the taints, they'll know what's to be done—if anything's to be done."

As he got closer, George realized the Sphinxes were really as big as small elephants, and they both had their heads turned toward him. The faces were women's faces, as alike as identical twins, but not, somehow, the same. The Sphinx on the right had a kind, amused smile on her lips. The Sphinx on the left had the same smile, but something wasn't right about it. It wasn't kind. It was pained. George found himself edging toward the kinder-looking Sphinx. He heard the Gunner whisper under his breath.

"Good choice."

And then the Sphinx spoke.

"Thutmose *the Second*—to be exact."

"Not that we like to be exact," purred the other Sphinx. "We like to be enigmatic. Do you know what 'enigmatic' means, clever little boy?"

The Gunner nudged George.

"It means mysterious," he croaked. It really was very difficult having a conversation with a mythological creature the size of a minibus. You didn't know where to look.

"It means much more than mysterious. It means obscure, it means questionable, it means unreliable."

George couldn't help thinking they probably weren't the best things to come to for advice then, but he knew instinctively that it would be a really bad idea to mention it.

"You're probably not the best people to come to for advice then," said a tough little voice behind him.

"Who is she?" purred what George was beginning

to think of as the nice Sphinx.

"I'm Edie Laemmel," said Edie before the Gunner could answer for her.

"She's a glint," hissed the other Sphinx.

And now even the nice Sphinx didn't look so friendly either. They both tensed and drew back, like cats seeing a terrier approaching.

"Why did you bring a *glint*?" she asked the Gunner, using the word like it was something dirty. "We thought there were no more glints. We thought the gift had died out."

"She's not with us. She's just following us. She won't leave us alone."

"Of course not. She's a glint. They make pain for everyone. You shouldn't have brought her."

The Gunner spun and pointed at Edie.

"Back away. Double-time. Across the street. Now."

Edie stood her ground. Her lower jaw came forward and a strand of hair dropped in front of her eyes as she lowered her head, never breaking eye contact with the Gunner. George watched her nostrils flare and her lips whiten as she pressed them together.

"Look—"

The Gunner waved her off. "Go away."

"Listen—"

The Gunner stepped toward her suddenly. "Go away— please."

"I don't even know what a glint is."

The Gunner stopped. His head came back as if he hadn't thought of this possibility, as if he needed a beat to consider it. Edie stuffed her bunched hands into her pockets and looked at George.

"I'll go, if you tell me what a glint is."

It was George's turn to shrug helplessly. The Sphinxes hissed behind the Gunner. It was a cat noise, but coming from bodies their size it had the effect of a steam valve opening. The Gunner shook his head.

"No. You go. We ask these ladies our question. Then I'll tell you."

Edie's lips thinned down into an ever tighter line. Then she gritted out one word.

"Fine."

George watched her walk off down the pavement and lean against the wall, looking across the river as if she suddenly wasn't interested in them anymore. The Gunner put a hand on his shoulder and turned him back to the Sphinxes. They looked more relaxed—although, as they spoke he noticed one or the other of them was always looking over his shoulder, keeping an eye on the small girl silhouetted against the Thames. The Gunner edged him closer to the statues. George's head craned back as they loomed above him.

"We have a question."

The not-nice Sphinx spat an answer without taking her eyes off Edie.

"Everyone has a question. That's why they come to us."

"The boy, he's done something to stir up the taints. They're after him."

The other Sphinx, who wasn't looking so nice anymore, stared at him.

"So what?"

"So the question is, how can we stop them—"

"Killing him?" finished the Sphinx.

"That'd do for a start, yeah," said the Gunner.

"And that's your question?"

The Gunner looked at George. George nodded.

The Sphinx on Edie-watch suddenly turned her huge eyes on George. Her movement was so fast, and the headdress so like a cobra's hood fanned out on each side of her face, that George could only think of the three stone serpents rearing back to strike just before the Gunner had stepped off the monument. He could suddenly see exactly how half of her, at least, was a taint. The impression was reinforced as she hissed her question.

"You're sure? You're sure that is the question you want answered?"

Since George couldn't think of anything more important than not getting killed, he nodded again.

"Ask it, then."

He cleared his throat.

"How can I stop these things killing me?"

They looked at him expectantly.

"Oh, *please*."

The Sphinxes leaned against one another with a sinuous feline familiarity.

"Anyone can ask us a question, and we must answer, but only if the questioner first answers a riddle or a question we ask them. That is the way of the Sphinx."

George looked at the Gunner. The Gunner nodded.

"That's how things work with them."

"But I'm terrible at riddles."

The not-nice Sphinx smiled. At least, George thought it was the not-nice Sphinx. Since Edie arrived, it really was becoming harder and harder to tell them apart.

"Then you won't get an answer; and you can go away and take your glint with you."

"She's not *my* glint."

"You can take her away anyway."

George saw a look in her face, a flash of malice, a spark of the same bored unpleasantness he'd seen in Killingbeck's eyes. It made him angry. The anger flickered awake in his belly, like a flame in a woodstove when a log has been lying smoldering all night without flames, waiting for someone to open the door and let enough air in to reignite the blaze. It wasn't a blaze, it was just a cat's tongue of flame, but it was the first time George had felt anything except fear and confusion since the pterodactyl had unpeeled from the frieze, so he held on to it. It felt familiar, and comforting. He faced up to the Sphinx.

"Ask your riddle."

The Sphinx lowered its head to the pavement. George

could see its shoulders hunched high behind it. He knew he was getting the mouse's eye-view of a big cat. And he knew cats liked playing with mice.

Before they ripped them apart.

The Sphinx's head began to move in a small serpentine zigzag as it spoke. George wondered if it was trying to hypnotize him.

"I am a suit no men may wear, neither peasants
    nor kings,
Yet no man goes without me.
What's got by me shall be well known.
What lies at me is the reason for things.
All may touch me when I am soft, none when I
    am stone.
Lose me and you will falter—yet if I am taken,
    you will find courage anew."

The other Sphinx purred the question over the first one's shoulder.

"What am I?"

George stood there. Traffic hammered past on the road behind him. He could hear the hiss of tires on the wet tarmac. He knew the real world was right there, a world where boys didn't have to answer impossible questions asked by even more impossible creatures like giant bronze cat-people. But he also knew that answering this question was the only way he could get back to that other safe world. He didn't know how he knew it, but he did. And because he knew this, and couldn't begin to think what the answer to the riddle was, he let that flicker of anger build. Frustration hit the anger like pure oxygen hitting a flame, and the flicker turned into a blaze and a roar that blocked everything out. He clenched his fists and turned to the Gunner.

"It's not fair! I don't know the answer! It's stupid!"

He felt the rain on his face trickling down the side of his nose. Then he realized it wasn't raining, and that the rain on his nose was tears, and that made him angrier still. He swiped his hand across his face, wiping it off.

"It's not fair, it's just—"

The Gunner crouched down. Gripped his shoulders. Looked into his face. Shook him twice, hard.

"You're angry. Sometimes angry gets things done. This isn't one of those times, right? Angry stops you thinking. And this is one time you need to do exactly that."

George breathed in through his mouth, out through his nose. He did it again, trying to slow things down. It was something his dad had showed him how to do. Sometimes it worked. He looked up at the Sphinx.

"Can you say it again?" he asked.

"I don't have to."

George felt the flame flare. He tried to shut the oxygen off by controlling his breathing again.

"You must be scared I'll guess it, then."

The bronze eyes held steady.

"Must I?"

George tried not to blink. The Sphinx shuddered and stretched.

"I am a suit no men may wear, neither peasants
    nor kings,
Yet no man goes without me.
What's got by me shall be well known.
What lies at me is the reason for things.
All may touch me when I am soft, none when I
    am stone.
Lose me and you will falter—yet if I am taken,
    you will find courage anew."

The moment the Sphinx began to talk, George closed his eyes. He just concentrated on what he was hearing. He thought of different kinds of suits: business suits, diving suits, suits of armor, tweed suits, lawsuits, sailor suits—nothing made sense. It just didn't. It was like the crosswords his father used to do, clues within clues, cryptic like a code that only grown-ups understood. His father used to try clues on him, and he hardly ever understood the answers, even when he explained them to him. There were words that meant secret things, other words that meant you had to take words to bits and use their letters to make new words, and lots of shorthand winks at the puzzlers that the regulars would get to help them on their way.

He could see his father laughing at some particularly clever clue when he'd solved it. He could hear him saying it was simple if you remembered that words could mean more than one thing, saying you had to read the clues again because they might not mean what you first thought, saying that sometimes they were there to send you down the wrong alley.

He opened his eyes. The Sphinx's smile was especially annoying. He closed them again. Suits—what other kind of suits were—And then it hit him like a bright flash, and he was talking before he had finished the thought.

"Hearts. Hearts! You're a heart."

His eyes opened fast enough to see the surprise ripple between the two Sphinxes. The Gunner gaped at him.

"Heart?"

George knew he was right. It all fell together as he spoke, and he felt something like clean air blowing through his mind.

"*I am a suit no men may wear*—that's 'suit' like suits of cards, so it's got to be clubs, spades, diamonds, or hearts. *No man goes without me?* Well, it's got to be a heart, because if you don't have a heart you're like a thing without a battery, you don't go at all. *What's got by me shall be well known?* Easy—if you've *got* something *by* heart, you know it *well*. *What lies at me?* i.e. what *lies* at the heart of something—*is the reason for things . . .*"

He could feel the Gunner looking at him in amazement. More than that, he felt elation sweeping him onward, his mind becoming faster and clearer as the rest of the riddle almost seemed to solve itself as it tumbled out of his mouth.

"*All may touch me when I am soft, none when I am stone?* A *soft* heart is easily touched, but a *stone* heart isn't affected by anything; it's untouchable! If you *lose* heart, you *falter*, but if you *take* heart, you get your courage back. Heart. The answer is heart. You have to answer my question!"

He realized he was jabbing his finger at the front Sphinx, like he was in charge. It didn't feel particularly wise or polite, but it felt good.

"You want to know how to stop the taints killing you?"

"Yes. I answered your riddle. You *have* to tell me!"

The Sphinx sat back on her haunches and looked at her sister. The sister spoke.

"Your remedy lies in the Stone Heart, and the Heart Stone shall be your relief. To end what has begun, you must first find the Stone Heart, and then you must make sacrifice and amends for that which was broken by placing on the Stone at the Heart of London that which is necessary for its repair."

George looked at the Gunner. The Gunner looked at him.

"What's the Stone Heart?"

The Gunner shrugged. They both looked at the Sphinxes. The Sphinxes looked enigmatic.

"What's the Stone Heart?"

If a cat can shrug, that's what the Sphinx closest to George did.

"We answered your question. If you don't understand the answer, maybe you should have asked a better one."

All the good feelings that had been washing through George seemed to stop and start to curdle all at once.

"That's not fair!"

"We're not fair. We're Sphinxes. Now go away."

The second Sphinx looked a little shamefaced as it turned away and headed for its plinth. It was the nicer of the two.

"You cheated!"

"We answered your question."

"But . . ."

"But you didn't answer mine."

There it was again. That gravelly little voice. The Sphinxes turned back. George turned. So did the Gunner. Edie was standing right behind him.

"He's right. You cheated him. So now answer my question."

The Sphinxes got that cat with a terrier look again.

"We don't have to."

"Yes, you do. You're Sphinxes. Answering questions is what you do. You're just nasty about it. Both of you."

"Both of us?"

It was the not-nice Sphinx. Edie stood her ground.

"We're both the same, are we? You're sure about that?"

"Yes. No. Hold on—that's a trick, isn't it?"

"Is it?" The Sphinx smiled.

Edie nodded. She walked toward it. George wasn't sure what was going on, but he got the strong impression that the Sphinx was controlling the urge to shy away from the approaching girl.

"You asked me if you're both the same. I think you mean that to be your question, so I get it wrong before I even know you're doing one of your riddles and you don't have to answer my question. I think that's a twisted sphinxish way of tricking people."

"You have a very suspicious mind, little girl."

"Thank you."

Edie walked up one side of the Sphinx, then down the other. Then she walked over to the other one and did the same. Then she smiled.

"You look the same. But you're different. You"—she pointed at the nicer of the two—"you are perfect. You're smooth. Unlike you"—she walked up the side of the other one and pointed to its side—"you've got holes. Something has put holes in you."

George squinted. She was right. There were small jagged holes in the flank and foreleg of the bronze body. The Sphinx looked down at itself.

"Very clever. Very sharp. But I'm afraid that wasn't my question."

Edie shook her head.

"We both know it was. But if you want to cheat, ask me another."

Before the not-nice Sphinx could answer, the nice one spoke.

"How did we become different?"

The other Sphinx turned on its haunch and hissed in something that might have been anger but was also close to alarm.

"No! She's a glint. She's a *glint*! She'll—"

The two Sphinxes were suddenly eyeball to eyeball, tails writhing in slow irritation with each other.

"I know. But the girl was right. You were cheating. That's not being an enigma. That's lying. Let her answer. You have become too taintlike of late, sister—"

"Do you wonder I have turned against men after they made me as I was, then marred me as they did, as they did when—?"

"No, sister, enough. Let the girl tell us, if she can. . . ." The damaged Sphinx held herself still as Edie walked up to her.

"What's happening?" asked George.

The Gunner looked at Edie running her hands along the huge flank of the bronze Sphinx. Her hand stopped as she found a hole. He turned away and reflexively pulled his collar up, like a man expecting a sudden squall.

"Mind your shoes."

George couldn't take his eyes off Edie. Her hand disappeared inside the Sphinx.

"There's a hole."

The Sphinx stared at her, unimpressed.

"A hole isn't *how*. A hole is *what*. You told us I have holes already."

Edie closed her eyes. A small shudder passed through her.

"Wh—?" began George. Then it happened.

Edie stiffened. There was the sense of a silent detonation at her epicenter—the blast wave of whatever was happening to her blew her hair out in a fan, and before it had a chance to fall again, all the leaves on the trees blew flat and the street garbage blew away from her in a three-hundred-and-sixty degree arc. George opened his mouth.

Edie screamed. Her back arched, her eyes screwed shut, her mouth opened wide, her neck tendons snapped tight as violin strings, and a sound that wasn't a just sound ripped into George's head. He threw his hands over his ears to protect himself. It didn't make a difference. The scream was stuck inside his head and just seemed to get louder and louder as it echoed around with no way to escape.

Edie felt the past slam into her through her hands like a massive electric shock, as if the metal of the statue had been storing the memory of pain and horror deep within it, waiting for her to touch it and receive the full power of it in one distilled jolt.

Her eyes snapped open. Then shut. Then open.

Again and again. And as they did, she saw the past in fast juddering time slices, some freeze-frames, some slow-motion fragments of light and sound. Every time she closed her eyes to escape the unbearable pain that the past seared into her, she found an intolerable pressure built up in her head, and she knew it would burst if she didn't open her eyes and let the past in once more.

And what she saw in the jarring slices of her vision was this:

The Embankment was different. The road was thinner. The trees shorter, and some were in different places. The modern office blocks were gone. The bridges were not as they are now. People stood looking up into the sky. It was bright day. The city did not roar with the sound of thousands of unseen motorcars growling through its entrails. The people wore the long skirts and formal coats of the early twentieth century. A nanny in a uniform was smiling as she tried to fasten the bonnet on a laughing child. A newspaper seller was shouting something about the "British Expeditionary Force" and Flanders, though he stopped shouting and swore when he saw the thing everyone else was looking up at loom into view over the tops of the buildings.

A long slow rocket shape hummed overhead, whirring propellers pushing it between Edie and the sun. It was almost dreamlike in its slow immensity.

People stopped shouting and just stared at it. In the sudden calm Edie could hear the clopping of a horse approaching as a hansom cab came out of Adam Street—the cabbie lowering his whip as his mouth fell open at the sight above him. She heard him swear softly, "Bloody hell. A zeppelin!"

Then small dark dots fell slowly out of the belly of the zeppelin, and time broke into fragments again. But like shards of glass, the fragments seemed to cut deep into Edie's brain and increase the pain tenfold.

She saw the dots get bigger. Closer. Resolve into bomb shapes. She saw a woman scream and a man throw her to the ground, covering her body with his.

She saw the newspaper seller jump over the edge of the Embankment, down into the Thames.

She saw the first bomb hit the road.

She saw the flash.

She felt the blast rip her lips back off her screaming mouth.

She felt the blast heat sucking into her lungs.

She screamed louder.

She saw the holes blown in the side of the Sphinx.

Saw a child's bonnet blow into the iron railings of Adam Gardens.

Saw the man and the woman blown into the top of a tree.

Saw the horse in two parts, slowly pinwheeling twenty feet into the air; wet bits of it, that should never be seen, ribboning apart in a hideous mind-scarring arc.

And then it stopped.

And the present was back.

George and the Gunner were bent double, shielding themselves. The screaming noise suddenly stopped scouring around George's head. He convulsed as the rising wave of nausea hit him, and he threw up for the second time that night, a thin spatter of bile all over his feet.

The Gunner tried to force his face out of the pained grimace it was stuck in.

"Told you to mind your shoes."

George sat down on the pavement. Every joint was aching, and the nausea had changed to something like ancient dread or deep sadness, or the memory of both. Edie was staring at her hand. She sat down suddenly, a plan her body had decided on without consulting her mind.

"That was—bad," George managed to say.

The Gunner nodded. He looked as shaky as a solid bronze man can look.

"She's a glint. I told you."

Edie was looking up at them from across the pavement. Behind her, the Sphinxes were dragging themselves back onto their plinths. They still looked like big cats. But now they looked like big sick cats. The Gunner rubbed his face.

"Glints are people bad things happen around. Glints can make even the stones weep."

Edie looked at the Gunner. Then at the Sphinxes.

"Why?"

The closest Sphinx stopped and looked at her.

"How can you not know what you are? Everything knows what it is."

Edie pulled herself to her feet.

"I thought you answered questions. Not asked them. A bomb put holes in the one of you that's damaged, right? Now answer my question."

"You want to know why glints can make stones weep?"

The Gunner stepped forward, between the girl and the crouching giant cat.

"No."

Edie pushed him aside. George was struck by the fact that such a small girl could make such a big statue move out of her way. In fact, he'd later wonder if the Gunner hadn't sort of shied away from her hands pushing at his knees.

"It's my question. I earned it," she spat fiercely.

"But—" began the Gunner.

"No buts. No more buts or waits or go-aways!"

She punched her finger at the Sphinx's face.

"Answer my question!"

# CHAPTER THIRTEEN

## How a Stone Weeps

The Sphinx settled back on its haunches. The one behind it rumbled a growl like distant thunder. Its tail lashed lazily and was still. Edie put her finger back into a fist and buried both her hands in her pockets.

The Sphinx still facing her—the nice one—looked like it had returned to its normal unmoving state. Edie kicked at the plinth.

"Hoi. I'm still here!"

"Scarcely," sighed the Sphinx.

"What do you m—" began Edie.

"If you keep interrupting you'll miss the answer, won't you?" the Sphinx whispered, raising an eyebrow. Edie closed her mouth. She had to do it twice, but eventually it stayed shut.

"You are here. I can see that. But to know what a glint is, to truly comprehend, you must see things on a longer scale. And on a longer scale, you, him, all *people* are scarcely here at all. Compared to the life of stone or metal, you're as important as a splash of rain that falls in a summer shower, and then dries out and is gone. What people do passes, but the rocks remain. Not forever. Just a lot longer than people. And the rocks remember."

"That doesn't make sense. Rocks can't remember. Rocks can't think—"

"Do you want an argument or an answer?"

"I want an argument that makes sense."

"Glints bring the spark of what happened out of the rock."

George suddenly understood.

"You see the past!"

Edie turned on him as if he had somehow betrayed her.

"I don't! I mean, it's not, it's—" Edie stuttered.

"It's more than that," said the Sphinx softly.

George felt his mind spinning wild, but it spun on a center, and that center was the conviction that he was right about Edie, that he knew her gift.

"But you *do* see the past. When it's happening, when you did that thing, when everything went, you know, sickening like you've been kicked in the stomach, when your hair stood on end—"

Edie shook her head angrily.

"I don't know what 'thing' I do. I don't think *I* do anything. Something does it to me!"

"But you were just there, and your hair kind of blew out and—"

"Look! I wasn't 'there,' I was, I was—"

Surprisingly it was the Sphinx that came to her rescue.

"She was 'then.' Bad things that happen leave a mark on their surroundings. Good things, too. But people respond more strongly to bad. And glints, when they touch stones that have a mark in them, channel it. The past plays through them again."

George, in the midst of everything, found himself enthralled by the idea.

"That's so—amazing! What's it like when you—"

Edie cut him off tersely.

"Terrible."

The Gunner looked over their heads.

"It's a waste."

Edie looked up at him.

"What do you mean, a waste?"

"Using your question to ask them about it. I could have told you that. Any spit could. But you had your precious question and now it's used up."

The Sphinx looked at them with a cat-that-got-the-cream smile. George found himself hating it.

"So we just answer another of its riddles, and get another question."

The not-nice Sphinx lashed its tail and turned on them.

"It doesn't work like that. You get one question each day."

Edie looked on in silence as George took this in.

"And you don't have a day. Not to wait. Not to live, probably."

George felt panic drop the bottom out of his stomach again. The Sphinx's voice had a mocking triumph in it that he didn't like one bit, mainly because it sounded so sure of itself. He turned on the Gunner.

"What does she mean?"

The voice of the other Sphinx came over his shoulder.

"Ask the shaveling."

George spun on it.

"The what?"

Something was happening to the Sphinx. He realized it was retreating back into motionless, blank bronze. He asked again, urgently: "The what? Please, the *shaveling*? What shaveling?"

The Sphinx's eyes lost life and dulled before them— its voice retreated too, as if it were coming from farther and farther away.

"The dark shaveling. What is to be known, he knows. . . ."

And as an echo of a whisper, before the sounds of the traffic still hammering past them on the Embankment drowned everything, George was sure he caught, on the edge of his hearing, the other Sphinx's mocking whisper.

"And much that is not to be known—not by you, thing of flesh, little rain splash, so shortly here, so soon gone. . . ."

George looked at Edie. Edie looked at the Gunner.

The Gunner shrugged. Edie looked unimpressed.

"You don't know what a shaveling is?"

The Gunner shook his head.

"Do you?"

Edie shook hers. They both looked at George.

"Someone who shaves?" he tried.

"Oh, nice one," said Edie. "Someone who shaves. Can't be more than about four million of them in the city. You going to ask them all?"

The Gunner grimaced at her and stretched out a kink in his shoulder.

"Don't give him grief, you're the one should have asked about the Stone Heart."

"Why?" said Edie, looking up with an intensity that stopped him stretching and made him look, unexpectedly, uncomfortable.

"Because we need to know what it is, don't we, missy? Because we're in big trouble and—"

Again she cut him off flatly.

"What 'we'? Is there a 'we' here that I don't know about? Because all you've done since I found you is try to lose me and tell me to stay away. That's not being 'we.' That's being 'you.' And I don't think I owe 'you' anything."

"But—"

"And don't call me missy."

The Gunner swallowed something. George wondered whether it was frustration or something closer to fear.

Then he found himself wondering why—whichever it was—that Edie provoked such a reaction in the large soldier.

"But you were going to ask, weren't you? That's why you answered their question. . . ."

George joined in.

"You did. You were going to ask, he's right—"

Edie swiveled her eyes without moving her face, and George, caught in the flatness of her gaze, knew exactly what it was about her that perturbed the Gunner. Her eyes, when they were like this, were not particularly human, or if they were human, they seemed so old that no human could have lived long enough to own them. They were eyes that had gone elsewhere and seen awful things and come back different. He realized that the flatness of her gaze was not dullness. It was as if her eyes were worn or bleached out by too much weather.

"I was going to ask. Then I changed my mind."

"But why?" asked George.

The Gunner exhaled in frustration.

"Never trust a glint."

Edie stood her ground. "You going to start asking everyone who shaves, then, hope that you find the right one, the one who can tell you about your precious stone heart thingy?"

"No," said George, bridling. "I'm going to find a dictionary and look 'shaveling' up."

"Good," said the Gunner unexpectedly.

"You saying a dictionary's a good idea?" asked Edie incredulously.

"Dunno," said the Gunner cheerfully. "But it's a good thing he's having ideas and not just panicking or pissing and moaning. Because, unless you missed all that the Sphinx said, whatever he's got to do, sounds like the clock's running. Come on."

George jogged to keep up with the Gunner, who was crossing the traffic and heading away from the river.

"You know where we can find a dictionary? A book-shop maybe, or—"

"I got no idea where we can find a dictionary, son, but I can do us one better."

"Better than a dictionary?"

"Yeah. I know where we can find a man what wrote one. Come on. Mind that taxi."

George hopped up on to the curb as a cab whined past, narrowly missing him. He looked back. He couldn't see Edie.

# CHAPTER FOURTEEN

## The One Who Walks Behind

The woman in the red raincoat pulled it a little tighter around her neck and hurried through the light drizzle toward Cannon Street station. All around her, people swerved and stutter-stepped past each other on the pavement. The traffic was moving slowly enough for some of them to walk on the edge of the road instead, and all of them had, in some way, the same thought: home.

These were the professional commuters, London's foot soldiers, each determinedly plowing their own way homeward in the way they had done yesterday, and the way they would tomorrow. Almost all walked on autopilot. People with trains to catch walked faster than those who just needed to take the tube. People who needed a bus walked irritably between stops, gauging their speed with one eye constantly darting back over their shoulders in case a red double-decker should unexpectedly materialize where there had been none a moment before.

The only ones displaying any kind of self-consciousness were the ones looking for a taxi. They were the only ones looking at the other pedestrians too, in case someone darted ahead of them and pulled a cab from under their noses.

The woman in the red raincoat had no thought of a taxi on her mind. She was looking forward to the Northern Line and twenty-five minutes—she hoped seated—head down over the paperback now bumping on her hip in the pocket of her coat.

And then, like a deer in the forest when it catches a sound or unexpected smell, her head came up. She felt something behind her. She turned, not knowing why, and saw no one. Or rather, she saw everyone but nobody in particular, nobody looking at her.

Except, someone *was* looking at her. In the city someone is almost always looking at you, even when you think you're alone. And when you think you're most alone—say, on a dark street, late at night, when everyone honest and sober is safe in bed—and you get that prickle between your shoulder blades that tells you someone is watching you, and you turn quickly and see no one, and you sigh with relief—don't kid yourself: there's always someone there. Just because you can't see them doesn't mean they aren't there.

The walker behind the woman in the red coat had had a long time to perfect not being seen. He had had a long time to perfect his walking too, and if you had the knack of seeing him, of noticing him even though he was making sure that no one saw him, you might notice that he was never actually still—he never stopped walking. Even when he looked like he might be standing still, he rocked from foot to foot, walking on the spot. Sometimes he walked on the spot, so slowly and deliberately he looked like an animal pawing the ground just before it springs on its prey. If you were able to keep him centered in your eyes and, perhaps more important, your mind, then you might begin to see that this perpetual motion hung on him like a curse.

And if you thought that, you might be more right than you knew.

He walked tall, a long once-green tweed overcoat flapping at his heels. His face was hard to see, as he wore an old green hoodie with the hood turned up. Long tendrils of gray and black hair escaped into the night breeze. The coat partially obscured the yellow outline of a prancing stag leaping across the front of the grimy sweatshirt, below a John Deere logo. The faintly hippy-ish atmosphere about him was enhanced by the jewelry he wore around his neck—a rough stone hanging from a thick silver chain, worn tight as a choker—so tight that the stone bobbed up and down in sync with his Adam's apple.

The Walker felt the thing that had pulled him from his normal meandering passage through the city tug insistently at him from the side of the building across the

road, like a dark magnet. His tongue made a rare appearance and flicked over dry lips. It was the sinister pull
dragging at him with a renewed intensity that made him
forget to prevent the woman from seeing him. She
looked around a second time and gasped to find this tall,
ominous figure so close behind her.

The dry lips parted in something like the almost-for-
gotten memory of a smile. His hand reached out and
touched her lightly on the shoulder.

"It's not all right," he said gently, as if comforting her.
Her eyes widened. His voice was like the dry rustle of
leaves blown across a tombstone.

"It's not all right at all. None of it. And it never will
be."

And because she had heard him and because he had
allowed her to see him, she started to scream. She
dropped her bag and opened her mouth and screamed:
not at him—because being instantly forgotten was
another skill he had—but at everything else.

As he walked across the street toward an undistinguished office building, the woman in the red coat continued screaming, her high voice cutting sharply through
the endless growl of the traffic. The crowd eddied and
parted around her as the commuters noticed and avoided
another lone street-crazy howling at the city in the growing darkness.

The Walker crouched in front of a low wrought iron
grille set into the side of the building. He reached his

hand through and rocked slightly, his feet flexing beneath his bent legs, as if trying to push the building. He stared intensely through the grille, listening. He nodded.

"I see."

He listened some more.

"If the taints fail again. I will bring him. We will bring him."

His hand jerked out from behind the grille—and it was hard to tell if it was being spat out or he was just relieved to get it back—and he rocked up onto his feet and started walking north. As he did so, he tugged at the bulging hood around his head. A large black bird hopped free and shook its wings out, perching firmly on the green tweed shoulder of his coat.

"Go and find the ones that failed."

The bird clacked its beak and lofted into the sky, sideslipping between two tall buildings, and was almost immediately lost to sight.

Back on the street, the Walker waited unnoticed in a phalanx of uninterested pedestrians for the lights to change, before striding off to the north. As they waited, a police car sirened past and stopped farther down the road, where a screaming woman in a red coat was being helped by two other women who were finding it impossible to calm her, or discover what it was that had filled her with such deep horror.

The lights changed and the Walker paced until he

found someone heading in his direction to follow. And then they were gone as the swirl of humanity closed in behind them.

# CHAPTER FIFTEEN
## A Man Called Dictionary

The Gunner walked fast, and George jogged to keep up. The Gunner had something on his mind. He cleared his throat, as if approaching a difficult subject with a delicacy he wasn't used to displaying.

"He herks and jerks a bit. Don't mind it. He doesn't. Unless you let on you notice."

"Herks and jerks?" said George, who was getting quite used to not understanding what anyone was saying to him.

"Yeah, slobbers. And twitches. He don't mean anything by it, he can't help it; but I'll tell you what, he's got a brain on him. He knows all about words and history, and London . . . and anything else you can think of, I reckon."

The Gunner walked on a few paces.

"Mind you, he is sensitive about the twitching. And he'll make funny noises all of a sudden, like he might bark out a strange word, maybe like he's a bit, you know . . ."

He tapped his tin hat.

"Mad?" George ventured.

"Nah, not mad. As such. Not Dictionary. But you might think he's got a few tiles loose on the roof, so to speak. He hasn't, though. His bark's worse than his bite, and his brain—well, way he tells it he wrote a whole dictionary by himself in half the time it took a roomful of Frenchies to do it, so his brain's top of the line. He don't much like Frenchies, of course, but that was the way of it when he was alive—"

George stopped in his tracks.

"When he was alive? So he's *dead*?"

"He's not dead, you idiot. He's a statue, right?" Edie was walking right behind him. He didn't know how long she'd been there, and he jumped a bit at the sound of her voice so close in his ear.

"Right," growled the Gunner. "He's the spit of a man who lived three hundred–odd years ago, which was a time when little misses was meant to be respectful and silent, so you keep a mind of it when we talk to him, right?"

Edie's expression said anything *but* it was all right with her, but she didn't say a word as they came up out of the side street and into the Strand, heading east into the flow of pedestrians hurrying toward Charing Cross station.

Strangely enough, although no one noticed the

Gunner, everyone got out of his way, so George and Edie were able to make good progress by tucking in behind him and staying close.

"Weird how they can't see him, isn't it?" puffed George.

Edie said nothing. After several yards of nothing, George decided he wasn't going to speak to her anymore. When he had first realized she could also see the Gunner, back in the underground garage, he had felt a flicker of relief that at least here was someone else who might share his nightmare and make it less horrible. He now realized this had been the fear talking.

Edie might be his age, she might be able to see the unbelievable things he saw, but there was no inch of give in her. He'd tried to talk to her and she'd started out by hitting him—and things had gotten worse from there. Much worse. He could still taste the bile in his mouth from his reaction to her glinting with the Sphinxes. Nothing good had come from her yet, and he'd be a fool to expect anything from her. Least of all a conversation.

"It's horrible," she said.

Despite himself, he looked around at her. She shrugged, her eyes on the ground.

"When I first saw them moving—the statues—I thought I'd gone loony. I thought the first one I saw was some kind of trick for the tourists, some bloke dressed up, covered in black paint or something. I thought it was a good trick. Then I noticed no one else paid him any attention at all. And after a bit I got sc— I got what you said. Freaked out. Then I saw you running through the park with him, so . . ."

"So you ran after us."

"I thought it'd make it less horrible."

"Here we go, come on, mind that bus. . . ."

The Gunner suddenly lurched into the traffic, making for a small, pale stone church marooned on its own island where the Strand was joined by the curved tributary of the Aldwych, just before they both hurried on to become Fleet Street. The church's spire ascended to the sky in elegant steps, sharply defying the taller and more impressive buildings around it, flanked by a scrabble of twisted plane trees reaching up in half-hearted solidarity.

Three statues stood facing east in front of it. George looked at each one expectantly. There were two men in World War II uniforms and peaked caps; and farther off, the back view of a man in a long gown on top of a very elaborate plinth peered back down the Strand as if expecting something distasteful to appear at any moment. George looked at the Gunner.

"Is he the Dictionary?"

"Why d'you think it's him?"

"Because he looks like a professor. In his robes. He looks distinguished."

The Gunner shook his head.

"He's not distinguished. He's just a politician. Come on."

George eyed the two statues in peaked caps as they approached them.

"Is it—"

The Gunner pointed past the stautes.

"Not them. He's at the other end."

George felt odd walking past the statues, as if either one might suddenly jerk into life at any minute. Despite their uniforms they both looked a bit schoolmastery. Edie eyed them both carefully. She nodded at George.

"I know what you mean."

"I didn't say anything."

"They look like each other. But they're different. You can sense it."

"No, I can't. I was just thinking it's really weird not knowing when or if they're going to come alive."

"Oh. I thought you got the vibe."

He looked at her. She looked disappointed.

"What vibe?"

"Dunno." She nodded at one of the uniformed men. "But there's a lot of death there."

George realized something else about Edie. Nothing she said ever made anything better. He shivered and followed the Gunner around the corner of the church.

"There's a lot of death everywhere," grunted the Gunner. "This is London. Lot of life, lot of death, lot of everything. Here he is."

"Here who is?" said a new voice.

George looked up. A statue of a man in eighteenth-century dress looked down at him, a bird perched incongruously on top of a wig that in real life would have been powdered, but now was peppered with pigeon splat. Between the bun-shaped sides of the wig, his face hung fleshy and lopsided, mouth working silently, as if he were chewing his tongue.

The Gunner tipped his helmet back on his head and nodded a greeting.

"Dictionary, if you can spare a moment of your time, we'd like a word."

Dictionary cleared his throat explosively and spoke. His voice was deep and rough and had the flattened vowels and blunt consonants of the Midlands. George couldn't help noticing that he sounded more like a farmer than a man who knew all about words and London.

"What time I have is not my own, but that granted by an unknowable Providence and so not mine to give. However—" Dictionary nodded at a thick book held in his left hand, as his right—as if it had a life of its own—plucked at a frock coat and knee breeches. "—what words I have are in this book, and placed there by mine own labors, so of them I may make free as I will, and they are, as ever, at your pleasure."

George's eyes edged sideways to look a question at the Gunner.

"He says yes."

Edie spoke quietly under her breath, "Well, he takes a lot of words to say it."

The Gunner fired a look at her. Dictionary squirmed briefly, like a man surreptitiously trying to dislodge an ice cube someone has slipped down the back of his shirt.

"Well, it is not often that we see children who see us as we are, Gunner. I'll warrant there's a history here, eh?"

Dictionary plucked at his breeches and dropped creakily to one knee as he looked down at them.

"You might say, Dictionary. The boy here's in a spot of bother—"

"*Tchah*—the 'boy' has a name, no doubt?"

The Gunner brought George forward. George looked up at the lopsided slab of Dictionary's face and decided that it was a face that appeared angry and forbidding until you looked closer, when you saw something kinder in it. It was a face that wasn't used to smiling—but wanted to.

"He's called George. George, this is Dictionary Johnson. Dictionary—George."

Dictionary spasmed suddenly, as if trying to jerk himself out of his coat in one fast movement. His neck twisted twice in a stuttering reflex, and he barked something that may have been a word but might have been mere noise.

"*Gah*—pleasure of your acquaintance, sir."

Gunner prodded George in the back.

"Oh. Pleased to meet you."

Dictionary looked at George, which made him feel uncomfortable.

"I observe you are exercised, sir, exercised by some strong emotion."

"Yeah," said George, "I'm confused."

"Confused—or scared, perhaps?"

"Perhaps," muttered George quietly, looking away from Edie.

"When I was young and fearful, a wise woman gave me this advice, which I treasured and now pass on to you: just as hope enlarges happiness, so fear aggravates calamity."

"Ah," said George, still trying to untangle the words into some kind of sense.

"You make things worse by worrying about them," explained Edie.

He turned on her.

"They can't be much worse than things trying to kill me, can they?"

"Of course they can. They can be much worse."

Before he could ask her what she meant—or even ask himself whether he wanted to ask her, in case she told him—Dictionary cleared his throat.

"You would perhaps oblige me with an outline of the events that bring you to my humble plinth? I am starved of conversation, you understand, which is vexing, pinioned as I am here on this lonely outcrop as the life of the fair city swirls round and past me. There is no wit, no variation to divert me from the depressing spectacle of the gentlemen of the law strutting in and out of that magnificent theater of lies opposite."

He jabbed his book at the vast white stone jumble of pinnacles and arches across the road.

"That's the Law Courts," said George.

"Indeed." Dictionary nodded. "And a fine excess of architecture it is for such a plain purpose as deciding right from wrong. It is my observation that on the outside, all the light exuberance of spires and turrets point upward to the heavens in order to distract one's attention from the fact that inside, within the dark chambers of the law, all points downward, into the fell attorney's pocket. 'Tis like paint on a tart's face, mere distraction. Why—"

The Gunner interrupted.

"The boy has a problem, Dictionary. Pardon me for breaking in, but it's a serious one. We've come from asking the Sphinxes—"

"The Sphinxes? *Gah*—then you'll be none the wiser and twice as confused, no doubt. Only a jobberknowl would go to a sphinx for an answer—"

"Jobberknowl?" George looked at Edie, who shrugged.

Dictionary's fingers flew through the pages of his book.

"A blockhead."

"A thicko," explained Edie helpfully.

The Gunner prodded George in the back again. George cleared his throat.

"The Sphinx sort of gave us a half-answer, and told me to go to the 'dark shaveling.' Only, I don't know what a shaveling is."

Dictionary's fingers flew through the pages of his book, slowing down as he got nearer the word he was looking for. He stabbed it in satisfaction.

"'Shaveling: a monk.'"

"So I'm looking for a dark monk?"

"A monk or an abbot, a friar—"

"A dark friar."

The air went a bit still. The children gazed up at the two statues, who were looking at each other with that look people exchange when they're busy not saying something.

"A dark friar who knows all about London."

Dictionary straightened and looked east, up Fleet Street.

"A black friar, then."

The Gunner nodded slowly with a grimace.

"The Black Friar. Should have known."

"What's wrong with this Black Friar?" asked George, trying to watch the two statues at once.

"Nothing," they both replied rather quickly, looking away from each other.

"Still," harrumphed Dictionary, "not a man to disturb lightly. Perhaps I can help. It is mere vanity, but I pride myself on a tireless knowledge of the metropolis."

"The boy's got the taints stirred up. He don't know why, but they're after him. That's why we went to the Sphinxes, seeing as how they're halfway between us spits and the taints."

"And what crepuscular illumination were they able to shed on this dilemma?"

"What does crepuscular mean?" interrupted Edie.

"Dim," said Dictionary, with a sour twitch of his shoulders. George could see he didn't like being disturbed while he was talking.

"Well, why not say dim? All these long words are like talking in code."

Before Dictionary could reply, George broke in. He wanted answers, and he didn't want Edie starting another argument.

"The Sphinxes said I needed to find the Stone Heart. I think they said the Black Monk—"

"Friar," said the Gunner.

"The Black Friar could tell me what it was."

"'Course, it'd save a lot of time and—you know, if you happened to know what the Stone Heart was, Dictionary," said the Gunner hopefully. "Then we wouldn't have to bother the Friar at all. And that would be . . ."

He seemed to run out of words.

"More convenient?" suggested the other statue.

"There you go."

"So we need to fathom the meaning of the Stone

Heart," said Dictionary, suddenly swiveling and lowering himself so that his stockinged legs hung off the edge of the plinth. He riffled through the book in his hand, but came up with nothing. He clutched it to his chest and rocked back and forth, eyes closed in thought.

"Stoneheart? Stone heart? A heart-shaped stone, perhaps. Or the heart of a stone—but that could be any stone, and looking for any stone in this great city would be like trying to find a grain of wheat in a wheat field. No. Stone Hart perhaps—'hart,' as in a statue of a deer, a male deer, carved of stone?"

He opened one eye and looked at them. No one nodded, so he closed it again, rocked some more.

"Or Stone Heart, perhaps being a disease of the affective organ, in need of physick, as in gallstone, kidney stone?"

George nudged the Gunner and spoke quietly.

"I don't understand what he's saying."

The Gunner put his finger to his lips and looked at the rocking figure above.

Edie's voice cracked the silence.

"Neither does he. He doesn't know what it is."

The rocking stopped. Dictionary opened the other eye and focused on her.

"Why, in faith, what I took for a helpmeet and a paranymph is no more than a mannerless"—his fingers fanned the pages of the book at speed. He found the word he was searching for and speared it with his finger—"a mannerless sprunt."

"Sprunt? He called me a sprunt!" bristled Edie.

"I know," said the Gunner wearily. "He found it under the S's. If he was looking under P's he'd probably call you a pest. Or a pain in the—"

Edie jutted her chin suspiciously at the figure above her and tugged on his buckled shoe.

"Is a sprunt like a glint?"

Dictionary shuddered and pulled his foot up out of her reach.

"A glint? Not at all. 'Glint' does not appear in my dictionary, being an ungodly word, a mere superstition beyond even the wildest Frenchified imaginings of the Romanists. A sprunt is a common word, widely used, as any child even of the female inclination knows, meaning anything short that will not bend."

George looked at her. His lip, despite itself, twitched.

"What?" she asked dangerously.

"You might be a bit of a sprunt."

"You might be getting a puffy one if you start calling me names, too."

Edie pushed George hard. He had to grab her jacket to stop falling backward. There was a ripping noise and the clink of glass hitting stone. She swung at him, punching his shoulder hard enough to make him let go. Dictionary looked scandalized.

"Now, children, there shall be no occasion for snick-or-snee here in the very shadow of God's house!"

"Snick-or-snee?" said George, floundering again.

"A barney. A bust-up. A fight," said the Gunner wearily.

"With knives, mark you, with knives," harrumphed Dictionary.

"It wasn't a fight. She pushed me. Look, I'm sorry but—"

He stopped talking. Edie was crouched over the thing that had fallen out of her ripped pocket and clinked on the pavement. It was the weathered disk of glass. Her eyes were transfixed by it.

"They're here."

The warning glass was blazing blue-green light, brighter than she'd ever seen it.

"There's taints. Here. Now."

They all looked up into the evening sky—still stained orange by the fluorescent city lights—except Edie, who swept the glass into her other pocket and zipped it shut.

For one terrible moment George felt his gut turning to water as a winged shape dropped out of the sky and flapped over them. He relaxed when he saw it was just a large black bird, not some gargoyle.

"It's just a bird," he said with relief.

It flapped around them above their heads, flying as if in slow motion. Dictionary waved his book at it, trying to shoo it away.

"A strick," he said wonderingly, almost to himself. "A strick if ever I saw one."

"Strick?" asked the Gunner, not taking his eyes off the eerily slow bird.

Dictionary waved his book at the Gunner, as if trying to shake the meaning out of it and onto him.

"Strick. A bird of ill omen."

He twitched and jerked, and George found himself shivering as if the movement were contagious.

"What do we do now?" His arm was gripped in a small vise. Edie yanked at him. "Run."

She dragged him stumbling into the traffic. After two stutter-steps he was running faster than she was.

The Gunner looked around from where he had been watching the wheeling bird. Horror flashed across his face. He kicked into a sprint and shouted in one movement "No! Not that way!"

George and Edie had to stop short as a red double-decker bus turned in front of them, blocking the way down Fleet Street. George heard the Gunner shout, and spun around. He got a glimpse of the big man running toward him, pointing, yelling something—then another bus turned behind George, and for a moment, he and Edie were sandwiched in a narrow red canyon as the two buses passed each other.

It was like being in the eye of a hurricane—a beat of quiet as the two red walls ground past them in opposite directions.

Then, with a whoosh of sound and diesel fumes, the bus ahead of them swept away, and Edie tugged him onward—a good three fast steps until she saw what they were running into. The thing the Gunner was shouting about behind them as he ran around the other double-decker bus. The thing with the fiery eyes and the scales and the wings that cracked like thunder. The thing that saw them from the top of its tall stone perch planted in the middle of the street.

Then she braked, and George stopped, still looking back to see what the Gunner was trying to say, not realizing what they had just run into.

"What is it?"

"I think it's a dragon."

And he turned, slowly.

And it was, exactly, a dragon.

And then there was nowhere to run.

# Chapter Sixteen

## The Dragon at the Bar

Dragons come in all shapes and sizes, from vast night-mares whose wings unfold with a thunderclap and block out the sky, to tiny furry mascots that dangle in a harm-less but irritating way from people's rearview mirrors. The first thing George and Edie noticed was that the dragon that guards Fleet Street is *not* one of the fuzzy cuddleable ones. Its wiry body looked like that of a lion crossed with a muscular greyhound, and then covered in scales like chain mail.

The thin spiny tail cracked like a whip and the wings snapped wide as it reared back on its hind legs. The front claws—and these were proper cut-you-to-shreds claws with talons like curved daggers on them—picked up the large shield it rested on and clashed it twice on its chest scales, making a warning sound George could feel vibrat-ing the ground he stood on.

But its head was the nastiest thing about it. It sat on

top of a long reptile neck that grew out of the lion's body, with a crest of spikes bristling along its top side. The head had ears pricked like a horse's and a snarling mouth that showed a lot of hooked fangs as it looked right at George and Edie. And the eyes that it was doing the looking with glowered out from under angry brows with a heat and an intensity that seemed to weld George to the spot. The eyes were like looking into the heart of a banked-up fire. They were the deep red of burning coal, and as George watched the intensity of the red fade into a hotter, white heat, black tendrils of smoke whisped out of the eye sockets and rolled up and over the jutting brows into the night sky.

Edie tugged at him.

"I can't move," George said.

"Neither can I."

The dragon's head snaked back, turning its whole body into a coiled S shape. The narrow chest expanded and the scales on the neck stuck out in angry spikes. George had once seen film of a frilled lizard expanding its neck in anger. This looked like the grown-up end-of-the-world version of that.

And then the Gunner was skidding to a halt in front of them, between them and the dragon.

"Don't look into its eyes! It's got you stuck! Don't look into the—"

*Whoomf.*

The dragon's head struck forward, the mouth

opened, the barbed tongue jabbed out like a sword, and then the flame jetted out, and there was no question, no way in the world that George and Edie or anyone who could see it *wouldn't* watch it.

The flame hit the street in a twisting spiral of wildfire, ropes of red and orange and purple and yellow blaze twining together before slapping into the ground with the massive controlled force of water from a fire hose. The flames spread wide across the street and rushed toward them like a building wave.

Still rooted to the spot, George and Edie could do nothing but shield their heads from the wall of heat racing ahead of the flaring crest.

The Gunner spun and knelt in front of them, pulling his rain-cape wide, trying to protect them from the rolling incineration slamming toward them. There wasn't enough cape to block out the sight, and George couldn't tear his eyes away from the inevitable conflagration anyway.

"Get down!" shouted the Gunner.

George couldn't move. Couldn't even shut his eyes. He knew he was a heartbeat away from ignition and conflagration, but he didn't blink. He felt the heat hit his eyeballs and dry them out in an instant. Then he blinked reflexively to wet them, and when his eyes opened, he saw the flames stop dead, as if they had hit an invisible wall ten yards in front of them.

The Gunner looked at George's face, at his reaction,

then turned to look behind him. Flames lapped up against the invisible barrier like water hitting a glass wall.

"Bloody hell!"

The fire built up behind the wall, rising higher and higher, taking shape as if filling a mold. And as they watched, they saw that in the midst of all this, London carried on. Cars drove through the wall of flame without noticing. A cyclist wove around a taxi, his whistle shrieking angrily, unaware that he'd missed the cab by inches but ridden straight through a studded gate of fire.

Whatever was happening was happening to George and Edie and the Gunner but not to the rest of London, not to normal everyday London. Normal everyday London just got on with getting home and going out and not making eye contact with anyone else, in case something odd happened.

Something odder than everyday odd was happening, of course. The flames were building a gate spread from side to side of Fleet Street. Or rather, they were swirling into a sharp-edged flame sculpture of a gatehouse with three openings underneath it. There was a wide central gate, with two narrow man-size arches on either side. Above the main gate rose a flattened classical arch with blocks of stone sharply outlined by different colored streaks of flame. On top of this arch was a gatehouse room, with an elegant window flanked by two alcoves, and on top of that a shallow arched roof. Even though he was terrified and obviously going mad again, George couldn't help noticing that it was beautiful.

An ugly single-decker bus with a jointed middle drove through the side of the flame gatehouse, the driver blankly chewing gum with a sour expression on his face, unseeing eyes fixed on the back of the car in front.

"What is it?" Edie asked, eyes transfixed by the barrier.

"Temple Bar," whispered the Gunner.

"What's Temple Bar?"

"One of the old gates to the city. They took it down, hundred, more'n a hundred years ago. Put up that dragon instead. Same purpose though, I reckon—"

There was a crash from behind the gatehouse. The flames blurred and jumped, then sharpened their edges again. You could even see the studded panels in the sturdy gates.

"What purpose?" George croaked out of a dry throat.

"Guard the ways into the city. Keep out the unwanted."

The wide gates beneath the central arch shook. Something reached over the spiked top and pulled angrily.

It was the dragon's claw.

"Move!" shouted the Gunner, hand scrabbling for his holster.

And then all the magic and the beauty of the fire-building was gone, and terror returned as the gates wrenched open and the dragon stepped through the arch.

The building heat inside the beast had turned it from a dull metal monster to a shining white-hot dragon.

Its head swung hypnotically as it searched for someone, and then it stopped, finding George. The neck was swollen as the fire-crop beneath bulged the scales into an angry frill framing the burning, unavoidable eyes.

Everything in George's body tried to run, but everything in his mind stopped sending the right signals. The Gunner grabbed him and pulled—and nothing happened. George seemed to have become as immovable as a rock, even to the Gunner's great brass-bound muscles.

"Bloody hell!" said the Gunner again, this time with more disbelief in his voice.

The dragon's head cocked back. Its mouth opened. The fangs sparkled like blue diamonds.

"No, you don't," growled the Gunner.

His gun hand snapped out, cocking the heavy revolver in one determined movement.

The dragon didn't even look at him.

*Blam!*

The revolver bucked in his fist.

*Splat.*

The bullet hit the white-hot dragon where its heart might be, and melted on impact, splashing a darker color over the creature's skin.

"Ah," said the Gunner.

*Blam! Blam! Blam!*

*Splat. Splat. Splat.*

Three more bullets splashed across the dragon's front, with as much effect as paintballs on a tank. The dragon looked down on the molten lead hissing across its chest, noticed the Gunner as if for the first time, and spat flame.

The Gunner spun and tried to grab George and Edie before the lance of fire hit. His sweeping fingertips grazed George but scooped up Edie just as the flame-burst punched into his shoulder and sent him spinning and rolling across the street, curled around her in a protective ball.

George couldn't imagine the power behind a fire jet that could send a bronze man skittering across the ground like a crumpled paper cup being hosed into the gutter.

And he didn't *want* to imagine what that *felt* like, because the dragon flamed again, and this time the fire was a different color—a kind of shimmering violet—and he had time to decide on the exact color because the flame didn't go away but stood like a fiery wall, bisecting the road between him and Edie and the Gunner.

A lorry overtook a cyclist and drove right down the center of the wall of fire, which closed in behind it as it passed. The driver's head turned and grinned toward George.

"Oi oi!" he shouted, and stuck out his tongue, making a rude licking motion.

"Arsehole!" replied a girl's voice on the other side of

George, and he dragged his eyes away from the dragon for a flicker, long enough to see a pretty blond girl smoothing a wind-caught dress back down over her legs as she struggled to control her cycle in the evening traffic that, horribly and inexplicably to George, seemed to be going about its own business and ignoring the dragon in their midst.

The dragon wasn't ignoring George. It was watching him intensely. George still couldn't move his legs. He had to shade his eyes to see the dragon, but when he did he was sure it looked different. Still angry, because that's the way dragons are made, but something else. The heat shimmer coming off the creature made it hard to be sure, but it seemed to be raising an eyebrow. He didn't know what that meant. It was probably trying to make its mind up on how to roast him, George decided bitterly—and then there it was again. The unwanted bit of himself, the black, biley-treacle taste in his mouth, the prickling behind his eyes, the dark cable that seemed to twist through him, the thing he didn't think about, the thing he usually forgot was inside him, the thing he didn't understand. The thing that made him angry.

"What?" he shouted.

The dragon's eyebrow was definitely raised.

"What are you waiting for? Cooking instructions? Medium-rare or well-done? Make it well-done then, get it over faster!"

And then the dragon cocked its head, looked at him,

and spat fire. It spat fire into its own front claws, which twisted and tumbled and turned the fire into a ball, and then it spun the fire in one claw, looking at George.

He breathed again. Maybe it wasn't going to roast him. Maybe things were, unbelievably, going to be all right.

The white dragon cocked its arm and hurled the ball of wildfire straight at George.

Time seemed to go slow—or maybe, because George knew that time was about to be up for him, he savored the microseconds more and it just *seemed* like time was going slowly. He saw the bolt of flame spinning toward him in a long arc, and he knew from the rooted feeling of his feet that he was never going to be able to dodge it. And for a reason that had nothing to do with logic or sense, but everything to do with a lifetime of being the last boy picked for football and always being the goalie, he bunched his hands into fists and, throwing his shoulders one way, lashed out at the ball. He hit it a glancing blow, felt the hiss of fire as it made contact, a moment of searing heat, and then saw it spin away behind him.

The dragon roared and slashed a claw toward the ball, which spun faster and continued to curve, tighter this time, looping behind George and coming back around the other side of him in a gravity defying orbit.

And as it began to circle him, faster and faster, it leaked flame from where he had hit it, and where it leaked, the flame stood in the air and stayed, so that he found himself at the center of a rising cone of fire.

And very quickly he could see nothing of the rest of London beyond the flames, and was alone, trapped in a fiery tornado that whipped at his clothes and lashed at his hair, and sounded like an express train full of screaming people thundering around and around him. And despite himself, he jammed his hands over his ears and shut his eyes and added his own scream to the rising crescendo.

Upside down on the other side of the road, beyond the wall of violet flame, Edie opened her eyes. She was jammed under the hunched body of the Gunner, like the victim in a car crash. The Gunner's helmet had come off and rocked upturned on the pavement in front of her like a black bowl. She shifted a little and saw his face was shmooshed on the concrete. She struggled to free herself. He turned and looked at her. She stopped struggling.

"You see what he did? The boy?" There was something like wonder leaking through the pain in his face. She shook her head.

"He was a goner. Dragon threw a fireball with his name on it, and he"—the Gunner winced—"he done something. Dunno what, but he dodged it."

"Are you okay?"

"Yes."

He didn't sound convincing. He looked even less so as he painfully lifted his head from the ground and unkinked himself to let her free.

As soon as she rolled to her feet she saw what had changed.

The flame-built Temple Bar was fading in jerks, like a candle guttering out. All the fire was now concentrated on a vortex whirling around a small figure she knew was George. And standing in front of the blazing cone, claws raised to the sky, was the white dragon, somehow controlling and molding the fire, with its shield slung over its shoulder, flashing a blood–bright red cross over the road at them.

She turned to the Gunner, who was staggering to one knee. A jangling line of Hare Krishnas jogged between them, chanting and smiling and banging tambourines, oblivious of the cone of fire or the Gunner or Edie. She pointed at George.

"Can you save him?"

"Yes."

He still didn't sound convincing. His shoulder hung low and unmoving, still smoking from where the dragon had hit him. He winced as he fumbled his rain-cape over one shoulder and fumbled at the jangling bridle chains hanging there.

"You're hurt!" she said, sounding strangely betrayed, somehow not wanting to believe it was possible.

"Yes," he growled, this time convincingly. "Help get these bloody chains off me. . . ."

She saw he had only one hand that worked properly. Without thinking, she clambered up on his knee and reached under the folds of his cape, surprised at the way what looked like metal moved and felt like material. She tugged at the chains.

"What are you—?"

"Don't talk. You talk too much. Listen."

She was about to fire back an answer, when she saw his face. It was hurt, but he wasn't looking at her angrily. For a moment he even looked kind.

"He's got to get to the Black Friar. He's in a pub at the end of Blackfriars Bridge."

She kept looking at the cone of flame across the street.

"You'll take him—" Edie said.

"No. I won't. I don't even know if this'll work, but if it does I won't be able to and you will. Your problem is the dragons."

"There's more than one?"

"There's one guarding every street that leads into the City. And the problem—*one* of the problems—with the Black Friar, is that he's *in* the City. So you can't take the streets—"

"We can take the Underground—"

He clasped her arm.

"No. I dunno what or who George is, but if he's who or what I think he might be, the only place more dangerous for him than aboveground is under it. Never, ever go underground, you got it? I done it once in the parking garage and we got away with it by blind luck and ruddy ignorance, but don't do it again!"

Edie nodded.

"So if we can't go by streets . . ."

He took the chains from her and looped them around his good fist, eyes on the fire and the dragon as he spoke.

"There was a road here before there was streets. It's a wet road, but you take it. There ain't much can save you once a taint's got your number, but what's uncanny and evil's always hated two things: cold iron and running water. So your way ain't by land. And one more thing—"

Edie pointed. Across the street, the dragon had lowered its arms. It flicked out a claw and gently sliced an opening in the cone of fire. They saw a brief image of George standing in the middle of the fire, and then the dragon stepped inside the burning wall, and the opening slapped shut behind it.

George felt a blast of cold air suck inside the cone and opened his eyes. And of course once he did, he wished he hadn't, because the dragon was towering over him—and he would have screamed, but he was all screamed out; so he shut his mouth and clenched his teeth and all the screaming stopped at once, and he was alone in the spiral of flame with the dragon.

As he looked up, he saw its white head outlined against the disk of night sky at the top of the cone. And behind the head he saw the flashing light of a jet flying across London, and somehow the fact that there were still jets full of people being told to fasten their safety belts and eating airline food off those tiny trays made him shake his head in wonder.

The dragon mirrored his movement with its own head.

George shook his head again to see if that was what was happening. The dragon copied him. George found he was laughing, at least part laughing, part crying. And as he choked and snuffled, the dragon did the same, soundlessly pantomiming his motions.

George looked at the friendly blinking airplane light just about to leave the circle of normality above him, and tried very hard to wake up. He didn't, and he got angry again.

"You're not real!" he spat at the dragon, who was watching him very closely. He pointed at the sky.

"That's real, that's a *plane* and it's *real* and *science* is real and jet engines and crappy food and pepper and salt in little packets and seat belts and bad movies with the cool bits taken out and boiled hard candy when you land and ears popping anyway and everything about that is real and NOT YOU!"

The dragon's eyes changed and it roared something that might have been a wordless screech, but sounded a little like a hot metal throat trying to shout.

"RRREAL—"

The noise bounced around George and made him flinch. He looked into the creature's mouth and saw a flame at the back of the throat, behind the tongue with its flat spear-tip end, like a pilot light waiting to ignite the stream of wildfire brewing inside the dragon's fire-crop.

"NOT REAL!" shouted George, and spat—spitting being all that he could do in defiance of the inevitable. The spit sizzled and instantly evaporated off the chest of the dragon. He held his hand up to ward off the heat.

And the dragon suddenly snaked out a claw like a switchblade and jagged it over George's outstretched hand so fast he couldn't avoid it.

George had never felt pain like it. But he had imagined pain like it. It was as if all the bone-snapping, hand-shattering pain that he had expected, but miraculously *not* felt when he'd hit the head off the tiny dragon at the Natural History Museum was suddenly happening, only a thousand times more intensely. He felt his body spasm, totally out of his control, as he curled over his injured hand.

His mouth rictussed wide and wider, and his neck tendons snapped tight as whipcords, but no sound came out. It was pain past screaming. It was pain so bad that it became suddenly dull and distant, as if happening to someone else; and as darkness crept in on the edges of his sight, he welcomed it like a friend, though he knew he shouldn't. And where he had felt fear and anger, he felt more sadness than he knew there had ever been in his life, and his heart slowed and shriveled under the world-crushing weight of it.

He sensed the dragon stepping over him, and then the last thing he saw—as his brain decided to focus on self-preservation and close down his eyesight—was a darkness that burst through the wall of fire in the shrinking center of his vision. And the final bit of George that was George, and not just the pain and the sadness, thought he recognized the shape of the darkness and wished he could remember why it wore a tin hat.

The Gunner leaped through the wall of flame and found himself on the dragon's back. Before it could turn and throw him off, he scrambled as high as he could using the ladder of spines, his hobnailed boots kicking sparks off them as he pushed higher up the dragon, which was nearly twice his height.

It jerked around and roared.

George had tumbled to the ground in a motionless heap. The Gunner swung his good hand, and the chains of the bridle lashed down and around the muzzle of the dragon just as it puffed its neck out to blast him off it with a torrent of flame.

"No, you don't!"

Grimacing with pain, he cinched the chain and pulled hard, muzzling the dragon. As it realized what was happening, the dragon tried to get a claw under its chin to rip the chain off, but the Gunner yanked harder, trapping the claw under the dragon's jaw and jamming its mouth shut as the chain tightened.

The dragon flailed lopsidedly at the man on its back, and now it was its turn to buck and struggle. Its wings beat at the Gunner, but he rode it like a man in a rodeo trying to break a horse.

He gripped its shoulders with his knees, pressing down hard, pulling back on the bridle chains. The sharp scales beneath his legs began to spang upright as the pressure from the fire-crop built, like a boiler about to burst. The whole body of the dragon began to bristle like a porcupine as its scales all stood up. It shook more and more savagely. The Gunner arched back, hands grinding on the chains, pulling the dragon, like a man bending a bow.

Which was a mistake. He leaned so far back that the dragon's tail was able to whip around the Gunner's neck from behind him, and pull at him in turn, whipping him in different directions, trying to pull him apart.

He saw a small figure dart between the dragon's legs and crouch over George.

Then the dragon staggered backward, and the Gunner couldn't see George and Edie anymore. The dragon's strategy of pulling the Gunner backward was a bad one in the end, because of course in trying to strangle the Gunner, he was adding his own strength to the Gunner's pull on the muzzle, and the dragon desperately needed to open its mouth and relieve the pressure of its swollen fire-crop.

They crashed to the ground and scrabbled at each

other. The Gunner's grip slipped a little. Sparks shot out from between the dragon's clenched teeth. One of the chain links melted on one side—the O of the link becoming a C, whose gap got wider as the dragon struggled to open its jaws and point its head toward the children.

The Gunner saw a round metal manhole cover in the road beside them. He jabbed his two fingers into the holes on it, and ripped it out of the tarmac.

"No you bloody don't, snakey."

He wrenched the dragon's head away from the children and forced it down into the manhole. Metal shrieked on metal as the two of them writhed against each other, and then there was a distinct *ping* as the C-link gave way and became an *I*, and the pent-up flame burst out of the dragon in an uncontrolled magma jet of pure wildfire, straight down into the sewer beneath the street.

The Gunner felt the back blast slam out of the manhole, searing at his face.

The jet of flame filled the sewer and raced along the main drain, spilling sideways, up and down into the pipes and drains that fed it. It traveled like the pressure wave in front of an explosion, swelling and finding new ways to burst out and spaces to expand into.

On the surface, still wrestling to keep the struggling dragon's head underground, the Gunner had a street-level view of the fire's progress. Flame gouted from drains all the way down each side of the street, and a hundred yards down the road, another manhole cover popped into the sky on top of a geyser of wildfire.

A truck's front wheels bounced into the hole and out again, making the driver spill the packet of chips he was eating all over himself. Then there was a clang as the manhole cover landed in the back of his truck.

The Gunner turned back to look at George and Edie.

They were gone.

# CHAPTER SEVENTEEN

## Single Handed

George was already walking when he truly became conscious. Edie was dragging him, her shoulder under his armpit, her arm around his waist, staggering down a sloping alley that led away from the light. He was aware she was talking to him, but the echo of the screaming still filled his ears, accompanied by a heavy pounding bass backbeat that he recognized as his heart pumping. He felt his injured hand throbbing in time to the blood, pulsing with a pain that was bone-deep and too intense to be sharp anymore, just a pounding blunt pain that was both too hot and too cold all at once. He tried to look back at his hand on the end of the arm Edie had jammed over her shoulder.

She shook her head and said something he couldn't hear. Panic hooked out of nowhere and hit him in the gut.

Maybe his hand was too badly shredded to mend.

Maybe?

Certainly.

The dragon had slashed it with a white-hot dagger-claw.

His hand *had* to be maimed, that's what she was trying to stop him seeing.

He yanked his arm, tugged his head around, tried to see, tried to stop—but she carried on, and they became tangled and fell in a painful scrabble of knees and elbows on the wet concrete. As the impact pain shot up his leg, the echo of the screaming stopped dead, and the roar of the city came back, and he could hear.

". . . said you were an idiot— OUCH!" yelped Edie, as she hit the wet concrete. "Why?"

George felt the slime on the ground beneath him and realized that it must be—had to be—his blood. You don't get your hand shredded without a lot of blood, he thought. He'd played enough computer games to know that.

Nausea rose in his stomach as he looked at his good hand.

It wasn't blood. It was just city slime, gray and brown street dirt slicked with rain. He disentangled his hurt arm from behind Edie, and even as he did so, he knew it was a false hope—this absence of gore, because, of course the dragon's claw had been white-hot, so it would have sliced up his hand and sealed the wound at the same time.

He scrabbled back against the wall and made himself look at the throbbing pain at the end of his arm.

The shock hit him and he started to shake. He clenched his fists to try and stop the tremors. Fists, because he had fists—as in, two good ones.

His hand was still there.

He opened and closed it again, in disbelief.

The more he moved it, the more it hurt. But he couldn't help moving it, because he could; because, against all the odds, it was still there on the end of his arm, and there was no blood and no gore; and for a brief glorious moment he didn't care about what the future held, because whatever it was, he, George, would also be able to hold it with two hands. He couldn't stop himself laughing, and that began to hurt, too.

"What's so funny? We've got to move."

Edie got to her feet on the other side of the alley and tried to brush the slime off her knees.

He held up his hands, like they were the punch line of the funniest joke in the world.

And then he stopped laughing.

Edie stared at his hand and moved across the alley as if drawn against her will by what she was seeing. And he looked closer too, and saw what he'd missed. He had been so happy to have both hands work that he'd just been clenching them and staring into his palms, and hadn't looked closely at the back of the one that the dragon had slashed.

There was a red and purple mark, a pulsing scar-branded into his skin, cut and seared closed in the same zigzag fiery slashes, and it looked like this:

Edie shook her head.

"That's not good."

He put his hand away in his pocket. Hiding it seemed the right thing to do. It found the wodge of plasticene and kneaded it between finger and thumb.

"The dragon slashed me."

Her face showed no emotion. It was as blank as if people told her that dragons slashed them every day of the week. As soon as he'd said the words, George started laughing again. He repeated his words, just to see how deranged they sounded.

"The dragon slashed me!"

She watched him get up, wipe the tears from his eyes, and stumble off down the alley toward the river.

"Where are you going?"

He stopped at the pavement edge, looking at a red and blue Underground sign that shone out against the dark glitter of the Thames beyond the traffic on the Embankment.

"Home."

She stood in front of him.

"You can't."

"Watch me."

"We can't go home. Not from all this."

"I can."

He looked for a break in the traffic.

"We can't just pretend this isn't happening, you have to get to the Black Friar—"

"You go to the Black Friar. I'm going home."

Edie actually stamped her feet in frustration. He hadn't thought people really did that, but she did. She did it again. She looked as if she were going to explode.

"Listen, you idiot, we—"

"Hey, you're the one who said there's no 'we'! I'm agreeing, you're right, okay? I'm just not doing this any-more. . . ."

He waved at a taxi that was pulling away from the Temple tube station across the street. The driver saw him, waved, indicated for a U-turn and waited for a gap in the traffic. Something flapped between George and the streetlight, and he flinched, but when he looked up he saw it was just a big black bird, not a dragon or any-thing made of stone or metal, so he relaxed.

Edie looked desperate. He felt guilty, but he didn't know why, or if he did, he didn't want to know. He felt his brain was about to melt anyway, and the pain in his hand was rising again.

"I'm just stopping this. I'm just going home. And I'm just going to crash out, and then I'm just going to wake up tomorrow and this will—this will just be . . . over."

"What about me?"

"I don't know. You should go home, too. Everyone should go home and this should stop."

"It won't."

"You don't know that."

Edie jutted her jaw. The streetlight glistened in her eyes. At her feet the black bird swooped in and tugged the guts out of a discarded burger in a bright wrapper. She took a deep breath.

"I do. It never stops."

"You don't know that. You can't know that. You're just—just a kid."

The taxi found its gap and U-turned to park next to them. She put a hand on his shoulder.

"So are you. You can't go home, George. I'm sorry, but you really can't. The Gunner said—"

The bird hopped with them as George pushed past her to the driver's window. It left the burger uneaten. George shook off her hand and leaned into the taxi.

"Thirty-seven St. George's Square, please."

"All right, son, hop in."

Edie reached for him, but the black bird chose this moment to launch itself into the air between them in a flurry of black feathers, and Edie stepped back for an instant, and in that instant George slipped into the taxi.

She reached an imploring hand across the gulf of air between them.

"Look. Don't do this—it's dangerous—"

"I'm sorry."

He closed the door. The window was open. So was Edie's mouth. She couldn't believe this was happening. He tried to find something to say that would make what he was doing feel better.

"Good luck."

*"Good luck?"*

She stood there as if she'd been hit. George looked at her and tried to say something better, but the taxi moved off, and he didn't have the words, so he just shrugged and held up his hand in half a wave, and their eyes stayed locked on each other until the taxi turned onto the Embankment and George couldn't see her anymore.

He took a deep breath. Then another. Then he curled himself around the pain in his hand, the hand still thrust deep in his coat pocket, and sank down in the corner of the seat with his eyes closed.

Of course, if he'd looked back he'd have seen the bird flapping lazily along behind the taxi until the big dark mass of Waterloo Bridge swept up and over them, and the bird wheeled north, up and over the brightly lit classical pillars of the long building on the side of the bridge, in the general direction of St. Pancras station.

Edie wiped her eyes. She felt in her pocket. The glass was still there. It just reflected the lights of the city. It had no inner warning flame now. She reached beyond the glass, to the scrabble of coins that jingled like shrapnel at the bottom of her pocket. She counted the heavier coins into one hand, dropped the others into her pocket, and took off her shoe. There was a banknote inside. She slid it out carefully. Her hand closed around the paper and the coins as she wriggled her foot back into the shoe and set off toward Temple station.

# CHAPTER EIGHTEEN

## The Walker in the Circle

Beside the steep gothic roof of St. Pancras station and its highly decorated brickwork is another big red-brick building. They are as alike as chalk and Chinese food. Brick color and size is all they have in common. Where St. Pancras sweeps the eye into the curve of its facade and then throws it upward to enjoy the exuberance of its peaks and spires, the other building stops the eye dead with windowless slopes of brick bunkered down in a defensive hunch, as if expecting something nasty from the road in front.

Between it and the wide raceway of Euston Road is an open stone and brick piazza, which feels less like a pleasure spot than a featureless killing ground for the giant brick fortress squatting on two sides of it. Of course, it isn't really featureless. There is a massive statue of a heavy-browed man crouched over a pair of dividers, as if measuring the world—or at least the few yards in front of his feet. And it isn't actually a fortress, either. It's a library. The British Library. You can tell that because there is a tall gate and a metal screen where it announces itself repeatedly in a frozen cascade of thickening fonts.

And there is also a sunken circle.

The sunken circle has stone benches all around its interior. On the top rim, there are roughly round boulders. If you were to look closely at the boulders you'd see there are crudely carved human figures that appear to be starting to emerge from them.

The descending black bird took no notice of the statue or the stones. It did, however, fly through the gates because it was no ordinary black bird. It was a raven, and it chose to fly beneath the arch because it did have, among many things rooks didn't come equipped with, a sense of style.

It banked right and overflew the sunken circle. The Walker paced back and forth on the curved bench, a thin roll-up cigarette smoldering in the side of his mouth, eye squinted against the smoke.

The Raven sideslipped down to land on his shoulder. The Walker didn't look at all surprised that a large black bird had alighted by his ear.

The Raven shuffled up closer. Its beak clacked quietly. The Walker listened.

"St. George's Square, you say? By the river."

He turned decisively. The Raven pushed off and hung in the air in front of his head, flapping unnaturally slowly, lazily defying all laws of gravity and several of the general advisory guidelines of nature as it did so. The Walker pointed to the rookery of gargoyles on St. Pancras.

"Tell him not to fail this time, rain or no rain—or by the first stone and the chisel that cracked it, I'll be the one he answers to."

High above them, the cat-gargoyle with the flaked wing and the corroding waterspout watched the Raven rise toward it. It shook itself in anticipation. It stretched its wings, and when it looked around it saw that all the other gargoyles were very busy not looking at it at all.

Back in front of the bunker building, the only sign of the Walker was a pinched-out dog-end of cigarette smoking slightly on the brick floor of the stone circle.

On the other side of the Euston Road, a man walking down Judd Street with earphones on had the sudden sense that he should take them off because he wouldn't be able to hear someone coming up behind him. But when he turned quickly, there was no one there.

# CHAPTER NINETEEN

## Going Home

George paid the cabbie. He got back very little change from the ten pounds he gave the driver, and he realized that his lunch money for the rest of the week was gone. He didn't care a bit. He was home. He winced as he reached for the change with his bad hand.

"You okay, son?" asked the cabbie.

"It's just this," said George, holding up his hand.

The cabbie shrugged. George realized with a shudder of horror that the man couldn't see the mark on his hand.

"Looks okay. You sprain it or something?"

George nodded. Of course the man couldn't see the scar. There was no scar, not in the real world. This was, in some way he didn't understand, all in his mind. He just wished his hand was not where all the pain still was.

"Yeah. A sprain."

"Tiger Balm," advised the cabbie. "You tell your mum

to get you Tiger Balm. Works every time. G'night."

George stepped back as the cabbie drove off, and looked up at a modern apartment block wedged in the middle of a terrace of older buildings, like a gate-crasher at a party. He punched the number into the security pad on the door and headed across the gray foyer to the lift. He got in and hit the top button. As the door slid shut he felt something relax inside him and realized he felt strange, and he realized the strangeness was that he was safe.

He felt in his trouser pocket and pulled out his house keys. A small bronze airplane, a Spitfire hung off the key ring. His dad had made it for him. They'd both loved making plastic models, but George had kept breaking the planes when he played with them afterward. His dad had made him this "unbreakable" for his tenth birthday. He decided to stop thinking about his dad, and stopped looking at the plane. He held it by its side and impatiently tapped the elegant sweep of its wing against the metal wall instead.

The elevator announced the top floor by saying "Top flat" in a tone that always seemed to George to be ever so slightly boastful. The door sighed open, and George walked across the narrow hall and unlocked the door to his apartment.

"Hi, Mum," he said as he entered.

All the lights were off, except for in his mother's room. He walked along the corridor and looked in. A white bed sat on a white carpet. White blinds blocked out the night. A white cupboard door in the white walls stood slightly ajar. But apart from that, there was nothing to disturb the calm absence of color except the picture on his mother's white bedside table—a picture of her, in tasteful black-and-white.

George walked to the cupboard, peered inside. He saw the gap where the suitcase was usually rolled in and parked, and knew that his mother was not home. He turned off the lamp and walked into the kitchen, knowing what he was going to find on the microwave, knowing so well that he didn't even bother to turn on the lights. He peeled the sticky-note off and cracked open the fridge. In the blue light from within he read familiar words:

> Sorry G, an audition came up! Kay will keep an eye. Turn your phone on and I'll explain! Love M

Auditions came up quite a lot for his mum. Kay was a friend who lived in the flat below—another actress. In fact, Kay was the reason that his mother had moved to the apartment after his parents split up. Kay was a very old friend, and supposedly good at "keeping an eye," which is what his mother called babysitting. Kay was actually less keen on keeping an eye than his mother thought, but his mother was good at keeping focused on what she thought rather than what others did, so Kay got asked to watch George more often than either of them liked. The advantage was that she left George alone, and he didn't bother her much. In fact, he stayed in his mother's flat and—humiliatingly—they switched on a baby monitor that reached Kay's flat underneath.

"We're as close as if you were just upstairs in my house," Kay always said, and George knew that it was fine and easier, and meant that she didn't have to have him in her guest room, which she used for yoga and not guests. She was good at waking before him and coming up and being sure he ate something before he went to school, he had to admit that. He wasn't what his mum called a latchkey kid. Like most things, however, it just reminded him of the times when he'd had other stuff. Like a dad and a garden and a rabbit and no need for neighbors to babysit when his mum's career came calling.

He picked up the phone. After the shock of the day, dropping into the rut of familiar routines felt okay. More than okay. It felt calming. He'd call Kay, say he was home, say he was okay; she'd ask if he wanted to come down for his tea; he'd say no thanks, and then he could be alone until tomorrow, when the sun would rise and a new day would begin and life would be back to what it was.

"Hi, Kay."

"Hey, G, I heard you come in up there. You okay?"

He suddenly wanted to tell her no, wanted to tell her everything: tell her about the pain in his hand, about the nightmare he's just lived through. . . .

"I'm fine."

It came out by itself. No matter; she'd ask if he wanted to come down and then he'd tell her. . . .

"That's great, love. Listen, bang on the floor if you need anything. I've got people to dinner, but we'll try not to keep you up with sad middle-aged dancing, okay?"

"Okay," he lied.

"I got a summer pudding. I'll save you a slice for breakfast. Your mum left your supper, yeah?"

"Yeah."

"Sleep tight, not too much screen time, come down if you get the weirds, okay? You can always curl up in the yoga room—it's quite comfy."

It wasn't. This was just part of the ritual.

"I'm fine. Thanks."

"G'night, superstar."

"'Night."

He noticed the light blinking for messages when he hung up. He listened, in case it was his mum. It was Killingbeck, explaining that George had walked off a school trip and would his mother call this evening if he wasn't at home, and call tomorrow if he was, to discuss the seriousness of—"

George deleted the message.

He went back to the fridge, opened it, and stared in

for a bit. Then he retrieved peanut butter and jam, and took some bread from the white bin on the white counter, and made some brown bread into a sandwich. And then he took some milk and turned that brown with some cocoa powder, and then he took the sandwich and the chocolate milk across the white carpet, past the bronze head of his mother placed center stage in the living room, past the dark picture window and the balcony, and into his room.

He hit the lights and stopped in the doorway. His room was a jumble of color. It was a jumble of every-thing. It looked like burglars had been through it in a hurry. They hadn't, of course, but that was how he kept it most of the time. The walls had shelves, and on them were his toys and models—the ones he'd made and the ones his father had made, and the ones they'd made together: soldiers and goblins and orcs and knights and space marines and skeleton armies and Spitfires and Tiger Moths and Totoros—and then on the upper shelves the grown-up things his dad had made, the things from his studio, the castings, the clay models, and the imagi-nary animals he used to make for George when he was a very little boy indeed. There were even little busts of George at different ages, quickly made "clay sketches" his dad had called them. They were all there, where they should be, in his room, on the upper shelves, where they could come to no harm, or indeed good or anything else, not now his father's studio was gone.

He wandered back into his mother's room, chewing his sandwich. He picked her cordless phone off the side table and went and slumped inside the cupboard, sitting in the little slot of space where the suitcase lived. He'd started doing this a long time ago. He must have noticed that he was the same size as the suitcase-shaped hole on one of his mum's earlier absences. He used to like the smell of his mother's clothes above him, because it reminded him of her, he supposed. Now it just smelled of dry-cleaning. He still liked the podlike safety of the space, though he knew he'd be really *really* embarrassed if his mum caught him picnicking on the floor of her cupboard. As she'd once said, "Peanut butter and Prada don't mix." He stared out at the white room and munched his sandwich. He felt calmer, but his hand still hurt. He decided he'd go and get one of his mother's aspirin when he'd finished eating.

He dialed the number. It rang and rang, and just when he knew the answer-message was going to click in, his mother answered.

"MIGUEL?"

She was shouting. He could hear the noise of a party or a bar behind her, glasses clinking, people talking and laughing, music thumping in the background. He had no idea who Miguel was. The voices in the background didn't sound English.

"Hi, Mum."

He could hear the gears switching in her head.

"G! My darling. I thought you were Miguel. I'm in Madrid. It's a thriller. Just the kind of thing you like!"

He presumed the thriller was the audition, not Madrid. As it happened, he didn't like thrillers much either.

"G? Are you okay? I tried to call. You get my messages, darling?" The phone went a bit muffled, but not enough to stop him hearing her say, "Stop it. It's my son," and giggle throatily. The phone unmuffled and she continued. "So you're okay with Kay and everything, yeah? And how was your day?"

He felt it all welling up inside him, all the madness and the terror, and he wanted to tell her about it, he wanted her to tell him what to do, he wanted her to listen and tell him it was all a dream. He wanted it with a sweet, sad pain that rose in his throat like a sudden wave.

"So you're okay, baby?"

"No," he said quietly.

"Didn't hear that, darling. I'm with some people. So you're okay?"

He longed to tell her everything and have her make it all make sense, make it better, stop it hurting. He longed for her to be able to hear him.

"I'm fine."

"Great. Love you."

"Yes."

He hung up and took a bite out of his sandwich. It

didn't matter what he wanted. She couldn't do any of those things. This was one of the many reasons why he'd decided to be a loner, to stop relying on people. That way they couldn't let you down. He felt very tired by the thought, but he knew once more that it was the right thing.

He closed his eyes. The sandwich tumbled stickily to the floor. After a moment the glass toppled to the carpet and made a small brown map of Madagascar on the white pile. George noticed nothing of this. His mind had shut down so his brain could start trying to knot itself back together.

# CHAPTER TWENTY

## A Wolf in the Night

The Walker, for a change, wasn't walking. He was standing on the open back platform of a Routemaster bus, holding on to the pole. His hair streamed back out of his hood in the slipstream. The Raven flapped steadily behind him, at head height, a couple of feet back, so as not to draw attention to itself.

The conductor asked him for his ticket. And then thanked him, even though he didn't produce one.

The conductor started to climb the steps to the upper level, brow furrowing as if he'd forgotten to say something. He turned.

"Oh, er, please come inside, sir. It's dangerous. . . ."

The Walker didn't look at him. "I'm not going to hurt you."

The conductor nodded, as if that made perfect sense. "Okay."

The conductor disappeared up the stairs, unsure as

to why he felt strange, and relieved, but what he wasn't thinking about anymore was the Walker. Because the Walker was able to be forgotten as easily as he was able not to be seen. That was why he'd been able to walk for so long without people noticing he was always there, always walking, always, more or less, the same as he had been when they'd seen him as children. Or when their grandparents' grandparents had been children and had seen him, for that matter.

The Raven got tired of flapping along and flew onto his shoulder. It tucked its head in against the slipstream. After all, it thought, there was no point tiring itself out trying to remain unobtrusive when the Walker could do it for both of them. The Walker watched a street name pass on the corner of a building.

"Lupus Street. From the Latin *lupus*—a wolf. Nearly there."

Since the Raven didn't react, it was hard to see if it was interested. In fact, it wasn't. Even older than the Walker, from its perspective, Latin was just another of those Johnny-come-lately, here-today-gone-tomorrow modern languages that caught on for a bit then fizzled out.

# CHAPTER TWENTY-ONE

## Uninvited Guests

The door buzzer woke George, firstly because it was loud, and secondly because it wouldn't stop. He stumbled to his feet, squished across the map of Madagascar, and pressed the intercom.

Because it was that kind of flat with that kind of intercom, a blurry black-and-white image of the doorstep came to life on the screen by the controls.

Edie's face filled the frame, eyeballing the camera, mouth in a determined line.

"Hey, stop that!"

She took her finger off the buzzer.

"How did you—"

"Shut it," she hissed. Her eyes flicked up and out of frame. She loomed back in again and whispered.

"Have you got a back door?"

George felt woozy. His hand hurt. His head was catching up fast.

"Wait a minute, how did you find me?"

"You gave the taxi your address, I heard. Now—"

He was still trying to find a way to explain that she could not know where he was, so that he could start believing that she wasn't there at all, and go back to sleep.

"No, but how'd you know which is my buzzer?"

She hopped up and down with frustration. Her hand dived into the front pocket of her jacket and struggled to remove something.

"Easy. Had to be the top flat. The one with the gargoyle on the balcony."

George snorted.

"We haven't got a gargoyle."

She held the sea-glass up to the camera. It was so bright it left ghost trails on the screen as she waggled it back and forth.

"See? You have now. It's walking up and down, sniffing."

George realized there was a noise outside the kitchen. A noise coming from the balcony. It was more a scraping noise, but he could hear sniffing and whistling behind it. His guts went cold and watery again.

"Hang on."

He slid over to the doorway and peered around the edge into the living room. Beyond the brass bust of his mother, beyond the sliding door to the balcony, something moved. And as it moved the motion-detector light on the balcony clicked on, and it wasn't a cat or a burglar, but the gargoyle with the cat face and the broken wing and the whistling rainspout. Its blank sandstone eyes were peering into the room, and its talons were scraping along the glass, looking for something. They were heading toward the handle.

George dived back to the intercom.

"I see it."

Edie looked up and nodded. She pocketed the glass.

"So since it's on the front of the building, I wondered if you had a back way out. Oh."

He could see her staring at the glass.

"What?"

"The glass changed color." She looked down the road, both ways. "I think something else is coming."

The Raven flapped around the corner into St. Georges Square a moment before the Walker strode into view. The bird flew higher, until it was almost at roof level. It perched on the balcony of George's apartment. The gargoyle was still scrabbling at the door handle. It sensed the bird and turned. The bird returned its look with an unblinking black eye, then stepped back off the railing and dropped like a stone.

The Walker arrived at George's door and stepped up onto the porch at just the moment when the Raven landed on his shoulder. This was the kind of stylish touch the Raven prided himself on. The Walker ignored it, leaned into the keypad, and appeared to peer at it.

Edie was nowhere in sight.

A young couple bounced up onto the step behind him. The man carried a paper-wrapped bottle of wine in his hand. The woman pressed the buzzer and said: "Kay? Sorry we're late!"

The door buzzed and three of them walked in, though if you'd asked either of the young people, they'd have sworn they were only two.

They got into the lift and pressed the next-to-top button. The only clue that somewhere in their subconscious minds they might have been aware that they were sharing the small space with a tall hooded man in a green coat with a bird on his shoulder, was that they stopped talking. And looked as if they suddenly were having less fun than they had been moments ago.

The lift announced the floor and they stepped out. The Walker watched them. As the door closed he muttered: "You forgot the wine."

The young man made a face at the girl.

"I forgot the wine!"

She looked at his empty hands.

"Idiot."

In the lift, ascending, the Walker looked at the paper-wrapped bottle in his own hands. He slid it into his pocket as the lift announced the top floor.

The door slid open, and he stepped out onto the landing. The door to George's flat stood wide. The Walker remained still. He shrugged his shoulder. The Raven flapped through the door.

Most birds panic when flying in a confined space. The Raven didn't. It flapped around the apartment with slow gravity-defying wing beats, seeing everything: the whiteness of the main rooms, the jumble of George's room, and the absence of anything resembling an actual George on the premises.

It paused on top of the bronze head of George's mother, which it streaked with a thin splash of drop-pings, and peered through the glass at the gargoyle on the balcony. It shook its head.

The gargoyle hoot-whistled through the corroded pipe in its mouth and turned away, wings cracking open as it launched into the night sky. The Raven flapped back out of the door, to where the Walker was pacing the hall.

"Gone?"

The Raven just hopped onto his shoulder. The Walker strode into George's apartment and closed the door behind him.

George emerged from the underground parking at the back of his apartment building to find Edie already there. She flashed the glowing sea-glass at him.

"Let's run."

"Okay."

And because that seemed to both of them to be all that needed to be said, that's exactly what they did. They

ran out of the small backstreet, and across a major
street, and along a narrow empty road that turned
sharply into a busy riverside four-lane, and then kept on
running on the wide pavement.

Edie grimaced.

"I've got a stitch."

He nodded.

"Me, too."

Neither of them stopped running. Neither of them
focused on the buildings or the people they were running
past. All they worried about was getting away from whatever was behind them. Edie knew a lot about running
like this. All that mattered was that you didn't stop, that
there was always a space in front to run into that you
didn't run into a dead end, so that whoever was behind
you didn't catch up.

They ran into Parliament Square and had to cross the
road to escape the barriers that ran at street level
beneath the ornate gothic cliff on their right. In the middle of the square George came to a halt and bent double,
trying to get his breath. Edie tugged at him.

"Come on!"

He shook his head, too out of breath to speak.

"It's not safe here. Look!"

She grabbed the back of his hair and pulled his head
up, pointing around the square. Statues loomed all
around them. Big Ben looked down on them, its lit clock
face hanging in the sky like a second moon.

"Too many     ings here."

"Taints," he   asped.

"Too much    erything. Come. We need to keep to the river."

He followed   er across the street, every muscle in his legs begging h    to stop. A thick mass of traffic lurched past, penned in   y crash barriers, cutting them off from the continuatio    of the Embankment beyond the Houses of Parliament.

Edie starte    to climb the barrier. This time it was George's turn    pluck at her. He pointed at the well-lit underpass to t   ir left.

"This way!"

She shook    r head and hopped over the barrier.

"No. Never    derground"

"What?"

"Never und    ground. The Gunner said. It's more dangerous."

"Oh, come    —" he began.

"For you,"    e said.

He followed   er over the barrier and waited for a gap in the cars.

"Where are   e going?"

She didn't    ar him, or if she did she must have decided not to    swer.

"Edie, whe    are we going?"

She looked    him quickly, then went back to watching the cars.

"It's 'we' now, is it?"

He flashed the memory of driving away from her in the taxi. It hadn't felt good then, and it felt worse now.

"I guess it is."

"And why's that, all of a sudden?" she spat.

"Because you came and found me again."

"Found you?"

He shrugged. Opened his mouth, but before he could speak, Edie saw a gap in the traffic and dived across the road. He followed her, weaving path through the headlights and the horns. A Porsche flashed him and blared a warning as it refused to slow enough for both of them to reach the safety of the Embankment. Edie nipped in front of it and George had to slam to a halt. He saw a blur of pinstripe and an ugly shouting mouth from the driver, then it was gone and he ran across the lane.

He couldn't see Edie, only the benches and the Embankment wall and the lights of the South Bank reflected in the river beyond.

"Found you?" She was behind him. He exhaled in relief.

"Saved me."

"Did I?" Her eyes were unblinking. He met them with a level look of his own.

"Yeah. You did."

She waited, lifted her shoulders briefly, then dropped them.

"I guess that's a thank-you then, is it?"

He had no idea what it was about her that infuriated him so much, but he felt it every time he looked into her eyes, and almost every time she spoke. Only, the truth was she had warned him that the gargoyle had found him, and she had no reason that he knew to have done that. Maybe it was that that he found so infuriating. He matched her shrug.

"I guess so."

She let his eyes go.

"We need to keep moving."

He stayed still.

"Where to?"

She snorted at him.

"The Black Friar. Or did you forget?"

He shook his head. The pain in his hand was returning.

"How do we get to it? Or him, or whatever he or it is?"

"Come on."

He ran just behind her shoulder. The pace was slower now—not much, just enough to talk as they went. She pointed with her chin.

"Black Friar's at the end of Blackfriars Bridge. We just follow the riverbank until we get to it."

"That's . . ." He couldn't find the right word to fit their situation. So he chose a hopeful one. "That's good."

"No it's not. The Black Friar is in the City, and all roads into the City are guarded by dragons like the one we ran into."

His stomach lurched as he had a horrible flashback of the dragon's head staring at him, and his hand twinged sharply as he relived the pain of the talon zagging the wound on his hand.

"So that's bad."

"Would be if the Gunner hadn't told me how to get round them."

He asked the question that had been hanging unasked between them.

"Where is the Gunner?"

"Now you ask," she said bitterly.

"Edie. Where is he? What's wrong with you?"

She stopped dead, so fast that he ran into her back. She turned on him, and her eyes, he was shocked to see, were wet.

"He saved you. He jumped on the dragon, even though he was hurt bad, and he saved you. Probably saved us both. And he told me what to do and how to get you to the Friar, and you know why? Because he was pretty sure the dragon would kill him. But he jumped in and saved you anyway. And you just turned your back and ran, and only now bother to ask about him. How selfish is that?"

He couldn't believe her. He felt gut-punched. The Gunner couldn't be dead.

"He can't be dead," he said.

"How would you know? You were too busy hailing taxis."

"No," he said quicker now, remembering. "If he gets back on his plinth by midnight, he'll—he'll recharge. He'll heal. It'll be all right. It's how it works. If he's on his plinth by turn o'day—"

"George." Her voice hit his small flicker of hope like a bucket of ice-cold water. "He was having trouble walking *before* he jumped back on the dragon. He didn't think he'd be all right. And I think he knew what he was doing. More than you, right? He was sacrificing himself to save us."

"But I didn't—"

"No. I don't want to hear what you 'didn't.' Save your breath and figure out what it is *you're* going to sacrifice if we ever find this Stone Heart thing."

"What?" He was still trying not to feel so awful about the Gunner.

"What the Sphinx said. 'Your remedy lies in the Stone Heart, and the Heart Stone shall be your relief. . . . You must find the Stone Heart, and then you must make sacrifices and amends for that which is broken by putting on the Stone at the Heart of London that which is necessary for its repair.' she recited. "Or did you forget?"

"No."

"Good. Because it'd be a bloody shame if you get to this stone, and he's sacrificed himself to help you, and you still haven't got a clue about what to do, wouldn't it?"

"Hold on," he said quickly. "If I'm such a pain, why did you come back?"

"Because he told me to look after you. Actually, he said we had to look after each other, but you're as much use as a dolphin on a bicycle. . . ."

She turned and pulled ahead of him, and he was too busy trying to keep up to think of an answer. And what energy he did have left over for thinking was suddenly being used for thinking about the Gunner.

And the worst part of thinking about the Gunner and what he had done, was that he hadn't done the one thing George knew people did to each other. He hadn't let George down. George, on the other hand, had let him down. Grief and guilt are a nasty combination, and the more he absorbed them, the sadder and more exposed he felt, out here alone in the dark street with the black water to his right pulling at him as he tried to keep up with Edie.

# CHAPTER TWENTY-TWO

## The Gunner Alone

The Gunner sat with his back propped against the wall of the church. He looked broken. The bridle chains lying beside him on the pavement still smoked. He was staring up Fleet Street. The dragon, no longer white-hot, was climbing up onto its plinth. It was clearly too worn out to fly. As it climbed, it looked, despite its lion's body, more lizard-like than ever before.

"Well, that was something out of the quotidian, I'll grant you that, Gunner." Dictionary spoke without looking around. Like the Gunner, he was not going to take his eyes off the beast scaling its high plinth.

"Say again?" coughed the Gunner.

"I don't see that every day," Dictionary said, after a brief pause.

"You think he's done, the dragon?"

"Most certainly not. It is not his nature to be done. It is his nature to guard. And, as with any guard, he will not

long leave his post, lest whilst in the pursuit of one inter-
loper he leaves the way open to another."

"That right?"

"That is how he was made."

"Well, what a maker meant, the made must mind,
right?"

"So I have heard it said. So I feel it in my bones."

"Got bones, have you?"

Dictionary paused. He jerked his head and barked
wordlessly.

"*Tchah*—I *feel* I have bones. Aching bones."

"I know what you mean."

The Gunner got to his feet painfully. He tucked the
bridle chains into his belt.

The dragon's head came up at the sound of metal
clinking against metal, and there was a shadow of red in
its eyes as it peered straight down the center of the street
at them.

"He heard that," Dictionary observed mildly.

"Then he'll know me next time," grunted the soldier.

"Where does your path take you?"

"The long path? I got no read on that. But tonight?"
He stretched. Took a few steps that were really limps disguised as walking. "Tonight, like snakey there, I need to
be on my stone for the day's turn, or else . . ."

Dictionary looked at the clock sticking out from
the facade of the Law Courts like an unexpected pub
sign.

"Fewer than three hours to midnight."

The Gunner dragged his eyes from the dragon and looked up at the jerking wigged figure.

"Better get a start, then. S'only a couple of miles, but it feels like it's gonna be a long slog after the going-over he gave me."

"And the children?"

The Gunner suddenly sat down again, exhausted. He busied himself with attaching the bridle chains to his belt as if this was what he had sat down for. Actually, he was barely able to stand. He just didn't want to talk about it. Dictionary watched him, unusually motionless, not twitching at all. A gray bird settled on his head and squittered white down the back of his jacket. When he spoke again his voice was flat and harsh as a church door slamming.

"And the *children*, Gunner?"

"What must be, must be. And I must get my breath, and be on my stone at turn o'day."

The Gunner finally met his eye. "—The children are on their own."

"Not if you send a pigeon."

The Gunner's head came up. He shook it to clear it. He wasn't thinking straight. He should have thought of that.

"Well?" said Dictionary. "Is that not your conceit? Is that not how the brethren of military spits communicate between themselves?"

"Worked in the trenches. Works in London," mumbled

the Gunner. "You're right. But I'll need to get a—"

Dictionary raised his hand. The gray bird hopped off his wig and onto it. He slipped off his plinth and crossed to the Gunner. The Gunner nodded and pulled a stub of pencil from one pocket and a tiny roll of paper from the other. The effort exhausted him.

"Shall I?" said Dictionary, and exchanged the bird for the writing materials.

The Gunner sat against the cool stone, eyes closed, gently holding the bird as Dictionary wrote. Then he took the minute scroll from him and attached it to the bird's leg. He breathed into its ear.

"All the Jaggers. All the soldiers. Watch out for gargoyles. You're a messenger, not a taint's teatime snack."

He gently lifted his hands, and the gray wings fluttered and the bird lofted gently into the night sky.

The Gunner watched it disappear into the night.

"Thanks, Dictionary."

Dictionary just handed him back the pencil and paper and harrumphed. The Gunner got to his feet.

"Better make a start."

Dictionary watched him stagger off. The Gunner turned.

"If I don't . . ."

Dictionary nodded.

"It'll not be just Jaggers and soldier-spits keeping an eye out for the children, Gunner. You have my word."

The Gunner held his eyes for a beat, then nodded back.

"A word from you. That's a thing well worth having."

Dictionary inclined his head in something like a bow.

"You do me a kindness. Godspeed."

# CHAPTER TWENTY-THREE

## Mudlark and Frost Fair

There weren't many people on the Embankment where George and Edie found themselves. Edie had slowed to a fast walk. Ahead of her, George saw a familiar shape silhouetted against the river lights.

"Oh, great. We're going around in circles."

"Only because you ran away."

He didn't have a good answer for that. They approached Cleopatra's Needle, both of them watching the Sphinxes. Nothing happened.

George cleared his throat.

"You think we should . . ."

"What? Stop and say hello? You haven't got time for that. And remember. The Gunner said they're half-taint anyway, and that's half too much for me."

Nevertheless, George noticed she trailed her hand along the flanks of the Sphinxes as they passed.

"Why did you do that?" he asked, as they left

the Sphinxes behind them.

"Show them I'm not scared," she replied, as if that made all the sense in the world. She suddenly right-angled and sat down on an ornate iron bench, facing the river. The ends of the bench had been cast to look like crouching pack camels, presumably to continue the Egyptian motif along the riverside from Cleopatra's Needle.

"Now what are you doing?" asked George, watching her take her boots off.

"Making a banana meringue," she said irritably. "What does it look like?"

"It looks like you're taking your shoes off."

"Bingo. Bring the boy a genius badge."

"I don't know what you're doing."

"I do. Simon says, take your shoes off, too."

"Why?"

"Because that's how it works. If I say 'Simon says,' you just do it, and then we don't have to have a debate and waste time that you don't have."

He opened his mouth.

"Simon says, hurry up. Before that dragon notices us."

His head snapped around in the direction she was pointing with her chin. A long way down the Embankment—though not long enough to make him any-thing like comfortable—there was another dragon holding a shield emblazoned with a red cross. This dragon was silver, and stubbier that the one guarding Temple Bar, but stubby in a bunch-of-compacted-muscles kind of way, and the frozen snarl on its face showed teeth that George wanted to see no closer up than this.

He sat on the bench. He took off his shoes. Edie was stripping off her tights too.

"Simon says, trousers too."

"What?"

There was a sudden hiss and snap from the region of his knees, and the bench bucked as the camel tried to bite him. He stumbled forward, scrabbling away from the hissing creature. Edie rode the convulsion out, gripping the seat with both hands.

"It tried to bite me!"

He leaned back against the lamppost on the edge of the river wall. Something roiled and squirmed under his hand. He moved it away just fast enough to stop the iron fish that wound around the base from closing its gaping mouth on it. He hopped into the no-man's land between the bench and the river wall.

"What's going on?"

"They're little taints, aren't they? Let's get out of here before they get the attention of one of the big ones. We got to get past that dragon to get to the Black Friar, and we got to get to the Friar before turn o'day. Meaning midnight, I reckon. It's what the Gunner said."

He looked up the road at the dragon, which seemed a lot closer than when he last looked, though it hadn't moved at all.

"How do we get past it?"

"Simon says, follow me."

And she crossed to a gate in the river wall, and vaulted over. In two steps she was out of sight. George grabbed his shoes and followed as fast as he could.

Edie was at the bottom of a flight of stone steps, gingerly putting her foot into the inky blackness beyond.

"You're joking!"

"No," she said, without stopping as she went knee-deep in the dark water. "I'm wet and I'm cold and I reckon we should get this over with as fast as we can."

"We're swimming?"

She finished tying her bootlaces together and hung her boots around her neck.

"You swim if you want. I'm going to wade. The tide's going out, I expect." She set off along the greasy river wall, one hand trailing along it for balance. "I hope there's not broken glass here."

George stepped into the water. His feet sucked into silt below, up to his calf. It was cold and oozy, and in the ooze there were lumps like pebbles and sticks, and when he looked off to his right there was nothing but water between him and the south of London. He had the strong sense of something untamed and dangerous out there beneath the ripples in the center of the river. It felt—in a way he couldn't quite explain to himself—like walking on the edge of a cliff: only, instead of a gulf of air sucking at him, there was a dark undertow coiling past. He found that, like Edie, he was keeping one hand on the river wall, and not just for balance.

A thought occurred, uncomfortably.

"How do you know it's going out?"

"What's going out?"

"The tide. How do you know it isn't coming in?"

"I don't."

"Oh."

They splashed on, passing under the gangplank leading to an old steamer permanently moored to the riverbank. As they negotiated the canyon between the river wall and the rusting upsweep of the boat's hull, they could hear laughter and music coming from the deck. A lit cigarette arced into the darkness and fizzed out in the water between them.

"Simon says, think positive."

"Does Simon say how far we have to do this for?"

"One more bridge."

He splashed on. He remembered a summer's afternoon, walking along the river with both of his parents. He remembered looking over the edge to see people walking on mudbanks exposed by low tide, people with spades and buckets. People looking for things.

"People come down here at low tide and look for things," he said.

Edie grunted.

"It's like beachcombing, only there's no beach. Just mud. It's called mudlarking."

She didn't even bother to grunt this time. Just kept on going. He scowled at her and wondered if she was as cold and miserable as he was.

And then she fell and was gone.

George didn't think. He stumbled forward, lurched into the water, and reached for where she'd last been. His hands closed on nothing but river.

His hands sculled blindly beneath the water. Edie had been snatched from the face of the earth as abruptly as someone throwing an on-off switch.

"Edie!"

He found stuff in his hands and he tugged it to the surface, but it was just a black bin-liner leaking fruit peels and plastic packaging. He tossed it and plunged back into the water.

The blackening undertow winding out in the deeper part of the river was pulling at him.

"Give her back!" he shouted as his arms flailed in the icy water, churning faster and faster. He had no idea, when he later reran the moment, why he was shouting or who he was shouting at—only that it was something out there, something beyond his depth. His hand smacked at the water surface, as if trying to waken her from a sudden sleep.

"EDIE!"

Then his foot hit something and he reached for it, and it was her, and he yanked, and then they both stumbled to the side of the river wall and spluttered for a bit.

She looked smaller. Her hair rat-tailed down on either side of a face now streaked with river mud.

"You okay?"

She spat Thames water back into the river and nodded, still coughing too much to speak clearly.

"Hole," was all she could say, as she wiped slime from her eyes.

"You're okay." He smiled encouragingly.

She looked back at the patch where she'd disappeared.

"Sucked me in."

He lost the smile.

"It didn't."

"George, it sucked me in. Something sucked me in."

George thought. He fumbled at his belt.

"Bit late for that, George. I told you to take them off. You're soaked now—"

"Simon says, shut up and hold on to this. . . ." He pulled his belt through the belt loops on his trousers and held one end out to her. His voice was firm. "That way, if you go in again I can find you quicker."

After a long beat she reached out and wound one end of the belt around her fist. She nodded.

"Or we both get pulled in."

"I thought Simon said, think positive," George said, pushing his way in front of her. "I'll lead. I'll go first."

"Simon says that saying Simon was a stupid idea,"

she said, almost sounding like she was apologizing. "Not like the belt. The belt's a good idea."

Without needing to say another word, they set off along the river wall.

They passed under a complicated switchback pontoon and pier that made creaking noises as the water slapped at it on the river side. On the road above, a police car sirened past, blue light splashing on the underside of the trees that overhung the Embankment above them.

Edie stumbled and got her balance quickly. He started to ask if she was okay, but she got her question in early, as if heading him off.

"So you're rich, are you?"

He took a moment to register what she'd said.

"What?"

"You're rich. I saw the street you live on. The house. All shiny modern, like the adverts."

"We're not rich. My mum rents it."

"Gotta be rich to rent it."

"We're not rich. She's an actress."

"Actresses are rich."

George thought of his mother and his father and all the shouting, all the arguing about bits of paper that came in long brown envelopes or stiff white ones that had to be signed for.

"Not all the time."

Edie walked on. Unimpressed.

"How many bedrooms you got?"

"Two. And a sort of third one that's a sort of study."

"You and your parents live there, and how many brothers or sisters or whatnot?"

"Just me and my mum."

"Two of you and sort of three bedrooms? You're rich. And I bet your dad's got a house too, right?"

"He's dead."

Edie absorbed this.

"Oh."

They walked on. The water was getting lower again, as if there was a mudbank humping to the surface beneath their feet. Both of them were beginning to shiver with the cold. George clamped his mouth tight to stop his teeth chattering.

"What about you?" asked George through clenched teeth, eager to take the spotlight off himself.

"Me, too."

"You're rich?"

"No. My dad's dead."

"Oh."

They splashed on. It felt very lonely down here in the lee of the Embankment, below the lintel of the city, wading through the icy mud.

"So you live with your mum?"

"No," she replied after a pause. "She's not around."

"So where do you—"

"I stay in hostels. For runaways. It's crappy, okay?"

"Okay," he said.

"I run away from them too." She sniffed defiantly. "I'm freezing."

They trudged on a bit.

"When I'm hungry, I think of food," she said. "I think of when I was the most stuffed, when I couldn't eat another thing."

"Should think it makes you more hungry." George shivered.

"No. It works. Try it."

"I'm not hungry," said George.

"Not hungry, you mung. When were you the warmest?"

"Oh," said George.

He sploshed through a flotilla of fish and chip wrappers.

"I was in a barn. In the hay. With my dad."

"Your dad is a farmer? *Was* a farmer, sorry?"

"No," said George, remembering. "He was making a bull."

"He was whatting a bull?" she asked incredulously.

"He was an artist. Someone wanted a bull. So he got this farmer who had a bull, and he had him put it in a stall, and then we went down and he sketched it."

Just for an instant he smelled the memory of warm hay and his father's cigarettes. Then it was gone.

"I wasn't meant to be there. But my mum had an audition. She's always having auditions. And so he had to take me with him. It was great. I was quite little and it was winter and you could see the bull's breath coming out in two snorty clouds when he breathed. He even had a ring through his nose—I mean, he was a real bull."

"Doesn't sound very warm," muttered Edie.

"No, it was. It was great. Dad wrapped me in this blanket from the car and he made a hay bed, like a hole in the hay, and I sat there next to him, and we had thermoses of tea and that bright-orange tomato soup that stains your lips, and he drew and I drew too, except I got so warm in my hay bed that I fell asleep. I mean it was really toasty, and it smelled great, and when I woke up it was getting dark and he was finished and just lying beside me. . . ."

He remembered it all. The glow of the lightbulb in the roof, making all the hay golden. And the massive black bull, big as a small car, quietly chomping on its feed. And the sound of his dad smoking. He'd always smoked when he was working, but only outside. When George was old enough to know that smoking was a really bad idea if you liked things like lungs and living, his dad had made a pact. He'd half stop smoking. Never inside. Only while working. And never in a pub. So that's how George remembered him: the sound of his dad concentrating, one eye screwed up against the smoke drifting up his cheek, hands steady, always sketching or making something. And the regular quiet pop-and-suck sound he made on the cigarette parked in one side of his face: the sound of a man smoking without using his hands. Even though smoking was such a bad thing, he still found the memory of the noise soothing.

And it hadn't been the smoking that killed him anyway.

"That's the warmest I remember being," he said to eradicate the next memory that was winging in out of the dark, out of the place where he banished it as often as he could.

"I went to a farm once," said Edie. "School trip. A goat peed on me."

He smiled, and then felt something sharp under his foot and skipped sideways before it broke his skin. Off balance, he yanked them both away from the wall. The mud got thinner under his feet and he dipped in, falling on one knee.

"I'm sorry," he blurted.

Edie stumbled after him—falling down on all fours, dropping her end of the belt in the effort to stay upright, chin above the water.

"I'm not—"

And her hand closed on something solid in the mud, something that felt like old slimy wood, like an ancient stump or a piling, and she felt a surge of energy weld her hand to it, and she couldn't pull it away, and then . . .

"Oh, no," said George, seeing her with her eyes wide and her chin barely breaking water.

And the rippled surface of the water blew flat around her, the shock wave of the past winnowing out from her at the epicenter, and her wet hair fanned wide in dripping spikes, and her eyes convulsed shut, and the two-century-wide gap between where they were and what she was seeing hit her like a down-bound freight train.

It was dark but it was lighter.

There were fewer lights across the wide river but there were many more on it, and what lights there were were softer. No sharp-edged electric light reflected off the fast moving ripples on the Thames, because there was no electric light at all, and more important, no ripples, only white ridges of ice—and they didn't move a bit.

The river was frozen.

And covered in snow.

The lights were lanterns and flares and braziers, and in their light, reflected off the snow and ice beneath, there were people.

There were men in top hats with their necks swaddled in scarves. There were women in bonnets and long wide skirts that trailed on the ice as they walked carefully, hands hidden in fur-trimmed muffs that hung in front of them. Everyone's eyes reflected the torch flares and the fires and a general excitement at the otherness all around them. Everyone seemed happy, and there were laughing children everywhere, running and sliding, long mufflers flying out behind them in the night air.

A child launched herself into a slide, her bonnet snapping back off her head, held on by the ribbons, her red cheeks and red nose framing the redder hole of a mouth stretched wide in an excited shriek. She stopped herself by grabbing on to a thick pole set upright in the ice, and hung there, laughing as her friends caught up with her.

From the top of the pole stretched a banner, with crude writing swirled across it in blue and green, reading: FROST FAIR, and below it, in smaller script, the invitation: COME ONE, COME ALL!

It all looked like a dream, and the unreal quality was heightened by the mist that seemed to rise from the ice and surround everything, softening the edges of people and things, creating haloes around the burning torches illuminating the street that ran down the center of the river toward the bridge ahead of them.

It was a street of tents and rough shelters, in all shapes and sizes. From the back, most of the structures had a hurried shipwreck quality to them, but at the front, in the mouth of each one, there was light and painted billboards and colored lanterns and cheery activity. Beneath flags and looping swags of bunting, London's merchants and innkeepers had taken to the ice, and wherever Edie looked it seemed like there was someone selling or shouting or serving hot drinks that gave off thin skeins of steam that added to the eerie fog hanging in the air.

And there was laughter and shouting and the sound of different kinds of music fighting each other to be heard. Edie could hear the distant skirl of bagpipes and the rattle of snare drums, and closer, she could hear fiddle players, and something like a barrel organ jigging and popping away in between.

She heard a *chunk* to her left, and when she looked she saw three men with pickaxes chopping ice out of a channel dug between the river ice and the bank. The men were thickset and unshaven, with outdoor faces and high boots turned back at the knee. They all had brass badges hanging from their necks, which swung as they threw the picks into the ice. Farther along the channel, another group of similar-looking men had put a plank across it, and were busy charging finely dressed people for the privilege of crossing the water onto the snowy pleasure ground beyond.

As Edie watched, she saw a heavy-jowled man question the charges, as if he thought that paying for crossing three feet of water the lowest and most impertinent sort of insult. They showed him the brass badges and mouthfuls of discolored teeth. She heard a snatch of what they said, and heard that they said it with pride.

"Watermen, sir—with your leave—ancient custom and tradition of the river. Safe and efficacious carriage across the hazardous flow, sir."

The jowly man was about to continue his protest when a little girl in a green cape started jumping up and down at his side and pointing to the ice beyond.

Edie followed the line of her finger and saw that everyone was now moving in that direction, drawn as if by a large magnet to the spectacle now progressing down the impromptu tented mall in the center of the ice.

First came a drummer. Then men carrying large flaming torches that smoked darkly into the air. Then came three bagpipers in full Highland dress, cheeks bulging as they played, long horse-tail sporrans swinging in time as they marched slowly ahead of another pair of torchbearers. And then there it was, its massive feet lurching it forward in time to the leisurely swing of the sporrans ahead of it.

An elephant.

A white elephant.

Edie was used to horror and pain when she glinted the past, but sometimes the past didn't come in sharp hurtful jags that sliced at her. Sometimes, very rarely, it was even close enough to something else for her to actually enjoy it and not be too scared.

But it had never, until now, seemed to be like this.

She exhaled. Some knot deep in her chest loosened, and she took a breath of air that felt cleaner and almost refreshing, despite, or maybe because of, the sweet and smoky smell of roasted chestnuts that came with it.

"It's beautiful."

She heard the words before she recognized the voice, and knew that she had said them herself.

And the elephant on the ice was indeed beautiful. Walking with slow deliberate steps, it swayed past the open mouths and the garish bunting with an otherworldly dignity. On its back it carried a howdah, which was a sort of tented castle that swayed from side to side as it moved. More flaming torches were fixed to each of the four corners of the little pavilion, and from inside, a very beautiful woman in a white fur cloak and bejewelled turban waved at the onlookers.

A small dark-faced boy in a smaller fur coat sat behind the elephant's ears, waving at the crowd and flashing his own white teeth at them as they passed.

The elephant was not only white, but patterned. In the torchlight Edie could see that someone had painted garlands of flowers along its sides and on its face, and even made bands of pale colors all down its trunk. As it moved through the crowd, every eye was on it, and the low-hanging ice-smog only added to the dreamy beauty of the spectacle.

Edie was transfixed.

And then she thought she heard someone call her name. She looked up and saw someone, someone shorter than a man, running toward her, away from the crowd, the only face against a sea of backs.

And he seemed to be shouting something, hands cupped in front of his face to make a megaphone—and she couldn't hear, and then she could, just an urgent snatch: "Don't look at the elephant!"

And then the beauty stopped, and time went jagged and the past ceased to be a soothing dreamy flow, and hit at her in juddering slices.

The running figure tripped and fell before she could make out its face in the fog.

There was a shout to her right.

Her head snapped around.

Another figure, a girl in a bonnet was running toward her, arms waving, shouting and shaking something bright. And behind the brightness, Edie caught a glimpse of something big and burly and man-shaped lurching out of the fog.

And then time sliced.

And, closer now, a big man was struggling with something that was fighting like a wildcat.

The something broke free and was, suddenly again, the girl, running for her life straight at Edie.

The man bent and pulled steel from inside his double-caped coat.

The steel of a long burnished knife.

Torch-flare reflected redly off it as he started to run after the girl.

Time sliced again, and the girl ran toward Edie, stumbling blindly, really close now. Her bonnet had been mashed forward over her face by the struggling.

Edie saw her.

Saw the three-foot-wide channel of freezing water in front of her.

Saw the girl could not see it through the bonnet blindfold.

Edie tried to shout a warning but her mouth was

already at full stretch, just screaming with the unexplainable pain of the past flowing through her.

And then time jumped forward again, and the girl was in the water and under it, and her face broke into the air covered in hair like a thick flap of seaweed, and the one visible eye seemed almost to see Edie, and she was shouting something, and all Edie caught was: "He's not what he seems! Tell—"

And then a rescuing hand reached over and grabbed her hair, only it wasn't rescuing at all. It was pushing her back under, and all there was were bubbles and splashing and black water, and then the girl broke free for an instant and fishmouthed for air; and Edie heard her scream like she was shouting directly into the core of Edie's being without going via the ears. And the words had the terrible panicked urgency of last words: ". . . gates in the mirrors . . ."

Then the man's hand spread once more and grabbed the bonnet and plunged the spluttering face under the water for the last time, and the hair spread apart, and Edie saw the distorted face suddenly clean and white under the water, eyes wide in terror, mouth still shouting and then breathing water. Edie couldn't tell why, but she felt she knew the face, and then the mouth stopped moving and the eyes went still, and something dark swooped between Edie and the "then," and she was gasping for air in the "now." The Frost Fair and the elephant and the drowned girl were gone, and she was staring across a moving river and electric light made hard edges of every-thing, even the blackness.

George was at her side, looking sick and perturbed.

"What happened?"

And all she could say, with a heart full of a new and inexplicable sadness, was: "I missed it."

"What? What did you miss?"

She lurched out of the deeper water and stood for a moment, gazing across the river as if she were trying to conjure the past back into being one more time. Then she shook her head and wiped her face.

"I don't know."

She started walking toward the bridge louring over the water ahead of them.

"I was looking at the elephant."

# CHAPTER TWENTY-FOUR

## Rough Edges

The Walker was pacing around George's room, looking at all the toys and models and clay animals. He pushed back his hood as he paced, and grimaced.

His mouth was the kind that settles in a permanent scowl, the sides pulled back to expose teeth and gums, as if the very air were distasteful to him. His eyes were a dark violet, sunk deep in their sockets. He had a small beard around his mouth, although his cheeks were, in a grizzled fashion, clean-shaven. The beard hooked into a goatish tuft on the end of his chin. There was a single pearl dangling from a gold hoop looped through one ear, and he wore a black rimless cap on the back of his head.

He looked like a magician turned pirate.

But not a kind magician or a good pirate.

He suddenly reached up and took a small clay model of George as a baby and stuck it in his pocket. Then he pulled a long dagger, with a surprisingly ornate jeweled handle, from a scabbard hung at the back of his belt, under his coat, and pulled open a drawer.

He removed a T-shirt, smelled it, and discarded it.

He crossed to a laundry bin and pulled out a dirty T-shirt.

He smelled it and smiled.

He took the dagger and ripped out a section of it in three jagged slices.

Then he pocketed the scrap of material and left the room.

As he walked across the living room he paused in front of the bust of George's mother. Her head was thrown back in a laugh, hair caught in a permanent swirl of joy. His hand stroked the naked shoulders and the exposed curve of her neck and traveled on to the edge of the piece, where the smooth sensual curves suddenly ended in a sharp jagged edge, as if someone had taken a hacksaw and angrily removed something from a sculpture that was—when you looked closely at it—a little lopsided. His fingers enjoyed the rough edges a second time, and then he suddenly turned and left the room to itself and the night.

# Chapter Twenty-Five

## George in Charge

A metal ladder was fixed to the embankment wall, leading up the greasy slabs of stone toward the orange fluorescent lights above. George climbed as far as he could, then came to a sheet of hinged metal that had been padlocked in place on the top six feet of the ladder, to stop people climbing down into the river. He hunched his feet up closer to his body, and used the slope of the metal and his two arms to brace himself as he climbed up the last bit of ladder, his feet held in place by friction and willpower.

He took a deep breath and stuck his head over the parapet. His arms were burning with the strain of holding his weight, but he wasn't going to climb onto dry land until he saw if they'd come far enough to be safe. He peered to his left and, with relief, saw no sign of the dragon. They were a long way past it. He checked right and saw nothing more threatening than the river walkway disappearing under the bridge almost directly above him.

He turned and gave Edie the thumbs-up. She wasn't watching him. She was still looking back along the river.

"Hey!"

She looked up, her eyes taking their time to return from a long way off. He gave her another thumbs-up.

"It's safe. We're in the City. No dragons."

He clambered over the wall and onto the river walk. Below him, she began climbing.

"No dragons doesn't mean we're safe."

Her gravelly voice sounded even rawer than usual. He wondered if it was the cold. And now that he thought about it, he noticed what he had been ignoring, that he was soaked and muddy and very very cold indeed. Now that he was on dryish land, his body let him feel the full force of the exposure they'd just put themselves through. The body works on autopilot when you're running scared, and pumps adrenaline into your system to help you fight or—as in George and Edie's case—flee. Sadly, there's only so much adrenaline in the system; and it runs out. George felt like his was running out through the soles of his feet and making him notice every detail of how uncomfortable he was, all at once. Even the stone under his feet felt like a jagged sheet of ice.

But one thing was good. One thing had changed. Maybe it was the jolt that Edie had given him telling him that the Gunner was gone, or maybe it was pulling her out of the water when she'd disappeared and he'd thought he was alone again: but since he'd decided to take the lead, he actually felt less out of control. He didn't expect Edie would accept he was leading anything, but for the moment he was, and it felt good. He was less panicked because he had someone else to think about rather than just worrying about himself. It was strange.

He pulled his shoes out of his pockets and tried to put his feet into them. Wet feet resisted the leather lining, and his feet seemed to have grown two sizes anyway, so he gave up—just as Edie slid over the wall and joined him and dripped onto the pavement. They both shivered uncontrollably.

Edie looked terrible, as if the wet and the mud had dampened her normal fire. Her shaking was like a flame guttering out. Her lips were tight and tinged in blue.

George knew that she was colder than he was, and he knew he still had to stay in charge.

"Come on. Let's run."

Her eyes came up, their normal light frosted over with sadness and cold. For a change she didn't say anything, didn't argue or jab or complain. He jerked his thumb toward the bridge.

"Is that Blackfriars Bridge?"

She nodded.

"Then let's run up there and find this Black Friar."

"I don't want to run."

She hunched down on her heels, trying to curl her body around the last flickering lick of heat in her core.

Her hand found the sea-glass, and she checked it. It was dull and safe and wet from the river. Seeing it wet reminded her of the seaside, the beach where she had first found the glass and pocketed it. She realized even that first moment had been surreptitious: she had seen it at her feet in the wet pebbles, and had picked it up without thinking much, but once it was in her hand she had realized that she felt something about it, and hadn't wanted him to see it or touch it or take it away from her.

He hadn't noticed her crouch and scoop it up, because he'd been awkward and looking out to sea and trying to light a roll-up at the same time. He'd been awkward because he'd taken her onto the beach to tell her that her mother was not coming back, and that it was just the two of them for now, "until things sorted out."

On the train that had brought Edie into London, she had sat next to two happy families returning from a day at the sea, and one of the posh mothers told the other that the thing she always loved about the seaside was that you never saw unhappy children at the beach. And the other mum had laughed and said no, not until it was time to go home. And Edie had wanted to scream. All the worst things that had happened to her had happened at the beach or—if they hadn't—the news of them was first given to her on a beach, in front of an uncaring bloody sea whose waves rolled in endlessly, their greeny-brown

George in Charge

surfaces flaked and scalloped by the wind, hard and relentless as liquid flint.

It was one of the reasons that she'd got on a train to London when she had had to run away. All the other trains went to places that she knew were by the sea. She hadn't come to London because of the bright lights, or because it was the capital.

She'd come because it was inland.

George shook her shoulder, snapping her out of her reverie.

"Edie. Come on. We have to keep moving."

"Just give me a minute," she shivered back, grumpy with cold. "Frozen."

He jogged on the spot. His dad had taken him walking and camping one snowy Christmas way up north. He'd told him how to keep moving to keep warm, how to check for frostnip, how to cuddle together in the tent to keep warm at night, and he'd felt in the grip of a real adventure then, sleeping in a tent in the snow with no noise except the wind buffeting the side wall and his dad's snoring in his ear. It had felt like an adventure, but it had also seemed safe. Remembering the long-gone warmth from the bearlike curl of his sleeping father made his eyes prickle, made him notice how very cold and alone and *not* safe he felt right now. He snapped at Edie.

"Edie. I'm serious. You need to move. We're going to get pneumonia or something."

She just crouched further in on herself. He had to

make her move, and looking at her hand, he saw how to do it.

"Edie. You can stay here. But if you want this back, you better run."

And he snatched the sea-glass from her and ran off.

Her hand closed on air, and her head snapped up and she was on her feet despite herself, already running before she was aware she'd decided to move.

"Wait!"

George looked back to check she was following and then just ran on. The river walk continued under the span of the bridge. The stubby pillars that decorated the piers of the bridge were floodlit, and he was so starved of warmth that he felt the heat of the lights on the side of his face as he ran under the red-painted metal arch.

From Edie's point of view it looked like he was running into the mouth of something.

"George!"

He already felt fractionally better because he was running and warming up. It was good that she was following him. He lifted the sea-glass over his head to lure her onward.

"Come on! Catch up!"

She watched him run into the dimly lit gullet under the metal ribs of the bridge. And first she thought it was a reflection, and then as it grew she realized with horror what she was seeing: the sea-glass was beginning to glow, then blaze. Its light strobed off the vertical iron bars that ran along the landward side of the river walk, sending long lazy stripes of shadow across the strange caged space beyond.

But it wasn't that that made her shout a warning.

Not only that.

Ahead of George, two helmeted figures were approaching at speed, although their legs didn't move at all. They appeared to be statues eerily gliding over the ground toward him, and in their hands were weapons—spears maybe, or scythes.

One held his weapon ankle-low, the other carried it poised on his shoulder casually, but ready to strike. Their silhouettes were bulky with armor, and light reflected off the greaves on their lower legs.

Edie shouted George's name just as the lead figure swooped into motion, his legs pushing from side to side in a slow powerful gliding movement, adding to his momentum as he bore down on the running boy.

Her warning shout scarcely made it to George's ear before the leading figure put his weapon out and ran it along the iron bars, making a harsh ratchetting noise of wood against metal as he skated up to George.

Only, he wasn't a monster or a taint or a statue, or even interested in anything other than making a noise with his hockey stick to amuse his friend, who took the stick off his shoulder and powered after him on his own Rollerblades, making the same noise on the cage bars as he passed George.

As they caromed out from under the bridge, laughing and skating, Edie saw them for what they were, street hockey players heading home on their Rollerblades.

She exhaled with momentary relief, and then doubled her speed to catch up with George.

"Hey!"

He waved the glass, still without looking at it, and jinked left into the mouth of a tunnel. The glass still blazed its unseen warning.

"No! NOT UNDERGROUND!"

He didn't hear her.

Ahead of him, the tunnel angled beneath the old riverbank and the roundabout at the end of the bridge.

As he ran into it, he felt the heat rise, and he was glad of the way it seemed to have trapped the day's warmth.

# CHAPTER TWENTY-SIX

## Going Underground

It was a long anonymous box of a tunnel, like any underpass in any city. The walls were lined with vertically ribbed panels, and the floor was a checkerboard strip of yellow and black paving stones. It was a space that just goes from here to there, the kind of nothing space you don't notice because it isn't designed to be noticed. You forget dozens of spaces like this every day, the moment you pass through them. When you picture yourself in your mind's eye, you're always *somewhere*, never in a limbo space like this at all. And if there's any point of human contact in this kind of space, it's usually no more than the downcast gaze of a busker, or the smell of an opportunistic pee someone's had against the wall when they were desperate and no one was looking, or maybe just the thought that the footsteps behind you might be a mugger. Because, of course, a rarely traveled and largely unnoticed space, out of sight, beneath the skin of the city, is just the place for a mugging.

George wasn't thinking of mugging when he looked back. He was just checking that Edie was still following. And because he was looking back, he didn't see the hand that grabbed him, though he heard the crunching, cracking noise that preceded it by an instant.

As the hand clamped tight on his arm, he knew it was a mugger. In his subconscious, like all of us, George had known that one day he'd be alone in a place like this and the mugger would appear. Though, as he turned he was wondering where the mugger had been hiding, because the tunnel had been perfectly empty a moment before.

The hand twisting and coiling around his upper arm came from no mugger.

It came from the wall.

Or it came from a split that it had punched in the wall, with a crunch and a crack. And with the crack came a blast of warmth that ramped up the heat in the passage, as if someone had just opened an oven door.

He had one moment of calm clarity before the panic hit him, and in that frozen extended instant he saw the hand and the arm with almost scientific detachment and detail.

It wasn't a human arm, because the hand had too many fingers and no discernible joints in any of them. They twined around his arm like a team of small competing snakes, pulsing and constricting and growing longer and thicker in front of his eyes.

It wasn't a human arm, because it wasn't covered in skin. It wasn't covered in anything, and what wasn't covered was not flesh or bone, but the very soil of the city, the living earth and mud that is always only a few inches beneath the surface layer of stone and tarmac. As he stared in shocked fascination, fragments of gravel and larger pebbles popped out of the clay and writhed and rippled along the surface of the forearm, forming themselves into stony trails that flexed and twisted together like tendons.

And finally, it wasn't a human arm, because it was already four feet long.

Panic finally arrived, and George dropped the sea-glass and jerked and tugged, trying to get free. The heat intensified and seemed to thicken the air around him, making it as hard to breathe as soup.

"EDIE!" he screamed, trying to look backward and kick at the arm at the same time.

A rhythmic growing *chunka-chunka* noise turned his head back to the front, and froze him for a second time. Something was speeding toward him at floor level, like a shark attacking from beneath the pavement, rippling the yellow and black paving stones into a menacing bow wave as it came for him.

Though he was still firmly pinioned by his arm, he managed to lurch away and run his legs up the side of the passage, desperate to get his feet up out of harm's way. Sweat was pouring from him, and he could see his wet clothes beginning to steam in the heat of the air that closed around him.

"EDIE!"

He was stuck, jammed horizontally across the passageway, his feet scrabbling for purchase on the wall.

The under-floor attacker just switched tack. The rippling paving stones headed to the edge of the floor and then up the side, and the wall itself bulged in its own bow wave and the thing broke surface with a ripping noise. A single clay finger jagged out and developed into a roiling knot of tendrils, like a giant clay model of a sea urchin on the end of another arm, heading right for George's ankles. In a final surge of panicked energy, he found himself contorting in horror, trying to run even farther up the wall and onto the ceiling, before the tendrils slapped into his right leg and whipped around it in a grip that was, if anything, tighter and more painful than the one on his arm.

Edie ran into the end of the tunnel and bounced off the side wall before she got a fix on what was happening in front of her. Or rather, she didn't get a fix, so much as an impression. There were two Georges it seemed: one standing in the middle of the passage, unmoving, and then another George being held in the air, at right angles to the standing George—or a maybe-George because it was a wispy image, see-through and almost invisible, like a skein of smoke with a faint moving picture projected on it. She couldn't see exactly what was holding the nearly-

George, but she could see from the way he was struggling that he was fighting it, and fighting it hard.

And then she saw the ceiling ripple, as if a ghost-ceiling was flexing, and then the ghost-ceiling split and she thought, very, very far away she could hear someone quietly whispering her name—

"Edie!"

George saw the solid brown mass rip out of the ceiling in front of him, and he shouted louder than he could ever remember doing before in his short life—a life that looked like it was not going to get any longer than the next second or so.

A column of clay dropped out of the gash in the roof and hung in front of him. As he watched in horror, it started to whirl slowly, as if being kneaded and shaped by an army of invisible hands. The bottom of the column spread out, while the top thinned into a sinewy cable as thick as a telegraph pole. When the column had morphed itself into a rough cone shape, the cable flexed and bent, and tilted the base of the cone toward George.

George stopped shouting. He stopped doing anything. The only movement he made was a reflexive blink as his brain dealt with the stinging sweat pouring into his eyes. He just stared.

The base of the cone was a mouth, and in the mouth were teeth: teeth that moved and ground and clashed and shattered against each other: teeth that weren't really teeth, but sharp flints and jags of broken glass, torn and rusted soda cans and shards of broken china. And they were constantly churning and rotating in the earthy maw of the cone, chipping and skreeing against each other.

George was looking into the heart of a slow whirlwind of mud. And what he saw was a meat grinder.

The hand and the tentacles holding his arm and leg pulled apart and twisted, and the pain screwed through him as he was stretched, wrung out like a dishcloth, and he realized that he was being held for the mouth like a cob of corn about to be bitten into. The grip on his ankle was especially tight, and as it twisted he felt his leg being pulled out of its socket, and he realized the pain was about to become beyond excruciating, and that he was going to pass out. And simultaneously he realized that passing out would mean that he was dead meat in the grinder, and he found a treacly blackness within himself that pushed the pain down to a place where he could find it later, and he used every ounce of strength left in him to chop his hand at the arm attached to the tendrils holding his leg.

And again thinking two things at once, he knew it was a futile gesture, and he knew sometimes all you have is the lost hope. And his hand hit the arm and felt thick wet earth and sharp pebbles and long dead roots and then air again, and his feet were suddenly free, and gravity did its thing and his body dropped from the horizontal to the vertical.

He felt the air move as the mouth lunged for where

he had just been, and he heard the teeth gnash. And then he felt the pain in his arm double as it took all his weight, still clenched in the other earth hand. His feet were dancing six inches in the air, looking blindly for pavement to relieve the pressure, and as the cone of teeth pulled back, like a snake preparing to strike again, he lashed out at it.

Again he felt earth and stone and debris and then air, and this time he saw what his hand could do: the cone simply stopped being a cone in front of his eyes and just dropped to the ground in a spatter of soil and pebbles, as haphazard as a thrown shovelful of dirt splayed across the checkerboard at his feet.

He grabbed at the many fingers boa-constrictoring around his arm, and found that they too dissolved into a formless scrabble of soil as he touched it with his hand, as if it were just as simple and easy as brushing dirt from his sleeve.

He dropped to the floor and stumbled a little.

Edie saw the floating almost-George lash and fight and then drop into a stumble, and then the two Georges were one, like something coming into focus. And then there was one boy and no ghost images, and Edie ran for him.

"George. Out of here, now!"

She had no idea what she'd just seen, but she knew it wasn't good, and she knew it was to do with being underground, and she needed to get them both into the open air as soon as possible. She grabbed his wet arm and pulled. He took a step forward, then stopped.

"H-hang on."

He dipped and snatched something from the floor, and then they were both running up the steps and out into the night—and as they hit the air, George gulped it like a man drinking cool water after a day's work in a blast furnace.

And of course the cold air and the shock made him shake all over again, and his teeth rattled together until he looked at Edie.

"What?" she said.

He handed over the thing he'd dropped in the underground passage. She took it and looked into it. If there was any light in it, it was very pale—so pale it might just be her imagination, she decided.

"I'm sorry I took it. I did it so that you'd run after me. I didn't know how else to make you move. . . ."

She slid the sea-glass into her pocket and zipped it up with an air of finality.

"Well, don't take it again. Ever."

"I won't."

She shivered and rubbed at her soaking arms. Her teeth began to chatter again.

"And if you do nick it, at least look at the stupid thing. It's what it's for, you mung. You ran right into whatever just happened."

He felt the ache in his arm and ankle, and thought of the earth rippling with gravel tendons and the mouthful of sharp forgotten debris, and decided he'd think about it later. He wanted to move on.

"Yup."

"Could have saved yourself a lot of trouble."

He nodded, just glad to be out of the tunnel, above-ground and breathing normally. He cleared his throat. Maybe he could talk about it if she'd seen it, and of course she *had* to have seen it. Maybe she could make sense of it.

"Do you know what that was?" he asked.

"Apart from horrible and frightening?"

"Yeah."

She shook her head.

"Not a Scooby. Just more nightmare."

"But you saw it?"

It was important to George, suddenly, that she had also witnessed it.

"I saw *something*. Like layers or—I dunno. Bits of a thing. You were there and just standing, and then there was like another wispy you floating about and fighting away, and then—it's complicated."

He nodded.

"Maybe the Black Friar can explain."

She shook her head.

"Just ask him about the London Stone, like the Gunner said. Keep it simple."

"Why?"

She shrugged and walked across the pavement,

heading away from the river, rubbing herself as she went, trying to stop her teeth chattering.

"Don't know. Every time we talk to one of these spits they're confusing enough without giving them more reason to get all ambiguous on us. London Stone's the key, so let's not give him the excuse not to give us a simple answer."

# Chapter Twenty-seven

## The Dark Shaveling

George followed Edie toward a narrow triangular four-story pub that jutted its sharpest angle toward the river, like the prow of an earthbound boat. On the first floor, above a green and gold mosaic number 174, a black statue of a large monk was positioned like a figurehead, his hands folded contentedly on the upper slopes of an expansive stomach kept in check by a long tasseled belt.

The children stopped beneath it. The pub was closed. Looking up at the Friar, all they could really see of his face were double chins and fat cheeks and a jutting nose. He appeared to be beaming merrily, but it was just an impression, since they couldn't see his eyes. Above his head there was a halolike yellow clock face. George looked at it in disbelief.

"It can't be five to seven! It's got to be later than that."

"It's always five to seven here, young man. Always such a convivial, promising time, five to seven; the day's work done, the evening spread before you like a banquet to pick and choose what diversion you will; a time for warmth and conviviality and conversation."

The voice boomed down at them, a rich, honeyed voice in which you could hear barely controlled laughter and good cheer ringing through like a peal of bells.

"Conversation is what we've come for," said Edie, stepping back for a better look.

The Black Friar jerked his head down to look at her, his pouchy face wobbling in surprise.

"You heard me?"

"Mind you, the warmth sounds pretty good, too," added George, jogging on the spot and rubbing at himself to try and get some heat going.

"You *both* heard me?" said the Friar, looking from one to another.

"We're both cold," said Edie.

"And wet," added George. "Cold and wet."

"Well I'll be jiggered," said the Friar. "Watch out below."

He stepped off the front of the building and dropped to the ground, his cassock billowing around him like a dark parachute. He hit the pavement with a crash that did justice to his considerable girth, straightened his legs, smoothed his robes, and looked at them both appraisingly. Close to him, they could see his eyes were indeed set in deep laugh lines, making him look a very friendly and cheery sort of monk—which was a relief, because his size was just looming enough to have been threatening in other circumstances.

"Conversation, you say? And what of? And why? And whence? And wherefore too, no doubt?"

George and Edie exchanged a look that translated as "Huh?" in any language you chose.

"Sorry?"

"Apology accepted. Think no more about it. It's forgotten," said the Friar, beaming down at them.

George began to wonder if the monk was a bit mad. Edie just thought he was annoying.

"The Gunner said you could help us. And we could do with the help."

"The Gunner, you say?"

"Please," said George.

"I know of several Gunners."

"We just know the one. He's a spit, like you."

There was a long pause as the Friar examined them. Then he chuckled and pointed to the door of the pub.

"Please. Any friend of the Gunner, whatever Gunner, is a friend of mine and so forth! You find us at a disadvantage; the hostelry doors closed due to a refurbishment of the lavatories beneath the bar, which were, I'll admit, a little noxious with age and overuse. But enter, please do. Hospitality is ever our watchword, no matter what the time."

George tried the door. It wouldn't budge. Edie

stepped in and rattled it to no more effect. She turned an accusing eye on the friar.

"It's locked."

"Ah, well, love laughs at locksmiths." He chuckled.

"What?"

He pushed in front of them.

"To the pure of heart no door is ever locked." He fumbled for a moment, then the door swung open. "As you see."

"You used a key," Edie observed quietly.

He gave a theatrical sigh, shoulders slumping good-humoredly, like a disappointed conjuror.

"Bless your sharp little eyes, we shall have to watch you, and that's a fact."

He stood to one side and the two of them walked into the pub. It was a narrow, awkwardly angled space. In the dark there were odd shapes and reflections that seemed to loom and then lurch away as the lights of passing cars swept past the windows. The bottles behind the bar and the brassware on it glittered with the fragmented reflections of the streetlights outside.

There were stepladders and other evidence of builders spread across the floor, and a dust sheet hung protectively over the bar surface, like a discarded shroud.

The door snapped shut behind them. The Black Friar swept past with unexpected nimble-footedness for such a large and bulky man.

"Come, come, mind the tradesmen's mess; into the chamber here, the alcove, and we will have heat and light and see what we can do for you, for it's clear that unless we do something, you will likely come down with the sniffles."

He bustled them through the left-hand of three low arches and pressed them onto a bench at the end of a dim vaulted space, and left them, suddenly ducking down a flight of steps beside the bar. Edie stared at George.

"Sniffles!"

"I know." He shrugged.

He was freezing again. His clothes stuck to him like soaked bandages.

"We're meant to trust something that says 'sniffles'?"

He could hear her teeth chattering in the dark. Before he could say anything more, there was a clattering and the Friar reappeared, dragging something heavy that clanged on each step as he came up the stairs.

He blocked out the streetlight as he lurched through the arch, and then bent to lower a gas canister and a stubby torpedo-shaped heater onto the floor in front of them.

"The tradesmen have been trying to dry out the cellar. I'm sure they would think it unchristian to deprive you of this warmth in your hour of need."

He lifted his arm, and a bundle of clothing fell to the floor.

"Dry clothes. Towels of a sort. People leave things," he explained. "Peril of overindulgence in a hostelry such as this, waking up at home having gained a headache and lost a topcoat, d'you see?"

He chortled at his own good humor.

"Everyday tragedy of the convivial man, no doubt! Help yourself, do. I shall give you privacy while you change. Perhaps food would be—"

"Yes," said Edie, so fast that George suddenly realized she couldn't have eaten in a long while.

She knelt over the clothes and lifted a handful of towels.

"These are beer towels. They're tiny."

"Good job there's a bunch of them," George said. He knelt by the heater and looked at it. He turned the knob on the top of the gas bottle. He heard a rustle of clothing from behind him and started to look back.

"Er, I'm changing," said Edie, the shiver still in her voice.

"It's all right. I'm not looking," he said, trying to make out the controls in the meager streetlight. "I'm trying to get us some warmth."

"You know how that works?"

He found an electric plug on the end of a wire. There was a socket by his knee, so he plugged it in. A fan started blowing inside the stubby torpedo.

"My dad had one like it in his studio. Used it in winter. Hang on."

He turned a taplike switch. Nothing happened. Edie snorted in derision.

"I thought you said you knew how to work it."

He carried on, counting to ten, then pressed a button. There was a click and a tiny spark noise, then a big *Whoomf* and the space heater roared into life. A circle of flame inside the metal casing was blown forward by the fan onto a grid that started to glow red. As George held his hand in front of the big opening, the heat began building fast. The flames went from blue to red to almost white, and then the heat was too strong for him to leave his hand in the way.

"Nice one," said Edie, almost impressed. "Oh, wow."

The flames from the heater were also lighting up the alcove they were in. It was a barrel-vaulted space, about two meters wide by five long, and every inch of it was decorated with smoky-brown marble shot through with black streaks. There were columns and pilasters and mirrors and ornate alabaster light fittings and pieces of statuary everywhere. Above their heads, the curve of a barrel-vault reflected back the light from thousands of gold mosaic chips, outlined in thin lines of black-and-white checkerboarding. In the center of the ceiling was a star-shaped compass, and all around the cornicing below ran ornate lettering, each one a quotation, none of which made any connection with the others around it. George was facing one that read: HASTE IS SLOW. He turned to read another that suggested: FINERY IS FOOLERY.

Out of the corner of his eye, he saw Edie pulling on a long man's sweatshirt. "Hey," she said.

"Sorry," he said, looking away quickly. "This place. It's pretty weird, no?"

"Weird is right."

"It's like being inside a church or something."

She pushed past him and spread her skirt and tights on a chair in front of the heat blasting out of the heater. "You want to get dry and change?"

He stepped back. She stood in front of the heat, looking up at the decoration around them, rubbing her hair with a beer towel. He noticed she clutched the sea-glass in her hand.

He stripped off his coat and shirt, and rubbed his chest with the bar towels. It felt great, and the ache in his arm and hand and ankle all seemed bearable now. He rummaged in the pile of clothes, found a woolen cardigan and put it straight on, next to his skin. He was so happy to be dry that he didn't mind the scratchiness. It felt comforting and real. He unbuckled his belt.

"'Don't advertise it—tell a gossip,'" Edie read from the far cornice. "Don't know what that means. Doesn't make sense. Tell you what, though, this heat is brilliant."

# CHAPTER TWENTY-EIGHT

## A Flick of the Wrist

On the Royal Artillery Memorial there are other statues. The Shell-carrier stands at the gun end, two big shell-holsters hanging on either side of his legs. At the breech end of the gun stands the Officer, legs apart, a coat folded over hands held together in front of him.

A motorbike's ripped exhaust growled around the unusually empty curve of Hyde Park Corner, making use of the temporary lull in the traffic to get some unaccustomed urban velocity. The rider was going too fast to have noticed the little movement, even if it had been one that he could have seen under normal circumstances.

The Officer flicked his wrist toward himself and flipped the cover off a lidded wristwatch. He looked down. Snapped the cover closed and resumed his normal position, staring toward the bottom of Buckingham Palace Gardens, where the queen presumably keeps her potting shed. And though he stood at ease, with his legs apart, his face was as blank and unreadable as if he were standing at attention on a drill square. It was a face made to endure.

The only sign of what he thought was a minuscule tic, as he sucked his teeth, making an irritable snapping noise.

# CHAPTER TWENTY-NINE

## The Maker's Mark

George rubbed at his legs with a towel, then pulled on a pair of plaster-spattered builder's trousers. They were about ten years too big for him, but he slid the belt through the loops and cinched them tight.

"I almost feel human." He grinned as he rolled up the bottoms above his ankle.

"I know what you mean, young fellow."

The booming voice entered the room ahead of the Friar, who ducked under the arch, carrying bags of crisps and rolls and a bottle of green liquid, all of which he placed on the table in front of them.

"Sit in the heat, and eat. Then when you've stopped shaking like a pair of Quakers we'll have our conversation. But first—drink this."

He uncorked the bottle and poured two measures of sticky-looking greeny-yellow liquid into glasses.

"What is it?" asked Edie, in a voice slow with suspicion.

"Made by monks." The Friar smiled. "Herbs and flowers, and a little kick in the tail. It'll warm you from the inside. Down the hatch!"

George picked up the glass and slugged it back. Fire, more than heat, slid down his throat, and he choked at the strength of it. It was sweet and pungent fire, though, tasting of honey and medicine and herbs he didn't know the names of; and when he'd finished spluttering he felt the fire settling inside him, as if something had been rekindled.

"It's not bad," he said to Edie, who was watching to see if he convulsed into a poisoned stupor. "Fine," she said, downing her glassful. She didn't choke or sputter, but her face grimaced so much that he could see her back teeth.

"*Gah!*" She shuddered. "That's foul. I suppose you think that's funny!"

"I thought it was okay," he said.

"Tastes like old ladies' foot baths. *After* they've used them. Ugh!"

She tore open a roll and ripped the top off a bag of prawn cocktail crisps. She emptied the crisps into the roll, closed it, and bit into it. The crunch of her teeth meeting the crisps preceded an ecstatic smile.

"Thath got rid of the tathte," she announced through a mouthful of bread and crisp shards. "Try thome."

It was George's turn to look disgusted.

"No, thanks."

She shrugged, finished the roll in two huge bites, and set about making another sandwich.

The Friar eased himself down onto a padded bench that ran along the end of the chamber. He beckoned the children with a smile.

"Now gather round and tell me what's what, my little friends. Tell me what you've been up to, to find yourselves in such a pickle."

"It's not a pickle," said Edie.

The monk chortled indulgently.

"And it's certainly not funny," she continued, before burying her teeth into her new creation with a defiant crunch.

"She's right," said George.

"Everything is funny from some angle, I assure you it is. It's just a matter of where you're standing."

George understood where Edie's frustration was coming from. He'd just been through a nightmare, and all this spit could do was laugh at them.

"From where we're standing, it's serious."

The Friar looked hard at him. Then he passed his hand over his face from forehead to chin, and as the hand passed, all the features had the smile wiped off them, and a dark and somber expression flooded in to fill the gap.

"Quite so. Quite so."

The monk leaned back and looked around the room. He looked at the four imp-cherubs that sat high in each corner, but George saw no answering movement in them. The monk stretched a kink out of his shoulders.

"And why should I help you?"

"Because you're one of the good guys," said George.

"Am I? I wasn't aware of that. Indeed, I wasn't aware of being a 'guy' at all. A 'guy' is something you burn on Bonfire Night, and I can assure you an incendiary finale is the very last thing I foresee for myself. My whole life's work has been committed to avoiding a fiery end, you might say."

The Black Friar clearly savored the taste of his own words rolling around his mouth, thought George with a strong twinge of irritation. It seemed like people—things, really—had been talking at him all day, and none of them had really given him a straight answer, just pushed him from one horrible experience to another. His voice was unexpectedly curt.

"You know what I mean."

Edie caught the tone and looked up at him in surprise. The Friar cocked his head to balance the irritatingly raised eyebrow.

"Not at all, goodness gracious. I only know what you say. Who told you I was 'a good guy'?"

"You're a monk," Edie cut in.

"And monks help, do they?"

"Yes. Monks are on the side of good."

"Well, let me tell you what I am." He spread his arms wide in the expansive gesture of a man with nothing to hide. The sleeves of his robe fell back, revealing strong muscular arms that didn't look as fat as George had expected.

"I am what I seem, no more no less. I am both a fat monk and a merry innkeeper, the halest of fellows well-met, and the watcher who stands at the road's fork. I am also a man who likes talking with men who like to talk. I provide mirth and happiness, warmth and cheer, and absolution for sins past, present, and even—for a fee—future. In short, I can soothe your needs and ease your passage through this vale of tears. I am a helpmeet to the needy and a bringer of quietus. If you see what I drive at . . ."

Edie squirmed irritably, pulling the sweatshirt over her knees.

"What I see, and what I hear, is that some spits have got a really annoying habit of using words we don't understand."

She looked at George. George nodded.

"What's a quietus?"

"A quietus, my dear boy, is a release, a discharge from the cares of life, a payment in full, as of a duty or a debt—"

"Look," interrupted Edie, "just listen. We nearly died getting here. This isn't time for an English lesson."

The Friar just beamed at her and waited. When nothing happened, he raised an eyebrow. And waited some more.

"She's telling the truth. She was sucked into the mud

in the Thames, and I was—grabbed by something in the underpass out there. . . ."

The other eyebrow lifted to join its twin. The grin stretched wider. George decided that there was something infuriating about people who talked too much when you didn't want them to, and then just dried up and smiled a lot, instead of saying anything when you *did* want them to—especially when the smile did the talking and seemed to say "You're exaggerating."

"It happened! In the underpass. The walls grabbed me."

The eyes opened wide and the grin pursed into a little "O" of pretend shock.

"The walls, you say?"

"Yep. The walls." George realized he was jutting his chin, just like Edie. The monk leaned forward and hoisted a single eyebrow again.

"Devil of a job for a wall to grab someone, wouldn't you agree?"

He laughed indulgently, jowls wobbling with mirth. Edie's voice cut in low and flat.

"It wasn't funny."

He chortled some more, then controlled himself with a great and visible effort.

"No. I imagine it wasn't. Walls grabbing him, you say. Why, I suppose they just grew hands and—what? Pinched and snatched at him?"

He started chuckling again, holding up an apologetic hand.

George wasn't enjoying the big monk's laughter at all.

"Pretty much. More snatching than pinching."

The Friar stopped laughing and looked at him.

"The walls grew hands?"

"And tentacles. And a mouth thing on a stalk. Like a big trumpet with teeth."

The room had gone very quiet, as if more things than the Friar were straining to hear what was being said. The Friar was no longer even smiling. The only sound was the gas heater hissing.

"And this happened? Really happened? To both of you?"

"Just to him," said Edie.

"But she saw it," George quickly added.

The Friar looked up at the other carvings and figures around the pub. None of them showed the slightest sign of animation, but George had the strongest feeling something was being said that he couldn't hear or understand.

The Black Friar rubbed his head and eyes with both hands as if trying to wake himself up. He shook himself and smiled at George.

"What were they made of, these 'hands,' the hands that clutched, might I ask?"

"Earth."

The smile mostly stayed fixed on the face of the Friar, but a little of it seemed to drain from around the eyes.

"Earth?"

"Mud. Clay. Gravel."

"And they caught you? They touched you?"

George nodded. He showed his ankle and his left arm. The redness was already turning into something harsher and bruisier. Even Edie was impressed.

"Wow. Something really did grab you hard there!" Edie exclaimed.

"I told you. You said you saw."

"I saw *something*. But it was like ghost trails. Like something on top of what I was seeing. Like . . ."

She ran out of ways to describe what she had almost seen, so she shut up. The Black Friar leaned in to George and parked his smile right in front of his face.

"If you were grabbed, and I certainly can see you have been roughly used by someone—"

"Some *thing*. Some *things*," George insisted.

"Quite, quite, my dear fellow, quite so. But, er, if this *earth* grabbed you, how, it occurs to me, how did you escape its clutches?"

"I just hit it."

Mirth crept into the Friar's eyes again.

"You *just* hit it and it *just* stopped? You'll forgive me, but it hardly seems likely, if the elements were raised to such a pitch that they found form and corporated so aggressively, that a mere—again, forgive me—boy could just slap them away. No, I fear this is a twice-told tale, a confection told you by another—"

"It's not a *confection*! It's not! They were pulling me apart, and I hit them like this and like this, and they fell apart—just went to, you know, mud and gravel on the floor and— What?"

The monk had been watching George miming his ordeal, and as George's hand had opened and mimicked the blows that had saved him, the monk's hand flashed out and grabbed it.

He pulled it gently but firmly toward him, his eyes fixed on the dragon's mark scratched redly into the skin.

"Where did you get that?"

"Get what?"

The monk twisted the hand gently, so that both children could see the scar.

"That. That maker's mark."

Even though he was sitting in front of a walking, talking statue, George felt the full absurdity of his answer as he said it.

"From a dragon. A dragon slashed me. At Temple Bar."

The friar sat back, still holding the hand, shaking his head.

"That's not a dragon mark, and if a dragon slashes you, young fellow, you get slashed and you stay slashed until you're burned and there's an end of you."

"It did!" George exploded in frustration.

"It did NOT!" replied the monk, raising his voice. "It is a maker's mark. And you, young scallion, are no manner of thing to be bearing it!"

George looked at his hand.

"I don't know what a maker's mark is!"

"I don't know what a scallion is," said Edie. And before the monk could answer, she went on. "But if it means liar, you're wrong. He did get slashed by a dragon, and something"—her eyes went shifty for a moment, then hardened as they met George's—"*something* bad happened in the underpass out there. So."

The monk looked from one to the other, then stood suddenly. Suddenly serious, suddenly slightly terrible in his mirthlessness.

"Stay here. Don't leave the building, don't leave the room, don't touch anything, don't talk to anything. I'll be back."

And in a sudden whirl of cape and cassock, he was up and out of the door; and the last they saw or heard of him was the snick of the key in the lock and his shadow striding away into the fluorescent-lit night beyond the frosted glass of the windows.

George looked at his hand.

"It's just a scar."

Edie shuffled over and looked at it.

"It is sort of a bit like a shape, isn't it?"

"Of course it's a shape!"

"No, I mean a *meant* shape. Like Chinese, or a symbol or something. . . ."

He closed his fist and shoved it in his pocket.

"Yeah, well—whatever it is, it hurts like hell!"

She looked at the pub door.

"You trust him?"

"Why not?"

"Dunno. I never trust people who smile too much."

George looked around the room. It seemed stuffed with faces and statues looking at them. In fact, the whole space was getting very warm because of the heater. It was claustrophobic under the vaulted roof. The brown and black marble seemed sweaty and unwholesome, like smoky mutton fat.

"So," she repeated, "do you trust him?"

He nodded around the room.

"I don't think now is the time. The walls have ears—"

"Yeah. And eyes and mouths and hands and hooves and talons and, hello—"

She stopped under an alabaster light fixture that came out of the wall. At first it looked like an upsweep of decorative swirls, from which hung a strange lamp made of metal in the shape of a buxom milkmaid. She was carrying the twin hanging lightbulbs on a yoke across her shoulders.

"What?" said George, trying to see what she was looking at.

Her fingers traced the raised letters on the bottom of the alabaster bracket. They read: NOON. Her hand stopped and she pointed.

"See?"

He looked closer. The carving wasn't just decoration. It was a faun: half-man, half-goat; but it was a winged faun, and it hung upside down, eyes closed, arms crossed across its chest, sleeping like a bat.

"It's a devil," said Edie.

"It's a faun. Half-goat, half-man. It's from mythology," George replied.

"It's not very monkish though, is it. Fauns, milk-maids, those cherub things up on the corners—what's that got to do with being a friar?"

"I don't know. But the Gunner wouldn't have sent us here if he was bad."

"If he was a taint."

"He's not a taint."

"Maybe there are bad spits too?"

They pondered this possibility.

"I wish the Gunner was here."

# CHAPTER THIRTY

## Dead in the Water

The Gunner was facedown in the mud and not moving. He'd walked down the Strand, every step hurting worse than the one before, and by the time he'd reached Trafalgar Square and turned left under the lofty pillars of Admiralty Arch, he knew he was in worse trouble than he'd imagined.

He carried the heat of the Temple Bar dragon's fire in him like a growing poison. It was a heat that sapped all his energy. Never before had he felt like he was made of bronze. He had been made to be a man in uniform, and if he had ever been asked, he would have said he felt like any other man. But no one asks statues these kind of questions, not even other statues.

Inside himself, where the poison of the fire was lodged, he felt looser, almost liquid. Where he had felt solid he now felt soft, and the outer skin, beyond the heat, felt like scrap metal that he had to drag along with him, metal that could burst or break at any moment. He hated the feeling. It was the memory and the pain of his birth, the time when something that was not him but just a possibility of him poured hot and molten from formlessness into his present shape; and in the birth memory was the realization that this is what his death would feel like, and in that thought was the corroding poison of the dragon's fire.

The pain he remembered was not the pain of the molten bronze pouring into the gunner-shaped cast at the foundry. It was the pain of cooling into that shape, of becoming solid. It was the pain of all the *other* things that the metal could have been made into dying as he became the Gunner and not them. And because the number of things the molten bronze could have been shaped into was infinite, so was the pain of their possibilities dying.

He stumbled up the Mall, and as he passed St. James's Park to his left, he caught the flat sheen of the lake through the trees. And he thought that if he could get to the lake and get into the water he might cool this burning, sapping pain enough to continue across into Green Park and from there to Hyde Park Corner, and get to his plinth before midnight. Although, by the time he thought it, the fire-poison was gnawing at him so badly that he really would have been happy to lie in the cool inky-black water until midnight came, and the consequences of not being on his plinth at turn o'day happened anyway.

The pain and the damage was so severe that oblivion and never moving or seeing again didn't seem so bad.

He hoped the kid would be okay. He was pretty sure the Friar wasn't as black as he was painted. Not like there was much choice. And the strange girl, the glint. All that hurt inside her. All that pain she would give to those close to her. Still, she was all he could trust.

The boy probably deserved better.

He splashed into the lake, sending a family of sleeping ducks skittering away across the ripples in protest. He fell to one knee, then sat back and laid his body in the cold mud just below the shallow water.

It didn't help.

He'd expected the water to fizz and steam off him as he lowered himself into it, he felt so hot inside. But the water didn't boil, and there was no hiss, no hot water vapor rising beneath the spreading plane trees.

It didn't help a bit.

And now he had used up all of his energy getting to the lake, and he had none left to get home in time. Maybe ever.

"Stupid," was the last word he said.

Then, with a last gargantuan effort, he rolled onto his great chest and tried to crawl out of the mud, knowing he wouldn't make it, knowing he'd try anyway. He almost made three feet, and then his arms and legs gave out and he slumped facedown into the mire at the water's edge. His head twisted sideways, and his helmet came off, and his cheek plowed into the mud and water.

And then he was still.

# CHAPTER THIRTY-ONE

## Little Tragedy

Edie sat in front of the heater, pulling on her tights. George looked over at her.

"Are they dry already?"

She tugged them on with satisfaction.

"Any drier and they'd be burning. You want to watch your jeans don't scorch."

He reached over and felt his trousers. They were pretty dry. He took them off to a dark corner of the pub and changed into them. Edie disappeared behind the bar, and from the crunching noise she was making, he knew she was taking more packets of crisps.

"What are you doing?" he asked.

"Nicking food. You want some?"

"No."

She carried on rustling. Then clinking. Then her head popped up over the bar and looked at him through the gloom.

"What?"

"I didn't say anything."

"Yeah, you did. I heard you, I . . ." She cocked her head, hearing something. It was George's turn to ask the questions.

"What?"

She shook her head and stuffed a juice bottle inside her coat.

"Nothing."

"Did you hear something?"

"I thought I did. It's this place. All the mirrors and the dark nooks. Feels like there's more people in here than you think."

"There *are* more people in here than you think," said a voice neither of them had heard before.

It was a puckish London voice, like that of a very old child with a swagger in it. They looked toward the pillared alcove and saw a mask hanging upside down in the archway, grimacing at them. Then a hand pulled the mask away, and they saw it was one of the imp-cherubs that had been sitting on the cornicing. His face was grinning and mischievous, and his hair hung down in an unruly mane beneath it.

"Really," said George, speaking slowly.

He had the impression that this small boy might disappear at any moment, a thought confirmed by the way the child kept one eye on the door at all times, as if waiting for it to open and the Friar to return.

"Ho, yes. And there are more 'heres' here too, if you know how to see them," said the boy.

Edie opened her mouth, but George waved at her to keep quiet—which she unexpectedly did.

"What's your name?" George asked.

"Me? I'm Tragedy. Or Little Tragedy. Or You Imp."

George pointed at the boy's grinning face.

"Shouldn't you be Comedy?"

"Garn, 'course not. That's why I got given the bleedin' mask, to hide my face. Comedy don't need a mask, trust me!"

"Why?" said Edie.

"Why what?"

"Why trust you? People wearing masks usually have something to hide."

Little Tragedy looked hurt and offended.

"Edie," said George in a low, warning tone.

"I ain't wearing it now, am I?" said the boy, waving the mask in the air beneath him.

"No," admitted Edie, after a sharp glance from George.

Little Tragedy's face split in a smile.

"There you go, then. Besides, everyone's got a mask of some kind, don't they? Everyone's not quite what they seem."

"Aren't they?" said Edie.

"No, they ain't. Blimey, sit under a pub roof without ever leaving for a hundred years, you see things. You hear things. And after a bit, you think things and all."

"What do you think?" George asked carefully. He sensed that the boy wanted to say something to them, but needed it to be teased out of him somehow.

"Well. It's all a lark, isn't it?"

"Is it?"

"So he says. Old Black. He says it's all a great lark, and that the trick of it is to have the last laugh, and the first laugh, and as many of the ones in between as we can." His face dropped the smile and became suddenly worried as he went on. "Only, my question is, who are you?"

"Who am I?"

"Who am *both* of you? Because, like I said, I seen things, but I never seen Old Black stop smiling—or looking like he's smiling—like he done when you told him what you been up to and how you got here. So what I'm thinking is, who are you?"

George shrugged. His fingers itched and felt for something that wasn't there. He picked his coat off the back of the chair where it was hanging and put it on. He found the piece of plasticene and squished it with his thumb.

"I'm just ordinary. I mean, today I can see spits like you. I mean, I hope you're a spit. . . ."

"Which I certainly ain't a taint, begging your pardon, I don't think so!" spluttered the boy in outrage.

"Sorry. No offense. And I see taints and I'm in this

nightmare. But most of the time I'm just ordinary."

"It's not seeing us as we are what makes you different. We seen people who can see us before—"

"What happens to them?" broke in Edie.

"Dunno. They don't usually hang around for long. I think they get got."

"'Got' by what?"

"Dunno. But something gets them, because they don't come back."

"Cheerful," said Edie grimly. "Thanks."

"I'm not saying they get snuffed out, mind. Not necessarily. There's other ways to go than popping your clogs, other *places*. I'm just saying they maybe go there."

"To other places?" asked George. Little Tragedy wasn't making much sense to him, but he still had the feeling that the mischievous-looking boy was bursting to tell them something. Or maybe, he thought, he wasn't bursting to tell them something at all, but just swollen with the big joke that he knew something he *wasn't* going to tell them. Despite his snub nose and twinkling eyes, there was perhaps something not entirely wholesome about him.

"What other places?" asked Edie.

He paused for effect, and his smile went from puckish to something closer to a leer. He said the words slowly and deliberately.

"Other 'heres.'"

"What other 'heres'?"

The boy grinned conspiratorially and reached out his arm toward her, little fingers beckoning.

"I'll tell you if you touch me," said the boy.

"What?" said George.

"She's a glint, isn't she? So if she touches me, she'll know."

"Know what?" asked George.

"Know if something bad happened to me. And if she can tell me that, then I'll tell her about the other places. I might even show her how to get to them, too."

Edie and George exchanged a look. She cleared her throat.

"Do you think something bad happened to you?"

Little Tragedy put the mask in front of his face. Then took it away. Then put it in front and then took it away again.

"See? Two of me."

"One's a mask."

"I know it's a mask," he said, as if explaining something very obvious to two people who were very slow on the uptake. "I'm just showing you what I feel like. Two people, two types of people, and I don't feel right. Like I'm made wrong. So if you glint me, you can see if I'm made proper. Or if something bad happened that I don't know about."

He smiled at Edie, and George could see it was a brave smile, as if he were trying not to cry. Edie walked toward him.

"I don't like glinting," she said. "It hurts me."

Little Tragedy reached out a thin arm and waggled his fingers again.

"Don't do it," said George sharply.

Edie stopped in the archway and looked back at him. "What?"

"All the other statues, the Sphinxes, the Gunner, all of them are frightened of you. Or at least they really don't like being around you when you glint."

"So?" she asked, the old challenging look rekindling in her eyes.

"So it's not right, him being so keen to be glinted. It might be a trap."

"A trap? You're joking," snorted the boy. "Bit late to worry about that, isn't it?"

George looked at Edie. Edie looked at the door. They both were remembering the *snick* the lock had made as the Black Friar had left.

"Are you saying we can't trust the Black Friar?"

"Trust Old Black? 'Course you can trust him! You can trust him for just about anything. Just as long as you trust him never to be what he seems. . . ."

Edie shivered suddenly as she remembered the drowning girl shouting "He's not what he seems!"

"George—"

*Click.* The door unlocked. Little Tragedy put his fingers to his lips and spoke very fast.

"I never said nothing and I wasn't here."

# CHAPTER THIRTY-TWO

## No Man's Land

The Gunner's face lay on its side, one eye in the water, one eye staring unblinking out at the night and the thin layer of ground mist rising off the grass in the park. There was no question of his ever moving again, but he was still—just—thinking. And because he was thinking at the very edge of his energy, the thoughts were not the thoughts of his time as a statue, of what, as a spit, he had endured and seen of life and London. They were the first thoughts, the spit-thoughts, the idea of him that the sculptor had put into him as he was made. And because the sculptor had not only been a maker of statues, but a soldier himself, the thoughts that the Gunner had came to him like memories of a life lived, a life in the war.

He no longer thought he was in St. James's Park. He couldn't hear the distant growl of traffic. He heard guns rumbling in a rolling barrage, far away. And closer, he heard the flat crack and slap of rifles firing overhead in random counterpoint to the mechanical stutter of machine guns. He heard men shouting orders, he heard other men screaming for their mothers. He heard feet rushing past, he heard the crack-thump of a grenade and fewer people screaming after that.

He focused on the gouged mud inches in front of his eye.

He knew where he was.

I'm in No Man's Land, he thought. And no bloody man's going to come out here to get me.

And no man did exactly that.

Shapes moved in the mist beyond the mud. A tall figure in a flapping mackintosh and a tin hat just like his walked toward him out of the haze. He saw the man's boots squish the mud in front of his nose. He felt a hand on his shoulder. He heard a snap of concern as someone sucked their teeth in frustration.

Then he felt himself hoisted in the air—high in the air, rising toward the sky—and he knew it was over, and the eye not clogged with mud stayed open, but stopped seeing anything.

# CHAPTER THIRTY-THREE

## The Way Marked

An instant after Little Tragedy disappeared, the Black Friar swept into the room, slamming the door behind him. He stared at George and Edie.

"You two look very . . . guilty."

George felt his face reddening. He'd always been like this. At school, whenever some crime had been announced at assembly, he always blushed, and was always sure that his face looked guilty even when he'd had nothing to do with it. He was sure the Friar could see they'd been talking about him.

Edie, on the other hand, looked as innocent as she could be, framed in the archway, standing between two mirrors on the inside face of each pillar. As the Black Friar looked back at George, she surreptitiously pulled the sea-glass from her pocket and snatched a look at him, then at the glass. She saw, with more relief than she'd expected, that it was *not* blazing a warning.

Then she saw it blazing somewhere else.

In the mirror.

In her hand it was dull, but in the reflection of the mirror it blazed blue. She caught another blaze out of the corner of her eye and saw that it was blazing green in the reflection of her hand in the mirror on the other pillar. Checking her hand again, there was no blaze. The glass was safe and dull. She sneaked another look at the two mirrors, and as she stepped back, she saw the mirrors reflecting each other again and again, so that you could see them disappearing away back into infinity, a tunnel of identical mirrors with a fragment of her hand carrying a blazing sea-glass in each one. Then she saw—thought she saw—something else, way down toward the end of one of those mirrored tunnels, something that broke the regular progression of this wilderness of mirrors.

It was something like a black bowl: more familiar than that, somehow, but it must be a bowl because there was a knife lying beside it. . . .

But before she could begin to realize what it was, what it might be, where she'd seen it before, the Friar's voice broke in.

"Do you have anything to confess?"

Edie shrugged and pocketed the sea-glass, which made a sort of rustling noise. George thought of the crisp packets jammed in her pockets. As if reading his thoughts, she pulled a packet from her pocket and emptied them into another roll on the table at her side.

"I took some crisps."

"You don't look guilty about crisps. Come now. I must hear your confession if you are to be shriven."

The smile had gone out of his voice. He loomed over them, waiting. Edie glanced at George. George looked into the dark face of the monk, trying to see if this was a new joke. The eyes were black and steady as a coal face.

"What's 'shriven'?" he asked, hoping the question would buy enough time for his racing heartbeat to slow down.

"Being shriven is obtaining forgiveness by confessing and doing penance."

George thought that coal faces probably didn't look this hard into people's eyes, as if trying to find all the secrets that might be hidden there. Edie's voice came through the wodge of her third crisp sandwich.

"We didn't come to you for shrivening."

Something like humor twinkled back into the upper reaches of the coal face.

"Shriving."

"Whatever. We didn't come for that. We came for help. For information."

"Yes," said the monk. "I've been out walking. You came via the river, which is in itself strange, and you disturbed something under the ground, beneath the road out there. I felt the walls in the underpass. You disturbed the clay in a way things have not been disturbed for a long long time, a much longer time than I have been standing on this building, for example. You, my boy, have roused the hunger of unmade things. Now sit."

He spun a stool and sat on it, legs spread apart, hands on his knees. He pointed to the bench in front of him. His movements had an authority neither of the children felt strong enough to resist. George sat down and rolled the plasticene in his pocket. Edie slumped at the other end of the bench and drew her legs up under her as she chomped away on the roll.

"By way of confession, perhaps you should tell me how you came here and what exactly it is your friend the Gunner thinks I can help you with."

George nipped ears out of the plasticene in his pocket, and started working on a nose.

"I don't know where to start, really. . . ."

"I think you will have to start at the beginning."

"I know. Start at the beginning. Go on to the end. Then stop," said George. That's what Killingbeck always said to them about how to write an essay. "The thing is, I don't know what the beginning is. . . ."

"And you're worried about the end."

"Terrified," admitted George.

"Terrified might be an understandable reaction. But terror's not much use, young fellow. Terror stops you thinking, and stopping thinking's a good way to let bad things catch up on you. No, I think you better get over being terrified. You can be terrified later, if this ends well. Then you can be as terrified as you'd like in the knowledge that you are safe and it's all over. If you get terrified now and stop thinking, then the things that want to terrify you will already have won. Does that make sense?"

"No," said Edie sullenly.

"Yes," said George.

"I'm glad you both agree," said the Friar.

"We don't," said Edie.

"Yes, you do. You're just someone who says what people don't want to hear. I know you know what I'm saying is true. If you didn't think fast, you wouldn't be here. And if you didn't have a strong mind, and I mean a really strong mind, you'd be mad by now, wouldn't you?"

"No," said Edie doggedly.

"Exactly," said the Friar, looking pleased as he turned his smile on George. "I'd start telling your story from when you first realized that things that you thought could never move, were moving. Or have you always been able to see the London of spits and taints?"

"Not until today," said George. "Worse luck."

"We'll get to the luck later," said the monk. "Start with today, then."

George squirmed on the bench to get comfortable. And as he squirmed, he felt the nub of dragon's head in his pocket dig into his side, the fragment he'd snapped off the facade of the Natural History Museum. He began talking.

He started with looking up at the belly of the whale and being accused of something he didn't do, and being made to wait in the hall under the dinosaur, and how he'd gone outside, and what he'd felt—and then the words just came faster and faster, like a torrent, and he couldn't stop them.

And he couldn't stop, or care, about the tears that rolled down his face as he talked, because they were just tears, and he wasn't crying or sniveling as he told the story of his day, of the Gunner's sacrifice and the Temple Bar dragon and Edie, and after a while the tears dried. He didn't even notice when Edie shoved across a wad of paper napkins and he used them to dry his eyes.

And as he spoke, Edie saw that his voice stopped being so scared and frightened and bewildered at the predicament he'd fallen into, and became a little deeper, a little darker, a little angry, even.

She realized it was as if his voice was mirroring the changes he himself had undergone on the journey here.

And because she wasn't talking, she was able to watch the Black Friar. He sat still as the statue that he was, face set in an encouraging smile. Because she was a good watcher, and because of what Little Tragedy had said about him not being what he seemed, but mostly because of the shouted warning from the drowning girl, she saw things about him that others might have missed.

She saw his eyes change as George went on with his story. Saw him flick a glance at her when George got to the bit about the Sphinxes. Saw his hands bunch a little tighter when George described the fight at Temple Bar. His eyes flashed from George to Edie again as he told about the near miss at his mother's flat. And then the Friar sat back and relaxed his body, but not his face, when George told about their passage from the river to the pub.

"And then we met you," ended George. "Can I get something to drink? I'm parched."

The Friar sat looking at him for a long beat. Then he stood suddenly, as if he had made his decision, and leaned back over the bar. His hands came back with two bottles of Coke.

"You know these are bad for you?" he asked.

And then he used his teeth like a bottle opener, twice: fast, in a gesture that Edie and George both thought was unusually un-monklike, and held out a bottle to each of them.

"Don't try that yourselves," he admonished.

He sat back down as they drank, and put the two bottle caps on the table in front of him. He doodled them around on the brown wooden surface, then left them next to each other.

"So," he began, "you're on your own."

"There are two of us," said George.

"Quite right," he replied, pushing the two bottle caps together so they touched. "The two of you on your own. And the Gunner sends you here. But he doesn't come himself."

"He was hurt. And he had to get the dragon before it got George," Edie explained.

"The dragon and George. George and the dragon," mused the monk. "Seems almost perfect, indeed it does."

He was getting jolly again. His eyes were retreating into the cracks of his smiling cheeks, which made them harder to see.

"Your hand again, George, if you'd be so kind."

George showed him the hand with the red mark zagging and curling in on itself in the middle of it.

"It hurts?"

"It aches now. It was worse before."

"Capital. Capital." The monk let the hand go. "And that was the hand you lashed out with, the hand that broke the carving on the museum?"

"Yes."

"And the broken carving, what of it?"

"It broke?"

"And then?"

"And then this pterodactyl came off the wall, and this all began."

"Quite so, quite so, as you say. But the carving?" His tongue popped out and licked his lips as he leaned forward. "Where is it?"

George looked up at the expectant, almost hungry face. He felt the carving jabbing into his side through the thin lining of his coat.

"Why?" he found himself asking.

"WHY?" said the monk, his bulk jerking forward and lowering over George like a storm cloud about to break. "WHY? Why ask why?"

Edie sat forward. And edged slowly toward George. "Because we don't know whether to trust you."

The words sat there, flat and unmoving as the bottle tops on the table between them.

"I see," said the storm cloud, settling back on his stool. He exhaled like a boiler adjusting its pressure. His eyes swiveled left and upward, although his great head didn't move an inch.

"I suspect the hand of a Little Tragedy has been meddling here. Or the tongue. Is that right, You Imp?"

There was a pause. Then a little voice came floating out of the alcove.

"Sorry, was you talking to me?"

"Yes, You Imp. Have you been talking to the children here?"

There was another pause and the sound of someone shifting uncomfortably on a cornice.

"Er. No?"

"No?" boomed the monk.

"Well, not 'no' as such. Perhaps . . . perhaps more as in a 'perhaps' sort of a way, if you see what I mean. They was asking me things, pestering me, by your leave—"

"We weren't," said Edie. "He's lying."

"Ooooh, I ain't!" squealed the voice. "Can't trust her, she's a glint, ain't she? By the hand that made me, I swear you should never trust a glint. Nasty probing things, upsetting the natural flow—you know they are, your worship—"

"He is lying," said George.

"Ooooh!" came another squeal "What tosh! He's a . . . well, I don't rightly know what he is, but he's not a canny thing, is he? Not run of the mill, so to speak. Why, I wouldn't—"

"SILENCE, YOU IMP!" shouted the monk, and they could hear the glasses jumping on the shelves behind the bar with the shock of it.

"He is lying," said George.

"Well, of course he is," said the monk in a voice that was strangely warm and calm all of a sudden. "You've heard of the father of lies? Well, as you'd expect, he has plenty of children, and that little imp there, that strutting Tragedy, is one of his by-blows. He can no more keep to the truth three sentences in a row than I could tip the great dome of St. Paul's and use it as my soup bowl."

A high-pitched "Oooh!" of affront crept out of the alcove and then was silent. The Friar shook his head and beckoned the two of them to come closer.

"You'll make your own choice who you trust, my friends. No coercion, no compunction in my house. It is, as I said, a place of hospitality. What did the Sphinxes tell you?"

Talking to the Sphinxes seemed such a long time ago

to George. It almost seemed like a lifetime ago, in a calmer, gentler age.

"They said if I wanted to know how to stop the taints killing me, and stop them hunting me, I have to find the Stone Heart, and sacrifice something."

"'The remedy lies in the Stone Heart, and the Heart Stone shall be your relief. To end what has begun, you must first find the Stone Heart, and then you must make sacrifice and amends for that which was broken by placing on the Stone at the Heart of London that which is necessary for its repair,'" recited Edie. The Friar looked at her, impressed. She looked unexpectedly self-conscious. "I'm good at remembering things. But they wouldn't tell us what the Stone Heart is."

"They might have, if you hadn't used our second question asking about glinting," muttered George.

"It was *my* question," she hit back.

"Yeah, but the Gunner could have told you, and then . . ." He ran out of steam.

The Friar looked at them both.

"Oh dear, dear. You really have no idea who to trust, do you? You'd rather fight than think after all—"

"No," said George. "I really just want to stop this and get home."

"Then stop squabbling and listen." He leaned in, and all the shadows in the room seemed to lean in with him. "You have less time than you know, and more danger ahead than you think. So listen. The way is hard, but it is marked. You have a day to repine and a day to repair. After that—" He picked up the bottle tops and scrunched them in his hand. He dropped the crushed remnants on to the table, where they rocked ominously as his voice broke like low thunder all around the room. "After that, the stones you have offended will rise up and grind you and crush you, and your life and very soul will be winnowed to the four winds on the great threshing floor, and a great fire will—"

He caught sight of their horror-struck faces and took a breath. When he spoke again it was almost apologetic.

"Well, it won't be good."

"What does that mean, 'a day to repine and a day to repair'? Is that like two days?" said George.

"No. It means you have one day to both be sorry for what you've done and to try and make amends. Those twenty-four hours will have begun when you broke the stone. I don't suppose you know what time that was?"

"About three forty," said George, remembering looking at his watch and thinking how long it was going to be before the school tour of the museum finished, just before he turned and lashed out a the little carving jagging into his back.

"Then you must reach the Stone Heart within a day of your offense, and it's already nearly the Low Twelve. Tomorrow is upon us."

"What's the Low Twelve?" asked George.

"Midnight. Turn o'day. The time of death and

ignorance, but also the time of rebirth, because what can be reborn that has not first died? You have until three forty tomorrow afternoon until—"

"Winnowing and crushing?" George interrupted gloomily.

"And so forth, yes."

"I don't even want to know what winnowing is, do I?" asked Edie.

"It won't help him, no," answered the monk. "But don't be downhearted. There is, as I said, a way—a marked way."

"And if I make my amends, it's all over? I'm safe?"

The big monk nodded his head, his eyes closed solemnly, his fingers lacing together over the crest of his stomach.

"Only by making your sacrifice can you be assured of the Easy Quietus. Any later and you are only guaranteed the Hard Way."

"What if he doesn't find the Stone Heart at all?" asked Edie.

"If he doesn't go to it at all, then the taints will undoubtedly catch him and make whatever the Hard Way is seem like a mercy by comparison. He must find the Stone Heart. And he cannot come to it empty-handed. He must bring what was broken."

"The dragon carving," said George.

"If you have it," said the monk. "If you don't have it, you better go back and find it. Do you have it?"

He leaned in. George, for a reason he couldn't explain but felt deep in his gut, shook his head.

"I did pick it up."

"Good."

"But I left it in my mum's flat."

"You idiot!"

The Black Friar leaned back.

"Well, easy then. Just tell him where the Stone Heart is, and we'll go get the thing he broke and bring it there, and Bob's your uncle!" Edie said.

"Bob is not my uncle and it's not that easy. There are, in a city like this, many things that may be the Stone Heart. For each, it is different. For each, the journey is a new path never walked twice."

"Well *what* is the Stone Heart?"

"From the way the Sphinxes phrase it, it could be anything, anyplace, anyone, even. Sphinxes spin riddles even when they give answers. And what could be better for them than an answer with two meanings? Except one with three. What is the Stone Heart? Who can say?"

Edie was losing patience. It felt like the walls were closing in.

"This is mumbo jumbo. How does he get to the Stone Heart?"

"Edie," George broke in.

The Black Friar closed his eyes and turned his head to the ceiling. He spoke as if reciting from memory.

"The Way is always marked, and these are the marks

of his way. He has to climb the Winding Stair. The Winding Stair will lead to the Memory of the Fire. Where the Memory of the Fire is caged he will catch a fire, and the caught fire will show him the path to the Stone Heart."

He opened his eyes and looked at them with satisfaction. They looked at each other.

"Is that another *riddle*?" spat Edie in disbelief.

"It's a map of words," said the monk.

"Why can't you just tell us?" asked George, feeling the fear and the frustration building in his chest again.

"Because I don't know the end, my dear chap. I only know the way. And the fact is, the way is hard. Though, if you had the fragment, I might be able to help more?"

It was the hungry look in his eye that stopped George thrusting his hand into his coat pocket and tossing the nub of dragon-shaped stone onto the table between them. It wasn't anything he could argue or explain. It was just something he felt.

"We're going to have to get wet again," he said to Edie.

"What?" she said in shock.

"We have to go back."

# CHAPTER THIRTY-FOUR

## The Man of Many Parts

The Friar stood at the door of the pub as Edie and George emerged under his arms into the night air.

"If you return with the broken fragment, I may be able to speed your quietus," he boomed. "Yes, children, bring it to me, and I will see what I can do."

"Thank you," said George. "We'll be back."

"And mind you, stay aboveground until you do. Because until you do, you are still prey to their hunger."

"What hunger?" said George.

"Whose hunger?" asked Edie.

"The hunger of unmade things," said the monk, as if that explained everything.

Despite wanting to leave, George turned back.

"That's what you said about what happened to me in the underpass. What does it mean?"

"Look at the mark on your hand, boy. If it is right and you are a maker, or if you are to be a maker, then you have broken an ancient bond by using making hands to mar." He looked at George's uncomprehending face and started again. "You have used gifted hands, hands made to make things, to break things in anger. All things that have been made—statues, spits, and taints—feel your power and the affront it has caused. Even things not yet made will reach out to you and crave the form you might give them."

"The ground was reaching out to me?"

"The clay sensed your mark and the gift you carry. Everything seeks form in a universe designed to break things down."

"How do you know I'm a maker?"

"How do you know you are not? You say your hand broke the dragon carving at the museum, and you say the same hands cut through the clay that was attacking you in the underpass. Maybe you're the maker the mark says you are. Or maybe you're something else. But your hands do seem to have power, wouldn't you say?"

Before George could register how little of that he really understood, the Friar stood back and waved.

"Safe home, my little friends. And safer back."

"Thank you," said George, nudging Edie.

"Yeah, thanks for the crisps and the heater and all," she said. And then, only slightly resisting George's hand clamped on her arm, she let him lead her across the road, under the shadow of an imposing white Art Deco building from whose heights clean-cut statues of women and animals seemed to watch.

As George looked back and waved, he saw the Friar raise a hand and then disappear back into the pub.

"Now run!" he hissed at Edie as they turned onto the Embankment.

"You're going to run straight into another dragon if we—" she began.

"No, I'm not," he said, jerking her hard to the right, up a narrow street like a canyon, with tall anonymous building facades running up both sides.

"What—?" she started.

"Later," he gritted, and ran faster.

"Good," she muttered under her breath. "So we're *not* going to get wet again."

The two of them flew up the street and turned. She could run as fast as him, he noted. They kept running. They passed a dark side street, and at the end of it he caught a sudden glimpse of a tiered steeple rocketing skyward like an illuminated wedding cake. It flashed past and he ran on, crossing another couple of streets and passing under an archway. As soon as they'd entered the space beyond the arch, he slowed.

"So what was that about?" panted Edie.

"We're not going back to my mum's," he replied, taking stock of where they were, still walking forward, eager to put distance between them and the Black Friar.

"But you need to get the carv—Oh!"

He had pulled the small dragon's head from his pocket

and showed it to her as he walked.

"I see. You lied to the monk."

She almost sounded impressed. He nodded.

"Did you trust him?" he asked.

She shook her head. "No. But that doesn't mean anything. I don't trust anyone."

"Well, he looked just a little bit too eager when he asked if I had it with me. I mean, if it's the key to my getting out of this nightmare, I'm not giving it to anyone. I'll take it to the Stone Heart myself."

He looked around as they walked.

They were in one of those quiet and occasionally magical oases that hide behind London's busier thoroughfares. It was, for a start, gaslit. The light was both softer and spookier than the fluorescent lights he was used to. If it hadn't been for the electric bloom of untended computer screens in the elegant windows of the sombre brick buildings around them, it would have been possible to imagine they'd passed under the arch into an era earlier than theirs by a hundred years.

He walked on through a gate and found himself looking across a big courtyard, toward a red pillar box. He stopped when movement caught his eye.

"What?" hissed Edie, bumping into his back as he pulled up short.

An imposing figure in a flapping robe was walking briskly across the space between them and the pillar box. He had a pile of papers under his arm, and a long gray wig that fell in rolls of hair down arou his neck, onto his shoulders. His face was angry and termined, and only looked angrier when a sheaf of pap s slipped from his grip and spilled across the gro d. He looked around, as if searching for some lackey pick them up for him, then doubled his scowl as he ent to retrieve them himself.

"It's a judge," whispered Edie.

George decided to turn around b re they were noticed. There was something very f idding in the scowl under that wig.

"What?" he said, as they doubled bac past a looming building on their left.

"He's a judge. I've been here during e day. This is where the judges and the lawyers are. C e here in day-light, you see them all strutting abou ke they know everything about everything. You see t m all twanged up in little wigs and cloaks and stuff."

"Twanged up" was a phrase her dad ad used. She'd never used it before. She didn't know w it had slipped out. It was the way he described wom who were all dressed up to go out. No matter how she ed to not think about it, bits of him kept surfacing en she wasn't expecting it. It was like walking along a l ch at low tide. Every day was a new one, and you n er knew what would be uncovered.

George turned right under anoth archway and decided not to worry about why a ju was walking about in the middle of the night, "twanged up" or not. He paused and got his breath next to a sundial. There was an inscription reading: SHADOWS WE ARE AND LIKE SHADOWS DEPART. He shivered and moved on through some arched cloisters and out into the space surrounding a louring church and its attendant company of plane trees.

He stopped and leaned against the railing surrounding the end of the church, which was rounded and defensive, more like a turreted bastion than a place of God.

Edie slumped onto a step and watched the shadows. She noticed George didn't look too relaxed, either.

"You think this is a good place?"

"I don't know. It's a church."

"Says it's a temple," she said, looking at the sign.

"Temple Church," he said, reading it. "Same thing."

"It looks more like a castle," she said, looking up through the plane trees at the curved wall, topped by defensive crenellations. "It doesn't feel like a good place, George."

"I know." He shivered. "I don't think you have to be a glint to get that. It feels haunted."

She wondered whether to tell him about ghosts. About how they existed, but nothing to worry about. About how it had taken her a long time to realize that they just hung about like echoes that had forgotten to diminish. They didn't, wouldn't, and couldn't do anything to the living. They weren't people. They didn't appear to have minds at all. They were just repeating loops of something that once was and now wasn't. They were insubstantial, like the memory of a faint hint of a smell. They were absolutely nothing compared to the reality of the past that slammed into her when she was glinting.

She'd almost trained herself not to notice them.

She wouldn't even bother telling him that the judge they'd seen dropping papers as he walked between the gas lamps was one. There wasn't any point, anymore than drawing George's attention to the discarded burger wrapper at their feet, or the irrelevant pigeon coming to roost in the trees above their head. For her they were just part of the streetscape, something you walked on by.

"Let's not hang around, then," she said, getting up. "Where are we going?"

"Somewhere we can be safe for the night. Somewhere we can work out what the Black Friar meant by the Winding Stair."

She sat back down again.

"You mean we don't know where we're going?"

"I mean we're stuck inside the City because of the dragons. But maybe tomorrow morning we can go to a library and look up this Winding Stair. Or buy a tourist guidebook or something."

"I haven't got any money. To buy a guide. I spent it all on the taxi getting to your house to warn you." She pulled a small handful of change out of her pocket. "About a quid left."

He jingled the change in his pocket, pulling coins out of the plasticene lump where it had got stuck.

"Eighty-five pence." He held it out to her. "Here. It's all I've got. But when this is over—"

He stopped. His wallet, stupidly, was in his backpack with his phone, locked away in the Natural History Museum. The world of school trips and cloakrooms and cash machines seemed a long way off. He felt a strong tug of yearning for that simpler world that seemed only a thin overlay away from where he was now. It was the same tug that he'd felt looking up at the airplane when he was stuck inside the cone of fire with the dragon. He would give anything, he realized, absolutely anything to be back in that humdrum everyday world. But all he had to give, right now, was the change in his hand. He pushed it closer to her.

"When this is over I can get you lots. Whatever I owe you. More."

"I didn't say that because I want your money!" she said, looking at the scrabble of coins reflecting the street-lights. She realized that she wasn't feeling angry because of the money. She was feeling angry because George had a way out. His saying "when this is over" made it clear that for him "this" was a temporary state that he might be able to get out of. And the truth for Edie was, she realized, that "this" was something she was stuck in. And she'd still be stuck here when he was out of it.

And realizing this, she asked herself why she was

sticking with him. She'd been frightened and alone before she saw him running across Hyde Park with the Gunner. But she had survived. She'd survive after he was gone, she thought. But she'd be alone again. Maybe that was what was making her angry.

She remembered the swoop of hope that had propelled her off the bus and made her run after them, in the hope that George would be like her, would be able to make sense of things. But she now realized that he was different, that his "this" was something he could—if he was lucky—escape. It was a layer of the world he'd fallen into, and if he could find the Winding Stair, he could maybe climb back out of it. Her "this" was set and sealed because it was hardwired into her being, bone deep and inescapable. Her "this" was who she was and how she saw the world, not something she'd fallen into. It was like living in the falling-apart seaside town she'd once had a home in: she used to watch smiling happy people come for the day, unpack their shiny cars, and play and sit on the beach, facing the sea with their backs to the grim warren of crumbling houses and failing shops behind them on the Front. They always took their laughter and brightness with them when they left as the sun went down. They were like George.

He was a tourist.

She was here for the duration.

So she stood and stuck out her hand and took the money and zipped her pocket tight so she wouldn't lose it.

"This isn't enough for a book. We'll have to nick it."

He pushed off the railings and jogged on.

"Come on, then. This place gives me the willies."

They retraced their steps through the cloisters, and went left through the courtyard and out the gate, and headed north, away from the river.

The Temple Church sat quiet and unwatched now that they had gone, keeping its secrets to itself. The only thing stirring was the irrelevant pigeon in the trees above where George and Edie had been.

The irrelevant pigeon—which wasn't, of course, either irrelevant or a pigeon—opened its eye and stretched its wings, then flapped off above the rooftops, like George and Edie heading north. It knew, in its dark raven heart, that of all the directions it could fly in, north was the one that gave it the greatest pleasure. It had no idea why. But flying slowly north always seemed the most suggestibly ominous way a raven could fly. It was a little detail, but when you were as old as it was, collecting points for style was one of the things that stopped you getting bored with the way history kept repeating itself.

Below the Raven's balefully slow wing-beats, George and Edie found themselves suddenly out of the quiet streets and on Fleet Street. Night buses cannoned past, racing minicabs and late-night drivers to the lights.

George looked at the lights and the colors and the shop fronts, and felt a little dizzy. He started to walk left, but Edie's hand stopped him.

"You in a hurry to go another round with that dragon, then?"

He only half heard her, but it still irritated him.

"I'm in a hurry for everything, or didn't you hear the Friar? I've got less than fifteen hours to sort this out before I get 'winnowed.'"

"You want winnowing, keep right on, then. Temple Bar's down that way."

He stopped. He saw the Law Courts and thought he could make out the spiky outline of the dragon silhouetted against the church wall beyond it. He crossed the road and hurried along a street continuing north instead.

"Fetter Lane," read Edie.

"Fetters are chains. Like handcuffs. On your legs," said George.

"I know," she said. "They don't go in for cheerful, do they, these city people naming their streets? I even saw a Bleeding Heart Yard once. Had a horrible atmosphere. I didn't touch anything and got out as fast as I could."

Above them, waiting for them to catch up, on a length of dripping guttering, the Raven thought of bleeding hearts and realized it was hungry. It watched them pass beneath and then flapped off over the roof of the building, heading northwest. It was thinking of the Walker, but it happened to look down just as it crossed the City boundary, and had a better idea.

It turned on a wing tip and dropped like a rock, heading toward a nondescript modern building faced in cheap-looking shiny pink stone on the north side of the street. You could tell the architect had liked drawing angles, because the building had nothing to say to the buildings on either side of it, and it said its nothing in a collection of meaningless lines and points that didn't even look decorative.

But in the front, at ground level, there was a nook: half sentry box, half downlit shower stall. And the nook was occupied. And it was into this nook that the Raven sideslipped, coming to a halt on the tarnished metal shoulder of a statue that was almost human, in parts. Or rather, the shoulder of a statue that was in parts. And almost all of those parts were human.

The Raven clacked its beak next to an ear in an almost-human part of the head.

Back in the canyon of Fetter Lane, George was trying to explain his plan.

"I'm looking for a park or something," George said after a while. "Somewhere we can sleep and no one will bother us."

Edie fired off one of her snorts.

"Parks are freezing. This isn't like *Babes in the Wood*, where we snuggle down under the trees, and kind birds drop leaves on us to keep us warm and toasty under a compost duvet. Parks are rubbish for sleeping in."

"What do you suggest, then?"

"A vent. Somewhere a building's letting off heat. And you sit on it on a nice opened-out cardboard box and you get old papers and stuff them up your clothes, and another box or two for cover."

They came to the junction with another big street.

"High Holborn," she said, looking up at the sign on the side of a building. "No parks around here."

"Fine," said George. He was feeling really tired suddenly. Tired of this. Tired of the nightmare. Tired of being scared. Tired of being confused. Tired of Edie snorting at him.

"You find us a nice warm vent, then," he continued. He just wanted to sleep.

"Fine," she said, and set off heading right.

"Why this way?"

"Because we'd better head away from the edge of the City, hadn't we? To stop us walking toward trouble."

They walked on. No more was said, because both of them were so tired that everything was getting to feel disconnected and distant—even the fear and thoughts of the taints. Only irritation with each other seemed immediate enough to keep them going. So they each, in different ways, nurtured that irritation so as to stop just giving up and stopping.

They walked under the overhanging eaves of an

ancient half-timbered building. It was different enough for George to stop and step back to look up at it, rising above him in a four-floored cliff of black timber and white plaster and leaded casements. It had a steep pitched roof and brick chimneys. It looked like something off a Christmas card.

And there was an arch leading to a small courtyard in the middle of it.

"We could go in there. Look!" He pointed back to the middle of the road. A tin-hatted fusilier stood on top of a war memorial, one foot resting on a rock, pack on his back, horizontal rifle held loosely in one hand as he looked alertly west, away from them.

"We've even got a guard at the door."

"He's not the Gunner," said Edie suddenly, exhaustedly, wishing he were.

"Yeah, but he's a spit. Come on. Let's see. It'll be safe."

And it would have been safe. Except, while they were busy heading away from the city boundary so as not to walk toward trouble, trouble—thanks to the Raven—had been walking toward them.

If George hadn't stepped back into the street to look up at the half-timbered building, they might have been safe, because the Raven had had to lose sight of them to go and alert the Grid Man. But George stepping back on the pavement was the thing that the bird's eye picked up, and then things started to happen.

The Raven swooped and clacked in the ear of the

Grid Man, and the Grid Man crossed the road, clanking and scraping as he came, so that the sound of metal protesting against stone was the second sound that alerted Edie and George to the fact that something bad was happening.

The first sound was the one that got them, though. It was the *clack shuffle clack* that he made. And as he got closer, first Edie, then George, turned their heads and saw him.

The Grid Man was roughly in the shape of a squat, muscled man with a heavy-browed head and backswept hair. He did not walk like a man, however. He walked like a toy robot that never takes either foot off the ground as it slides them forward one at time. That was the scraping shuffle noise. At that point they stopped seeing what was human about him, and started seeing the inhuman bits. George saw that he was made up of parts of a human figure, as if someone had cut his body into pieces and then stuck them back together, only leaving gaps between all the chunks, so that the statue looked like it was wearing its own skin as a disconnected suit of armor. The face was cut down the middle, the wide channel of the cut running down through the nose and mouth, and two horizontal cuts—one through the upper lip, one just above the eyebrows—divided it into six chunks. Each section moved slightly out of time with the other parts, which made its scowl seem to happen in stages. The pieces of body, some of which were more machine-part than human, moved with a similar out-of-sync quality. Rods of metal jutted out of the body chunks, as if holding the whole thing together, like meat skewers through a kebab.

The clacking noise came from two thick metal grids held in his hands, about the size and shape of tennis rackets. It was made by a metal ball that he hit from one grid to the other as he walked.

Edie, standing close to the building, looked at George. He didn't look at her. He spoke quietly, trying not to alert Grid Man to her presence in the shadows.

"Get out of here. They just want me."

The *clack shuffle clack* speeded up.

"Okay," whispered Edie. "Just run."

And she melted back into the archway, mingling with the shadows, not daring to run in case the noise of her feet drew attention to herself.

George paused to flick a glance at the Fusilier high on his plinth.

"I don't suppose . . . ?"

The Fusilier didn't look around. George decided he didn't have time to try and persuade a statue to move if it showed no sign of being able to, so he spun on his heel and exploded into a sprint, heading east. He realized he'd done so much running on these unforgiving pavements that his feet were bruised and painful. About ten steps in, he just forgot the pain and ran.

The Grid Man sped up, but he wasn't exactly built for

speed. The *clack shuffle clack* increased in tempo, then stopped abruptly. George noted it and kept running.

Behind him, the Grid Man tossed the metal ball in the air and swung the right-hand grid like a tennis player powering in a forehand smash. As he connected with the ball, there was a shower of sparks as metal hit metal, and the resounding *clang* was so loud that this time George did turn, which was fortunate, because it probably saved his leg.

He saw the ball hurtling toward him at ankle level, and he lifted his foot on reflex. He didn't get it quite high enough as the ball grazed the sole of his shoe, and at that velocity, the force of the graze was enough to rip a chunk of rubber off the shoe and take his legs out from under him. He managed to break his fall with one hand, but he still hit the gritty paving stone with enough force to knock the wind out of himself for a moment, and his right cheek slapped the ground in a hard snap of pain so jarring that he felt his teeth rattle.

The impact and the jag of pain blew the fear out of him along with the air, and in its place came that black treacly feeling, so strong he could taste it.

Behind him, the ball continued on its trajectory and then began looping up in a slow parabola.

He struggled to his feet and looked down the street at the Grid Man. He was now accustomed to the fact that the meager late-night traffic didn't notice what was going on in his London.

He wiped his mouth and stared at the statue across sixty yards of litter-blown pavement. Grid Man just looked at him, his eyes blinking out of time with each other. It felt, for an instant, like a showdown in one of the slow old Westerns his dad had tried to make him love as much as he did. George spat, expecting blood. There was none. Just that dark taste.

"Better luck next time," he muttered, trying to decide which way to run. He was relieved to see the Grid Man had no other ball to cannon at him. Something made him stand there, waiting to see what the taint would do next.

He didn't see that the ball had tightened the arc of its flight, and had now curved back in on itself, like a boomerang retracing its steps.

Grid Man raised one arm and smiled, an out-of-phase smile that spread across his segmented face in disconnected jerks. It looked like he was waving, or saluting. To George's eye the gesture had a mocking quality to it. He raised his arm in imitation, and waggled his fingers in farewell.

"Yeah, right. See you . . ."

Because he didn't have eyes in the back of his head, he didn't know that the Grid Man had just put his grid in the air like a baseball player's glove, in case the metal ball now hurtling home toward the back of George's head missed its target.

Because he didn't have eyes in the back of his head,

he had no way of knowing that the last thing about to go through his mind would be two spinning kilos of metal ball.

Because he didn't have eyes in the back of his head, and because she *could* see what was incoming behind him, Edie stepped out of the relative safety of her shadowed archway and screamed like a banshee.

"George! Behind you! Get down!"

He ducked without using his brain, the adrenaline doing the thinking for him. He felt the punch of air as the ball careened past his left ear, and saw the Grid Man twitch in disappointment as the ball clanged home into the grid he was holding in the air like a catcher's mitt.

George scrambled around and ran, jinking left and right, trying to be a moving target, looking for an alley to dive down, his shoulder blades itching in anticipation of another volley. None came, and he sidestepped into a slit that suddenly revealed itself between two buildings, bouncing off brickwork as he failed to complete the turn cleanly. He grinned in relief.

Just before he heard it.

"NO!"

Edie's voice.

"Geeoorge!"

He'd heard her shout before, but he'd never heard fear like this, fear mixed with pain. It froze him.

Grid Man had Edie. As soon as she had broken cover to shout a warning, one segment of his head had swiveled sideways at right angles, pointing his right eye at her, while the left side of his face stayed looking down the street toward George.

Grid Man saw her, and then moved toward her. She ran into the shadows under the arch and found she was in a cul-de-sac. By the time she turned around, he was blocking the way out. He shuffled forward, gently clacking the grids on the end of either hand together in a taunting mockery of a man clapping.

She really did have nowhere to run, and when she tried to duck under his arm and break past him, one of the metal rods that seemed to skewer him together shot out and caught her under the chin, like clothesline tackle. Her feet flew up and she crashed backward, and things went white then black as her head hit the ground. She can only have been knocked senseless for an instant, but when she opened her eyes again she was upright and moving. And then she tried to move her feet and realized they were kicking in the air, and the reason her head hurt was that he was carrying her by her head, holding it between the grids—not hard enough to crush her skull, but hard enough to hold her in the air. Her hands grabbed the grids in self-preservation, her small fingers lacing through the metal tracery as she took as much of the weight as she could off her head and neck. He carried her like a rag doll, and her body swung from side to side as he walked. She kicked at him with her heels as he emerged back into the street, and that's when he squeezed, and her head really did feel like it was being squished in a vise, and that's why she screamed, although she didn't know she was doing it.

George was still frozen in the narrow alley. His heart jackhammered away as if it were trying to punch its way out of his chest and keep on running away all by itself. He looked down the alley.

It was a dead end.

He caught himself looking around to see if he could reach a drainpipe and climb his way to safety and keep running away. He instantly hated himself for the thought.

Edie screamed again. Closer.

He hated himself even more for thinking of leaving her. So he stepped back into the street.

Grid Man was walking toward him, Edie hung from his grids, swinging like the clapper in a bell as he lurched from side to side.

George had no idea what to do.

"Put her down!" he shouted.

Grid Man lurched on. Now Edie could see George; she clenched her jaw tight shut. She wasn't going to scream in front of him. Only the treacherous tears squeezing out of her eyes betrayed her.

"Look," said George, "put her down. You don't want her!"

Grid Man's eyebrows rose and fell, one after the other. His smile was split into two halves and neither one of them was nice. He shook his head from side to side, with the jerkiness of bad robotic dancing. He opened his mouth to say something, and the sound of his voice came in an unintelligible mashed overdub, coming out of the divided mouth in different pieces. The deep disjointed voice didn't sound like any language George had ever heard. It ground out of the lip sections like an angry Italian trying to outshout a drunk Scotsman through a mouthful of ball bearings.

"*Nonvoglio*lassiewanyou*stronzo*weebasturt."

"You're hurting her. PLEASE!" shouted George.

The head nodded, grin widening, eyes rolling in pleasure. And George couldn't take it, and he couldn't run, because Edie wasn't screaming for him anymore, wasn't screaming at all, but was putting all her efforts into hanging on to the grids and not letting the Grid Man snap her neck by mistake. And maybe he could have run if her eyes hadn't been locked onto his like tractor beams.

So he lurched forward and kicked at the Grid Man, and as soon as he got within reach, the taint batted at him and sent him sprawling across the pavement with a casual backhand.

Edie tried to disentangle herself and escape, but the Grid Man clamped down on her. George rolled back onto his feet.

"Leave—her—alone! Please!"

Grid Man sneered and raised Edie high above his

head, and both Edie and George knew he was going to snap her neck or dash her against the pavement, and both knew there was nothing George could do.

"Run, George! Just run!" she shouted, the words coming raw and ragged from her throat.

"No!" shouted George.

And two things happened at once. A black bird hopped out of the shadows and looked at George and then at the Grid Man. Then it hopped onto the Grid Man's shoulder and clacked its beak, and the Grid Man smiled brutally and flexed.

And George heard a sound he'd heard once before. It was the crash of hobnailed boots. It was the sound of hobnailed army boots hitting the ground.

Just for a moment, both children's hearts leaped as they thought it was the Gunner come back from the dead. But a thinner, vinegary Cockney voice that they had never heard before cut in like a straight razor.

"Put her down, you nasty jerry-built pile of foundry slag."

The wiry Fusilier stood behind the Grid Man, rifle held ready to thrust the long-sword bayonet into its back. The Fusilier was a lighter-framed man than the Gunner had been, but he had the same dogged set to his jaw.

"*Chey*irprobbie*ignoto*pileatolieyirsel!" spat the mouth parts of the Grid Man. He didn't move an inch, although the bird did flap off to one side and watched from a more prudent vantage point.

"Or I'll gut you like a kipper."

The bird clacked its beak. Grid Man started to move, but the Fusilier moved faster and more decisively. With an explosive "HA!" he lunged forward and stabbed the sword bayonet into the gap running down the Grid Man's spine, between the segments of back. Sparks dropped from the bayonet's edge as he rammed it home to the hilt, like sparks from a grinding wheel.

Grid Man convulsed. He dropped Edie. As soon as she hit the pavement and rolled, George darted across the space and pulled her in to the wall. He felt her arm trembling with shock under his hand.

They both stared at the two statues, locked together by the bayonet plunged through the Grid Man's back. The Fusilier held the bayonet steady, but you could see from the strain on his face and the shaking of his arms—not to mention the tendons standing out on his neck—that he was fighting the efforts of the Grid Man to turn on the blade.

"Stop. Get back on your plinth. Or I'll do you. It's close to turn o'day, and taint you may be, but you ain't that stupid. . . ." hissed the Fusilier.

The Grid Man snarled, and then did something horrible to himself. With a series of grinding and shearing noises, he started to turn himself around on the bayonet, bit by bit, like a human Rubik's Cube. First, one section of head rotated and fixed an eye on the Fusilier, then a shoulder section turned itself around. Then the top of the head swiveled, then a lower leg, and so on. With a nasty final jerk, the two chest sections rotated in opposite directions on either side of the impaling bayonet, and the Grid Man was facing the Fusilier.

"Crikey!" he said, studiously unimpressed. "You are an ugly bastard."

Grid Man raised the thick ellipsoid grids in either hand and they started to spin, faster and faster, like a pair of angle grinders. He thrust them toward the Fusilier.

The bird clacked its beak encouragingly.

"Sorry, chummo. Your choice," said the Fusilier, leaning back.

*Blam! Blam! Blam!* He fired into the body of the Grid Man. The recoil jerked the bayonet loose and he stepped back.

The Grid Man didn't blow to dust as the pterodactyl had. He fell back and started to fall apart. His head snarled at the Fusilier.

*Blam!*

The head stopped moving and all the sections dropped into piles of coiling brass swarf, like the metal off-cuts from a lathe, squirming and writhing in on themselves in knots of shiny worms. They knotted and reknotted themselves tighter and tighter until there was nothing left on the pavement except the smell of burned metal and the suggestion of a man-shaped scorch mark on the stone.

The Fusilier rested his gun butt on the pavement and looked at it, breathing hard. So did George and Edie. The bird looked at it. Having had more experience in these matters than any of them, it thought faster and decided it was time to leave.

It opened its wings quietly and took a step forward into the air.

The Fusilier's eyes caught the movement. His hand moved in a fast blur.

There was a *click* as he unsnapped the bayonet and a *whirr* followed by a simultaneous *thock* and *squawk!* as he threw the sword-size knife hard and fast across the pavement.

The Raven found itself pinned to the side of the building, with a blade through the wing. It didn't feel any pain, just irritation.

"No, you don't," said the Fusilier, as he rapidly fed bullets into the magazine of his rifle through the open breech, and slammed the bolt home on a live round.

"*Squawk?*" clacked the Raven, trying to look friendly and unthreatening and cuddly, which is a problem if nature has fitted you out in greasy feathers, and decided you should wear basic bad-guy black.

"Not a chance," said the Fusilier, and *blam*. He blew the Raven into a cloud of feathers that would have been the makings of a very stylish feather duster, if your tastes leaned to the stricter end of the goth spectrum.

The Fusilier retrieved his bayonet and slung his rifle

over the shoulder. He looked all around, checking that the coast was clear before he looked at George and Edie.

"Thank you," said George.

"Thank the Gunner and old Dictionary," said the Fusilier. When he spoke more quietly, his voice was less vinegary and more of an astringent wheeze.

"The Gunner's okay? You've seen him?" said George, his spirits lifting even further. The Fusilier shook his head with a finality that sent George's spirits straight back into a tailspin.

"No. From what he wrote, I don't reckon there's much chance of any of us seeing the Gunner ever again. Not as a walking spit. Think he's done for. He sent a note. By pigeon. To all of us. Saying he was scuppered. Asking us to keep an eye out for you two, as it were."

"Oh," said George, a lump rising in his throat.

"Yeah," wheezed the Fusilier. There was a pause. "He was something, wasn't he?"

Before George could speak, or maybe because he couldn't quite trust himself to yet, the Fusilier switched attention to Edie.

"She okay?" he asked.

George saw that Edie was still shaking. Her face, always pale, now seemed almost translucent. Her eyes were open wide, but her dark pupils had shrunk to the size of periods.

"Edie?"

She heard his voice from a long way off. It seemed to

take a lot of effort to turn her head, and almost impossible to focus on him.

"You okay?"

She felt her ears. She was almost surprised to find them both present and attached. Her neck felt badly wrenched, and she rubbed it.

"Bet your head hurts from being squeezed in that waffle maker," he said.

"I'm all right."

She wasn't. She knew it. He could see it. But he could also see arguing with her would just make her dig her heels in and make it worse. He didn't have the energy for an argument, and she looked like what energy she did have was all being used to keep upright. He decided to keep an eye on her. She looked like she might faint at any moment.

The Fusilier just nodded.

"That's a good girl. Right. You need to get off the street, sharpish. Got anywhere to go?"

They shook their heads. He checked his watch. Scowled.

"Okay. Follow me, at the double. I know a place where you can get a bit of sanctuary. Dunno what you done, either, but upsetting that bird's not a clever idea. We better get away from here."

George look at the feathers twisting up into the night sky.

"But you blew it to hell!" he said.

"Which is a lot closer than you think," grunted the soldier drily. "So we better get moving."

He shouldered his rifle by the strap.

"You don't want to be here when he gets back."

# Chapter Thirty-Five

## The Impossible Door

The church of St. Dunstan's in the West stands on the north side of Fleet Street. It is—and it was this that was making George cast a nervous glance toward Temple Bar—the westernmost church in the city of London, close to the boundary. It is remarkable for several reasons, but the one the Fusilier was pointing at was a door. It was a perfectly normal, paneled Georgian front door, set in a handsome stone door frame. What made it remarkable was that it was set halfway up the side of the church beneath its own pedimented portico on top of a blank stone wall, with no means of getting to it.

It was guarded by two portly bearded men, who stood on either side, half-naked except for some animal skins loosely swaddled around their midriffs. They held clubs in one hand, and had the other cocked jauntily on their hips. For no reason—or perhaps it was the beards—

George thought of his geography teacher at school, though he suspected they were meant to be Hercules. Though, why there were two of them, he didn't know and hadn't the energy to care. Two bells hung above the door, and George suspected that they hit the bells when the clock dictated. The clock itself stuck out at right-angles on the blank wall below the portico.

"You'll be safe behind there, with them two guarding the door," said the Fusilier.

"But we can't get up there," George pointed out. "It's impossible."

"Of course it is. It's the Impossible Door. That's why it's safe," said the Fusilier. He cupped his hands and shouted up at the two Herculeses. "Oi! Shop!"

The right-hand club bearer jerked into motion, as if awakening from a daydream. He stretched the crick out of his neck and leaned over the edge. A torrent of words with lots of consonants and too few vowels poured out from behind the beard.

"What's he saying?" asked George. Edie was still not really present, though her shaking had stopped.

"Blowed if I know," said the Fusilier. "It's all Greek to me. . . ."

He grinned at the Herculeses. Pointed to George and Edie, gave a thumbs-up, tapped his watch, and then turned away.

"Five minutes to turn o'day. I got to get back on my plinth. Be good, and if you can't be good, be lucky!" and he was gone in a sudden tackety-booted clatter, heading back toward Holborn.

Edie stared after him. She felt at the end of her tether. She could hardly stand. She felt numb. And now, once more, she felt abandoned as the Fusilier disappeared around the corner.

"Edie," said George. "Edie! You don't want to miss this."

She turned, and through her numbness came awareness of a grinding noise. And as she looked up at the blank wall, she realized the shadows were all wrong. And then she realized they were all wrong because last time she'd looked, there had been no shadows on the smooth unscalable cliff in front of them. Only now, a zigzag shadow was growing.

And through the numbness that was clouding in on her, she realized that the shadow was being cast by stones that were pushing out of the wall, making a series of steps.

There was a clicking noise, and both of them looked up to the top of the steps. One Hercules was clicking his fingers at them and beckoning, while the other was scanning the night sky, club held at the ready.

"He said it was safe," said George, not sounding entirely convinced.

Edie used what felt like the last of her energy to unzip her pocket and check the sea-glass. It sat there, dim and dull and safe. She pushed past George and pulled herself up the stairs. He waited a beat, and followed her. The beckoning Hercules helped her up onto the step outside the Impossible Door, and pushed it open without a word. He smiled encouragingly. She checked her pocket and walked in under the portico, through the doorway.

George got up onto the step without any help and smiled at the Hercules holding the door. "Um. Thank you," he said. The Hercules smiled self-deprecatingly and hitched up his animal skin in embarrassment. It sounded like he said "In taxi," but George couldn't be sure. He nodded a half-smile and tentatively followed Edie in.

Once inside, they both turned and looked back at the door. The Hercules closed it slowly, as if trying not to frighten them. He pantomimed sleep, and mumbled another mouthful of consonants, making calming gestures with his hand.

"He's saying we're safe. I think," said George.

With a final nod and a smile, the door shut with an accompanying thud of finality. The air in the room sucked in a little, as if an air lock had been closed.

"Hope you're right," said Edie.

They looked around. There was light from a very dim cobweb-covered bulb screwed to the wall above the door, but not really enough to do more than cast shadows that just highlighted what couldn't be seen.

It was a strange room. The mechanism for the clock and the bells, by which the Herculeses outside the door struck them, filled the center of the space. There were beams and counterweights and pendulums and cogs. All the machinery threw sharp-angled shadows onto the sides of the room, where there were boxes and hampers and buttresses of broken-backed hymn books slowly falling apart against the walls. The machine room was obviously also used for storage.

Edie ducked under a large-toothed wheel and opened a hamper. It was full of oil lamps. She opened the next one. It was full of choirboy's cassocks and surplices. She moved some, and then lay down with them on top of her, curled up in the hamper like a short bed.

"Edie," said George. "What are you doing?"

"Sleeping," she mumbled. "Need to sleep."

Her hand pulled the sea-glass from her pocket and she gave it a final look.

"Safe. Sleep now."

George tried to remember what you were meant to do with people in shock. Or was it concussion? Maybe she had a concussion. He wished he'd listened more in the first aid class at school. Sleeping might be the worst thing she could do.

"Edie, I don't know if you should—"

She opened one eye. "Shut up."

"No, I mean you might have shock, and I—"

"George. Shut up . . ."

He did. The only sound was the heavy ticking of the clock mechanism in the middle of the room. Edie sat up.

". . . There's someone else in here."

George felt a cold trickle of fear slide down his spine. He looked around the room, through the strange shapes of the apparatus, into the shadows. Now that he concentrated on it, there were more shadows in the room than he was comfortable with.

"How do you know?" he whispered.

"I heard it."

George peered around the room. None of the shadows looked human shaped, though most of them were big enough to hide several people. He reached into the hamper full of oil lamps and picked one out.

"Stay here."

He held the lamp by its handle, ready to swing it like a club.

"Hello?"

There was no reply.

"George," said Edie.

"I'm fine," he lied, as he set out on a tour of the edges of the room. He walked the four walls in a clockwise direction. Then he checked out the roof and the top of the mechanism. He pulled himself up on a metal beam and had a look. There was just dust and pigeon droppings.

"No one's here," he said with relief.

"Edie?"

There was no reply. He dropped to the ground and ran across to the hamper.

Edie was fast asleep. The sea-glass was clenched tightly in her fist, and her fist was wedged under her cheek. He thought maybe he should wake her. Then he thought he'd let her sleep, because it probably wasn't bad. And beside which, he thought he might just sit down for a bit too.

He dropped to the floor and sat with his back on the side of the hamper. He pulled his coat around him and wished it weren't so cold. He still felt damp from the Thames. He tried to remember the warm day in the barn in the hay bed with his father sketching the bull, but the memory didn't bring him warmth now, only a deeper coldness.

And then his head nodded twice and slumped forward.

And for quite some time the only sound was the ticking of the clock mechanism, and the distant traffic outside, and the in-and-out of two children breathing.

And then there was something else as a kind of counterpoint to the ticking clock, right on the edge of hearing, but so quiet that you almost missed it.

George's eyes opened. He didn't move an inch.

"Edie," he whispered. He tried to nudge the hamper side without shifting too noticeably. "Edie!"

But there was no reply, no shifting of weight in the hamper behind him. Edie slept on, the glass clenched in her fist by her cheek, dull and safe.

"The clicking noise. I hear it."

"Him," said a voice from the shadowy corner beside George. The shadowy corner he'd carefully searched and found empty.

"Heard *him*. Or *me*, rather. Apologies. No intention to fright. Introduce myself perhaps? Wish you no harm."

The shadow moved jerkily and resolved into the tall thin figure of a man. He held one hand out, open with the palm forward, as if to ward off even the thought that he *might* mean harm. The other hand stayed down at his side and moved constantly, passing beads on a long loop of string through his finger and thumb, as if he were keeping count of something.

He jingled as he moved, and as he emerged into the dim light, George saw that this was because he was festooned with watches and winding keys and watch-maker's tools and little oil cans, all hanging from ancient ribbons pinned to his jacket. He looked like a human Christmas tree. The jacket was an old-fashioned cutaway tailcoat, so overmended and faded with age that it was hard to tell if it was black or dark green, or indeed where the patches began and the original coat ended. The needlework on the jacket and the repairs were done in fine regular stitching, clearly the work of a perfectionist.

His face, as it revealed itself in the pallid light of the single dim bulb, was not so much old, as timeworn, and actually much younger than it appeared to be when you got close and looked at it. It was just a very old youngish face, a face that had been young for a long time. His hair, scraped back into a queue tied with a frayed purple ribbon, wasn't actually the gray it seemed to be, but was—like his clothes—powdered with dust. He had a tall forehead and a long nose, which jutted out of his face like a challenge.

Perched on the bridge of the challenging nose was a pair of jeweler's spectacles, with extra-magnifying lenses on hinged arms ready to be swung into place over the main lenses, which were, strangely, dark blue. This gave him the unsettling appearance of a blind man who could see everything if he chose to.

Around his neck he wore a gray woolen scarf wound several times and tucked into a double-breasted waistcoat swagged across with three watch chains. His trousers matched the black-faded-to-green of his jacket, but retained the suggestion of stripes running through them, along with the strong hint of many more painstaking repairs.

"Had a name. Long gone. Not known by it now. Now known as the Clocker. Pleasure to meet. Apologies for shock. Etcetera."

And he clicked the heels of his boots together, inclined his head in a small bow, and stuck out the hand not tallying beads in greeting.

"You weren't there when I searched that corner a minute ago," said George warily, not taking his hand. He glanced over the lip of the hamper. Edie was sleeping, and the sea-glass was not blazing a warning.

"Was. Minute ago you asleep. Searched my corner hours ago. No mistake. Sure of it. Stickler for time, you see."

He spoke in short sentences, sentences so shorn of pronouns or verbs that they weren't really sentences at all, just clips of information. His left hand never stopped rotating the tally beads on his string. George got accustomed to the rhythm of it and realized he used the click of a tally bead as a kind of punctuation between the microsentences. And the microsentences were always fired in short bursts, so as not to waste a second.

George tried to shake sleep from his head. He looked up at the Clocker.

"Okay. Hours ago, then. You weren't there."

The Clocker coughed apologetically.

"Yes. Was. Ghastly trick. Hid. Rather, made you not see me. Again, apologies, etcetera."

His free hand whirled and curlicued as if trying to trace a giant watch spring, or maybe conjure the impression of a host of etceteras from the air in front of him. Then it returned to the offer of a handshake.

With his mind on the dull sea-glass, George tentatively shook it. The grip was surprisingly firm.

"I'm George."

"George. Good name. Stout fellow, no doubt. Saw you caring for girl. Right thing to do. Clearly taken a turn."

"She's just had a shock," said George, feeling unexpectedly defensive about Edie, resenting the implication that she had had a fainting fit. "She's pretty tough."

"Well, of course. A glint, I see. Never was a vaporish glint. Tough as the rocks they read. No offense meant."

"Er. None taken."

He suddenly sat down in front of George, folding his legs akimbo, like a well-oiled machine.

He lowered his voice.

"Better not wake girl. Shocked already. Was to see me? Chap out of ordinary? Straw on camel's back, perhaps? No need heap Pelion on Ossa. Etcetera. Follow, yes?"

"Yes," said George, who had no idea who, why, what, or even where Pelion or Ossa might be.

"Good man. Have chocolate, no doubt? Children often do?"

He smiled eagerly. George shook his head and disguised a shiver. The cold was blowing in under the door, which might be Impossible but wasn't weatherproof.

"Um no. No chocolate."

The Clocker looked disappointed. He looked closely at George. Clearly not closely enough, because he swung down a magnifying glass and looked even closer. Then he sat back and started unwinding his scarf from around his neck. It was a very long scarf, and as it unwound it also became apparent that it was also a very wide scarf. As he lifted the final loop over his head, it caught on his spectacles and swept them off his face and onto the floor.

The Clocker ducked his head on reflex, in a gesture that was half-squint, half-cringe. He scrabbled for his glasses, one eye screwed shut, the other looking for them.

"What's wrong with your eye?" asked George.

"Nothing," said the Clocker, crinkling the open eye in a smile. And he was right. Without the sinister glasses, George was surprised to see that the eye was a very friendly pale green with hazel flecks. It was an open eye, a generous eye, though its pale quality made it look a little washed out, or, like the face it sat in, worn by time. Seeing the face with an eye in it, not hidden behind a dark lens, George decided it was not a severe hatchet of a face, but a face that might even laugh every now and then.

"The other one," said George.

"Ah. Other one frightening. Upset you. Keep it behind these."

And he looped the earpieces of the spectacles behind his ears and hid his eyes behind the dark-blue lenses again. George could see from the way the creases in the face relaxed that he had opened the "frightening" eye behind the obscuring lens.

"Here. Let dog see rabbit. Half rabbit, anyway." The Clocker grinned and fumbled with the lens over the normal eye. He swiveled the blue lens out of the way. The effect changed from a sinister man wearing dark glasses at night to a more ordinary person wearing a dark patch over one eye. His face changed its proportions accordingly, and was almost cheery. He winked at George and held out the scarf.

"Borrow. Please. Ward off unseasonable cold. Take it as a favor, etcetera."

He delved into his pockets and rummaged.

"No worries about chocolate. Sure have some somewhere. . . ."

He produced a half-eaten bar of dark chocolate meticulously rewrapped in gold foil. He held it out to George with an encouraging nod.

"My guest. Good for you. Perk up, perhaps. Much as you like."

George bit into the chocolate and immediately realized he was starving. He tried to make the taste last, relishing the bittersweet sensation on his tongue, letting it melt a bit before he chewed it to pieces.

"Um," he said, "if it's not rude. What are you? Are you a spit?"

"Spit? No. Nor taint, rest assured."

He watched George eating with a kindly eye. He looked like he was trying to find short-enough words to explain the complex thing he was.

"Am tallyman. One of the Weirded. So to speak."

He smiled as if he knew he was probably just confusing

George all the more. Which of course he was.

"The Weirded?" said George, around a new chunk of chocolate.

"The cursed. Forgotten men. Thralls."

"I don't know what a thrall is," George said apologetically.

"Ah. Old word. Apologies. Thralls being curse bearers. Doomed to walk earth beyond natural span of years. Nonsense to your ears, no doubt. Detritus of old beliefs. Shards from midden of forgotten religions. Etcetera."

"You're cursed? To walk the earth forever."

"I am the Clocker. My curse? To keep an eye on the time. And vice versa, as you see. No alarm, please . . ."

He lifted the blue lens off the frightening eye. George couldn't help flinching. The eye was not an eye, but a small clock face. It had two regular hands for hours and minutes, and the uncanny and distressing effect was added to by the fact that the clock face pulsed red, then white in time with the second hand.

The Clocker hid his watch-eye behind the blue lens again.

"Eye to watch, and watch for an eye. My mark."

He grimaced apologetically. George glanced at Edie. She slept on. He cleared his throat.

"Can you tell me what's happening to me?"

"General terms? Certainly. Have found an un-London."

"Un-London?"

"Place with spits, taints, etcetera. Unseen by inhabitants of your London. But your London only one London. One of many. And what you see as London? Merely another's un-London. More things in heaven and earth, Horatio. Yes indeed. And more heavens and earths. More hells, too. Some slip. Some walk. Some fall. Between worlds, you see."

George thought about Little Tragedy saying there were more "heres" here than they imagined. His head was spinning.

"Is this like—magic, or something?"

The Clocker looked faintly appalled at the idea. He shook his head, and all the hanging objects jangled on his coat for emphasis.

"Not magic. Magic tommyrot. All done with mirrors."

"But can I walk between the worlds? I mean, is that what's happening to me?"

"No. You fell into an un-London. Didn't walk. Were pushed. Something about you. Smell it. Ever smell lightning rod after strike? Same smell. Hot metal and static electricity. Could be gift, could be curse. Probably both."

"I'm cursed? You mean I'm one of the Weirded?"

"Cursed maybe too strong. Sorry. But marked, certainly."

George felt the throb in his hand and folded it into his pocket.

"Why would I be cursed?"

The Clocker shrugged. "Done bad things?"

"No. No. Not bad enough for a curse, I mean." George said.

"A bad thing? People usually know why cursed. Start at baddest thing. Then work back."

"There isn't a baddest thing." Said George emphatically "Not like that. I haven't, don't—"

He stopped. A black feeling rising in his throat.

The Clocker looked at him with one kind eye and nodded.

"Better out than in. Or not. No wish to intrude. Englishman's secrets his castle, and all that. But may help."

"I said something. Something bad."

"Not likely cursed for bad language. Though would be appropriate. Ha."

"It wasn't bad language."

He felt he was suddenly unable to speak or breathe, and what was stopping him was like a huge bubble of air that was stuck in his chest.

"Don't tell me. Your business. Impertinent. Time my only business, really. Speak to others so rarely, forget myself. Impose too much. Apologies etcetera."

He offered George the last piece of chocolate. George wanted it but shook his head. The Clocker wrapped it back up in its foil and handed it over.

"For girl. Glint. Hungry when wakes, no doubt."

George took it and put it in his jacket pocket. Somehow, after all he'd been through, this kindness was a bit hard to take.

The Clocker smiled and looked away, giving George space and quiet. It was a surprisingly companionable silence.

# CHAPTER THIRTY-SIX

## Cold as Hell

If you walk up a stony mountain stream, and find a place where pebbles have been trapped by a certain combination of flowing water and flaws in the streambed, you can sometimes see an unnaturally perfect circular hole in the rock made by one of the pebbles—a pebble stuck in the eddying water—endlessly turning in the base of the hole. The pebble cuts a hole in the stone because it never stops moving.

The Walker, a man trapped by the flow of events in his own life, also never stopped moving and found the only relief from this curse in finding enclosed circular spaces around which to shuffle as he dozed in the between-state that was the nearest a man doomed to walk forever achieved instead of sleep.

He favored the sunken stone circle in the library piazza beside St. Pancras station, and had the habit of turning in its closed circuit for hours on end in the quiet times of the night.

Only it wasn't quiet this time.

His laps around the space were accompanied by a scraping noise, and the noise was one of metal against stone as he dragged the blade of his long knife along the stone bench curving him. His eyes were closed, but every time he completed a circuit, he paused, turned around, and retraced his steps the way he'd just come, thereby ensuring that the blade was honed on both sides equally.

He prided himself on the blade's sharpness. He'd had a long time to perfect this means of honing it. He was almost doing it in his sleep.

There was a *crump* and a *scree,* and something hit the ground at a low angle and skittered into the circle in front of him. Because he was used to noises in the city at night, he kept his eyes closed, and thus tripped over the hard icy bundle that had appeared. His knee hit the ground as his eyes snapped open.

He grimaced in pain and displeasure, and lifted himself back up into a walking position. He walked around the thing and kicked at it with his boot, raising a puff of ice crystals. It spun on its axis, and from within there came a faint and shivery *"Caw?"*

The Walker circled it two more times, then tapped it gingerly with the heel of his boot. The ice pod cracked, and a very sad-looking Raven staggered out, beak clattering with cold.

The Walker slid his dagger back into the scabbard.

"Where in hell have you been?" he asked, with a twisted smile that lasted no time at all.

The Raven shook snow from between its feathers and flapped up onto his shoulder, burrowing in beside his neck, finding a roost in the voluminous hood of his sweatshirt. It didn't answer the question because firstly it was rhetorical, and secondly it was the joke the Walker never tired of in this situation.

The Raven just took up its position inside the hood and closed its eyes and tried to stop shivering. It didn't need the Walker for his sense of humor. It needed him for his warmth.

# CHAPTER THIRTY-SEVEN

## Telling the Time

George and the Clocker sat in the dim light, watching Edie sleep. And in the end—perhaps because it was a companionable silence—George found himself filling it with unexpected words.

"I said something bad to my dad."

"Ah," said the Clocker, "most sons do. One day or another."

"Something *really* bad. I was angry and I said stuff that was bad and a lie, and I was just trying to hurt him. And I did hurt him. He told me I didn't mean it. And I told him I did. And I spat at him. I mean, I was a kid, I was ten . . . and he left and drove off. And there were—"

He stopped because it suddenly seemed very important to examine the peeling plaster on the wall to his right. The only sounds were Edie's breathing and the quiet click of the Clocker's tally beads marking off the seconds.

"You see, there were tears in his eyes, and I didn't say sorry or good-bye or . . . I didn't say anything. He wiped the spit off his cheek and said I didn't mean it, and I was just trying to hurt because I was hurting. And I swore I meant it, swore I would always mean it, and he looked stranger than I ever saw him look. I thought he was going to . . . then he left."

He paused to examine more plaster and wipe his nose.

"Don't know why I'm telling you this."

The Clocker smiled.

"Because you can. Everyone can tell the time."

"Sorry?"

"Joke. Wordplay. Lighten atmosphere. Bad habit. Apologies again."

"Oh," said George.

"Can tell the time everything. Won't change anything. Time ticks on regardless."

"Right," said George. And then he told the Clocker of how his father had driven off and never driven back, because someone else hadn't been looking and had driven into him the next day, and he'd been killed instantly, and so there was nothing left to say except a sorry that seemed as hollow and empty as a coffin now no one was there to hear it. And then because he had got over the hardest thing, the rest of the words came easy.

They flowed so fast that he suspected he was gabbling hysterically, but each time he checked the Clocker's

eye for a reaction, it was just smiling in friendly understanding. George told him about everything that had happened since the Natural History Museum, and the
Sphinxes' words and the need to find the Stone Heart and
the sacrifice that must be made, and he told him about the
Black Friar and his word-map of how to find the heart of
stone. He told him about the Winding Stair leading to the
Memory of Fire where the memory is caged, and how he
was to catch a fire to show him the path to the Stone Heart.

And then he was suddenly exhausted and talked out,
and he closed his eyes and wished he were home in bed,
where everything seemed real.

He jerked awake with the touch of the Clocker's hand on
his shoulder.

He hadn't realized he had nodded off.

"How long have I been asleep?"

"Too long and not long enough, perhaps. No harm.
Time to think."

"I wasn't thinking. I was asleep."

In rising panic he realized he had wasted time when
he could have been puzzling things out.

"No harm. Sleep good. Thinking done by self. Now,
re: Black Friar. Your worries? No reason to mistrust, per
se. None known to me, any rate. But right to mistrust all.
Your predicament? Wariness essential. Take pinch of salt
every time. Self included. Take pinch of salt with me. But
if interested, have thoughts."

George sat up straight.

"Of course I'm interested! It's all mumbo jumbo to me!"

"Memory of Fire? Hearts of Stone? Winding Stairs? Many things in London. Needles in haystack."

"I know."

"Many things. But only one Fire. Only one Great Fire."

The eye looked at George encouragingly. George thought of London and fires, and thought of the Blitz, and then he thought further back in history lessons—and he got it.

"The Fire of London?"

"Indubitably. Corroborating evidence? Memory of Fire? Memorial *to* fire?"

George scrabbled back in his own memory, raking over the lukewarm coals of past lessons. They'd done a wall chart of the Great Fire. Men in wigs pulling down flaming timbered houses, and the great plague that had happened before the fire. And after, he remembered helping cut out the tall cardboard outline of a pillar—

"The Monument!" he said.

"Exactly. Monument memorial to fire. And inside monument? Stair, circular. Winding, might say. Lead to top. And on top? Urn. Urn of fire."

"That," said George with a grin, "is just brilliant."

He began to get up. The Clocker pushed him gently back.

"That," he said, "is not open to public in middle of

night. You sleep. Bad time to be on streets. Low hours of night. Servants of the Stone walk."

"Servants of the Stone?"

"Doom-thralls like self. Thralled to ancient vows broken on blood stone. Self free of servitude to any but own doom. Keep eye on time as punishment. Not service like Stone Servants. Watch for them. They will watch for you. Now sleep. In morning can leave by other door. Via church. Will be open. Used by Russian Orthodoxes. Early risers. Better than alarm clock."

He clicked his beads with a smile and bent his head over them. Something in the way his head bent reminded George of the Gunner, and remembering the Gunner brought another question to his mind.

"Excuse me. One more thing. When all this began, when the Gunner saved me, he said something."

"No doubt. Startling event. Worthy of comment."

"He said I'd got no idea of what I'd started."

"Man of perspicacity."

"No," said George. "I mean—yes, but he didn't know about any of this, about the Stone Heart or the Heart of Stone or whatever. He was speaking about something else, I think. Something about spits and taints. . . ."

The Clocker nodded grimly.

"Spits, taints. Hostile. Uneasy peace allways. Equilibrium of distrust. Gunner kills four taints? Equilibrium gone. Things out of balance. Gauntlet thrown."

"What do you mean?"

"Don't know. Not fully. But has happened before. War between spits and taints always on cards. In background. Is why some statues walk and others don't. Non-walkers are—"

"Dead statues?"

"Precisely. Casualties of earlier wars. Taints, see, just voids with no spirit. Only lack and need to fill void. Appetites, envy, green-eyed monster, etcetera. Hate spirited statues. Hate meaning. Want it, too, always hate what can't have. But not worry self. If spit-war to come, beyond stopping."

"But you're saying I might be starting a war?"

"Only a 'might.' Never sleep worrying about 'might.' Especially if beyond control. Concentrate on what can do. Understand? Now sleep. Will keep watch."

There was no way George was going to sleep; his mind was racing with all this new information. He turned it over and over, and as he tried to sort it out, the loops in his thinking kept repeating themselves, and he returned to his fears and his memories in such a repetitive and inescapable pattern that it became soothing and regular—and this was the thing that did, in the end, send him to sleep.

# CHAPTER THIRTY-EIGHT

## The Dead Statue

The Grid Man stared fixedly across the street. A long bony hand waved itself in front of the eyes. He didn't move. The hand spread itself across the gap in its chest and pressed itself against the dull bronze, as if feeling for a heartbeat or some hint of a vital spark. The hand gave up and curled into a contemptuous fist, rapping a curled forefinger against the metal brow.

The Raven sat on top of the Grid Man's head. It squinnied a thin dribble of droppings down the unmoving face, leaving a whitish streak running vertically through the unresponding left eye.

"Exactly. No one here anymore, just a pile of metal," said the Walker. "Unlike your good Self. A bird of a quite different feather, so to speak. Didn't take you long to pull yourself together, did it?"

There were several things the Raven found unsatisfactory about the Walker. Not ever standing still made him a less than perfect perch, for example. And making snide jokes about his ability to rebirth himself. People didn't make jokes about phoenixes, thought the Raven. He filed it away for future brooding and resentment, and shook his feathers out. They didn't feel new. They already felt older than dirt.

"Right," said the Walker, having the bad manners to sound hurried and impatient while talking to a bird that daydreamed in eons. "We need something to find him. Something with a taste for children."

It was starting to rain heavily. He turned up the collar of his coat, unconsciously rubbed the stone on the choker around his neck, and pulled the torn scrap of T-shirt from his pocket and held it out to the Raven.

"It's time for the Minotaur."

# CHAPTER THIRTY-NINE

## A Day to Repair

George woke with a jolt. Edie was standing in front of him. She looked better. He could tell that because she was poking him with gusto.

"Hey, you were snoring!"

He looked around the room. He got to his feet and checked all the corners.

"He's gone," he said with disappointment.

"Who's gone?" she said, looking at him suspiciously.

And so he told her all about the Clocker, and what he'd said. He didn't tell *her* all of what he'd said to the Clocker, because it didn't seem any of her business, and besides, he'd said it to someone, and somehow that was what mattered.

"What was he like, this Clocker?" she asked.

George described him, starting with the way he looked and his clock-face eye, ending with his warning about the Servants of the Stone.

"And they're not taints. Or spits?"

"No," he replied.

"So what are they?"

"Weirded."

"They sound like it."

"It means doomed. They're cursed to walk the earth until they've undone whatever it was that got them in trouble in the first case. And the Servants of the Stone are—"

"In trouble with the Stone."

"Yup," he said, feeling the water deepening under his feet.

"And are you in trouble with the Stone?" she asked carefully, unconsciously rubbing her sea-glass between her fingers. She was remembering the warning from the drowning girl shouting, "He's not what he seems." She had a chilling jolt of doubt. She had thought the warning applied to the Black Friar. But what if the girl had been warning her about George?

"Yeah. But not their kind of trouble, though," he said, feet paddling a little desperately in the deep water of his ignorance.

"Not 'their kind' of trouble," she parroted. "Oh. How does that work, exactly?"

"The Clocker said they were beings who had made a pact with the Stone. I haven't made any pact. I've, um, wronged it."

"And wronging it is different?"

"Apparently."

Edie felt the room getting smaller. She wanted to be out in the fresh air, away from the dust and the dark, and away from the slightly uncomfortable feeling of being stuck in a locked room with George.

"How do we get out of here? I mean, it's going to be a bit harder climbing out of here in broad daylight. . . ."

George was suddenly aware of the time and the noises of the city outside the door. The grumble of traffic was full force, and with a shock he realized he must have slept again, and slept longer than before.

"We can go out from inside the church," he said hurriedly, crossing to the door the Clocker had shown him. "See?"

He gently undid the lock. Edie followed him cautiously. From the bottom of the narrow staircase came the sound of chanting in a language that wasn't English.

"What's that?" she whispered.

"Russians," he explained. "It's used by Russian Orthodoxes now, according to the Clocker."

"What are 'orthodoxes'?" asked Edie, following him down the stair.

"I don't know," said George, slipping out of a doorway behind a pillar in the nave of the church. "Unhappy, from the sound they make."

The front quarter of the church was mainly full of old people, with a sprinkling of younger people all facing away from them toward the altar. They were all standing, and the song they were singing wasn't really a song but more of a chanted moan of pain and apology, led by a bearded priest in long black robes. His eyes were the only ones to see George and Edie slip out from behind the pillar and head for the door to the street. By the time he had registered interest, the door was closing behind them.

They paused on the steps and looked at the bustling city splashing past in front of them. The relative emptiness of the night streets had been replaced by throngs of pedestrians, and where empty night-buses had raced minicabs on uncrowded streets, unavailable taxis now inched forward in a rain-lashed gridlock.

"Brilliant!" said Edie in disgust, looking up at the sheets of water dropping out of the lead-heavy sky. She pulled her coat tight around her neck. "Just brilliant."

"No," said George. "Edie. It *is* brilliant. Remember what the Gunner said? Gargoyles don't fly in the wet! It means we don't have to worry about them spotting us from the sky. The rain *is* brilliant. Come on."

"Come on where?" she asked, staying in the dry patch by the door. "I'm hungry."

"The Monument," he explained excitedly.

"Yeah, but we don't know what monument you need," she said, thinking that even if he did know, it wasn't a monument *she* needed, and wondered how or when she'd be able to work out if her new fear about George not being what he seemed would resolve itself.

"*The* Monument," he explained. "The Clocker helped me work it out." And he told her how the clues had been hidden in what the Black Friar had said.

"I didn't know whether we should trust the friar," she said.

"Me either," he admitted. "But the Clocker said it seemed to make sense. And he couldn't honestly see why the Friar wouldn't help us."

"And why do you trust the Clocker?"

Because he had kind eyes, thought George. Because he understood when I told him about my dad.

"Because he told me not to," he said. "He told me not to trust anyone, even him, not unless they were a spit without a hint of taint about them."

She shook her head as if this were the stupidest thing she'd heard all day.

"Could have been a double bluff though, couldn't it?"

"No," he said emphatically, sure he was right. "Here." He fished the square of chocolate from his pocket and held it out to her. "He left this for you. He said you'd be hungry when you woke up. He was that kind of person."

"The kind that gives sweets to unsuspecting little girls," she said, taking the chocolate anyway.

"I don't think you're that unsuspecting," he said.

"Too right," she said around the lump of chocolate already disappearing into her mouth. "Haven't been unsuspecting for a long, long time."

"Come on then, if you're coming," he said, looking up

at the clock above them. It was getting late. The Herculeses stared out at the street, eyes fixed and stony as if they'd never moved an inch since the sculptor had chiseled them out of the living rock.

"You got any more?" she said in a chocolate-muffled voice.

"No," he said, jogging into a narrow alleyway.

"Oh," she said disappointedly.

He didn't turn to see if she was following him. After a few yards he heard her voice behind his right ear.

"Why are we going this way?" she asked. "It's wetter than the streets."

"No one puts taints on the back of buildings or in alleys," he explained.

"Good thinking," she said grudgingly. "That one of your friend the Clocker's ideas?"

"No," he said. "I worked that one out all by myself."

# CHAPTER FORTY
## Absent Friends

Dictionary watched the early-morning lawyers walking into the Law Courts. He felt the pigeons landing on his wig, and enjoyed the warbling they made as they jostled for position.

"Your pardon, Mr. Johnson. A question. Amiable, assure you."

He looked down. The Clocker looked back at him.

"Introduce myself, perhaps."

"No need. You'll be the Clocker. I don't miss much up here, sir. We may never have had cause to converse, but I see you coming and going, checking the clocks and tallying away on your beads."

"Ah. Your fame precedes. Magnificent achievement. Man of many words, etcetera. Self man of few. But desire knowledge."

"Pursuit of knowledge is one of the things that elevates us beyond the ruminant bovine, sir. That and the ability to enjoy a pipe and a good dish of tea. If you mean no malice I have no objection to making your acquaintance and illuminating you, as far as my dim lamp of learning may cast its light into the tenebrous miasma that encircles us."

The Clocker bobbed a series of short bows.

"Eternally grateful. In your debt. Matter of boy."

"Boy? What's the matter with a boy? What boy?"

"Unusual boy. Travels with girl. Girl glint."

Dictionary shivered and shuddered.

"Oh. That boy. What of him?"

"Met him. Last night. Decent chap. In trouble. Seeking Stone Heart."

"And a bushel of trouble he caused too, in the pursuit of it. Perhaps you know of a spit that was known as the Gunner?"

The Clocker bobbed up and down in friendly excitement.

"Indeed. Absolutely. Well, no. But wish to. Wish to contact him. Tell him of boy and girl's movements. Need help, I feel."

"The Gunner may well be beyond help, giving or receiving. He left here in no state to get to his plinth before turn o'day, I fear."

The Clocker stopped bobbing, and slumped like a puppet with its strings cut.

"But. Oh. I see. Tragedy. Would like to . . . Unfortunate. Wish was something to do for 'em."

There was a pause. A harrumph. And the sound of a man grudgingly ripping a strip of paper from a very old dictionary.

The Clocker looked up. Dictionary cleared his throat in an explosive blast.

"The Gunner had friends, of course. Count myself one. But friends of a more martial aspect are probably more to the point at this particular juncture. The word could be put out, so to speak. Do you have a pen or pencil, sir?"

The Clocker held up a tiny curl of paper.

"Perhaps we may combine in essaying a pigeon?"

# CHAPTER FORTY-ONE

## As the Crow Flies

The Raven lofted up and over a sheer glass massif, heading northwest through the rain. Below him was a jumble of buildings thrown together with little rhyme or reason beyond the accident of history and the ravages of time, fire, and aerial bombing. Pitched roofs and piercing spires pointed to heights that had been unimaginable at the time they were built, but were themselves now looked down on by soaring office towers and mammoth blocks of flats alongside them.

The Raven caught an updraft from a building's heating system venting into the rain, and spiraled higher. As he did so he looked back on the cityscape behind him, where there were fewer towers and more blocks, all bisected by the sinuous river curving between them, tamed by the embankments built on both sides.

The Raven remembered the living river, remembered how its curves had sharpened and shallowed over the time it had known it, a snake moving over the land at a pace too slow for men to notice. And now it was banked in stone and concrete, tamed into a runnel, not a living river at all. He remembered when it had driven mill wheels. Now the only wheel was a massive upended bicycle wheel on the South Bank, where people paid to see what the Raven saw and had seen for generations.

The Raven flapped back on course, the scrap of George's T-shirt fluttering in its beak. Ahead of it, in the distance, it saw the densest cluster of modern high-rises, lit up from within against the gunmetal rain clouds behind them. He centered himself on the bulbous outline of the one that looked like a giant's cucumber thrust rudely end-first into the ground, and started to descend.

In a direct line between him and the cucumber, about half a mile in front of it, was the eastern edge of a massive complex of concrete and glass, like a fortress assembled from ziggurats and thin spiky towers. Inside the boundaries of this futuristic urban citadel there were fountains and walkways on different levels, and there was more concrete. The Raven knew that below the surface of the southern end of this sprawl had once run the ancient city wall. And he could remember when the dwarfed white church marooned within a startling patch of green in the cement bastion had once been the tallest building in the area.

It swerved around one of the spiky tower blocks and dropped suddenly into a forgotten corner of the complex. There were some raised flower beds being lashed by the rain. They were not full of flowers as such, but had been planted with hardy city-proof vegetation that almost matched the cement walkways for lack of color and decoration. The only piece of exuberance was a small grove of horse tail reeds.

The Raven dropped to the earth in front of the reeds and looked up at the feathery tips being buffeted by the wind and the rain squall breaking overhead.

Above it crouched a powerful figure, black and shiny in the rain, the wetness coursing over its hunched and massive body reflecting the surrounding streetlights. It was an unmistakeably male figure; below the waist, a man with strong overmuscled legs bent ready to spring out of the rushes at any unwary passer-by. But his principal feature was in the predominance of muscle and bulk curving up from the waist; not the muscle of a man, but the raw brutal power and bulk of a full-grown bull. The shoulders hunched massively below a bull's head topped by aggressively pointing horns; and so well had the sculptor shaped it, that the sound of enraged snorting seemed to lurk about it, even though it never—to the normal eye—moved or breathed at all.

The Raven hopped up on its shoulder. It dropped the piece of T-shirt into the flower bed in front of it as it sidled up to a pricked bovine ear and clacked its beak.

Above them, the spike of apartment block failed to keep the rain cloud pinned in place, and the rain moved on to drench other parts of the city. As the rain eased, and a small patch of fugitive blue appeared in the cloud-scape, the Raven could again be seen flapping south.

In the flower bed, beneath the rushes, for those whose eyes saw what was there and what really was not there, there was no Minotaur. Just a patch of newly turned earth, where a hoof had plashed the ground in anger and set off.

# CHAPTER FORTY-TWO

## After Pudding

George and Edie were working their way through a new part of the city. It was a part where modern buildings rose high on each side of them, but from streets whose names, narrowness, and random angles betrayed them as part of the very old plan of London. They turned down a thin sloping section of road called Pudding Lane.

"Don't know why you'd call a lane after a pudding," grumbled Edie, her collar held tight around her neck.

"It's where the bakers worked," explained George, happy to have found himself in a part of London that he knew about, if only from history lessons. "It's where the fire started."

"What fire?"

"The Great Fire. 1666. It began in a baker's oven around here."

"You know dates and things? Must be a brainbox as well as rich."

"I'm not rich, Edie. And it's an easy date to remember. It's a cigarette and three pipes."

"It's what?" said Edie, completely lost.

"Everyone gets taught that. The one looks like a cigarette and the sixes look like pipes. You know—like old men smoke?"

"I don't know any old men. And I didn't get taught about any fire."

"Well, if you don't believe me—"said George, turning left out of the bottom of Pudding Lane, "—look at that."

A tall stone pillar soared over their heads, dominating the small square that stood at the crest of a gentle rise. George thought it looked like a more homely Nelson's Column. It may have been the fact that buildings crowded in on it from all sides, giving you no place to stand back and appreciate its size; or it may have been that the square pediment it sat on had a door in the middle of it, with a yellow light burning inside. It somehow seemed more like a lighthouse than a triumphal column. And of course, there was no triumphal figure atop the fluted gray stone pillar. Instead there was a square cage running around it, painted gray and white. And rising from this unexpected cage was a gilded urn sprouting frozen gold flames. Even on a gray day like this, the aerial gilt sparkled against the city dullness around it.

Edie pulled him back into Pudding Lane.

"What?"

"Have you gone dragon-blind all of a sudden?"

"Dragons?" he said, floundering.

"On the top of the plinth!"

He stuck his head around the corner. Sure enough, he had completely missed the four roughly carved dragons clinging on to the corners of the plinth. They had a desperate teeth-gritted look to them, as if their legs were getting tired of gripping on to the corners, and they might plummet bottom-first to the ground below at any moment.

"I have to go up there," he said, looking up at the drizzle. "It's still raining."

"They're not waterspouts, George. I think the 'not flying in the rain' thing only applies to the gargoyles who are meant to be waterspouts. These look more—nasty."

She pulled out her sea-glass. It was lifeless and opaque, and told her that, despite their proximity and unpleasant grimaces, these dragons were—for now—no threat.

"They might be dead statues," he said "The Clocker said a lot of statues don't move anymore because they're dead. They died in the wars between the spits and the taints." He saw the trap his mouth was opening up for him to fall into, so he stopped.

"What wars between spits and taints?" she asked.

"Just ancient history," he finished quickly, wanting to move on. He made a great play of looking at his watch. "We better get a move on. I've not got much time."

He wasn't going to tell her that he might, by making

the Gunner save him from the pterodactyl, have triggered the beginning of a war between the spits and taints that was going to be anything but ancient.

"Look. We're probably fine," he said, nodding at the dull sea-glass.

She zipped it back into her pocket. "Huh," was all she could come up with at short notice, but she gave it all the feeling she could muster.

The two of them watched the dragons very carefully for the first sign of any movement as they walked in under the lee of the pillar.

"George," she said, nodding at a sign on the stone to the left of the door.

It showed the admission charges for the Monument. Children were one pound.

"We haven't got two quid," she said. "You'll have to go alone." He looked up at the cage in the sky.

"I'll be quick. You wait under cover over there." He pointed at a modern building faced in shiny brown marble.

She shivered. He took his coat off.

"Here. You wear this. Keep you warm. I'm going to be inside, running up those stairs. I'm going to be dry in there. Probably too hot by the time I get to the top."

She was unexpectedly thrown by his offer of the coat. She took it tentatively, and then thrust her arms into the sleeves decisively.

"Thanks."

"No bother."

"What are you going to do if it stops raining, and one of those dragons isn't dead and does wake up?"

He shrugged and tried to sound more confident than he actually felt. Although he already felt that trying to hide things from Edie was a bit pointless. Her eyes seemed to suck the truth out of things. Either that or he was getting light-headed with all this running around and sleeping rough. A hunger pang twinged through his gut. He ignored it.

"There's a cage up there. Like a shark cage. You know, for when you dive with sharks."

"I don't dive with sharks. How bored do you have to be to do that, anyway?" she asked.

After a long beat he decided it was a rhetorical question.

"I'll be fine."

She knew by now that "I'm fine" or "I'll be fine" was George's equivalent of whistling in the dark, a way of dealing with his nerves and fears. She decided to let him get away with it, because he'd lent her his coat and she was warming up.

He looked up at the drab mottled stone column and the matching clouds rolling past over its head.

"Better get on with it. It looks like it might clear up any minute."

He blew his cheeks out in a big breath, like a diver about to start his run up on the springboard.

"Though, how the heck I'm supposed to catch a fire anyway in all this rain I've got no idea. Right." He swiveled on his heel and headed for the door, one eye tracking the immobile dragons as he passed under them.

"Good luck."

She headed for the shelter across the square. Halfway there she turned, and was a little surprised to see him standing at the door to the stairs, looking back at her with a strange expression. He changed it as soon as he realized she was seeing it; but for an unguarded instant, she saw all the hesitancy and the tentativeness beneath the bravado he'd been adopting all the way here from Fleet Street. He switched to a confident smile and waved at her, before pushing at the door.

"George!" she shouted, and ran back through the thinning rain. And ever after she never knew why she did what she did next, but she unzipped her pocket and handed him her sea-glass. "It'll give you warning if things change. You know."

He felt a lump in his throat. He sensed how much the sea-glass meant to her.

"Edie—"

She waved him off and jogged away.

"Just don't lose it. Get a bend on."

He watched until she made the shelter of the build-ing overhang. Then he pocketed the glass and pushed in through the door.

Inside, there was a two-way turnstile and a narrow little booth on the right where a man was reading the paper and drinking steaming tea out of a thermos. He scarcely looked up as George dropped his coin into the depression in his narrow counter. He produced a ticket and a pamphlet and went back to his paper with a grunt that sounded like "No monkey business."

George cleared his throat and walked into the center of the plinth, and looked up. Illuminated by the regularly spaced lightbulbs, a stone staircase spiraled up the inside of the column, a black-painted safety railing, framing the narrow void of air in a snail's whorl. At its center, two hundred feet above, was a core of whiter light where the door opened onto the cage and the sky beyond. Despite the lightbulbs, the space felt very old and distant from the city beyond. It had the clean smell of dry stone despite the rain outside.

George checked the sea-glass and started climbing. He climbed three steps at a time and counted as he went.

By the time he got to thirty, Edie, on the outside, was feeling worried. It wasn't a specific worry. Though, with statues jumping off buildings and chasing her and trying to waffle her head flat, she didn't suppose she really needed anything to be that specific about. In fact, it wasn't specifically worry as such. It was more like a nagging void or a suddenly noticed absence. She'd once had an earache, and it had been really horrid, and she hadn't known how she would go on bearing it. And her mother had read her a story, and that story had led to another. And after a bit she'd forgotten about the pain—which was fine and dandy, but all stories come to an end, and the ones her mother had been reading to her were no exception to the rule. And when she'd stopped listening to the last story, the real world returned, and she remembered the pain, and then it had throbbed back into action. What she felt now was exactly what she'd felt in the gap between realizing the story was over and knowing she'd forgotten the pain in her ear, and the sure and certain knowledge that it was about to come back, big time.

She was missing the sea-glass more than she'd expected, she realized. It must be that. It couldn't be that she was missing George, who she wasn't—she reminded herself—even sure if she trusted.

Though, why had she lent him the glass if she didn't trust him? She pulled the jacket—his jacket—tighter. And in doing that she felt something bump against her, and she felt in the pocket and found the broken dragon's head. Its blank eyes stared back at her, and she quickly put it back in the pocket, suddenly worried that it might rouse the nearby dragons by some sympathetic process she didn't understand.

She wished she had the sea-glass. It had been with her for so long. It had only revealed its purpose once she had come to the city—but maybe that was because there weren't things like taints at the seaside, or at least not where she'd grown up. Her seaside was not affluent enough to pay for bins to put your dog's mess in, let alone statues or gargoyles.

A dark shadow flew between her and the sky. Her head came up on reflex, but she relaxed when she saw it was just a bird, not a dragon or a gargoyle.

And then she froze again. The rain was stopping. In fact, by the time she had realized it was stopping, it had stopped. And although Edie was right to be alarmed, the thing she was about to be terrified by was something else entirely.

It was behind her.

Something emerging from the shadows, like darkness becoming visible.

# CHAPTER FORTY-THREE

## Behind Edie

Everything goes in circles: if Edie hadn't lent her sea-glass to George, she wouldn't have been thinking about the seaside and the day she was told her mother wasn't coming back. If she'd had the sea-glass, maybe she'd have sensed something. Of course, if she'd had the sea-glass in her hand, maybe it would have sensed it for her. But she hadn't, and it didn't, and so she had no idea anything was behind her until one hand closed over her mouth, and the other one pulled her into the unseeing darkness of the shadows surrounding the square.

George was puffed and had lost count of the steps. He was at three hundred and something when he got to the door at the top. He stumbled out into the wet breeze and looked at the lowering skies hanging over the disordered jumble of buildings around him. The gloom was lit with treacherous flashes of low bright winter sun that was breaking through over his right shoulder. The Thames rolled past, surprisingly close, spreading wide and flat under the familiar silhouette of Tower Bridge to the east. As he turned north he saw a cluster of taller and more aggressively shiny and modern buildings sprouting above the older grubbier office blocks. The gherkin-shaped building jutted perkily above the polished jumble of a steel and pipe work that he recognized as the Lloyds Building.

He saw a lot of tall and spindly cranes spiking like transitory weeds between the finished and half-built buildings as he kept turning westward and came to a stop facing the reassuring half-globe of St. Paul's Cathedral. It would have been a perfect view of the dome and its supporting colonnade of pillars, were it not for a modern black block that obscured the view halfway between it and the Monument. The black tower was sheathed in a distinctive diagonal grid of silver metal reflecting the few hopeful rays of sun poking through the cloud base.

As he got his breath back, he thought how sad and unloved all these roofs seemed, like the orphan bits of buildings that no one looked at or thought about unless they were up in some unusual place, like he was. And just as he checked himself for letting his mind wander, he realized the wetness in the breeze was water being blown off the cage that surrounded the walkway, not from raindrops actually falling anymore.

He looked up at the golden urn of frozen fire above him. Some of the sun was hitting it, and it glittered against the underbelly of a sooty cloud buffeting overhead. A bird flapped past and came in to roost.

He decided the flames in the urn above him looked more like a gilded thistle, or maybe an artichoke. He thought the bird perched on top of it looked like it was going to have a very uncomfortable time roosting among those spikes, no matter how golden they were.

And then he remembered how it had just stopped raining, and thought of the crouching dragons with their tigerish grins below him, and he fumbled for Edie's glass.

It was dull, but somehow humming, filling his hands with a slight but persistent vibration. He stared around at the city below.

Above him, the bird stepped off the crown of flames and occupied the air in between the sun and the glass. The shadow falling on his hands seemed to still the vibration. Without thinking, he moved the glass back into the weak sunlight and it purred into life again, just for an instant. Then the shadow flapped across it and hung there. George moved the glass, and this time the shadow anticipated him and kept the glass out of the sun. George looked at the bird.

It was a raven.

And though the whole bird/beak arrangement might well have been designed to prevent the raven from smiling, he had a strong sense that the flash of life in the beady eye was mockingly challenging him, as if to say, "Try again."

He did try again. He faked left, then thrust the glass right. The Raven moved with him, as if connected by strings. Its eye blinked sympathetically at him. And he knew for sure that this was the Raven. He noticed that the way it hung in the sky did seem to defy the basic laws of avian aeronautics. And he remembered exactly where the Fusilier had said he'd blown it to, and where, therefore, it had come back from.

The Raven looked as if he knew just what George was thinking. It seemed to nod its head in acknowledgment as it hovered there.

Knowing that it was doing everything it could to stop the sea-glass get in the sun made George determined to beat the Raven and get the glass into the light. How difficult was it going to be? As he jogged around the corner, the Raven slid through the air between him and the glimpse of sun, keeping station with him as if on rails.

"What do you want?" he shouted at it.

"*Caw,*" it croaked almost maliciously.

"Bog off!" he yelled, and held the glass out at the end of his arm. That brought it quite close to the bars on the cage, and in a move that was quick as thought, the Raven punched forward in the air, stuck its head through the bars, and tried to snatch the glass from his hand.

"No, you don't!"

George leaped backward and found himself jammed

against the stone of the Monument. He hid his hands behind him for extra safety. The Raven clung on to the bars and just cocked its head this way and then that, as if quizzically wondering for how long George thought it was going to keep this up? It looked even blacker than it normally was, with the sun directly behind it. It seemed like a hole in the light.

George felt a narrow ridge on the wall at his back. He had an idea. He placed the sea-glass on it. Then he closed his hand as if he still held it, and faked left again, then went right. The bird followed his hand as if it still held the glass, keeping it in shadow.

George spun as fast as he could. The sea-glass sat on the wall where he'd left it, caught, as if in its own spotlight, by a ray of sun. The glass hummed and vibrated and suddenly ignited in a burst of pale flame that rolled around its edges like a fiery wreath.

"Yes!" shouted George.

"*CAW!*" croaked the Raven, as near to a yelp of surprise as a beak could make.

The vibrating fiery disk shook itself off the little ridge and clinked to the floor of the cage. The Raven made a hopeless lunge for it, but missed by a yard because of the restraining bars. George dived for the sea-glass. The fire flickered greedily, so he decided not to pick it up, but he crouched over it, staring into the smooth glass rimmed by the fire.

He didn't know what he was expecting to see. Maybe

words written in letters of flame. Or a map. Or something like a swirling crystal ball. What he saw was—
nothing.

Just an opaque glass surface with a ring of flames
licking around it.

And then the flames died, and it was what it always
seemed to be—the bottom of a bottle broken long ago,
worn smooth by the sea and the beach.

He was so disappointed that, when the flames gut-
tered out, he reached for it without thinking, with his
scarred hand.

If the dragon's bite had been unimaginably painful,
this was worse, because the other bite had only hurt his
hand. This pain began in his fist as he clasped the glass.
Then it spiraled out from the pain of the mark in his
hand, coiled around his wrist, and serpentined down his
arm. It felt as though a twisting briar had grown at
immense speed, twining its thorns around his forearm,
climbing over his elbow and tightly puncturing its way
over his upper arm. And then, instead of continuing to
hurt his arm or his skin, the pain plunged inside him at
his armpit, as if the thorny briar were stabbing its roots
down into the core of him, tightening them around his
heart and his lungs and his guts. He couldn't breathe, his
heart pounded irregularly and he felt sick, sicker than
he'd ever felt before. The only thing stopping him from
throwing up was the tight grip the pain had his guts
clenched in.

And then he started to jerk and shudder as the message of the fire caught in the glass spoke to him. He suddenly felt a brief lifting of all the pain and the shuddering, and in the treacherous instant of relief, he had time to realize that this was what Edie must feel when she glinted. And then it hit him.

But what hit him wasn't the past, like with Edie.

What hit him was the *now*.

It felt like a huge and inexorable hand was forcing his head down over the glass. His eyes were wide, and he found he couldn't blink, even when they began to sting and dry out. In massive jerks of pain and nausea, the glass revealed an image, then another, and another. And what the image was, the thing that George saw, was the view from the top of the Monument. He saw the view in the direction he was facing, sprawled on the floor of the cage.

It was of a narrow square of turbid river, framed between the horizontal stripes of concrete cladding on an office building on one side, and the partially domed spire and tower of an old church on the other.

Then the view jerked forward and sideways, and he was looking at the top of an office building, where an unlikely wooden pergola twined with dying plants bordered an immense block venting steam into the sky.

Another sickening jerk and zoom, and he was looking at the curving wall of the building beyond it, a modern stone facade echoed by the contrasting curve of a line of old victorian buildings next door.

And then as the view jerk-zoomed onward in its lurching fly-through of London, he saw something he recognized: it was the base of the Black Tower, the one caged in diagonal silvered steel braces.

The pain and tightness in his guts released in the moment of recognition, and he had to focus on not throwing up as the next jerk of perspective showed him St. Paul's, before suddenly diving down and around the base of the Black Tower, and swirling to a halt in a final frame that was, he knew—because it was suddenly outlined in flames—what he was looking for.

The London Stone.

Only it didn't look like anything mythic.

It didn't look magical

It didn't look especially historical.

It didn't even look interesting.

It *did* look like one of the dingiest, saddest, most forgotten buildings in London; a building without even the dignity of age.

True, there was something at pavement level that throbbed with dim light, but the rest of the building was a ratty looking 1960s office block, dull-eyed with neglect and lack of tenants.

George stared at the final frame, trying to control his clenched gut and pounding heart, trying to make sense of how it could be that the end of his nightmare and the end of his quest seemed to lie in a place that looked like somewhere an import-export business might rent an office for a month or so, before failing and leaving without paying the rent or emptying the wastepaper baskets.

# CHAPTER FORTY-FOUR

## Old Friends, New Betrayals

When the vision glinting into George through the sea-glass stopped, and the opaque disk was just a bottle end again, he dropped it and knelt there on his hands and knees, just trying to remember how to breathe normally.

The relief he felt was huge. It was so huge that he didn't notice the first tentative tugs as the Raven managed to get its beak through the railings and grip the end of his shoelace. It was a tough bird, and what it lacked in size, it made up for in strength. On the third tug, he noticed it and turned awkwardly. The Raven already had his foot at the bars, and was determinedly flapping backward.

"Hey!" shouted George, kicking at the bird with his free leg.

The Raven jerked his foot out between the bars with unexpected force and continued to fly backward.

"Hey! Stop that!" George shouted, so appalled at the small bird's strength and persistence that he was almost laughing as well as riding a new wave of rising panic. Hysteria, he thought as he kicked at the bird again. All that happened was that he connected with the unforgiving metal bars and felt a real and wholly unimaginary pain lance up his foot and ankle.

Alarmingly, the bird took no notice and jerked George's leg out over the two-hundred-and-two-foot drop, and things suddenly didn't seem so absurd or funny anymore. It also didn't seem like he was in real danger of falling because of the metal bars, but now his upper leg was jammed through them and his hands were on the cage. He yanked his dangling leg back, and the bird stayed put.

Something gave.

It was his shoe.

His foot slid out of it, and the Raven hovered for an instant with the shoe dangling from its beak, looking like a bird that had tugged up a worm only to find it was wearing a full-size Doc Marten. The Raven spat the lace out and lunged for the disappearing trouser leg.

By the time the shoe had clomped and bounced off the paving stones below, the Raven had caught the end of George's trousers and was yanking his leg back out over the drop. He grasped the cage and pulled in the other direction, but the bird just seemed to hunch in the air and double its efforts.

"You won't get me through the cage! So let go!" George yelled. His thigh was beginning to hurt as the bird yanked it through the gap.

And then the pain eased—because the bars started to pull apart.

Something flew in and attached itself to them and began to yank them wider and wider in a hideous scree of resisting metal. It pulled them by the ugly hooks on the end of its uglier batlike wings, and as it pulled, it whistled with the effort through the length of corroding piping stuck in the middle of its wildcatlike face.

It was the cat-gargoyle from St. Pancras, the one that he had last seen on the balcony of his mother's flat.

And like the Raven, it seemed to have a strength way out of proportion to its size. It grunted and hooted through its water pipe as it tugged and strained, and George realized that it was probably strong enough to rip the bars apart, and that if it did, he was in for a long drop and a short sharp splat.

It prised the bars enough apart to get its head in and snarl at him. Instinctively he reached out to protect himself. His hand closed around the waterspout jutting at him like a verdigris-encrusted gun barrel, and he pushed at it, trying to push the gargoyle off.

"Go away!" he shouted. "I'm not scared of you!"

The gargoyle shook its head like a terrier with a rat, and George held on and kept pushing it back outside the cage.

"I'm not!" he shouted, trying to convince himself. "You're just a waterspout! An ugly bloody waterspout, made to look frightening, but you don't!"

Lying as he was, on his back, he cocked his raven-free leg for a stamping kick into the gargoyle's face.

"Get away, spout! Just get away." And he booted his heel into the thing's chest with all the strength he could muster.

There was a graunching noise as the gargoyle flew back out of the cage. One of its hooks came loose from the bars, and it swung drunkenly over the gulf of air for a moment. George tried to pull the leg being tugged at by the Raven, but the Raven seemed to be anchored in its block of air.

Then the gargoyle swung back in toward George with horrible speed and ferocity. He had just enough time to realize that its mouth was wide open and shrieking because something had changed; and then he felt the reason in his hand. A length of corroding metal pipe. He had pulled it out of the gargoyle's mouth when he kicked it, which had freed it to open its fanged mouth wide and come at him with renewed ferocity.

*Blam!*

The gargoyle was kicked to one side by a shot slamming into it from below.

*Blam!*

A second shot knocked its remaining grip off the bars. It seemed to George that it hung there in the air, like a cartoon coyote that's run out of desert and found itself bicycling on the spot over a thousand-foot canyon drop.

The gargoyle even looked comically surprised. Its newly freed mouth opened in a recognizable "Huh?" expression.

"See you, spout," said George.

*Blam!*

Spout fragmented into shards and dust, dust that whirled in the eddy of wind around the Monument, and then winnowed north-westward, toward the great train sheds on the other side of the Euston Road.

The Raven paused in its tugging, and without giving more than an inch, looked down in the direction the shots had come from. George didn't know how the Fusilier had found them, but he knew that's who it had to be.

The Raven looked back at George. It looked very disappointed. It looked very much as though it shrugged. Then it wrenched at George's leg with a fury it had only hinted at before. George's fingernails scrabbled for purchase on the gridded metal floor plates.

*Blam!*

The Raven was hit and spun like a black tufted propeller on the end of his leg. George felt a sudden release as the bird opened its beak to comment.

*"Caw!"* it said. And then:

*Blam!*

It was suddenly a puffball of oily black feathers, and

George was not only free, but running.

He descended the spiral staircase with giddying velocity. He crashed through the turnstile at the bottom and bounced out the doors, knowing he was going to see the Fusilier and Edie, and he was so elated and adrenalized that he didn't see his shoe lying on its side, where it had fallen. So he tripped on it and cartwheeled to a painful halt on the curb before he looked up at the dark figure calmly reloading its revolver.

It wasn't the Fusilier.

"You should look where you're going, young 'un," said a gravelly voice George had thought he'd never hear again. "You don't know what kind of trouble you'll run into like that."

It was the Gunner.

Edie stuck her head around his side and just grinned at George. It was the first really wide smile he'd ever seen on her face.

It opened her up like sunshine.

Her dark eyes actually sparkled with excitement and relief. He knew he felt relieved to see the Gunner, too. He felt more than relieved. He felt like . . .

"Steady," said the Gunner as George rolled to his feet and lunged at him. The Gunner put a shovel of a hand in between them, and George, who had been an inch away from embarrassing himself by hugging the big man in the full flush of his relief, gripped it and clenched it and pumped it up and down in gratitude and excitement.

"You're okay!" he exploded. "I mean, you're . . . OKAY!"

"You're not too bad yourself," grunted the Gunner, reclaiming his hand and scratching the back of his neck in something like embarrassment. "You was fighting those two like a good 'un. You've found yourself some pluck, I'd say."

"They'd have had me," admitted George. "I was just struggling, really."

"Sometimes all you can do is struggle. But long as you're struggling, you ain't giving up, and that's the half of it."

Edie was still beaming.

"He came out of nowhere. And I thought he was a taint, and then I saw it was him and then the bird came, and he was about to shoot it and then that taint *did* come, and you were fighting and he couldn't get a clear shot and then—*blam blam blam*!" She mimicked the Gunner shooting. "It was awesome!"

George looked up at the distant cage at the top of the Monument. He grinned at the Gunner.

"That was brilliant shooting!"

"It was okay."

"No, I mean, you could have missed."

"I'm not paid to miss," said the soldier, holstering his revolver. "I'm the Gunner."

George's face was aching, he was smiling so widely.

"And you're not dead."

"Not last time I looked, no."

"Last time I looked, you were badly hurt," said Edie. "You talked as if you were going to die. Then the Fusilier said your message said—"

"I thought I was. I nearly did. Snakey don't take prisoners. And he fired me up bad. I made it as far as St. James's Park and pegged out in the mud. Half drowned in one of those ponds. Thought that was my ticket punched, and that's the truth of it."

"But you got back on your plinth. Before midnight—"

"No." He rubbed his chin. "One of my lot come and found me. Carried me home. The Officer. Saved my bacon."

"And you saved mine," said George, lacing his shoe back on.

"Did you do it?" asked Edie. "Did you catch a fire?"

"I did." He grinned up at them and pointed. "It's over there. Opposite a black tower block that's sort of caged in a crisscross silver lattice. . . ."

"Cannon Street," said the Gunner. "Right. Follow me. And, Edie—try not to get lost, eh?"

He led off. They jogged after him. Edie grinned despite herself. George caught the unfamiliar expression pass across her face.

"What?" he said.

"Edie. He called me Edie." She tried to stop grinning and went red instead.

"Well, it's your name, isn't it?"

"He usually calls me 'that glint' or 'her.'"

"Well, you grow on people," George grinned at her embarrassment.

"Yeah?" She almost looked pleased.

"Mind you," said George, "so do warts. . . ."

She threw a friendly punch at him as they jinked across the road in the Gunner's wake.

"I'm glad he's back. I'm glad he's here," she said, eyes locked on the Gunner's back.

"Yeah," said George. "I'm glad you're here, too."

"Shut up."

"No, I mean it. I owe you," he said decisively.

"No, you don't."

They paused for a beat as a taxi U-turned in front of them.

"Sure I do. I mean, seriously, why are you still with me?"

"Because you came back for me. Without thinking. With that taint that had me by the head. That's why I gave you the sea-glass."

George felt uneasy. He stopped smiling. He kicked the ground.

"Edie. I didn't come back for you without thinking. I mean, I did in the end, but I did think about just running away first. . . ."

She looked at him, absorbing the truth of what he was saying.

"I'm sorry. I wish I'd been braver. Without thinking

about running away. More like him," he said, pointing with his chin to where the Gunner was waiting impatiently for them on the other side of the narrow street. The taxi finished its slow squealing maneuver and drove off. She tugged his arm and they ran over.

"Maybe it's braver to think about running away but then stay anyway. And it's not just because of that," she said. "Maybe it's because I lost my temper when the Sphinxes gave me another question. If I'd asked about the Stone Heart you'd have got there quicker."

"We'll get there quicker if you two stop gassing and keep up," said the Gunner, snapping his fingers at them.

"It's not just terror and fear that stop you thinking," Edie went on in a low voice. "Anger can do that, too. So all the stuff, some of the stuff we've been through, it's my fault. If I hadn't asked about glinting, you'd have got there in a lot straighter line."

"Or I might not have got there at all."

"No. You'd have got here. You were meant to. The mark on your hand, being able to make stuff. It's *meant*, George. I mean, I haven't a scooby what 'it' is, but it's gotta be meant. I mean, your dad—he was a maker, right? Haven't you got that far?"

He didn't want to talk about his dad. So he ignored it.

"Edie. Seriously. How could you *not* have asked what glinting was? I mean, being something, something so—I don't know—weird and frightening, and *not knowing* what it was? That'd do anyone's head in. There's no way you couldn't have asked!"

"Stop jabbering and watch the skies," said the Gunner, pausing to let them catch up. "I may have only winged that bugger."

"Yeah," said Edie, running alongside. "I don't think winging him quite does it—if it's the same bird we saw blown to pieces last night."

"It would be," said the Gunner. "You can't kill him. Any more than you can kill Memory, which is what he is."

"What?" asked Edie, stumbling on a badly laid paving stone. The Gunner caught her and put her steady on her feet without looking down. The instinctive gentleness of the gesture surprised her enough to stop her asking about the bird. She didn't know whether to say thank you or not. She was unexpectedly confused. She didn't know why.

"What do you mean?" said George.

"Memory always finds a way to survive. Even if there's no one left to do the remembering, it locks itself away in stones and waits for one of her sort to pole up and unlock it."

Edie tapped George on the arm as they ran on.

"Can I have it back?" she asked.

"What?" he said, just as the realization of what she was talking about hit him.

"My sea-glass."

"Oh," he said.

She stopped dead. He stopped a couple of paces later and turned, trying to think of a way to explain.

*"You left it!"* She choked in disbelief, saving him the trouble. "You're joking, right?"

"It was very confusing. I was being attacked. I didn't think. . . ."

Edie looked at him. The pit of her stomach dropped like an elevator with the cable cut, creating a deepening void as it plummeted. The betrayal was so sudden it made her feel giddy and nauseous.

"We'll go back for it later. I mean, soon. But after we've been to the Stone," said George, aware that the Gunner was walking back to them.

All the warmth and happiness and relief she'd felt since the Gunner came back drained away as if it had never been there at all. In its place was chill and loneliness and, at her center, the old familiar hole—the lack. She couldn't think of anything to say to him. She knew what betrayal felt like, and this was worse.

She just spun on her heel and ran back the way they'd come. In four paces she was around the corner.

The Gunner looked at George, face set and unreadable, and all the worse for that. George suddenly felt outraged. He was so close. This was nearly over.

"What?"

The big square jaw swung slowly from side to side as the Gunner shook his head in what looked suspiciously like disappointment. George's sense of outrage ramped up and spread redly across his cheeks and neck.

"What? I didn't do it on purpose! Things were happening! Remember?"

"You don't understand, son—"

"Well add it to the pile, then," spat George. "Add it to the pile of things I don't understand. I don't understand any of this, I don't want any of this, I didn't ask for any of this, I—"

"You left her heart stone behind."

"Her what?"

"The sea-glass—her heart stone. A glint's heart stone is essential to them. It's vital to what they are."

"But we're nearly there! I mean, look! We're here!"

George pointed up the alley at the Black Tower and the faceless building beyond.

The big chin swayed in a more definite negative shake. "You're here." His thumb pointed back over his shoulder. "She's there"

"But—"

"She's there. And she's without her heart stone. And she's alone."

# Chapter Forty-five

## Don't Blink

Edie ran into the little square at the foot of the Monument. The door into the pillar was closed. She couldn't believe it. They'd just been here. It had been open then. She banged hard on the painted wood, before she noticed the scrap of cardboard wedged in the glass window.

BACK IN FIVE MIN'S it apostrophized in a blotchy scrawl of red marker pen.

She stepped back and looked up at the cage in the sky. Her heart was pounding and her knees felt weak. The sea-glass would make her feel better. All she needed was to get it back close to her. As soon as she got it in her hand, she knew she wouldn't feel this hole in the core of her.

She tried to control her breathing. She kept her head tilted to the sky and closed her eyes. Five minutes was three hundred seconds, which was three hundred elephants. She counted elephants in her head, trying not to speed up, trying to make each elephant last a whole second. . . .

As Edie counts, take a snapshot of the city.

Take a frame of the scene: a girl faces a door at the foot of a tall column, her eyes closed, rocking nervily from foot to foot, long sweep of dark hair swaying in counterpoint, counting elephants in her head to keep calm.

Keep her company. Count a couple of elephants yourself.

Take another frame.

Something's missing.

The column is there.

The door is there.

The girl is gone.

Look back at the first frame, the one with the girl. There's something else, something black and blurred on the left of the frame. Something black and blurred and bull-like. Something charging at the girl.

Now look at that second frame. The two-legged bull-shaped blur is just exiting the frame on the left edge. And in its arms is a girl-shaped bundle, mouth gaping in shock.

That's how fast the Minotaur moves.

So fast that the attendant removing the card-board sign from the door at the very moment the

Man-Bull stampeded past and grabbed her, didn't see a thing.

That's how fast Edie was deleted from the scene.

Blink and you miss it.

# CHAPTER FORTY-SIX

## Walker's Deal

The Gunner's eyes bored into George's, making him want to curl up and roll away to escape the heat of their gaze. He felt the tug of the Stone at the end of the alley.

The Gunner blinked twice.

"Bloody glints. Right, then."

And he swiveled and ran off after Edie. George was shocked.

"Hey!"

The Gunner stopped and looked back.

"Where are you going?"

"Where I'm needed."

And then he turned the corner and was gone.

George wanted to help Edie. And he wanted to give back the thing he'd broken and make amends with the Stone and stop this. Maybe he could quickly—

He wasn't wearing his coat. Edie was. And the nub of dragon's head was in the coat.

"Bloody glints."

And in a surge of anger, blacker than the tower ahead of him, he ran back after the Gunner and Edie; and every step he took away from the promise of safety tore at him and made him angrier with her and her unreasonable attachment to the sea-glass.

The Gunner reached the base of the Monument. There was no sign of Edie. He craned his head and tipped the brim of his tin hat, trying to see if she was already at the top of the column. There was no one, and no sign of movement visible in the cage above.

The Gunner did a quick circuit of the plinth. By the time he got back to the door, George was running into the square.

"Where is she?"

The Gunner shrugged and pointed at the door.

"Maybe she's climbing inside. . . ."

George shook his head.

"She didn't have the money to get in." He showed the Gunner his ticket stub.

"Well, you better get in there and see. And if she's not, you better get her heart stone and all."

George thought of the three hundred and something steps, and he got angrier.

"Fine."

Then something else hit him.

"Heart stone?"

The Gunner shrugged.

"Heart stone, memory stone, seeing stone—they calls it lots of things. Oh—"

George's head was whirling.

"Hold on. I'm looking for the Stone Heart, and I've been looking for it with someone who you just remember to tell me carries something called a heart stone—and you don't think that's *important*?"

The Gunner scratched his head in embarrassment.

"Well. Yeah. No. But they never calls it 'the Stone Heart,' you know, mostly they calls it the memory stone or the heart stone. Besides"—he pounced on the thought that was going to get him off the hook he suddenly found himself on—"besides, you said the glass just showed you the Stone Heart, and it's on Cannon Street. So it's not like the glass itself, or the glin— Edie—was the stone heart all along and we missed it, is it? So no harm done, as long as we get it for her, sharpish. Talk after, eh?"

He pushed George toward the door.

He showed his ticket to the doorkeeper. The Gunner heard him explaining that he had left something at the top and being waved through with a bored mumble.

The Gunner felt relief. George had made him feel stupid, like he'd missed something. And it wasn't just because he had missed something. It was because the boy had changed. Whatever he'd been going through was making him stand straighter and take charge. He wasn't a sniveler like he'd seemed when the Gunner first saw him. He grinned.

He paced around the column again, and then something caught his attention. It was a smell. His nostrils wrinkled and he bent over a scar on the pavement. It was a scuff, but it had raised the stone slightly, as if it had been done while the paving stone was wet concrete. Except the paving stone was not concrete. It was an old stone slab. But from the grit that the Gunner picked up and rubbed between his fingers, the mark was new. And it had been made by something with the power to paw a groove in a stone slab.

He moved a yard farther back and found something that stopped him dead. It was a hoof mark, plashed into the tarmac on the edge of the road. His head came up and his hand went for his revolver.

But there was nothing to see. An office building disgorged a small crowd of men and women in dark business suits. They walked away from the Monument, chattering and laughing, their colorful ties flapping in the gathering breeze.

And then he saw it, a lone figure walking toward him against the good-humored flow of the lunchtime office workers. A tall figure in a long flapping green tweed coat, hair whipping in the wind as it escaped from a grimy John Deere hoodie.

The Walker headed straight for him.

Without trying to draw attention to what he was doing, the Gunner straightened and casually walked a few yards to his left, to stand in front of the door, in case George came out. He didn't know what the Walker wanted, but he knew he didn't want George to run into him. And he had, he realized, been expecting him ever since he'd seen the Raven trying to tug George out of the cage above his head.

"I thought you'd be along. Never far from that bloody bird, are you?"

The Walker came to a sort of pacing halt in front of him, edging from one foot to the other as he looked the Gunner up and down. He threw back the hood of the sweatshirt, exposing his gray, gaunt face to the elements. "And have you, pray, seen that damned bird? He's never quite where he should be. Were he to have been, no doubt I should have got here sooner."

"Sorry about that, mate. He had to go."

The violet eyes looked the Gunner up and down with distaste. He looked at the revolver hanging loosely in his hand.

"Had to go?"

"He was being a nuisance. If you know what I mean."

"I know exactly what you mean. He's very good at being a nuisance. It's one of his finest qualities," said the Walker.

They stared at each other.

"He'll be very annoyed when he gets back."

"Not my problem," said the Gunner.

The eyes flashed. The scowl curved into a momentary

smile of anticipation, like a hungry man smelling a bakery in the distance.

"Oh, but pardon me, I think it will be. One thing he doesn't do is forget—" The smile bubbled into a fleeting and quite unappealing simper. "—being what he is, and all—if you get my allusion."

"I get nothing from you. Where's the girl?"

"The girl?"

"I've seen the Bull's marks, Walker. Where is she?"

The Walker began to pace more obviously: three paces one way—turn—three paces back.

"I had no intention to mix my plans with the girl. The girl is a distraction to the stratagem."

"Talk English."

"I assure you that I am talking an English older and better than the oaf grunts that drop out of your mouth, my mock-martial friend," sneered the Walker. "The Bull was given an item of the boy's dress. I nearly had him at his house. The Bull followed the smell. You know how children excite his appetites."

"So why'd he get the girl?"

"In every finely judged enterprise there is the possibility of an unexpected variable. In this case it appears the boy gave the girl his coat. The Bull is not to blame."

"Where's he taken her?"

"I met him pawing his way up the path of the old Fleet Ditch. You know where he lives. Disappointed to find he brought me no boy, but a girl, I let him continue homeward with her. All you have to do is find the boy and escort him there and effect an exchange. It is an endeavor so simple that I believe even so rude a mechanical as your stolid bronze self may effect it without confusion."

The Gunner clenched his fist and decided not to plant it in the middle of the sneer. Not until he knew more.

"Just let her go."

"When you bring the boy to the Bull. And then the Bull will bring the boy to me. I don't need the girl. I need the boy. I need what he has."

"Why's that, Stone Servant?" spat the Gunner.

"There are amends to be made."

"He's going to make his amends. He's been trying to do that ever since he realized what he's done."

"Or what he is."

"He doesn't know that yet."

"You haven't told him?"

"I ain't told him because I ain't sure what he is. All that matters is that you're out of order. He's going to make his amends—"

The Walker suddenly exploded, spittle flying across the gap between them as he screamed, "Damn HIS amends! I don't give a Spanish fig for HIS amends! You think I like being a Servant of the Stone? I was a Man of Power! I HAD servants, and not just flesh and blood! I want what was broken so I can make MY amends."

He glared at the Gunner. The outburst had only intensified the fury of his gaze. The Gunner shrugged.

"Way I heard it, you have to serve the Stone because you offended it out of greed and wanting more power and all. The boy crossed the Stone without knowing what he was doing."

"So his ignorance trumps my intelligence? I think not."

"Compared with what you must have done to end up as cursed as you are, he's done nothing."

"You plead for him? How moving. Sadly, the Stone is not sentimental. If I make his sacrifice, some fraction of my curse is lifted. And maybe . . ."

His hand reached inside his John Deere sweatshirt and pulled out the figurine he had taken from George's room.

"I have his image, too. Made by a maker. The Stone may swap one servant for another—"

"Walker, I can't let you do that."

"You can't stop me."

The Gunner raised the revolver in his hand. The Walker sneered and rolled his eyes. He flicked his long straggly hair out of his face with a bored snap of his wrist.

"And you certainly can't kill me."

*Blam! blam!*

Two shots, fired so fast as to almost blend into one. The little figurine of George exploded into chips of clay and dust as the force of the bullets pinwheeled the Walker backward, his long coat scything through the air as he hit the pavement.

"But I can stop you putting his likeness on the Stone," said the Gunner flatly. "You'll not claim his soul that way."

The Walker lay there for a moment, winded. Then he snapped back to his feet in a surprisingly limber move, and dusted himself off.

They both calmly looked at the two bullet holes in the sweatshirt. By chance—perhaps—the bullets obliterated the end of the logo on the sweatshirt, turning "John Deere" into "John Dee." There was no blood.

"I liked this garment," said the Walker slowly.

"You should thank me then, Mr. Dee," said the Gunner, holstering the gun. "At least it's spelled right now."

The Walker was making a great play of examining the back of his coat, where the bullets—again without a trace of blood or gore—had emerged. Actually, he was trying to control a great rage boiling up inside him. He smiled unconvincingly, lips white with tension.

"You're just a thing. Made of metal. Made by man. Remember that. A man made you—a man can unmake you. I am a man."

The Gunner shook his head.

"You ain't a man, Walker. You ain't anything like a man anymore. And you ain't been for a long, long time."

The Walker held his hand out.

"Shoot first, think later is always a poor stratagem, Gunner." He fingered the holes the Gunner had blown in his sweatshirt. The flesh beneath was not even scarred. "These holes will cost you, because they reminded me of your—capability. Give me the bullets. I *don't* want you meeting the Bull with an unfair advantage."

"You're dreaming!"

"The trouble with being a soldier is you think you can solve any problem by pointing a firearm at it. Well, not next time. Give me the weapon or the bullets, or by the hand that made you I will let the Bull do what he will with the girl-child—boy or no boy!"

He held his hand out and snapped his fingers. "By the hand that made you, Gunner, *all* the bullets!"

The Gunner tore a small pouch off his belt and held it out. The Walker looked inside.

"And the ones in your gun, Gunner. All the bullets, none hidden, and swear it by the hand that made you."

The Gunner looked sick. He broke the revolver and upended it, holding the cylinder between finger and thumb with a dainty kind of disgust as he dropped the bullets out of their chambers into the bag in the Walker's hand.

"Swear it!" snapped the Walker.

"By the hand that made me, that's all of 'em."

"You know the penalty for breaking a Maker's Oath?"

"Oath-breaking's more your line. But I know the deal."

"Break the oath and you Wander. Forever. No child is worth that. You can only begin to imagine the pain Wandering brings."

He eyed the Gunner. Then strode off all of a sudden, his head twisted back over his shoulder.

"Find this boy. Take him to the Bull. Life for life. Fair trade. Those are my terms. And if he tries to approach the Stone without giving me what I want, if he tries to make *his* amends and not mine, I can still cause more harm to a mortal than you or any of yours can dream of. Or prevent."

And with a cloaklike swirl of his ragged tweed coat, he was gone.

# CHAPTER FORTY-SEVEN

## The Bull's Roar

Edie could breathe again. When the Minotaur hit her and scooped her off the pavement, the impact had knocked all the air out of her lungs, and she had gaped in shock for a breath that just wouldn't come. Then things had gone swirly and black, and she'd lost consciousness.

The pounding impact of the Minotaur's hooves must have jerked her awake, maybe even kick-started her lungs back into action.

She swallowed a mouthful of air that was half diesel fumes, and gagged again. Then she started to struggle. She was being crushed against a massive black chest, curved like the keel of a great boat, shaggy with rough hair that moved—despite being made of metal—like an animal pelt.

She could hear the thudding of a massive heart against her right ear. Her right eye was squashed into its chest.

She could hear the deep grunt of an animal's breathing.

She could see a fraction of London with her left eye. Enough to see that whatever was carrying her was running with the traffic, in pace with a red bus.

All these impressions whirled in and hit her at once, like a kaleidoscope.

She struggled.

She kicked.

The beast stopped dead, with a suddenness that winded her all over again. Then the hands gripped her and held her out in front of the beast's face, and she saw what had grabbed her for the first time.

She saw the head of the Minotaur.

Forehead like an anvil.

Big sledgehammer snout.

Tiny angry eyes.

Sharp curved horns sweeping out and up in an evil, man-gutting curve.

And behind the horns, behind the flattened ears, a gargantuan hump of hunched, impossibly muscled back that loomed over her like a dark mountain.

She felt blackness seeping back in on her brain, and knew she had to fight its dark pull. She knew she had to fight.

She opened her mouth to shout, to yell, to scream, but before she could think which, the Minotaur beat her to it. The head reared, the mouth opened and revealed sharp predator's teeth that were designed for anything but chewing grass, and then the Bull roared.

No words. Just a bull roar of pure fury and hunger and sound that hit her in a thunderous rolling broadside.

It contained bass notes so deep that her guts began to squirm and loosen in a fear so ancient and hardwired into her, as to be beyond explanation.

It contained notes so high that she thought her ears were going to burst with the keening pain they contained.

And as her eyes reflexively shut, her hair was blown back in a hot blast of breath that smelled of fresh meat and old charnel houses. And Edie did the only thing she could do to stop the blackness sweeping her under. She found what energy there was left in her, and screamed straight back, right into the dark wet cavern of the Bull's mouth.

Trying to outshout the devil.

# CHAPTER FORTY-EIGHT

## Time to Go

Back at the Monument, the Gunner watched the spot where the Walker had disappeared around a corner, and slowly exhaled.

"You get all of that?"

There was no reply. The Gunner turned and snapped his fingers impatiently.

"It's all right. You can come out now. He's scarpered. Gone to guard the Stone. To stop you getting there without him adjusting things a little."

George emerged from the door in the plinth. He looked white and exhausted. His eyes were fixed on the distant corner that the Walker had disappeared around.

"Who was he?"

The Gunner crouched down and picked up the two empty shell casings from the ground at his feet. He looked at the empty cylinders and put them in his pocket as he straightened up.

"The Walker. You get her heart stone?"

George pulled the sea-glass from his pocket. The Gunner grunted.

"Don't lose it. She's gonna be in a bad enough way as it is. If we manage to get her out of this and you don't give her the heart stone, she's gonna be scuppered."

"What's happened?"

"The Bull's running," said the Gunner, sniffing the air and peering into the distance.

"What?" asked George.

"The Minotaur's got her."

"Minotaur?"

"Half-bull, half-man. And all bad. Man half of him hates the bull part, and the bull part thinks the man part's what makes it unhappy. Primitive, ugly bastard— pardon my French. Dangerous too, dangerous for her."

"Why?" asked George, his mind racing back to Greek legends he barely remembered his dad having read him one long-ago holiday on an island in the Mediterranean.

"Because Minotaurs think they can make themselves less bull and more man by eating the thing they want to be."

"He's going to *eat* her?"

"Not as such. He's gonna be pulled that way, but he's under the Walker's orders, see. The Walker's a Servant of the Stone. Cursed, like—"

"Weirded."

The Gunner looked at him, impressed for an instant.

"You been getting an education while I been getting my strength back, I can see that."

"I met the Clocker."

The Gunner looked closely at him.

"Did you now?" he said slowly.

"Is he good or bad?" asked George, all of a sudden needing to know very urgently why the Gunner had used that tone.

"Plenty of time to talk about that after we get the glint."

"Edie," said George firmly. She's called Edie. "And how are we going to stop a Minotaur? I mean, that man, that thing, he took all your bullets."

The Gunner looked ashamed for an instant.

"Yeah."

"Why'd you let him?"

"Because he's a tricky bleeder. It was give him the bullets, or he gave Edie to the Bull. You heard that, right?"

"Yeah, but I didn't understand. About the oath either."

"The oath's the thing a spit can't break. Swear by a Maker's hand, and you're done if you break the oath."

"Done? Like a statue that isn't on its plinth at turn o'day? Like the Grid Man?"

The Gunner's head jerked around at the sound of a distant roar that added itself to the rumble of traffic.

"Worse. You Wander. Now shut it and let's go. We

don't have time," he said fiercely, closing George's mouth with a look as he ran off.

"Where's he taken her?" asked George, running alongside him.

"Ain't you had an education? Where do Minotaurs always take their victims? Where do they live—in the stories?" he said, leading off at a fast clip.

George racked his brains. He remembered the Greek hero and Ariadne, the king's daughter, who helped him with a spool of string so he could find his way out of a—

"Maze! He lives in a maze?" he shouted.

"In the Labyrinth. That's right."

Then questions were out of the question for a while, as George needed all his breath for keeping up with the Gunner as they crossed roads and sprinted along pavements, always heading gently uphill, mostly north, always away from the river.

The Gunner stutter-stepped on the curb edge as a bus punched past, then grabbed George and carried him in a fast jinking run across a busy, crowded street. George saw unseeing drivers racing at them, and lurched in the Gunner's arms from side to side as the Gunner dodged them, so much that he felt nauseous when the Gunner deposited him on the opposing pavement.

"But there isn't a labyrinth in London," said George unsteadily.

The Gunner snorted in derision and set off northward again.

"Some say the whole boiling lot's a labyrinth. But don't worry . . ."

He pointed to a tall dark swerve of brick buttress ahead of them. Signs for the Museum of London flashed past, and a sign reading: LONDON WALL.

"We're nearly there."

George was struggling to keep up. It seemed like he'd been running forever. His life was divided into the past, when he hadn't really run after anything except footballs, and now, when he ran all the time.

"I never heard of the London Labyrinth," he gasped.

The Gunner pointed at a wall of concrete, pierced with walkways, topped with narrow spiky high-rises.

"Lucky you. Because this is it. As dark and labyrinthine a maze as any Minotaur could want."

He pulled George into a stairwell and pounded up the steps. George read a sign and an arrow as they passed.

It read: BARBICAN.

# CHAPTER FORTY-NINE

## The Hands of the Minotaur

Screaming had done no good. Edie had never put much faith in screaming anyway, but screaming into the Minotaur's roar had been like throwing a snowball into an avalanche and hoping to stop it.

She'd heard it stop when it was all roared out. She'd felt it shake itself in the rain, like a dog. And she'd seen the look in its unexpectedly small eye as it looked at her before it ran on.

It was a look that hated what it was, and hated what it wanted.

She bunched her fist and thought about swinging at it, but the void in her sapped all energy now, and the hand just twitched.

The void was growing, and there was less Edie and more nothing because, in a horrible way, the mad bull's-eye of the Minotaur was scooping out what was left of her. It was a hungry eye, a hot eye, a horrible eye.

The Minotaur ran into a spiral staircase and, as its hooves stomped up the concrete steps, Edie tried to think of something to do. She felt she was dissolving from the inside out.

They emerged into the rain on a raised walkway. An old man with a cane was ahead of them, shuffling along in the wet. Edie reached a hand out and shouted.

"Help!"

He didn't react. Of course he couldn't see her. His mind wouldn't let him see something as unbelievable as a wet girl being cradled by a striding, bestial statue.

The Minotaur stopped. Looked at her. At the old man. And its bull's mouth twitched in a sneer and it roared again.

Now she was feeling so empty, the sound seemed to echo around her hollowness and shake every bit of her. She felt the rising blackness at the edge of her vision, and knew she wouldn't be able to fight it this time.

The Minotaur suddenly pulled her close to its muzzle, and its nostrils sucked in long and hard. It shivered as if the smell of her was some exquisite stimulant, and then, most disgusting of all, she felt the thick swollen weight of its tongue curl out of its mouth and lick her, from her neck to her ear, then over her eye and into the hair over her forehead.

And the last thing she felt before the dark closed in were the hands of the Minotaur squeezing her body, her legs, her arms, the soft bits around her kidney, like a butcher testing his meat.

And then he swept her up and ran on, as her world went, mercifully, black.

# CHAPTER FIFTY

## London Labyrinth

The Gunner led George out of the stairwell, leaving the faint smell of urine-soaked concrete behind them as they skidded out onto a raised walkway.

George slipped. The ground beneath his feet was slick with rain, a thickening downpour that was just beginning. Running in under the storm clouds felt like running toward something it was infinitely more normal to run away from. As fast as you could.

The Gunner caught him and pulled him to his feet. He stopped and looked hard at George's hand. At the scar left by the dragon. He grunted.

"What?" asked George.

"Maker's mark. The glint—Edie—told me, just before the Raven got hold of you. That mark means you got a choice, and I'd say you've made it."

"What kind of choice? I haven't chosen *anything* about this!" George protested.

"Yeah, you have. You've chosen a lot, son. You're here. You could be at the Stone, putting your world to rights. But you're here."

He nodded as if he approved of something George didn't understand.

"Standing taller, you are; taller and straighter than when I first saw you. You ain't apologizing for yourself. You're fighting."

"I'm just trying to stay alive."

"No. If you was doing that, you'd be at the Stone, making your amends, not thinking about anyone else. Not with me, trying to help her."

He looked George up and down.

"You come a long way, mate, and not just miles. And you know why you're fighting and not just sniveling?"

"Not because of this mark," said George.

"You're fighting because you got something to fight for. The mark is what got you in trouble, but it's also what might help you out of it. The mark says you might be a maker."

"I'm not a maker! I don't make anything."

But his hand was, he noticed, back in his pocket, kneading away at the plasticene blob.

"You may not know what you are, but I'll tell you what, the taints know it, and after I seen you with that dragon at Temple Bar, I think I know it. It's in your blood and it's in your bone. You done well, son. You looked to be made of pretty dodgy stuff when I first seen you. Just goes to show. It's like Jagger used to say in his studio—it's not just the clay, it's what you make of it."

George thought of his dad, quietly sucking at the cigarette parked in the side of his face, hands working at the clay in between them. Before he could think further, the Gunner ran on.

"We can talk later. We got our work cut out."

George ran after him. He realized they were in a new self-contained complex within the City. The raised walkways that they were sprinting along gave it a futuristic feel, especially if your vision of the future involved grime and blank windows staring at you as you passed.

The Gunner pulled ahead, and George followed him along a path that ran parallel with the busy street below. He could see speeding cars and taxis racing past through the glass wall on his right. George had to swerve to avoid an old man with a cane, and bounced off a dustbin that looked like it was made of rubber but felt like it was made of rocks.

He ignored the pain and kept going.

Ahead of them, the four lane street disappeared under a vast arch in a big brick and stone building, as if it were being swallowed by a whale. The top of the arch was glassed in, and he saw people blankly staring out from their tables in a restaurant, chewing under the blue neon "Pizza" sign.

They ran into a covered atrium alongside the arch, and suddenly there were shiny floor surfaces and noise and color and bright artificial light. Diagonal steel pipes pierced the glass wall on his left, buttressing the polished pink granite to his right. A sign reading "Bastion Highwalk" slid past. They ran around a statue of two frozen tango dancers out in the open air. George wished he felt as light-footed as they looked. He felt like he was dragging lead in his shoes.

He was tired, and as he and the Gunner turned and twisted, he began to feel deeply out of control, with no idea where they were going. He was getting lost in the maze.

He had an impression of open spaces to their left, a flash of green, an unlikely white church by some water, and then they were out of the fresh air again and running in a low-ceilinged space. The walkway seemed to hug the roof as it right-angled through a forest of thick concrete columns.

In this long vaultlike space he felt underground again, although his sense told him they were still high above the ground-level of the city. He found it harder and harder to breathe.

"Come on, son. Dig in," said the Gunner.

They ran toward the square of light at the end of the dim passageway.

When they clattered out into the rain, they were on the edge of a huge rectangular space, entirely closed in by balconied flats raked back like pictures of Aztec pyramids that he had seen at school. The lost-city feel was added to by the vegetation sprouting from every balcony, startlingly green against the gray concrete and the reddy-brown bricks. On the floor of this elongated piazza was an impressive stretch of water, where fountains were fighting a losing battle with the wild downpour that was eclipsing their more ordered sprinkling.

They splashed through a sheet of water on the brick beneath their feet, then along another covered walkway.

George gave up trying to keep his bearings. He just concentrated on not losing the Gunner. He stopped noticing the things and places he was running past as anything other than a blur. Except, at one point, he looked right, and found himself glimpsing something like a giant's greenhouse, with tall lush tropical vegetation and groups of schoolchildren standing beneath it, looking out at the rain.

He couldn't believe he'd been as uninvolved and bored as they looked on his own school trip only a day ago.

He felt the rain on his hot face and thought about how he'd stood out on the steps of the Natural History Museum and been so angry and so sure that being a loner was the safest way to protect himself.

Right now he'd have given anything to be part of that mindless group behind the fuggy windows—not happy, maybe, but also not scared; not exhausted, not where he was now. He couldn't believe that all he'd been through had been going on for nearly twenty-four hours.

And then he remembered that the clock was ticking down, and that unless he got to the London Stone soon, he was going to be living—perhaps not for very long—something that the Black Friar had called the Hard Way.

Ahead of the Gunner a tall new office block swept into the sky, its bottom floors flaring out like a ski jump. Lit from within, against the dark clouds and driving rain, it somehow lifted the spirits. Maybe because it was glass and light, and not wet concrete.

George felt a bit better.

The Gunner turned a corner.

And then the Minotaur hit him.

# CHAPTER FIFTY-ONE

## The Bull and the Bullet

The Minotaur hit the Gunner as he rounded the corner, coming out of nowhere, hard and low, powerful as a speeding car, horns hooking evilly up and sideways.

There was a concussive thump of impact, and the noise of the air being knocked out of the Gunner mixed with the fierce grunt the Minotaur made as it bunched its massive neck muscles and tossed him up and over its back.

The horns caught in the bridle chains on the Gunner's belt, and sent them jingling across the wet pavement.

The Gunner hit the ground and rolled and skidded to a halt against a concrete tub in a great spray of rainwater.

The Minotaur turned.

And it was only when it turned that George saw that its arms were crossed over its chest, in a grotesque parody of cradling a baby—except the thing it was cradling was no baby, but Edie.

It was no Edie that George had ever seen. She was so pale she seemed a pearl-colored ghost of herself clutched against the blackened bronze of the Bull's chest like a rag doll. Her eyes were shut, and George had a horrid thought that she was dead—until he saw the working of her lips as they repeatedly tried to say something, like a sleep talker.

"EDIE!" he shouted.

Wherever she'd gone inside her head was a place from which she couldn't hear him. The Minotaur stamped the ground with one of his hooves, and George felt the whole walkway shake like worlds colliding.

The Minotaur held one hand out and made a very human beckoning gesture at him.

"Stay put," growled the Gunner, hoisting himself to his feet and stumbling in between the beast and the boy.

"What are we going to do?" said George, voice catching in a suddenly dry throat.

"I'm gonna drill the beggar."

He pulled his revolver and pointed it at the Minotaur.

"Oi. Bully-beef. Over here."

The Minotaur tensed when he saw the gun.

"But you haven't got a—" began George.

"Yeah, I have," said the Gunner without breaking eye contact with the Bull over the notch sight on the revolver.

"But you swore—"

"Too clever by half, the Walker. You want to fool a bloke who thinks he's made of brains, try something simple. Kept my thumb over one chamber when I shook the rest of 'em out. We got one shot here."

"But you broke your oath!"

The Gunner's face tightened, all the planes flattening into a defensive mask of indifference.

"My choice. The girl didn't sign up for this. Can't let it happen."

"But you'll—"

"Don't want to hear it," snapped the Gunner. He raised his chin at the Minotaur. "Put her down, Oxo. Nice and gentle."

The Minotaur didn't put Edie down. He shook her out of his arms, hanging limp and ragged as a tea towel, and held her by the shoulders in front of his torso like a shield.

"Nasty blighter, aren't you?" said the Gunner.

The Minotaur snorted.

*Blam!*

The revolver rocked in the Gunner's hand. The Minotaur didn't move. The detonation woke Edie, and her eyes struggled to make sense of where she was.

"Wha—?" was all she managed to say.

The Minotaur threw back its head and roared in a blast of rage and, George realized, triumph. The sound of the roaring echoed off the concrete buildings around them. Then it lowered its head and growled dangerously.

George couldn't believe his eyes.

"What happened?"

The Gunner swallowed.

"I missed."

George felt like the walls of the world were falling in on him. His chest felt tight, and breathing started to be a problem.

"What do you mean, you *missed*?" he asked jerkily.

"I didn't hit it." He looked at his gun in disbelief. "My luck must have started to turn already."

"You're the Gunner. You *don't* miss!" George hissed. "You said so!"

"I also said don't believe everything people tell you."

There was a pause as George's brain wobbled alarmingly on its gimbals.

"No, you didn't! You didn't say that!"

"Oh." The Gunner looked faintly embarrassed. "Well, I should have." He cleared his throat and spat into a puddle. "I'm saying it now."

The Minotaur was pawing the ground. Actually, he was pawing concrete and raising nasty ridges with his hoof as easily as if the concrete had been butter.

"Shoot it again," said George urgently. He wasn't thinking straight. He was in full pre-panic mode. "Shoot it before it charges."

"With what?" asked the Gunner. He broke open his revolver. The spent shell casing hit the puddle at their feet in a mocking, empty tinkle and plop.

"I'm out of bullets. Remember?"

Now it wasn't just the walls closing in. The floor dropped out of George's world.

"WHAT?"

The Gunner showed him the empty gun.

"Bu— Wha— Then how are you going to rescue her?" George burbled.

The Gunner shrugged with a fatalistic gesture George felt was entirely out of keeping with the seriousness of their predicament. Twenty feet away there was death, calmly plowing concrete with its hoof.

Edie just stared at them, her eyes spread wide in shock.

"Dunno, son. I mean, with another bullet maybe I can blow him into tomorrow, and we'll be long gone; but without a round to put up the spout"—he pointed at the Minotaur—"he'll rip me open from stem to stern. And you and all. And you know what Minotaurs do to little girls?"

"No"

There was a pause. The Gunner sniffed.

"Lucky you. Best not think about it. They're messy eaters."

George was hopping up and down in frustration.

"So what can we do?"

"Go down fighting?" said the Gunner.

George didn't want to go down, fighting or no fighting. The Gunner's attitude was tough and brave, but for the first time he found it—annoying. He needed to think. . . .

His hand thrust into his pocket and reflexively kneaded and shmooshed at the plasticene blob. And suddenly he knew.

"Give me the empty shell."

"What?"

"DO IT!"

The Gunner reached into his pocket and pulled out one of the empty casings. He flicked it over his shoulder. George's scarred hand reached out and caught it on reflex.

"I'm going to make a bullet."

The Gunner turned one stunned eye on him.

"You what?"

George was already wodging the plasticine into the empty shell casing. The Gunner snorted.

"Out of *plasticene*?"

George didn't even look up. His hands were working fast.

"If I'm this 'maker,' if this scar is the mark of a maker, then why not? I'll make a bullet!"

"Yeah, but plasticene . . ."

"You're made of bronze, but you're soft enough to move. No reason why it shouldn't work the other way. If I make it well enough. Like you said, it's not just the material, it's what you make of it," said George. "Keep your eye on the Bull."

There was new mettle in George's voice, and the Gunner found he was swiveling both eyes forward as he'd been told. As he'd been *ordered*. He whistled slowly.

"You're the boss. But speed up a bit, because he's about ready to steam in and try to hook us."

There was a scuff of hoof on paving stone, and a soft thud as the Minotaur dropped Edie.

"Here he comes."

"Slow him down. Buy me time," snapped George.

"Yes, sir," said the Gunner through a tight smile. "Here. Cop hold of this. I'm gonna have my hands full."

He handed the revolver backward, fast, and then turned to meet the charging Minotaur head-on.

The horns went to either side of his waist, and the Gunner threw himself into a backward roll, letting the force of the impact keep them going. George had to leap sideways to avoid being steamrollered flat by the two falling statues. The bullet shape got mashed flat in his fall.

He ran across to Edie, who was sprawled over the edge of a concrete planter. He heard a crash behind him, and saw that the Gunner and the Minotaur had rolled in a complete somersault. The clash had been the Gunner's boots hitting the ground again and bracing himself. He held the Bull's horns like bicycle handles as the Minotaur bulldozed him across the paving toward the edge of the walkway.

Sparks flew as the hobnails on his boots were

scraped back across the stone beneath.

George grabbed the sea-glass out of his pocket and closed Edie's limp hands on it. He heard her murmur, but didn't get what she was saying because he was busy rolling the plasticene in his hand.

"Hurry up, son!" shouted the Gunner.

George was already repairing the bullet he was trying to make.

Edie saw what he was doing. Her eyes were suddenly blazing, as if the intensity of the sea-glass were coursing through her body and beaming out of them.

"Good, George. *Make* it work."

He didn't have time to nod. He rolled and molded the plasticene.

The Gunner was backed up against the railing. A drop beckoned beyond, down into a busy street. He was fighting the immense power of the Minotaur's bovine muscles. He clenched his teeth and pushed back.

"Thing . . . about you, Oxo, is that . . . you'd make someone a very . . . nice . . . stew. Or a rissole."

The Minotaur shook its horns. The Gunner held on and rode the spasm.

"You know what rissoles are, don't you, Oxo?"

The Minotaur snapped his head right and left. The Gunner only just held on.

"They're sort of meatballs. Now—there's a thought."

And his iron-shod ammunition boot swung brutally upward between the straining legs of the Minotaur like a sledgehammer. He kicked with all the pent-up force in his body, and the Bull's feet jerked an inch off the ground as his boot clunked home.

The Minotaur bellowed in pain and fury. George felt the force of the roar hit him like a shock wave. The earlier echoing bellow was a whisper in comparison. The Bull shook loose and tried to gore the Gunner right through the chest. The Gunner twisted sideways, and the impact sent more sparks flying off the railing behind him.

"Make it, George," said Edie urgently.

He ducked his head and concentrated on the plasticene and the empty casing. He worked it into a flattened cone. As he worked he tried not to hear the grunting and clashing beyond him. He thought of bullets. He thought of what they can do. He thought of what he'd seen them do. He saw them pulverizing the salamanders at the Gunner's memorial. He saw the Raven blown to feathers, twice. He saw the gargoyle blown to powder on the cage at the Monument. He remembered the bullets in the Gunner's hands as he calmly reloaded. He imagined the force that a bullet carries as it crashes through its target. As he thought of what a bullet was, of what he'd seen, of how they looked, he found his hands loosening and almost working by themselves, almost as if they knew what he was doing. And, he noticed, the pain of the scar stopped completely.

He smoothed the top of the plasticene bullet, and

with the nail of his thumb, traced a delicate circle around the top of it, just as he had seen on the real bullets.

He broke the gun and stuck the bullet in it, as he'd seen the Gunner do.

There was a sudden whirlwind of flailing legs and hooves and horns as the two statues crashed past. They hit a concrete tub of plants so hard that it cracked and spilled earth onto the ground around their scrabbling, brawling bodies. George ran across and held out the gun.

"Done it!"

And the Gunner looked at him, and in that instant the Minotaur saw an opening and hooked a horn through his midriff.

It flashed and sparked like a grinding wheel as the sharp point went in low and to the side.

"Uh," said the Gunner in shock.

George couldn't believe the Gunner was gored.

Not after he'd come back.

Not after he'd thought he was dead.

The Minotaur jerked its head, twisting the horn in the wound with the ferocity of a terrier shaking a rat, pushing the Gunner back to the railing high above the street below. The Gunner took the railing in the small of his back as he raised his hands to club down on the Bull's neck. His hands changed direction and scrabbled ineffectually at the rail.

George was horrified. The Gunner surely hadn't just

come back to die again? He felt the black taste in his mouth, felt it tingle spikily in his nose, and found he was running forward, cocking the gun with both thumbs and aiming right at the thick-boned crown of the Bull's head.

"Eye," grunted the Gunner.

George stepped around the side and adjusted his aim. Not for an instant did the blackness give him room to think that the gun would *not* fire. He'd made a bullet. That was all he knew. And now he was going to use it to save his friend. His friends.

The Minotaur's eye rolled up and looked down the barrel of the gun. It was full of nothing but hate and appetite, and as it roared and pushed, George took up the slack on the trigger.

And then, before the gun fired, there was a *crack,* and the Minotaur and the Gunner were gone.

George's world had narrowed into such a tightly focused cone of vision that he had to step back to make sense of what was happening. His finger loosened on the trigger as he did so.

The Minotaur had pushed the Gunner over the railing, which had buckled, sending them both into thin air over the busy street.

George swung over the void to see what had happened.

*Crash!*

The Gunner and the Minotaur sprawled in impact on the red roof of a double-decker bus. As they hit, the

Gunner twisted, and the horn slid out of his side like a sword leaving its scabbard.

He had enough strength to boot the Bull's face and send it over the edge of the roof. The Bull's hand clamped onto the side as the bus pulled away, unaware of the Minotaur hanging from its offside rear and the Gunner spread-eagled on top of it.

Edie joined George at the railing.

"He's hurt!"

"Yeah," said George, hoping she hadn't noticed that it was him talking to the Gunner that had caused him to take his eyes off the Minotaur for the crucial second it took for him to get gored. "We better get after him."

They ran for a staircase.

"Hide the gun," said Edie.

He snatched a look at her.

"People don't notice us when we're with the spits because they can't see them and so we don't make sense. But two kids on the street, one carrying a cannon like that? Do the math!"

He saw she was back to her old self and decided not to comment on it as they descended the spiral staircase to the street, three steps at a time.

# CHAPTER FIFTY-TWO

## Death from Above

The bus picked up speed. On its roof, the Gunner got painfully to his knees and bent over the hole in his side.

"Just a hole. None of the important stuff. People live with worse."

He pulled a field dressing from his webbing and loosened his jacket. He pressed the dressing to his side and grimaced as he quickly wound the tapes around his midriff and tied them off.

"Sound as a pound," he grunted. Nevertheless, he slumped back and sat with his legs wide.

"Get me breath back."

His breath was coming hard. He leaned his head back and looked at the sky and the clouds and the rain dropping into his upturned face.

An angry roar snapped him back into the now.

The Minotaur was hauling itself back onto the roof at the rear of the bus.

The Gunner looked around. He couldn't see anything he could use as a weapon. The bus was accelerating toward an intersection. The traffic light hanging over it had just changed to green. The Minotaur got to its feet.

The Gunner dragged himself upright and braced himself to meet it.

"Come on then, Oxo. Do your worst."

He knew that the longer the bull kept its mind on him, the longer the kid and the glint had to make themselves scarce. He flicked a look behind him at the approaching intersection.

"I don't approve of hurting dumb animals, but in your case I'll make an exception."

The Bull roared and charged. The Gunner braced, and as the Bull was about to hit him, he squatted low—and as the Bull made contact, the Gunner used all the remaining strength in his body to thrust upward. He put everything into it, and felt the just-tied straps on his dressing break as he flexed.

If it hadn't been for the scything horns and the Minotaur's shriek of rage, it would almost have looked funny, like two ungainly ballet dancers, one throwing the other into the air in a clumsy lift.

The Bull's impetus met the Gunner's upthrust. Its hooves left the roof and its legs bicycled in midair, and then there was a *thunk*, and the Gunner dropped back on the roof of the bus and the Minotaur stayed where it was, suspended over the intersection, its horns jammed over the steel arm holding the traffic lights above the unseeing traffic.

It roared in rage as the Gunner pulled away on the top of the bus. Its roar was loud enough to turn the rainwater that was beading on the bus roof into a spray that hit the Gunner in the face. He blinked and waved at the Bull.

"Cheerio, cock. Always say beef should be well hung, don't they?"

He couldn't bring himself to grin at his joke. He watched the struggling Minotaur until the bus turned a corner and he couldn't see it anymore. Then he bent over his burst wound dressing and concentrated on reattaching it.

At least the kids were safe now, he thought. And that thought did give him an reason to grin as he hunched over the growing pain in his side.

George and Edie sprinted down the street in the wake of the bus. The revolver bumped heavily in George's pocket as he ran. Luckily, it was a one-way system, so there was no chance of losing the bus if they moved fast. A tall lorry kept pace with them, blocking out the sky.

They rounded a curve to find there was a lot of traffic, but no bus to be seen. The lorry pulled away from them.

"Where did they go?" panted Edie.

"Dunno," answered George. "He'll probably be okay, don't you think?"

"I hope so."

She rummaged in her pocket for the sea-glass.

"We're okay, aren't we?" he said.

The glass was blazing.

"No," she said.

They turned around, scanning the street. They could see nothing.

"What is it?" said George, his hand closing around the suddenly comforting shape of the revolver handle in his pocket.

"*Where* is it?" said Edie, puzzled.

There was a noise. A small one. A creak, from above them. As one they stopped panning the streetscape and looked up, straight over their heads.

Something dark and horned wrenched itself free from the traffic lights over their heads and dropped like an anvil.

They had time to jerk out of the way of its hooves as it crashed to the ground, but not enough time to escape the grabbing hands that caught them—Edie by the upper arm, George by the throat.

They had no time to cover their ears and escape the blast of victory that roared from between the Bull's teeth as he lifted them in the air and bellowed triumph at the storm clouds above.

George could see Edie struggling and kicking and trying to shout something at him, but he couldn't hear a word. And before he could think what to do next, the

Minotaur had jerked him down to its muzzle and was sniffing at him, and then tasting his face with a tongue like a thick slug.

George gagged, and then he was lofted in the air, and he saw Edie being sniffed at in turn. And as the tongue lolled out and swirled over her hair and head, he saw the plea in her eyes and the way she flinched; and he saw too how the flinching pleased the Minotaur, and saw its strange mouth twist into an openmouthed panting smile; and it was much more than George could take.

It wasn't the beast's leer, so much as the look and the flinching shudder in Edie's eye that spiked the protective anger that made his hand pull out of the jacket with the revolver in it.

He held steady and tried to keep still as he pointed it at the Minotaur.

And as he did, Edie managed one tight little word of reminder.

"Eye."

And he adjusted his aim and found the hot eyeball rolling up to meet his over the gun sight, and the Bull began to roar, and the black prickly feeling flushed up into him. And not for a moment did he think the bullet he'd made wouldn't work; only that he might spoil this by missing. And so as the heavy gun shook in his hand, he thought of nothing but controlling the shake; and everything was suddenly still, and the tiny eye he was targeting suddenly seemed big as a barn door and:

*Blam!*

George felt the gun buck in his hand. The roaring was cut off like a knife. The Bull's hands spasmed open, and George and Edie dropped to the ground.

The Bull's head rocked back, then forward, then back again, shaking faster and faster, its mouth straining to make a noise as it juddered horribly like it was trying to shake the bullet—George's bullet—out of its head. Then it stood up, looked at George with an eye leaking something like molten bronze, snarled, and began to lunge at him—then dropped like a stone.

For a long beat, all George could hear was his own breathing and heart pounding.

"Bull's-eye," said the Gunner.

George pulled Edie to her feet, and they watched the soldier limp toward them behind a battered but defiant smile.

At their feet the Minotaur's carcass began to collapse into a fizzing heap of bronze filings that the wind caught and began to disperse.

"Bloody brilliant. Now tell me you ain't got a maker's hands. And just in the nick of time, eh?"

The Gunner was hurt, George and Edie could see from the way he walked, hunched to one side, one hand holding the dressing tight around him.

"At least he can walk. Probably means it's going to be okay, don't you think?" said Edie quietly.

George checked his watch. It was 3:13. He reached

for the pocket in his coat, the coat Edie was still wearing. He found the dragon's head.

"Look. I've got to get to the Stone in less than half an hour," he said. "I better go. Then I'll come back, and we can figure out a way to help you back to your plinth before midnight."

She took off the coat and passed it to him.

"We go together," said the Gunner. "We've come this far together, we end this together."

"But you're hurt."

"I know. My luck turned—"

"Because you broke your—"

"Enough talking. We need to move. And you need me, son, because the Walker's gonna be guarding the Stone, and I ain't done all this to have you walk into his hands at the last minute, right?"

He led off, straightening with every step, visibly pushing the pain out of his consciousness as he went.

# CHAPTER FIFTY-THREE

## Black Tower

Opposite the neglected facade of the office building, in whose unprepossessing facade the London Stone is embedded, is a railway station.

Outside the station, like most stations in London, there is a stand for a man selling newspapers.

People have been filling the streets of the city with the noise of them crying their wares ever since the idea of trade arrived. The man advertising the name of his paper had ruined his voice through a combination of all-weather shouting and three packs of high-tar cigarettes a day. The sound he made was a raw shorthand rather than a clear description of his product.

"*Stannid*! Gitcha *Stannid*!" he shouted every twenty seconds.

He spent the remaining time hawking and spitting and wiping a runny nose. The noise was beginning to annoy the Walker, who was pacing the meter of pavement behind him, in the shadow of the Black Tower.

He avoided a splat of phlegm that the news vendor hoiked behind him, and decided enough was enough. If the Raven were here he could be more relaxed, as the Raven's eyes missed less than it forgot, and of course, it forgot almost nothing. As it was, he had to stand sentry on the Stone across the street, and this yelping coughing man was distracting him.

He put his hand out and touched him. The man turned, shocked to find someone had been so close to him all this time. Before the man could say anything, the Walker smiled and spoke quietly.

"Go home. You're sick. You're probably very, very ill. You may die."

The news vendor started shaking. He forgot he'd just seen the Walker. He didn't realize he'd been spoken to. He just felt terrible—ill and full of fear. It was the bloody smokes.

He snapped the lid on his metal stand closed and locked it. He felt panic building in his chest. He wondered if he'd get home before his heart attacked him.

The Walker smiled in satisfaction, unconsciously rotating the stone fragment on the chain around his neck with one hand as he watched the man shuffle off in an explosion of coughing.

He backed around a pillar and reached into his pocket. He was sure he could make the boy not see him if he came close to the Stone, but he knew that the Gunner, if he was still with them, would see him. So he pulled a silver disk from his pocket. It was the same size and shape as a woman's powder compact. He twisted the disk. There was a click, and it revealed itself to be two mirrors that clipped together for carrying. He pocketed one, and held the other around the edge of the pillar. He angled it so that he could get a good view across the street, and paced imperceptibly on the spot, eyes fixed on the Stone. As he watched, he licked his dry lips, one hand loosening the ancient dagger in the scabbard at his belt.

# Chapter Fifty-four

## Tempered Steel

The Gunner stopped them on the corner of the road leading onto Cannon Street, where the Black Tower rose into the sky in its cage of angled silver tubes.

"You don't move until I whistle. When I whistle, you know I've got him, or the coast is clear."

George checked his watch. It read 3:31.

"I've got eleven minutes." His voice was calm.

"You've got time. Don't show yourselves. I'm gonna go around the back. See where the evil bugger is."

Edie put her hand out to stop the Gunner. As she touched him, a wave of impressions flowed into her. It wasn't like glinting. It wasn't fear. It didn't have the slicing inalterable pain of the past. It was fluid, but it had a dark underthrob to it, like a tooth about to go bad.

"Wait," she said. "Something not good's going to happen."

He gave her a long look. Then a short smile.

"Glints see the past. Not the future. And bad stuff happens all the time. That's why we keep doing what we do."

"It's not that—"

He headed off at a trot.

"Later, eh?"

"What did he break?" said Edie, her eyes glued to his disappearing back. George leaned against the closed box of a newspaper stand as he answered.

"He swore an oath that he wouldn't bring a bullet against the Minotaur."

"What does that mean?"

"He put himself in harm's way, like taking on a curse or something. To save us."

"You mean me," she said dully. Then some of the old fire returned, and her chin jutted tightly. "I didn't ask him to."

She kicked angrily at the newspaper stand. It clanged satisfactorily, but it didn't make her feel any better.

"Sorry. It's my bloody temper. It's always my temper. If I'd kept it . . ." She looked away.

"What?"

"Nothing."

George's hand reached for her shoulder. She shrugged it off. He didn't, however, let go.

"Edie. What?"

"If I'd known how to control my temper, I don't think I'd be where I am now. I wouldn't be alone. I'd have a family." She fired out a short laugh that sounded half a sob. "I'd have a dad, anyway—of sorts. If I'd controlled myself."

They stood there for a long time, his hand on her shoulder, his eyes on her back. Her eyes somewhere else entirely, somewhere with the sea on the horizon and pebbles underfoot, and a train rattling past full of unseeing eyes and a driver waving happily, misreading everything he was seeing and turning away before he saw what she had had to do to the man behind her.

"It just comes. It blows through me. Like a wind. I can't close the doors and keep it out. It blows in like this black wind and I go with it, and then it's . . . and then I . . ."

"It's okay. It's going to be okay."

"No, it's not," said a voice corroded by ill humor. "Not for you. Nothing is ever going to be okay again."

The Walker had materialized behind George, holding the dagger's long blade at his throat.

# CHAPTER FIFTY-FIVE

## London Stone

The Walker's free hand patted George's coat pockets. George couldn't move. The razor-sharp blade brushed his Adam's apple so closely that he didn't dare swallow.

"Please," he said, trying to keep his voice steady. "I just want this all to be over. I just want to go home."

The Walker's teeth appeared in a humorless snarl.

"No one goes home. No one ever goes home."

Edie's leg began to shake. She stamped it to stop the tremor. It didn't work.

It wasn't just the knife, or the man in the big green coat, or the venom in his voice. All that was bad; all that was very, very bad. But it was as nothing compared to the thing that really terrified her.

What terrified her, what dropped the floor out of her world, was the fact that she'd seen the long burnished knife and the Walker before.

And she knew he was capable of slitting George's

throat without losing his smile, because the last time she'd seen him he had been drowning a little girl in a hole in the ice, at the Frost Fair.

But even that was not the worst thing. The worst thing was too awful to think about, so she stamped down on it by screaming at him.

"Leave him alone!"

The Walker ignored her completely as his hands scrabbled more and more desperately in George's pockets.

"Where is the thing you broke, boy? Just tell me. All I want is the thing you broke. All I want to do is put it on the Stone. . . ."

He felt the dragon's head in the side pocket of the coat. George could smell his breath, sweet with decay and hunger as he talked into his ear.

"Here we are. Take it out, boy, and hand it over. I shall make amends. The Stone will smile on me."

Edie felt a tug between her and the Walker. He was so busy watching George pull the broken carving out of his pocket that he had stopped looking at her. She had felt the tug before, but it was usually when something especially nasty was trying to make her touch it. Things with deep sadness exerted this kind of pull. She never went into churchyards, for example, because some headstones yanked at her like magnets. But no human had ever exerted such a tug. And then she saw what it must be.

The stone with the hole in it.

The one on the choker around the Walker's neck.

"Leave him alone!" she shouted.

The Walker raised his violet eyes and stared at her. Took the blade off George's throat and waved it at her in fast steely zigzag.

"Shut up, milady, or I'll open you up like a sack of peas. You'll spill all over the pavement, and you know what? Nobody will care."

"Yeah, they will," said George. And while the blade was still waving at Edie, and not brushing his throat, he gripped the stone dragon's head and smashed it back over his shoulder into the Walker's face with all the strength that he could put into it.

The Walker staggered back, one hand going to his eye, the other slashing the wicked blade at the space where George was. Only, George wasn't quite there. He was rolling sideways, out of the Walker's grip, trying to get free. He nearly managed it.

The blade lightly scraped his ribs, cutting a foot-long slash in his shirt, and jabbed through the tough wool of his jacket. The dagger held fast, and the Walker used it to yank George back toward him. George desperately tried to get his arms out and escape the jacket, but there wasn't enough time.

"Now you die, boy! You didn't have to, but now you do—by the Stone I swear it!" screamed the Walker. "And if you have blinded my eye, by the Stone I will make you SUFFER on the way to your quietus!"

"NO!" yelled Edie. And she leaped at the Walker like

a wildcat, giving in to the tug of his stone, suddenly, intuitively knowing what she was going to do.

The Walker saw the girl spring at him, dark hair swinging, eyes blazing, and though he tried to wrench the dagger around to impale her, he felt not rage or anger, but something he had almost forgotten about, something he had not felt for centuries.

He felt fear.

George smashed the dragon's head down across the Walker's knuckles, sending the dagger skittering across the pavement.

Edie's right hand went for his throat. It closed around the stone on his neck. Her left hand grabbed on to the Walker's ear and clamped tight. She felt the metal of his earring press painfully into her hand, but she kept holding on like a terrier.

And the past slammed into her in the old familiar juddering slices of pain and nausea.

Her hair blew out in a radius as the shock hit her. The Walker's head snapped back. His coattails also flew out in a fan, as what she was glinting hit him, too.

George managed to rip out of the sleeve of his jacket just as the first time-sliver sheared into Edie's brain.

And this is what she saw.

A room in a palace.

Courtiers in doublets and hose, swords at their sides. White ruffs around their necks.

Leaded-glass windows reflecting candles.

A woman in a dress as wide as a galleon sweeping across the floor, hair red as flame, a ruff around her neck. Face above it whiter than the ruff. She said something to a bowing man.

". . . not fail us, John Dee," was all Edie heard, as the woman handed him a purse and swept on. The man raised his head and watched her go.

It was the Walker.

Time sliced. Edie rode a wave of nausea. Tried to close her eyes. They jerked open again.

Now she was in a dark workshop.

The only light came from a candle and a brazier.

A skullcapped figure poured liquid fire from a metal pot into a mold.

As the liquid fire cooled, the light dimmed, and in the reddening glow she saw the man turn and shout something angry.

Again it was the Walker.

Time jerked her nightward.

Now she saw a street.

Old London by moonlight.

Half-timbered buildings overhanging the cobbles.

A church.

Beside the church, in the road, a square pillar.

By the pillar, the Walker.

Beneath the pillar a carved sign reading LONDONE STOUNE.

A flash of metal.

The clink of a hammer.

The Walker chiseling a lump off the stone.

And the wind rose and winnowed the leaves across the cobbles. And there was a rushing noise, like many wings suddenly appearing.

And the Walker froze guiltily.

And then the perspective lurched and tore in toward the back of the Walker's head, as if about to attack it, and he turned, and his eyes widened in sheer horror and he screamed, "NO!"

The past finished, and Edie was back in the present, and the Walker was still screaming, wide-eyed in the here and now.

She released the stone and backed away.

A dark figure slammed in past her shoulder and grabbed the Walker from behind in an immense disabling bear hug. Then turned and looked at them.

It was the Gunner.

"I thought I told you two to keep out of sight!"

And even though she was still feeling sick, Edie joined him and George in a grin.

"Now, what's the time?"

# CHAPTER FIFTY-SIX

## Sacrifice

The Gunner held the Walker tight in his massive bronze embrace, his arms pinioned to his side. The Walker's head was slumped forward, his black and gray hair tumbled over his face in greasy straggles. Whatever it was Edie had glinted had sucked the will and energy out of him, it seemed.

George looked at his watch.

Four minutes.

"I better go."

"Yeah," said the Gunner. "And good luck."

There was something in the way he said it that made George stop and turn.

"What happens? When I put the head on the Stone?"

"You get what you want. It's over."

"And what does that mean?"

"Hurry up," said Edie.

"Tell him," said a vicious voice. The Walker's head

raised a little, and a violet eye peered at George. "Tell him to say good-bye."

George felt there was a long list of questions that he should know the answers to, but that he now didn't have enough time to ask.

"What happens?"

The Walker shrugged.

"It ends. You make your amends. You return to your vision of safe happy London, *sans* spits, *sans* taints, *sans* anything strange and unexplainable to disturb your soft happy life. And good riddance to you."

"But I'll remember all this, right?"

"Edie," said the Gunner, "get George to the Stone."

"If I put this on the Stone Heart, are you saying that I—what? I forget you all?"

The Walker spat.

"Stone Heart? That isn't the Stone Heart. It's the London Stone. And yes. Make your trifling amends and return to your even more irrelevant existence," said the Walker.

"Edie!" snapped the Gunner.

She took his arm and pulled him toward the shabby building with the stone embedded in its facade. His mind was racing.

Behind them, the Walker struggled, worming his hands into his coat.

"No, you don't," said the Gunner, squeezing him tight.

Edie pulled George up to the low grating in the building side. Behind it the Stone sat there, innocent as any other lump of masonry. Except, Edie could feel a dark, massy pull reaching out from it. She stepped back.

"Go on, then."

He checked his watch. One and a half minutes. Ninety seconds to say something that made sense. Except he didn't think anything made sense. Especially what he was really thinking.

He looked at Edie. Her jaw was set in its habitual jut, but there was a smile, and above it were shining eyes nearly as dark as the hair that framed them.

"I'm a bit scared," he said.

"Everyone's scared," she said.

"If I do this, I think I won't . . . I mean, you'll be . . . or I'll be in a London, where none of this makes sense. So I won't believe you." He cleared his throat. "I won't know you. I mean, you'll still be in this—this un-London. This scary place. And you'll be alone."

"I'll be fine," she said, hearing that she was saying his words back at him. "Hurry."

She widened the smile, and her eyes seemed to shine that bit brighter. He looked at her.

"You're not scared of anything."

"I know. So I'll be fine. Go on."

He looked at her. Wanting to remember it all. Her face, the jaw set, the chin jutting at him below a tightening little smile.

442

"Edie, what if the Sphinxes gave me an answer that has two meanings? I mean, that would be perfectly like them, right?"

"George, get a bend on, will you? You know what the Sphinxes said: 'To end this, you must find the Stone Heart, and then make sacrifice for that which was broken by placing on the Stone at the Heart of London that which is necessary for its repair!' Do it! Time's running out. Remember what the Friar said about that!"

And the mention of the Friar jolted George, and it jolted him because he remembered what the Friar had said about Sphinxes spinning riddles even when they were answering. At the same time, out of the corner of his eye he saw the Walker trying to squirm out of the Gunner's grasp, and he thought of the derision with which he'd said the London Stone was not the Stone Heart—

—and then he thought of the Friar again, and it was with such a sharp immediacy that he almost believed he could hear the rolling, cheery voice as it chuckled, *—What could be better for them than an answer with two meanings? Except one with three! What is the Stone Heart? Who can say?*

He turned on Edie, the new thought bursting out of him in a geyser of words.

"Edie, wait, stop talking, just listen. Just listen! The Stone Heart and the Stone at the Heart of London? What if they are two *different* things, instead of two ways of describing the same stone. What if this London Stone is the Stone at the Heart of London, but the Stone Heart is something else entirely, something we're missing?"

She shook her head. Not wanting to entertain anymore talking, wanting to get this over.

"Like what? I mean, forget it—"

"I don't know what the Stone Heart would be then, but you know what the Friar said, he said it could be anything, anyplace, anyone—"

"No time for this, George—" she said flintily.

He felt desperate, like he was almost grasping it.

"No, seriously, what if there's more to this than me just making good what I broke and going home to extra maths and a bunch of kids who don't like me any more than I like them? I mean, Edie, look!"

He showed her his hand, the one with the maker's mark.

"I made a *bullet*, Edie. And it *worked*! What if—?"

She shook her head and cut him off.

"There's no time for 'what if,' George. This is when you do what you do—and good-bye, yeah? There's no point us both being stuck here, right? It's like climbers: one falls off and is dangling by the rope, and the other one holds on as long as he can, but in the end he's not strong enough—and why should they both fall off the mountain? So come on, George. You're safe now. You get to go home. No one gets to go home, he said—but you do! Yeah, you're special, George. You get to do the thing they said you couldn't; you beat them, don't waste it by *not* going home. Make it mean something by going home and being happy! Cut the rope! It's not your fault I'm dangling. If you were dangling I'd cut the rope without a thought, so do it!"

"No."

He looked at his watch.

"I'm not leaving you alone here. I'm not forgetting any of this."

"You idiot! You could be free!"

"But you'd be stuck here. Alone."

"I got on fine before I met you."

"No, you didn't."

"So what? If you forget all about this, you wouldn't know about it, so you wouldn't even have to feel guilty— you idiot, you total absolute idiot!"

And she hit him, openhanded.

In the face.

And he just stood there. And she hit him again.

And he just looked at her, something hardening in his eyes.

"GO!"

And this time her open hand constricted into a fist, and when it hit him, his face rocked back and there was blood on his lip.

"I told you never to hit me again," he said thickly.

"And I told you not to tell me what to do," she retorted, cocking her fist.

"Still here?"

He turned and bent over the grille.

"Fine. See you."

"Yeah. See you," she said with a last look at his back. Then she turned away and walked back to the Gunner, wiping something from her eye.

"S'all right," said the Gunner. "You'll be all right."

"Oh, please," said the Walker, sounding exquisitely bored. "Glints are never all right. They almost all come to bad ends. Tell her the truth."

"Excuse me, miss," It was George's voice. She turned.

He was standing there looking confused. There was no recognition in his eyes. It was horrible. He was hunched over and apologetic like when she first saw him. All the steel that completing his quest seemed to have put into him appeared to have drained back out of him.

"I'm sorry, but I'm . . . do you know where I am?" He looked embarrassed. "Sorry. But I don't know how I got here. I think I've had a bit of a turn."

His arms flapped helplessly. She remembered the boy she'd disliked at first sight.

"Sorry. No idea."

And she walked away.

"Edie."

She stopped. And it hit her. And she whirled.

George grinned at her. Standing straight and unapologetic.

He threw the dragon's head up in the air and caught it.

"Thought I'd keep a hold of this. See how hard the Hard Way really is." And there it was, in his wink. A flash of steel. "You don't get rid of me that easily."

And to their great embarrassment, they both started laughing and found each other hugging—though the moment they realized this was happening, they stopped it immediately and just beamed at each other.

"That was a horrible trick," she said.

"Yeah. You deserved it. All that 'cut the rope' rubbish."

"You didn't have to do it, George. I mean it. I'm not scared of anything."

"I know."

There was a long beat as they stopped smiling and looked at each other. She took a deep breath.

"I'm scared of everything," she said.

"I know that too."

George didn't know what to do. So he hit her companionably on the shoulder.

"How very sickening," said a nasty voice behind them. "You have found your own little Stone Heart."

The Walker was still gripped by the Gunner, who was smiling and shaking his head.

"Unfortunately, we have to go now," said the Walker, squirming his hands out of his pockets. He could only move his lower arms, but in the end it was enough. There was a flash of glass in each one.

He held them parallel with each other. And before anyone could do anything, he had raised a knee, and with an eye-twisting motion, stepped into one of the small mirrors.

As soon as the foot touched the mirror, there was a splash of light and the Gunner's head snapped back so violently that his hat fell off. And then there was a small *whoosh* as air rushed in to fill the place where the Walker and Gunner had been, as they appeared to be sucked into the mirror.

For a horrid moment two mirrors hung in midair, held by no hands, facing each other, with the Gunner's hat and the dagger on the ground between them like a black bowl and a knife.

And then all four objects were gone.

George and Edie stared at the emptiness in horror.

"He took the Gunner!"

Edie slumped to the ground, needing the building wall to support herself.

"The Gunner's gone." She couldn't believe it. "We don't even know where he's taken him!" she finished.

George sat next to her. He felt tired. Very tired. But he also felt certain.

"It'll be okay," he said.

"How?" she said exhaustedly.

"Dunno," he said, watching the people spill out of Cannon Street Station as if nothing strange ever happened. "But it's our turn now. Boot's on the other foot."

"What?"

"We'll have to rescue him." He smiled, trying to look confident. "It'll be okay."

She stared at him in horror and sudden frustration.

"It won't. It . . ."

She looked away and stared at the spot where the Gunner had been, and tried to remember where she'd seen the hat and the dagger lying together like a black bowl and a kitchen knife before. And the memory of someone shouting: ". . . gates in the mirrors!" at her across an expanse of ice came to her. But before she could make the connection, the memory of that ice took over, and the other terrifying thing, the thing that she had suppressed by shouting at the Walker, was swimming back up into her head—and she realized it was so big that she had to tell him.

"George. I saw him! The one that took the Gunner. I saw him before—"

"You saw the Walker before today?"

She nodded, fear rising nauseously in her throat as she knew what she had to say, knowing that saying it out loud would be like making it real.

"About a hundred years before today, maybe two hundred!"

"What?"

"I saw him when I glinted in the Thames. I saw him at the Frost Fair."

"You can't have . . ."

"I did. And he was drowning someone. It was—it was . . ."

She couldn't go on.

"It was . . . horrible?" he ventured.

"It was me."

He stared at her.

"It was a girl in a bonnet, and he drowned her, and it was me."

And for a long time they looked away from each other and said nothing.

"Well," George said finally. "We can't let that happen either, can we?"

Then, as the sun dipped, they stood up without any more words and walked together toward the light.

# ACKNOWLEDGMENTS

All the statues, spits, and taints in this book really are out there on the streets waiting to be found. If you feel like discovering them, or even just your own "unLondon," I really recommend sticking Ed Glinert's *London Compendium* in your pocket as you wander about. I did and do, and find it indispensable. Equally indispensable but less portable books were Christopher Hibbert and Ben Weinreb's *London Encyclopedia* and Peter Ackroyd's *London—The Biography*. The latter's *Hawksmoor* was one of the two books that got me out of the rut of my London and made me go and find other ones in the first place, a provocation for which I'm very grateful. The other book was a dusty copy of H. V. Morton's *London*, a strange brew of impressions that I'd also recommend searching secondhand bookshops for.

Closer to home, I'm very grateful to Katie Pearson for the D. H .Lawrence quotation at the front of this book. I'd also like to thank my (then twelve-year-old) godson Alexander Darby for reading an early extract from the book and telling me I really ought to describe things better. And finally, thanks to Jack and Ariadne and most especially Domenica for being such good sounding boards, first listeners, and strong believers. The only thing that was more fun than writing *Stoneheart* was reading it to you in the evenings. This is for you.

Don't miss the next exciting adventure in

THE STONEHEART TRILOGY

# IRONHAND

# IRONHAND

# CHAPTER ONE

## Darkness Falls

The Walker and the Gunner fell into the dark, pitched into a deep abyssal blackness beyond the memory of light. But though there was no possibility of seeing anything, the Gunner sensed they were plummeting through a succession of layers, as black flashed black in an unpleasant negative strobing, which he felt rather than saw.

And then the horrible movement through the void stopped abruptly as they hit something solid.

The Gunner's knees crunched down into wet gravel, and his free hand instinctively palmed out to halt his fall, sending a jarring shock up his arm as it smacked into an unseen stone wall in front of him. He hung there, head low, angled between the wall and the ground, panting for breath. He felt wrong, more wrong than he'd ever felt, more wrong than he'd known it was possible to feel. He felt it in ways he couldn't begin to list or explain; it was as if an invisible hand had reached into his core and wrenched everything off-true and left it hanging there, twisted and broken.

He heard the birl of gravel beside him as the Walker moved his feet. Using the last of his strength, he swiped a hand into the darkness, but his fingers only caught air and blackness.

He opened his mouth in an "oof" of pain at the effort, instantly clenching it shut and cutting off the giveaway sound. Whatever was happening to him, he was damned if he was going to give the Walker the pleasure of knowing how much it hurt.

And then the lights came on.

The first thing he saw was the upturned bowl of his tin helmet lying on the stones in front of his thick hobnailed army boots. Then he saw the protective legging cinched on to his right calf with three buckled straps like the residue of an ancient piece of armor. On a real soldier the legging would have been leather; but in this case, since he was, of course, a statue, it was made from bronze, like the rest of him. His left calf was unarmored, tightly wound with bandagelike puttees instead. Above that he saw his hands, strong blunt fingers splayed on the knees of his army britches, as he took a breath.

He scooped up the helmet, smoothed the front of his uniform tunic, and adjusted the cape around his shoulders. It wasn't a real cape. It was a canvas groundsheet from a one-man tent, to keep the weather off, tied in place with a piece of string through two grommet holes. He put on the helmet and stood up straight, every inch the battle-worn World War I veteran that he'd been sculpted to be.

And then his mouth, despite his best intentions, fell open again as his jaw dropped in shock.

They were in a large and ancient underground water tank. His feet stood on a small shelf of pea gravel that sloped against one wall. This tiny beach took a bite out of a rough square of black water, about ten yards on each side. The irregular blocks of stone lining the walls of the tank were greasily mottled with age and tumored with sickly blooms of damp fungus, which hung around them at what looked like a high-water mark. Drips from the stone roof of the chamber plopped concentric circles into the dark surface below.

But it wasn't the claustrophobic dimensions of this doorless chamber, with its dark water floor and half-moon gravel beach that made the Gunner gasp in surprise.

It was the lights.

Each wall had an outline of light blazing from it, a shape about the height of a man and perhaps a third as wide. The shapes were made from irregularly placed pieces of broken glass, and all had the same distinctive outline of a squat turret, the kind of thing a child might draw when trying to represent a castle. The light blasting forth from each of the four tower shapes intersected at the center of the water tank, where a silvered disk about the size of a plate spun lazily on the end of a piece of chain, reflecting the light randomly around the room.

"What is this?"

The question croaked from the Gunner's throat before he could stop it. He heard a sniff of contempt and focused on the gaunt figure, up to its knees in the water at the edge of the gravel bar. The Walker wore a long green tweed overcoat with a hooded sweatshirt underneath. He swept the hood back and ran his fingers through long rat-tailed hair brindled with gray. He had a skullcap on the back of his head, and a jutting goatee framing a mouth twisted into a permanent half-open sneer. His hands held two small circular mirrors, which he clipped together and stowed in his coat pocket. He bent and lifted a long dagger from the edge of the beach. He unpeeled a thin sour smile as he gestured around the water tank with the gleaming blade.

"This is a dream of four castles," he replied, indicating the turret shapes on the walls around them. "It is a vision that came to me in a dream, long ago, when I was a free man. It is a vision that I have made real. It is nothing that you could begin to understand."

He shifted the blade in his hand and sliced angled reflections of light around the room, revealing more edges of the subterranean tank.

"It was a void, and darkness was all it contained until I came across it. Now it is a place of power. My power."

The Gunner felt squeezed by the great pressure of earth above him. He felt as lost, as if he had been spirited into the bowels of the earth and pinned beneath a mountain. But he was damned if he was going to let the Walker enjoy his discomfort.

"Where are we? Where is this?"

The Walker spun slowly in a full circle, sending the reflected beams of light around the dank edges of the chamber.

"We are under London. A city you will only ever see again in your memories."

The Gunner would have swung a fist at the Walker, but the wrongness inside him seemed to have sapped his normal strength and had left him needing all his energy just to stay on his feet. And besides, he had to know what was going on. He was nowhere he'd ever been, feeling like nothing he'd ever felt, and he could always try to flatten the Walker later, when he came within easier reach. Although, he had a suspicion that escaping or even surviving whatever was happening to him was going to require more than swinging fists.

"Talk plainer."

"This is where you stay. Forever, perhaps. Enjoy the light. When I leave, it goes too."

The Walker looked at the Gunner with something like pleasure. "You feel it, don't you; inside, the emptiness, the rising horror, the loss of strength, the sense that you're not master of yourself?"

The Gunner made himself stand straighter. "Don't you worry about me, chum. I'm right as a trivet."

"Oh, I'm afraid you're not. You broke an oath sworn to me by the maker. You have to do what I say."

"Not happening," the Gunner snorted tersely.

"Oh, but it is. You're a proud man. I won't offend you by treating you like a lackey. After all, all I require of you is that you die. And all I have to do to effect that happy outcome is to forbid you to dig your way up out of here. And I do. I order you not to try to dig up toward the light and the clean air. Simple, isn't it? One instruction and you're doomed. Midnight will come, your plinth will be empty, whatever animates you will die, and you will be just so much scrap for the smelter."

The Walker's eyes burned bright with banked-up malice.

"Do you still feel master of yourself?"

The Gunner tried to lift his hands, determined to wrench one of the ceiling slabs down into the water to show the Walker he was wrong. But his arms wouldn't move. He shook his head in frustration. "I think I'm gonna grab you and shove your mirrors where the monkey put his nuts, that's what I think."

He lurched toward the Walker, but he was much too slow, and the Walker danced out of his reach. The Gunner stumbled against the wall, horrified by how weak he'd become. As he reached back to stop himself from falling, he dislodged one of the bright pieces of glass.

It fell at his feet. He stared at it, at the opaque surface, the rounded, sea-tumbled edges. And as he stared, his memory fired on reflex, and he saw a similar piece of tumbled glass in Edie's hand. Then it fired again, and he remembered the first time he'd seen her smile, like sunlight breaking cleanly across her face. He relived the surprise he'd felt when he'd realized that all it had taken to kindle that blaze was to smile at her and call her by her real name; and he remembered strongly how that realization had made him feel suddenly protective of this strange and outwardly flinty girl. It was that surge of paternal protectiveness that collided with the dreadful realization spreading slowly across his mind like a dark stain that made something shift uncomfortably inside him.

He bent and picked the sea-glass up between thumb and forefinger.

"These are heart stones."

He heard a dry humorless chuckle and looked up into the sour slash of the Walker's smile.

Then he heard the horror in his own voice as the question gritted out of his mouth, unbidden.

"What have you done, Walker?"

The gaunt figure above him just kept smiling, like a wolf airing its teeth.

"The glints, Walker. What the hell have you been doing to them?"

To find out what happens next, read

THE STONEHEART TRILOGY
BOOK TWO

# IRONHAND